Blood to Drink

Other books by Robert Skinner

Ficton
Skin Deep, Blood Red (1997)
Cat-Eyed Trouble (1998)
Daddy's Gone A-Hunting (1999)

Non-fiction
The Hard-Boiled Explicator: A Guide to the
Study of Dashiell Hammett, Raymond Chandler,
and Ross Macdonald (1985)
The New Hard-Boiled Dicks: A Personal Checklist (1987)
Two Guns From Harlem: The Detective Fiction of
Chester Himes (1989)
The New Hard-Boiled Dicks: Heroes for a New
Urban Mythology (1995)

Edited Works
With Michel Fabre:
Plan B by Chester Himes (1993)
Conversations with Chester Himes (1995)

With Michel Fabre and Lester Sullivan:
Chester Himes: An Annotated Primary and Secondary
Bibliography (1992)

With Thomas Bonner, Jr.:
Above Ground: Stories About Life and Death by
New Southern Writers (1993)
Immortelles: Poems of Life and Death by New
Southern Writers (1995)

Blood to Drink

A Wesley Farrell Novel

Robert Skinner

Poisoned Pen Press

Copyright © 2000 by Robert Skinner

First Edition 2000

10 9 8 7 6 5 4 3 2 1

Library of Congress Catalog Card Number: 99-068787

ISBN: 1-890208-33-7

Poisoned Pen Press
6962 E. First Ave. Ste 103
Scottsdale, AZ 85251
www.poisonedpenpress.com
info@poisonedpenpress.com

Printed in the United States of America

For Patrick Millikin
who's a true believer

"God will give him blood to drink."
Nathaniel Hawthorne,
The House of the Seven Gables, 1851

"In the hands of every individual is given a marvelous unseen influence for good or evil—the silent, unconscious, unseen influence of his life. This is simply the constant radiation of what a man really is, not what he pretends to be."
William George Jordan

"The night we got the heads-up about the kidnapping of Sallie and Clemmie Milton, I was having dinner in a Downtown restaurant. Because the crime was taking place in another parish, there was a lot of red tape to get through, and it was at least an hour before I arrived with units from the Louisiana State Police. Wesley Farrell had arrived on the scene before me. Nothing I'd seen in thirty years of police work prepared me for what I found there."

From the official records of Captain Francis Xavier Farrell Casey, Chief of the Detective Bureau, Orleans Parish, for the year 1939, a collection held in the City Archives, New Orleans Public Library

Prologue

September 23, 1934

Louis Bras and his Hot Six Combo were raising the roof on the bandstand of the Honey Pot, a 'tonk at the River end of St. Peter Street. Inside, the crowd was dancing and swaying to the music as Louis rattled the rafters with his cornet and came up for air now and then to sing the lyrics to "It Don't Mean A Thing" in his gravel voice.

In a corner, with his back to the wall, Wesley Farrell sat drinking beer out of a tall pilsner glass, unconsciously nodding his head in time to the music as his eyes moved restlessly over the crowd. He wasn't watching for anybody in particular, but he'd learned early that danger had a way of blind-siding you when you made your living in the underworld.

The Great Experiment, as the Volstead Act was sometimes known, was nearly over. For the first time since 1919, beer could be legally produced and sold. After fifteen years of enforced sobriety, it was possible to understand the boisterousness of the Honey Pot and the customers' half-crazed gaiety. Farrell wasn't by nature a sociable man, but he understood the occasional urge in others to cut loose a little.

For Farrell, Repeal wasn't particularly good news. He'd made a fair living importing illegal liquor past Coast Guard blockades and state and Federal Prohibition Agents. They all suspected him of rum-running and worse, but he had always eluded them. Now that racket was finished, and Farrell knew it was time to cut his losses and move on.

His eye lit upon a tall, well-built man in dress blues and a white peaked cap. Farrell saw from the little shield and two-and-a-half gold stripes on his sleeves that he was a Coast Guard lieutenant commander. He was a confident-looking man of perhaps thirty-five, with ruddy skin, dark red hair, and green eyes that inspected and evaluated everything around him. He seemed to be looking for somebody. He gave a word to the barkeep, and accepted a glass of beer.

Louis Bras had shifted into the lyrics for "Ja-Da" when the cork popped out of Hell. A huge man with a bulldog face pushed through the crowd and jostled a longshoreman, spilling beer down his shirt. In reflex, the longshoreman smashed bulldog in the jaw with his empty mug. The big man absorbed the blow, grabbed the longshoreman, lifted him overhead, and threw him across the room. The smaller man landed in the midst of a table surrounded by five dock workers, sending beer and food flying everywhere. The five bruisers rose as one, charging across the room at the big man, and the room erupted into a melee that swept up all and sundry. Louis continued to sing the bawdy lyrics as if the brawl was just another part of his act.

The corners of Farrell's mouth turned down in disgust. He sat where he was, hoping the fight would bypass him, but as he sipped his beer, a merchant marine officer crashed into his table. Farrell jumped up, and as he did so, the seaman turned on him, fists flailing.

Farrell gave into an instant of bitterness as he blocked the man's clumsy punch, drove an uppercut into his chin, then followed with a left-right to his gut. The seaman fell into a puddle at Farrell's feet.

He was gradually pushed further into the corner as more men crowded into his space. Farrell shoved men who bumped into him back into the chaos, occasionally clipping a jaw or temple with short, hard jabs when necessary. He fought smart, avoiding the main conflict, but the room had become a seething mass of kicking, biting, gouging, slugging men and shrieking women. It swelled like a cancerous mass in his direction.

Suddenly he was parrying the blows of three men, and was about to go down when the Coast Guard officer got thrown into the corner with him. By some unspoken understanding, they began fighting together, guarding each other's blind spots, using teamwork to get them out of the corner. Slowly, painfully, they worked their way toward the entrance and through it to the street. As they stood on the sidewalk, panting and checking themselves for bleeding wounds, they finally acknowledged each other. "Nice work in there," Farrell said. "You must've been in something like that before."

The red-headed sailor grinned wryly. "Only six or seven times. You didn't do so badly, yourself."

Before Farrell could reply, the wail of sirens could be heard in the distance. "Uh-oh," he said. "We better make tracks."

"I'm with you, brother. I got a car over here." The sailor sprinted toward an old green Marmon roadster. Farrell followed directly behind and stepped over into the shotgun seat. Within seconds, the car sped from the Honey Pot. As they turned the corner, a police cruiser passed them, the siren screaming like a banshee. Only a heartbeat behind, two more followed it its wake.

The sailor grinned without taking his eyes from the road. "You must be Irish to have that kind of luck."

Farrell cut his eyes at the man. "Part Irish, anyway. The name's Farrell, Wesley Farrell."

It was the sailor's turn to cut his eyes at his passenger. "I'm Commander George Schofield. I know your name. You've made a nice living out of running illegal booze past my boats." He turned his old roadster down Canal Street, and slowed as they drove past the darkened department stores on the famous boulevard.

Farrell reached a hand over to shake Schofield's and grinned. "If that were true, and I'm not saying it is, I wouldn't be in the business anymore. They repealed the Volstead Act, haven't you heard?"

"Full repeal isn't for another three months yet, Farrell. And until it is, I'm supposed to stop any smuggling I see and arrest those responsible."

"If you're such a Boy Scout, how come you were hanging around that crummy dive? Half the people in there made their living through bootleg whiskey for the past fifteen years. Bad company for a guy in your line."

"I was supposed to meet somebody in there," Schofield said, then he shut his mouth quickly.

Farrell registered his sudden reticence, and nodded as a flash of insight came. "I get it. Not very bright, though—agreeing to meet a stool pigeon in a place like that—you stuck out in that uniform like a sore thumb. You're probably lucky he *didn't* meet you."

"What?" Schofield sounded confused.

"Use your head, sailor man. If you wanted to get your throat cut, you couldn't find a better place than the Honey Pot. My guess is he was setting you up."

Schofield jerked his head at Farrell, and his eyes narrowed. "I don't believe that. This man has sent me good information on incoming liquor shipments several times. If he hadn't, I wouldn't have..." His face looked suddenly pale. "I guess I'm nuts to tell you this, but I think somebody's leaking our patrol movements to a gang. They've been slipping by my boats for a long time—how long I don't know. What I do know is that too much gets past us."

Farrell fingered his chin as he absorbed this unexpected confidence. "Well, it doesn't surprise me. When Sonny Bastrop was governor he drank Canadian Club on the lawn of the governor's mansion in plain sight. I know, because I delivered it myself. And I know of a half-dozen crooked state prohibition agents who've gotten rich tipping off one booze operation or another before the Feds closed in." He paused to get out his cigarette case. He offered one to the Coast Guardsman who took it and placed it between his lips. Farrell took one for himself, lit both cigarettes, then blew out a big cloud of smoke that disappeared behind them in the slipstream of the automobile.

"It isn't funny, Farrell. A hell of a lot of people have gotten killed over smuggled booze."

"I guess it isn't. Only ironic." Farrell paused and inhaled more smoke. "Is the turncoat one of your boys or a Treasury man?" Farrell knew the Coast Guard was an arm of the Treasury Department, so it could as easily have been a Prohibition agent as a Coast Guardsman.

"I don't know. We coordinate our movements and share intelligence reports with Treasury. Tonight I'd hoped to find out which." Schofield paused and looked over at Farrell. "You're pretty slick, Farrell. How do I know you're not mixed up in this?"

Farrell shrugged. "You don't, but for the record, I never needed cops on my payroll. I don't trust them. If one of them would sell you out, they'd sell me out just as quick. But you still haven't explained who you were looking for in the Honey Pot."

Schofield grinned. "I guess there's no harm in telling you now. I don't know who the man is—I've only communicated with him through typewritten notes addressed to my home. I received one this afternoon telling me he'd discovered the name of the man who was being paid off and which of the big gangs he worked for. I was told to meet him at the Honey Pot at 10:00 tonight, and to wear my uniform." He paused, fooling with the knot in his tie, then he said, "He's been straight with me until now. I don't think he was playing me for a sucker."

"Well, maybe not, but you won't find out tonight. I—" Farrell abruptly stopped talking as bright lights lit up the interior of the roadster. Farrell threw a look behind him, and saw headlights rushing toward them. "Schofield, step on it," he yelled. He reached into his coat for his .38 and leveled it over the tonneau of the roadster. A shotgun roared and buckshot whistled and hissed around them. Farrell fired back, his second shot extinguishing a headlamp in the pursuing car. He grinned until he heard a rear tire on the Marmon blow with a loud bang. The Coast Guardsman fought the wheel as the car skidded across the road. It sloughed sideways, giving the pursuer the opportunity he needed to pull abreast on the driver's side. As he did so, the shotgun cut loose with another load, and the Marmon fishtailed into the rear of a parked Chevrolet with a horrid shriek of tearing metal and breaking glass. Farrell hung on for dear life. As it shuddered to stop, he vaulted over the rear deck and took cover. Taking dead aim, he began shooting at the other car, a blue Pontiac sedan with Mississippi plates. He heard glass shatter as his bullets punched holes in the rear and side windows. Heedless of the withering fire, the invisible gunman fired again and again, driving Farrell face down in the street.

He heard the squeal of tires, and got to his feet in time to see the Pontiac tearing up Lakeward on Canal Boulevard. He threw two quick shots after it, his teeth bared in fury. As it disappeared, he stood there shaking with fright and rage until he remembered Schofield. He turned and ran back to the Marmon, jerking open the driver's door. The commander's body slid fluidly from the opening into Farrell's arms. His eyes were open, but bloody froth bubbled at his lips. Farrell saw several reddening holes in his shirt.

Schofield was trying to talk, but he was choking on the blood in his punctured lungs, his eyes full of desperation.

Farrell looked down on him with a feeling of impotence. He hadn't know the man long, but he had liked him. "Don't try to talk. Help will be here soon." Even as he said it, he knew it was a lie.

Schofield was no longer struggling, and his breath was ragged. At the last moment, the dying commander locked his eyes on Farrell's, a glassful of blood overflowed his gasping mouth, and the last breath shuddered out of him.

Farrell eased him to the ground. He'd seen men die before, but this butchery made his stomach roil. As he knelt there, he heard sirens for the second time that night. There were cops who wanted to see him in Hell with his back broken, so he knew he couldn't linger. He stood up, and began running. At Hennessey Street, he cut west, and kept up a ground-eating trot until he was five blocks away from the scene of the shooting. As he slackened his pace, he felt the vague nausea that always came at the end of a fight.

What he had just witnessed was a professional hit, as cowardly and sickening as murder got. As he'd guessed during the ride, somebody had set the sailor up. It was none of Farrell's business, but he knew he would remember how George Schofield had died. He paused and turned his steps back Downtown.

※※※

The blue Pontiac emerged onto City Park Avenue and headed back Uptown. In the front passenger seat, a big man with a deep scar running down through his right eyebrow propped a short-barreled Winchester shotgun against his leg. "You can slow down now." His voice was thick and gutteral.

"Right." The driver's face was mostly obscured by the turned-up collar of his coat and the brim of the brown fedora he had pulled low down over his forehead. His rough hands moved gracefully over the wheel without a tremor. "You get him?"

"You can't miss with one of these babies."

"Good. He'd have figured things out before long."

The big, scar-faced man reached into his jacket pocket and got out a package of Pall Mall cigarettes, tapped one out and grabbed it with his brutal lips. "Cigarette?" He offered the pack to the driver.

"Don't use 'em. They're no good for you."

The other man popped a match to life with his thumbnail, then shoved the end of his cigarette into the flame. He exhaled a long plume of smoke, blowing out the match at the same time. "No good for you. That's a riot." He tossed the spent match out the window, then rested his right elbow on the window ledge. "The chances you been takin' for the last coupla years." He laughed again.

The driver shrugged. "Some risks are worth takin'. 'Sides, I should go to the trouble to make all this jack, and then get sick and not get to enjoy it? A man's got to take care of his body, Mercer, if he wants to live to a ripe old age."

The big man sucked hard on his cigarette, and for a brief space of seconds the only sound was the sizzling of the flame eating into the tobacco. "Joe Earle, you still back there?"

"Yes, suh, Mist' Mercer." A negro boy, not older than eighteen, leaned out of the shadows in the back seat into the pale glow of the dashboard lights. There was sweat running down his face. "Didn't reckon on nobody s-shootin' back like that." His voice was shaky.

"That's why I give you the gun, knucklehead," Mercer snarled. "Somebody shoots at you, you shoot their face off—that's the way it works." Mercer paused to inhale the last of his cigarette and then threw the butt out the window. "Did you even shoot back?"

"Uh, reckon not." Joe Earle's voice was low and shamed. "I—I didn't get into this to do no killin'."

"You been gettin' good money for what you're doin', and if you have to let somebody take a shot at you once in a while, then that's just the breaks. But if you're just gonna hide in the corner when the fireworks start, I'll leave you back workin' on cars and find somebody who'll shoot when I tell 'em to." Mercer's contempt cut the air like a knife, and the young negro faded quickly back into the shadows. The .45 Mercer had given him lay on the seat beside him. He hadn't even cocked it when Farrell had started shooting, and had simply lain on the floor until he felt the car moving again.

"The car's a fuckin' mess," Mercer growled. "That guy with Schofield really tore it up. I wish I coulda put a round in *his* fuckin' head, but he was too good. Joe Earle, after we drop him off," he jerked his head at the driver, "I want you to take the car to Johnny and tell him to fix it up good, you hear me?"

"Yes, suh, Mist' Mercer." The youngster's expression was shrouded in darkness as the car hurtled through the night. He bit his lip to keep from crying, and the taste of blood was bitter on his tongue.

Chapter 1

March 12, 1939

The New Orleans police cruiser pulled to the side of Louisiana State Route 1 behind a pair of Chevrolets that bore the markings of the St. Bernard Parish Sheriff's department. Captain Frank Casey emerged from the right-hand passenger door as Negro Squad Detective Merlin Gautier climbed out from behind the wheel. The two of them stood there for a moment, staring at the deputies grouped around a blanket-covered form on the ground. There was a red smear at one end of the blanket, and a hand lay just outside the shroud.

Casey, a stocky man a shade under six feet with gray-shot red hair and mustache, looked coldly at the sight. Gautier stared too, unwilling to break the tense silence. A truck full of caged chickens went by them, leaving behind a clutch of feathers and the putrid smell of poultry floating in the morning breeze. As the truck passed, Casey strode toward the deputies. As he walked, he passed a campaign poster nailed to a nearby telegraph pole. On the poster was a photo of a serious-looking man in steel-rimmed glasses and a white cowboy Stetson. Beneath the picture were printed the words

> *"Tough on Crime—Paul Chauchaut—A Law-Enforcer For Governor of Louisiana."*

Casey had seen a hundred of them, and he paid no attention. When he reached the deputies, he took out his badge case and flipped it open.

"Frank Casey from the New Orleans Detective Bureau." He jerked his chin over his shoulder. "This is Detective Gautier from the Negro Squad. Tell us what you got."

A lanky man of mature years with an incongruously boyish face touched a finger to the brim of his cap. "Captain Luke Peters, sir. I'm the one who called. Deputies Gasso and Brisbois," he gestured with a bony hand to the other men, "found the body about 5:00 A M. I got here soon afterward. When we found the police badge and identification card on his body, I called from that store down the road yonder. We don't have much in the way of a crime lab, so we pretty much left things as we found 'em." Peters's voice was a pleasant baritone that held a trace of East Texas.

Casey knelt beside the body, gently pulled back the bloody sheet and swallowed hard. What remained of a negro of about thirty seemed to stare up at him. The entire left side of the corpse's face had been obliterated by a shotgun blast and the jaw hung bizarrely askew on the remaining hinge.

Gautier knelt beside his boss and began going through the dead man's clothes. He found a .38 Colt Official Police revolver lying on the ground near the right hand. Gautier broke the cylinder open and saw that three of the six rounds had been fired. He put it into a valise he'd brought, then went through the inside pockets of the man's jacket, discovering a wallet containing eleven dollars, a membership card for the Knights of Peter Claver, another for the Police Benevolent Association, and a photo of a pretty, dark skinned young woman and a grinning little boy. Gautier's jaw tightened at that, then he brutally closed the wallet and shoved it into his valise. The other inside coat pocket yielded a black leather folder with a gold star-and-crescent New Orleans police badge and a laminated police identification card in the name of Thomas William Blanton. The dead man's shirt pocket held a crumpled package of Old Gold cigarettes and a box of kitchen matches.

Casey had meanwhile been working on the trouser pockets, and had found a handful of coins and a nickel-silver Hamilton pocket watch on a silver fob. The fob was engraved with the initials TWB. He found the same initials stitched on a clean linen handkerchief in Blanton's hip pocket. He also found a three-blade Camillus pocket knife with green jigged bone scales and a small leather notebook with a pencil held in a leather loop. Casey opened the notebook and flipped through the pages, then he slipped it into his coat pocket. "No car keys," Casey muttered as he passed his other finds to Gautier, then he stood up to face Peters again.

"Let's talk to your men for a minute," Casey said. Wordlessly, Peters led him over to the other two men. They were identically dressed in pressed and pleated khaki uniforms with silver badges. Their waists and torsos were wrapped in shiny Sam Browne belts, and each belt supported a heavy revolver in a swivel holster. One was tall with fair skin and hair, the other short and stocky with swarthy, pitted skin and coal black hair. Black brows met over the bridge of his nose and his eyes were like jet marbles. He stood a bit to the front, indicating that he was probably the senior partner.

"This is Captain Casey from New Orleans, boys," Peters said. "Tell the man what you found."

"I'm Gasso," the short, dark man said. "We was doin' our reg'lar patrol through here, an' it was still plenty dark. Brisbois," he jerked a thumb at his partner, "was drivin', and when the headlights hit the body I told him to stop. I wasn't sure what it was, you unnerstan', but there was somethin' about it give me a cold chill. We got out with our flashlights and found the colored guy layin' there with half his head gone. We radioed the substation, and after a while Captain Peters come out."

"So you secured the crime scene, and nobody did any tramping around after you got here, right?"

"Right." Gasso nodded vigorously. "We didn't even touch the body except to find his identification."

"Good," Casey said. "I got our lab boys coming out right behind us. We can take it from here."

Gasso looked up at Peters, who nodded. Gasso and Brisbois each gave Casey and Peters a brief salute, and then departed. Within seconds they were back in their big Chevrolet heading east.

"I'll hang around, if you don't mind, Captain," Peters said. "The sheriff'll want a representative here since it's in our territory." He paused and tugged on his right earlobe for a moment. "Speaking of that, just why was one of your detectives this far out of his jurisdiction? The sheriff'll want to know how come he was here without notification."

Casey frowned and looked down at the tops of his shoes for a moment, then he looked up. "He was working undercover.

Whatever he was after must've brought him over here, but it's hard to say what. When we figure that out, we'll be glad to share it with the sheriff."

Peters' boyish face looked grave, and he tucked his thumbs into his belt. "Y'all want to play it close to the vest, it's fine by me, but sooner or later you'll have to fill in the sheriff, or he'll tell you to get the hell out of his parish. I don't want to cause you any extra grief, but you can't expect to operate here without letting him know what you're doing."

Casey stroked his chin with his thumb and forefinger as he stared at the tall deputy for a moment. "I'll have to ask for your forbearance while we sort this out, Peters. I'll come in to see the sheriff in a little while and talk it over with him, okay?"

Peters considered it for a moment, his eyes hooded and unreadable. "Okay. I'll tell him what you said. But you got to understand something about Sheriff Chauchaut—he's got a political reputation to protect, and he's not going to let himself look foolish." There was the barest trace of embarrassment in the rural policeman's voice, as though he found his boss's political ambitions a burden.

Casey nodded. "I understand."

The two policemen turned back to the body, and saw Gautier walking along the edges of the highway, searching the ground. Gautier looked up and then walked over.

"There's some foot tracks in the dirt on the shoulder comin' from that direction, Cap'n." He jerked a thumb to the east. "Toes are dug in hard. Looks to me like he might'a been running away from somebody when they caught up to him. He probably turned and got off three shots before they got him."

"See anything else?"

"He always wore a hat everywhere he went. Had a nifty Dobbs, dark brown, but it ain't nowhere around. We looked up and down the road, over in the grass yonder," he pointed toward the levee, "and across the road for about a fifty yards. It might mean something, but then again it might mean nothin'."

"Find any shotgun shells nearby?"

"Yep." Gautier held up a red paper cylinder with a shiny brass base on the end of his pencil. "Western twelve gauge, double-ought buck. It's good and clean—we oughta be able to get a picture of the striker and ejector marks in the microscope. Trouble is, repeating shotguns are prob'ly as common as dirt out here. We'll have a hell of a time tracing the murder weapon through a single spent shell."

Casey nodded. "Maybe—unless it's been used before. I see Nick Delgado's here. Go and tell him what you found, and give him the valise of stuff we took off Blanton. Stick around and hitch back with him. I'll drive down river—maybe I'll see something."

"Yes, sir." Gautier's lean brown face was hard and deep lines were etched alongside his nose and mouth. He walked toward the panel truck and waved at Delgado as the other detective got from behind the wheel. Casey walked back to his own cruiser, got behind the wheel, and stared for a long moment before starting the car and driving away from the crime scene.

⚇

Wesley Farrell sat staring out the window at Basin Street, idly rubbing his ear with a pencil, when the house phone on his desk rang. It startled him out of his daydream and he picked it up on the second ring. "Yeah," he said in his smooth baritone.

"'Scuse me for botherin' you, boss," bar manager Harry Slade said into his ear, "but there's a guy down here askin' to see you."

"He got a name?"

"He says he's James Schofield."

The name reverberated in Farrell's ear, causing a rush of memory to the night five years before when the Coast Guard officer with that name was killed beside him. The hairs on the back of his neck stood upright and he cleared his throat. "Okay, send him up." He put down the phone, trying to shake off an uneasy feeling.

In something less than a minute, he went to answer a knock at the door. A man stood there who could have been George Schofield's twin, except he was far too young. Farrell figured him for no more than twenty-six or -seven. "Mr. Schofield?" I'm Wes Farrell. What can I do for you?" Farrell betrayed no recognition, looking steadily at the other man.

The younger Schofield took Farrell's hand in a firm grip, shaking it several times before taking off his hat and walking into the office. Farrell gestured toward some chairs and Schofield went in, taking the chair directly across from Farrell's desk.

Farrell returned to his chair behind the desk, opened a cigarette box, and offered one to the other man. Schofield took it with a nod of thanks. He lit the cigarette and blew smoke into the air between them. "Thanks. I hope you don't mind my barging in like this."

"What is it that I can help you with?" Farrell spoke in an expressionless voice, watching the other man intently.

"Does my name mean anything to you?"

"Should it?"

"Answering a question with a question—that's not good manners, Farrell." Schofield's casual demeanor was no deeper than the silver plate on a two-dollar watch. Farrell felt the barely restrained anger simmering in him.

"Why don't you just get whatever it is off your chest so I can go back to work," Farrell said without heat. "This place isn't a stop on the historic tour of the French Quarter, and I'm not in the mood to do crossword puzzles with every stranger who comes in to pass the time of day."

Schofield reached into his jacket and pulled out a leather folder. He flipped it open and a badge identifying him as a U. S. Treasury Agent glinted dully in the room's muted daylight.

"So you're a T-Man." Farrell affected an attitude of boredom. "I don't recall breaking any Federal laws lately."

"Not lately. But during Prohibition, you fractured the Volstead Act six ways to Sunday. None of the resident agents could ever get anything on you, but your name was on the lips of every two-bit bootlegger and moonshiner between Pensacola and Galveston. If they'd had any luck, you'd be busting rocks in a Federal pen now."

"That's yesterday's news, even if it was true."

"My brother isn't yesterday's news. Lieutenant Commander George Samuel Schofield, United States Coast Guard. Deceased." Schofield spoke in a flat, hard voice. "He commanded a flotilla of seventy-five footers based here, and he was assassinated on Canal Street five years ago. Nobody was ever arrested or brought to trial for it."

"So why come to me? People get killed in New Orleans all the time without me being within a mile of them."

"Because you were neck deep in liquor smuggling. If you didn't have anything to do with my brother's death, you still might know who did."

"That's taking a lot for granted," Farrell said. "You have any idea how many people around here made their livings off illegal hooch between 1919 and 1934? At least a thousand would be a safe bet. Too many for me to know. Besides, who'd brag about shooting a Federal cop? You'd have to be dumb as a post to do that, and people that dumb don't live long in the rackets."

The logic of Farrell's words brought the younger man up short. With some effort, he smoothed the frown out of his features and spoke in a more reasonable tone. "Play along with me, Farrell. I don't want to cause you any trouble, but I want to know who killed my bother. This is personal. I don't give two hoots and a damn how much liquor you slipped through here. I want to know who killed George."

Understanding bloomed. "So this is private—Treasury has nothing to do with it?"

"I'm on an unpaid leave of absence," Schofield said stiffly. "I was in my sophomore year at the Coast Guard Academy in New London when George got killed. Afterward I resigned. It took me over a year to get accepted for training as a Treasury Agent. When I got into the field, for the next two years I volunteered for every bum detail and cold case that came along so that when I asked to do this I'd have too much on the credit side of the ledger for them to say no. Since then, I've studied the case up, down, and sideways, and I'm as certain as death that somebody here knows why George was killed—and by who."

Farrell shook his head. "Then you know more than I do, Agent Schofield. I'm sorry about your brother, but I can't help you. Killing cops is way out of my line—there's no future in it, and no profit."

"Don't pretend to be high-minded with me," Schofield said sharply. "You've killed before—not once but several times. You've been lucky enough to do some of it when you were cleaning house for the local law—which makes me wonder about them, too. No real cop I know goes out with a killer for a sidekick."

Farrell's face retained its emotionless facade, but his pale gray eyes grew paler yet and little lights began to jump in them. "You're about to run out of welcome, Agent Schofield. Since you're here unofficially and without any warrants, I can tell you to go to hell. I can even heave you out a window if the mood strikes me—and that mood's only about a hair away right now. So get lost."

Schofield got up, dark red circles burning in his cheeks. He crushed his cigarette out and put his hat back on. "Farrell, I smell lies coming off you like stink from a garbage dump. If you know anything about my brother's murder, I'll find it out. And by God, I'll come back with a set of handcuffs." He turned on his heel and walked out, leaving the door open behind him.

Farrell sat there for a moment, staring at the open door. His cigarette had burned down to nothing in the ashtray, so he got another out of the box, lighting it with the nickle-silver lighter on his desk. As he looked at the flame, he saw his hand was shaking. He closed the lighter and put it down on the desk. He let smoke feather gently from his nostrils as he remembered the sound of the shotgun and the stink of cordite rising hot from the barrel of his gun as he fired futilely at the departing Pontiac. After five years, it was like remembering a bad dream—a dream he had no desire to relive. But with the man's brother in town kicking over every spittoon and garbage pail, forgetting was a luxury he could no longer afford.

He'd done nothing to cause George Schofield's murder, but he'd done nothing to punish the people who'd done it, either. He wasn't a cop and he wasn't God, but something in him had always felt a sense of guilt that he'd let a good man get killed and then done nothing to avenge him.

Who had lured Schofield to his death that night? Schofield had said he only suspected there was a turncoat, not that he knew or had a guess as to who that man was. The supposed stool pigeon was supposed to identify the man for him, but more likely it was the turncoat and the gang he worked for who had lured Schofield to his death. Farrell's head was beginning to ache. He had a lot of cold ground to go over if he was going to get his questions answered.

⊗⊗⊗

In the back bedroom of a house on Castiglione Street, the scar-faced man named Mercer braced himself on his powerful forearms as he labored over a nude woman with short dark hair who lay face-down on the bed. She was groaning loudly as she neared a point of ecstasy that she could almost see behind her closed eyelids. The scar-faced man panted almost silently, his yellow eyes gleaming as he stared down at the woman's naked back, driving deeper and deeper into her. He slipped a hand under her belly and massaged the ripe flesh up to her heavy breasts, causing her to gasp and shudder. They went on like that for several moments more until the woman's groans turned to hoarse cries that sounded almost like she was in terrible pain. The cries deepened and became more distressed until she began to buck and writhe under him, screaming and convulsing with the orgasm that shot through her like a bolt of electricity. Mercer came as he plunged down into her like a pile driver, gripping her around the waist like a man holding on to a bucking horse. The two of them fell out of the bed, the woman still screaming until, exhausted, she collapsed on top of him.

The man laughed deep down in his chest as he rubbed his large hands roughly over her belly. She laughed too, but it was the laugh of someone who has finally reached the top of a tall mountain and is laughing as much from relief as from pleasure. After a time, she staggered to her feet and disappeared into the bathroom, closing the door behind her.

The scar-faced man got up and sat on the edge of the mattress, fumbling with a crumpled package of cigarettes until he got one shaken out. He stuck it into the corner of his mouth, lighting it with a kitchen match he scratched on the scarred night stand. He'd taken in a lung full of smoke when the telephone began to ring. He looked at it sourly and let it ring several more times before he reached out a hand to pick it up. "Yeah?" he said.

"Mercer, you trigger-happy fool," a man's voice said. "You just had to go and kill a cop, didn't you. What the hell are you using for brains?"

"The fuckin' guy had made us, pal. There wasn't nothin' else to do *but* kill him by then. What'd you want me to do—offer him some bonbons and tea, maybe?"

"He should never have gotten that close to you, Goddamnit," the voice shouted. "I'm paying you to think once in a while. How the hell'd he find you?"

"He suckered Hines into thinkin' he was in the hot car racket."
Mercer spoke casually, letting smoke drift from his nostrils. "When
he got to the hideout, one of the other niggers recognized him as
a cop who'd busted him a while back. I had no choice."

"So you had to do it on the road where a cop would be sure to
find him, huh? Christ Almighty, you could've just wrung his neck
and thrown the carcass in the river."

"Calm down, pal." An edge was growing in Mercer's voice.
"You weren't there, so I had to do the thinkin' for us. The guy got
hinky and broke away—wasn't nothin' else to do but run him
down and kill him—which we did. Pickin' up the body would've
been real smart—we could've been stopped by a cop, or even seen
by somebody else. We did it quick and clean—nothing to tie it to
any of us. As soon as I got back, I had Hines and the boys break
down the equipment and truck it across the parish to another
place I found out about. Nobody saw us—it was a clean getaway."

"So far as you know," the voice said pointedly. "Don't think
for a minute the New Orleans cops'll let this lie. They'll want
somebody to swing for it even if he was a nigger."

"But it ain't in their jurisdiction, pal." As Mercer spoke, the
woman appeared in the doorway, her eyes sleepy and her mouth
just slightly open. She came to the edge of the bed and stood
there, looking at him expectantly, her breasts bobbing elastically
from her pale chest. He looked at her with real satisfaction—she
was a good animal. She was the only pleasure he allowed himself,
and he wasn't going to let anybody spoil it with a lot of yapping.

The voice was silent for a minute, then, "Jurisdiction doesn't
count in a cop killing. And there's no statute of limitations on it.
I shouldn't have to remind you of that. If you got any more men
as stupid as Hines, take 'em out and kill *them* if you're so
Goddamned trigger happy."

He hung up the telephone in Mercer's ear, leaving the scar-
faced man sitting there with a frown on his face. It's always the
same, he thought. You always end up workin' with guys who want
the money but don't want to get their hands dirty.

He felt the woman put her hands and mouth on him as he set
the telephone down on the hook and crushed out the cigarette in
a tin ashtray on the night stand. He looked down at her, seeing
her pale skin gleaming with sweat. Her touch felt like a live wire

against his body, and he stretched out on the bed, no longer caring about the dead cop or the angry man on the phone. Mercer's fingers tangled in the woman's hair as he closed his eyes, feeling the blood surging through him like a river.

⪘

Across town, on the edge of a ghetto known as Gerttown, a skinny, narrow-skulled negro sat on the floor of a shotgun cottage, leaning against the bed while a prostitute called Violetta Dalton rubbed a hand softly across the man's close-cropped hair. The skinny man was half-way to drunk, his right hand wrapped possessively around the neck of a quart of Kentucky Gentleman. Violetta looked down on him with affectionate, troubled eyes as he talked in a dull monotone. He had begun talking about how he'd let his boss, a white man named Mercer, down, but gradually the monologue had shifted to what he'd done to make up for it. Violetta took in a deep breath and held it because it was obvious by how upset he had become that something terrible had happened.

"Yeah, I had that Chevvy of mine revved up, honey. We took off after that slick-talkin' brutha, I mean. Had him in sight 'fore he'd gone more'n a hunnert yards. He heard us, turned around, and Mercer, he—Mercer he—" his voice cut off in a strangled sob and he turned the neck of the bottle against his lips, sucking the bourbon down his throat like he was trying to drown his very soul with it.

"Stop it, Zootie, baby." Violetta spoke in a husky, alto voice. "Ain't no need in goin' over and over it. It's done now, and 'sides, you didn't pull the trigger." It was hard for Violetta to keep a tremor from disturbing the calm flow of her speech, but it had to be done if Zootie was to get what he'd done out of his system.

"Mercer's my pal." Zootie said this with great enthusiasm, but Violetta knew it was all movie-show emotion. Zootie's voice was hollow and his face was contorted with something between grief and horror. "He said we took care of that brutha but good. 'Magine, him a cop sneakin' up on us like that? He deserved it. You shoulda seen the look on his face when we come up on him. You shoulda seen—" Again, he had to resort to the bottle to keep from splitting down the middle.

Violetta stroked his head and gently massaged the muscles between his neck and shoulders. Violetta had seen him like this before after the white man he idolized committed some act of savagery on another black man. Zootie wanted more than anything in the world to believe that Mercer needed him, but it was plain to see that Zootie was just somebody to do his dirty work and to keep the other negroes in the gang in line.

Violetta had figured out some time ago that Mercer used people like Zootie because he knew a negro, particularly a negro raised in the South, knew how to blend so perfectly with the background that white people could ignore him, a factor that made stealing cars duck soup.

Zootie was his enforcer because Mercer had recognized early on that Zootie's need to be respected and feared was so strong that he would terrorize his own kind in order to get that respect, to feel important—to not be ignored. Violetta looked down on him with mingled feelings of tenderness and pity. There was sweetness, a kind of good in Zootie that could be reached with patience and love. Violetta had found it, and nurtured it whenever possible.

Zootie was good and drunk now, and he turned and looked up into the prostitute's large, liquid brown eyes. Light brown hair, chemically straightened, was arranged in waves around a pretty oval face the color of milk chocolate. Violetta was the first person Zootie had ever known who had shown him anything like love. He always turned to her when he'd seen and done things too terrible to keep inside.

After a time, he reached up a hand and Violetta took it, pulling him up into the bed until they were lying side by side, kissing and exploring each other's bodies. It was all Violetta had to give the miserable, guilt-ridden little man, and he took it gratefully, hungrily, even. He never stopped to consider the irony that a prostitute was the only person in the world who would show him love and affection. As their loving progressed, Violetta wondered what it would take to get Zootie away from Mercer, who had become father, mother, and brother to him. Violetta was tired of being a whore, and wondered if it were possible for them to have a normal life in which fear and degradation weren't the first two items on each day's menu. She wondered if she dared find out what it would take, and then if she dared risk it.

In an office in the U. S. Customs House, a man drummed his fingers on his desk as he read for the fifth time a communication from Treasury Enforcement headquarters in Washington. He looked anything but happy. He pulled a private telephone toward him and dialed an outside number. A man answered within three rings.

"Yeah?"

"This is Ewell. George Schofield's brother is supposed to be in town. He hasn't checked in here yet."

"You make anything of that?"

"Only that I don't like it."

"What do you want to do?"

Ewell scratched his ear. "Find him. Keep your ear to the ground. If he gets close to something, I want to know."

"He probably won't—not after all these years."

"I haven't lived this long by taking things for granted," Ewell replied. "I'm not starting now."

The other man was silent for a moment. "I hear you. I'll be in touch." He broke the connection.

Ewell put his receiver down very gently, then leaned back in his chair and stared across the room.

Chapter 2

Frank Casey drove slowly down Route 1, scrutinizing each side of the road. He was nearing the Lake Borgne canal lock at Violet when he saw something to the left; a ramshackle barn just visible through the trees at the end of a narrow lane. Casey turned the wheel sharply and headed down the dirt drive. About twenty-five yards in he discovered a disheveled cottage beside the barn, which itself seemed to have been used as a commercial garage at one time.

Loosening the gun in his holster, he got out of the car and walked to the barn door, shoved it open, and saw a Studebaker sedan sitting inside. It sported a maroon paint job and the chrome detailing of a deluxe model. "Well, well," he said in a low voice. "What do we have here?"

He leaned into the open driver's window to look at the registration on the steering column, discovering immediately that the car belonged to Blanton. His eyes lit on a dark brown Dobbs fedora on the seat. It looked like it had been freshly blocked. Picking it up, he turned it over and saw Blanton's name written in indelible ink on the sweatband.

Using his handkerchief, Casey opened the passenger door and further examined the interior. "Keys are still in it." His voice sounded hollow in the empty barn. He wondered if Blanton left it here, or if somebody else dumped it. He was betting Blanton drove here under his own steam, but something went wrong and he ended up running out on foot with the killers behind him, probably in a vehicle of their own. They caught up to him on the road, probably, and he put up a brief fight before they cut him down. Casey nodded as a picture began to form in his mind. Blanton was known as a scrapper—a dime's worth of luck and he might've made it.

As he stood up and looked about, he smelled the pungent aroma of paint. Over to one side there were paint-stained rags, canvas drop cloths, and remnants of masking tape. A pile of empty pails bore the labels of enamel automotive paint in a variety of colors.

The red-haired detective systematically searched the place from top to bottom. At the rear of the barn, Casey found a larger heap of discarded paint cans, suggesting that a substantial number of cars had come through here for repainting and body work before transport to another location. Under a drop cloth in another corner he discovered a pile of stolen license plates from Louisiana, Mississippi, Alabama, Florida, Texas, and Arkansas—undoubtedly left by accident when the thieves cleared out. He gathered them up and put them in the trunk of his own car. Casey guessed that after they'd killed Blanton, the car thieves had decided they couldn't operate that close to a murder, which meant they could be half-way to Mexico by now. But this was a big operation, he reasoned. They'd be more likely to move to another location, maybe in this same parish. He wondered how this could go on under the nose of a man who was selling himself to voters as "tough on crime."

He walked out into the bright light of morning and mounted the porch steps to the cottage. The door swung open noiselessly at his touch. Waiting briefly for his eyes to accustom themselves to the gloom, he moved quietly into the interior.

Surprisingly, the place was reasonably well-kept. He found the front parlor comfortably furnished with a sofa, a couple of armchairs grouped around a potbellied stove, and an old Crosley table radio with the veneer peeling off. A cheap braided oval rug brightened the cleanly-swept floor.

His search took him through two bedrooms, a bathroom with a flush toilet and shower stall, and a kitchen. There, Casey checked all the cabinets, the electric icebox, and the drawers in the kitchen table, finding nothing but a few old pulp magazines, a six-month-old newspaper, various kitchen utensils, and a few sets of paint-stained coveralls.

He was poking around in a hall closet when he spotted something that made his eyes light up—a box of Western 12 gauge double-ought buckshot shells. Using his pocketknife blade, he lifted the top and saw that the box was only partially full, with a few shells disordered from careless handling. Since they were wax-coated for weatherproofing, Casey knew there was a chance that one of the shells might have retained a full or partial fingerprint. He returned to the parlor for a piece of the discarded newspaper, returned to the bedroom and wrapped it carefully around the box before setting it down on the night stand.

The discovery of the shotgun shells seemed to quicken Casey's senses and he searched with a renewed sense of purpose. He returned to the bureau and pulled out each drawer, then turned them over and inspected the undersides. Most of them only had dust and cobwebs beneath, but the small top right-hand drawer yielded something of interest. It was a piece of paper about five by eight inches that was beginning to brown in the heat and humidity. Unfolding it carefully, Casey discovered that it was a receipt dated several months before from a photographic studio owned by Mrs. Florestine Paquet Connor on Rampart Street. Someone had paid two dollars and fifty cents for a photographic portrait. The photographer was a negro, so it stood to reason that this client was a negro as well. Two and a half bucks was a princely sum indeed for a negro to spend on a photograph. Casey refolded it and placed it in a clean white envelope he took from his inside breast pocket, then went over the house one more time before calling it quits.

He opened the trunk of the big Dodge police sedan and put the wrapped parcel of shotgun shells inside, then took out a ring-necked jug of water, a bar of soap, and some rags. As he washed and dried his hands and then used the damp rags to wipe the dust from his shoes, he stared at the barn. It had to belong to somebody.

He closed the trunk, got into the car, and headed back out to State Route 1, then turned in the direction of the Sheriff's Department in Chalmette. As he drove, he ruminated on what he knew of the sheriff. He was a big man, given to flamboyance, and tended to wear custom-tailored suits with a big, white cowboy Stetson. He'd been a sugar cane farmer and processor back in the early '20s, Casey remembered, and had developed political ambitions. Although he had no previous police experience, he had ridden into the Sheriff's Office on a wave of outrage when illegal whiskey traffickers had murdered the Violet town constable and his deputy. He'd promised to be ruthless in his extermination of the illegal manufacture and sale of alcohol, and had lived up to his promise when he'd personally led an all-out attack on the hideout harboring the notorious Ike Gelhard mob, which allegedly had been responsible for the murders of the Violet officers. A photographer for the *New Orleans States-Item* snapped a sensational photo of Chauchaut standing, wide-legged, over the body of Gelhard, himself, a riot gun cradled ostentatiously against his hip-bone. The picture had gotten national circulation, assuring the sheriff's reputation.

Thereafter, the sheriff was often photographed at the scene of high-profile arrests. He became friendly with Governor Sonny Bastrop and was known in political circles as one of the governor's supporters. The connection hadn't hurt him a bit with the people of his parish, many of whom were poor and had been helped by Bastrop's populist initiatives. Chauchaut had been returned to office in two successive elections by a substantial majority. In more recent times, he'd set his political sights higher, and was aiming to replace Bastrop when the governor's term ended later in the year. It was widely believed that he would win the election, thanks to the fact that he had plenty of money behind him. Casey had seen copies of his campaign poster everywhere.

It took Casey about three-quarters of an hour to reach Chalmette, the scene of General Andrew Jackson's dramatic rout of the British in 1814 and the home of the Sheriff's Department. It was a substantial three-story brick building with no architectural adornments, its third-story windows covered with thick steel bars. Two large white light globes were bracketed to the walls on either side of the entrance, and a metal sign bolted over the main door proclaimed the building's official nature. Casey was not surprised to see at least a half-dozen of Chauchaut's campaign posters on nearby telephone poles.

Casey parked, got out, and walked through the entrance. Inside, he found a heavy-set man with the chevrons of a sergeant busily working on a sheaf of papers with a pencil. He looked up at Casey with a bland, oval face decorated with a black mustache and eyebrows.

"He'p you, sir?" he asked in a voice lightly accented with Cajun French.

Casey took out his badge case and opened it for the sergeant. "Captain Frank Casey. I'm chief of detectives for New Orleans. Wonder if I might speak to the sheriff for a couple of minutes. He'll know what it's about."

The desk sergeant's expressionless face remained so, but his eyes gleamed brightly for the barest second before he picked up a telephone receiver and spoke into it quietly. He paused, listened for a little bit, then replaced the receiver in the cradle. "Go down de hall to your lef', Cap'n. It's de t'ird door on de right-han' side." That said, he picked up his pencil and returned to his work.

"Thanks," Casey said to the top of his head, then turned and followed his directions. When he came to a pebbled-glass door with the words SHERIFF PAUL CHAUCHAUT lettered in black paint, he opened it and stepped through.

Inside he found a male deputy typing a report of some kind on a big Underwood typewriter. The deputy looked up long enough for Casey to state his name, then he keyed his intercom and announced Casey's arrival. At the sheriff's word, the deputy pointed at the door to the sheriff's interior office.

Chauchaut stood as Casey entered. He was about six-four, and built to scale. The white clothing he affected made him look even bigger. His blonde hair was neat and close-cropped, and steel-rimmed spectacles gave him a stern, serious look. He was in his shirt-sleeves, but had his sheriff's star pinned to the breast of his white dress shirt. A hand-tooled Mexican belt holster hung on his left side with an ivory-handled Colt Detective Special riding in it. That amused Casey, who recognized it as part of Chauchaut's carefully crafted image. All he needed was a guitar and he'd have made a passing fair B-movie cowboy.

"Cap'n Casey," Chauchaut said in a big, hearty chamber-of-commerce voice. "I heard we got some trouble with one of your colored officers up the road a ways."

Casey nodded. "He was working undercover and was shotgunned, but Peters probably reported all that."

Chauchaut threw a hand at a pair of wooden side chairs that faced his desk. Casey sat down in one and dropped his hat into the other.

"We don't have any colored officers in this department," Chauchaut said musingly. "Kind of funny, a New Orleans man being in my bailiwick. Why didn't y'all fill me in that you had a man in my jurisdiction?" The sheriff's eyes narrowed as he sat down. His face seemed to harden.

"I'm sorry about that, Sheriff. He wasn't supposed to be here. Apparently his case brought him here—or maybe the people he was investigating led him here and killed him on the road. I can't see the whole picture just yet."

"Well, y'all sure do have my sympathy. It's bad medicine for a police officer to get gunned down like that—even a colored officer. What was he working on?" Chauchaut was good, Casey thought. His voice had just the right note of brotherly sorrow, and he'd slid that question right in behind it. But there was no good reason to withhold the information.

"He was trying to make contact with a hot car ring, which we originally believed was operating somewhere in Orleans Parish. Something, or more probably someone connected with that led or brought him to St. Bernard. What I found just before coming here makes it clear that the ring has actually been operating near Violet for some time, Sheriff." Casey could see from the hard intensity of the sheriff's eyes and the tightness around his mouth that he hadn't liked that answer. Casey decided to add a little sugar to make the embarrassing news go down a bit easier. "These guys are pretty slick. We've been looking for them for well over a year, so it's no reflection on your department that you didn't know they were here. My guess is that they've been damned careful not to call any unnecessary attention to themselves—up until now."

Muscles in Chauchaut's jaws were bunched so hard he looked like a squirrel with too many nuts in his cheeks. "What makes you think they've been operating here, Casey?"

"I found Detective Blanton's car in an abandoned barn a little this side of the Lake Borgne locks, not far from the murder scene. The barn looks as though it might've once been used as a commercial garage. There's a cottage nearby, and it's obvious that it's been in use for some time to perform body work and repaint cars. You wouldn't happen to know the name of the owner, would you?"

"Not right off-hand," the sheriff replied, his mouth barely moving. "But we can find out pretty damn quick."

The sheriff keyed his intercom and leaned toward the speaker. "Charlie, find Luke Peters and have him come in here, will you?" He didn't take his eyes off Casey as he spoke. After the secretary responded, Chauchaut got up and walked over to the window, turning away from Casey. The muscles in his back were tight under the white dress shirt, and the tension in his arms strained the fabric of the sleeves. As he stood there, Casey's eyes wandered about the room, coming to rest on a framed campaign poster on the wall adjacent to the sheriff's desk.

"How's the campaign going?" Casey said to fill up the silence.

Chauchaut turned "Very well, thank you. If I can get all the law enforcement officers in the state behind me—and I think I will—the governor's mansion will be mine. I've got the farmers, the labor unions, and even most of the colored preachers lined up behind me already." He smiled for a moment. "I'll be looking for some experienced lawmen to reorganize the State Police, captain."

Casey smiled. "It would be flattering to be considered." There might be a worse fate than becoming one of Chauchaut's pawns, but Casey couldn't think of one.

"Yeah, we got us a good state, but we still got a lot of bad elements left over from Prohibition. The right men could clean them up, and make this place a paradise. Think about it, Casey. I'm not as strong in Orleans Parish as I'd like. Your support would be—"

A knock at the door brought Casey to his feet. As he turned, Luke Peters entered the room. He wasn't wearing his hat or his duty belt, and he'd turned the cuffs of his shirt back from wrists matted with pale hair.

"You wanted to see me, sheriff? Afternoon, Captain Casey. I didn't expect to see you again so soon."

Casey nodded and smiled in reply as the sheriff began speaking.

"Yeah. You know an abandoned barn this side of Violet that might've been used as a commercial garage?"

Peters cocked his head thoughtfully to one side, his eyes examining the ceiling of the office for a few seconds. "Yeah, believe I do. Belonged to a colored man named Hope, Johnny Hope.

Nice fellow. Believe the Depression drove him out of business some time back. Good mechanic, though. Fixed an old Chevy of mine. What about it?"

"I found Detective Blanton's car there a couple of hours ago," Casey replied. "Along with plenty of indication that it was being used as a drop and body shop for a hot car ring. I found a pile of stolen license plates, empty paint cans, canvas tarps, tape—you name it. Except for the plates, it looks like they got all the important stuff out right after the killing."

Peters's face took on a pained look, and his eyes flickered from Chauchaut to Casey. "Damn. My memory is that Hope's living in your neck of the woods now. At least I recall that he moved in with some kin in Orleans Parish after he went out of business."

"That makes things a little easier. I'll have my Negro Squad find Hope and question him."

"Cap'n Casey, I'm mortified that all this happened in my parish." Chauchaut's face was stern and his voice earnest. There was a shadow in his eyes that might well have been embarrassment. "I'm going to put myself and every available man I've got on this, check out everybody who knew Hope. I suspect there are some other nigras in the parish who worked for him while he was in business. I'd be surprised if some of them can't tell us something."

"I appreciate that, Sheriff. I'll keep you posted on what we learn, and you can follow up at your end."

"Captain Casey, would you like me to get Detective Blanton's car and return it to your headquarters?" Peters asked. His expression was still pained, but it seemed obvious that he wanted to do something to redeem his department in Casey's eyes.

"That's mighty kind of you to offer. I'll head back to town and get my men to work locating Hope." Casey turned to face the sheriff, who had resumed his seat behind the desk. "I certainly thank you for all your cooperation, sheriff. Your men are as professional a group of officers as I've ever seen. I'll be back in touch with you later." He bent to retrieve his hat, shook hands with the sheriff and Peters, then left the office.

As he got back into his car, he reflected on the discomfort both Chauchaut and Peters had shown when he delivered the news about a hot car ring in their jurisdiction. They'd obviously been afraid a city detective had come to make monkeys out of them, but he couldn't complain about their willingness to help. Of course, Chauchaut had a lot to lose if the case blew up in his face.

He turned on to Route 1 and headed back to the city, dreading what he had to do next—deliver the bad news to Tom Blanton's widow. As he increased his speed, he passed yet another of the ubiquitous campaign posters with the sheriff's face looking out at him.

∞∞∞

"Is this gonna be trouble, Luke?" the sheriff asked when Casey had departed.

Peters turned a bland face to his boss. "Maybe not, sheriff. It might just be a golden opportunity."

"Opportunity?"

"Sure. It was an Orleans Parish detective that was killed, but the murder occurred in our jurisdiction. It's up to us to investigate the crime."

"Yeah," the sheriff said, nodding.

"Maybe it doesn't look too good for a hot car gang to be operating in our patch, but if we move quick, we can crack the case, arrest the men responsible, and it'll be one more thing in your favor with the voters—especially the colored voters."

The sheriff grinned. "You're gonna make a first rate commander of the State Police after I get elected, Luke."

"Reckon so, sheriff? Well, we'll see. I'll get some men to work looking up Hope's known associates in this parish. Once we got some names we can go talk to 'em, see what we can shake loose."

"Fine, Luke, fine. I got to work on a speech for the Chamber of Commerce."

"Okay, sheriff. I'll go back to work and get out of your hair." Peters left the sheriff's office and closed the door behind him. He had a thoughtful expression on his face as he walked back out into the hall and down to his office.

∞∞∞

It was nighttime in the French Quarter where music from Doc Pardee's clarinet drifted out of the open door of the Club Moulin Rouge like a sweetly aromatic smoke. Strolling passers-by on Rampart Street recognized the song he was playing as the old Duke Ellington number entitled "Louisiana," and heard the clear alto voice of Bonnie Celestine rising above the sound of the clarinet like a soft breeze. It was the kind of combination people had come to expect of them, and inside the club, all talking, dancing, and eye games between men and women came to a temporary standstill as the violet-eyed singer and the instrumental quartet worked their magic.

Savanna Beaulieu sat at her corner table on the raised platform and smiled to herself. It hadn't been very long since she'd returned to the city from Los Angeles, where she'd spent a long year of self-examination and inner torment brought about by a brutal rape at the hands of Sleepy Moyer, a pimp and gunman who'd subsequently been killed. She'd returned of her own free will to be with Wesley Farrell and to make a pact that they'd never willingly separate again. She'd come to know a peace and security that she'd never expected to have, and on days like this, when love songs filled the air of her club, it made her forget the day's petty trifles.

She saw from the clock over the bar that it was nearly midnight. Farrell would be coming through the door soon. He had his own club to run, and other business that took up his time, but the late evening and the hours between midnight and dawn they always saved for each other.

He came through the door as usual, pausing just inside to let his eyes track the room. Tonight he was dressed in a Palm Beach suit with a pale blue shirt and a tie the color of magenta, his pale yellow Borsalino tipped just a bit over his right ear. He smiled, removing his hat as he strolled through the crowd to ease into the chair beside her.

"Hi," she said.

"Hi. I heard Bonnie singing all the way down the street. I like that song."

"Me, too. I think that's the reason they play it every night. Where you been today?"

"My office mostly." He paused as a waiter brought a rye highball and placed it on a napkin in front of him. "I had a visitation from a ghost today."

"A ghost? I didn't think you could see them in the daylight."

"It was really a man, the brother of another man who was killed five years ago. He looks enough like the dead guy to be his twin. That's why it seemed like a ghost."

"You kill his brother?" It was an indelicate question, but their relationship was such that anything was fair game.

"No—the worst I can say is that I couldn't stop him from getting killed," he said ruefully. "Somebody out to get him ambushed us with a shotgun. I tried to drive them off, but they killed him anyway. He was a Coast Guard officer, so it's heavy odds that somebody in the whiskey smuggling business was responsible."

"So if nobody knows you were there, why did the brother come to see you?"

"The guy's a Treasury Agent. I think he became a T-Man in order to investigate the case, then got a leave of absence to come down here and turn over rocks until he found something that smelled."

"What could there be after all these years? And where did he get your name? It's not like you advertised you were a smuggler."

"It was no trick for him to find out my name—I made plenty in that racket, but I was mostly out of it by the time his brother was killed. I'm probably just one of two dozen names he found in some old files."

She turned her martini glass around in an aimless circle as she considered his words, her eyes vaguely troubled. "So what are you gonna do—ignore it?"

He shook his head. "Wish I could. Killing a Coast Guard officer in the line of duty is a Federal beef. If he can find enough to get the case reopened, it's barely possible I might get dragged into it somehow. I'm going to nose around and see what I can find out. Not many men would be crazy enough—or mean enough—to stalk a Federal officer in the middle of town and kill him. A man like that'll stand out. And somebody knows his name. I'll just have to find that somebody and get him to talk to me."

"Damn," she said. "There's no end to trouble, is there?"

He grinned. "If trouble was money, I'd own the world. Want to go upstairs for a little while?"

She grinned back. "You ask some silly questions sometimes, know that?"

⊗⊗⊗

As Wesley Farrell and Savanna walked up the stairs to her apartment above the Club Moulin Rouge, a telephone began to ring in the darkened bedroom of a house elsewhere in the city. It rang insistently until a pajama-clad arm emerged from the tangled bedding and took the receiver off the hook.

"'Lo," he mumbled.

"Got a hot flash for you, pally." A man's harsh voice cut through the darkness.

"Huh?" the sleeper said uncertainly. "Whozzatt?" Then the recognition came. "*Mercer*—What the hell do you want?" He rose up in the bed, a his face a pale shadow in the dark room.

"Pretty good, pally. You recognize me, huh? It's been a while, ain't it?" Mercer laughed, a nasty, phegmy sound in the telephone receiver.

"I said what do you want?"

"Just to let you in on some interesting news. I just got word that there's a Treasury Agent named James Schofield in town. Name mean anything to you?"

The man in the dark room said nothing, his mind working feverishly, trying to make sense of what he'd been told. "So why call me in the middle of the night?" he finally asked. "It's no skin off my nose."

"He's in town lookin' for his brother's killer." Mercer spoke in a flat voice. Even though the man in the bedroom couldn't see him, he knew somehow that Mercer's jaws were split in a nasty grin.

"That's your worry, not mine." The man bit the words off clean and hard.

"But you drove the car, and you set up the hit. I'd say you got your own share of worryin', cutie pie. If they get me, they'll hang you just as high."

"Listen, you, I'm through with you and all the rest of that, see? I did what I did, but that was a long time ago. Things are different now, get it?"

"They're different, all right. You got a hell of a lot more to lose now. I won't go down alone, in case you get some wild idea of feeding me to him in order to keep him off'n you. I'll roll over on you like a fuckin' oak log, pally. So keep cool, and remember what I said." As he spoke the final word, Mercer broke the connection, leaving the man staring off into the darkness of his bedroom.

A long time ago, the man in the bed had wanted some things, and the death of George Schofield had been part of the price. It had been tough all around, but a guy had to look out for number one. He got up and went to the kitchen, rummaging in the refrigerator until he found a quart of milk. Working in darkness, he poured some milk in the pan, added a healthy dash of nutmeg, and put the pan on the stove. He turned the fire on under the milk, and stood there until he decided it was warm enough. He poured the mixture into a cup, and sat down at the kitchen table, sipping the warm milk, letting the heat settle his mind.

He didn't care for Mercer very much, but didn't blame him for all the threatening and heavy breathing. Mercer, a man of limited intelligence, used bluster as a tool. He used it to get weaker men to do what he wanted. He suspected that James Schofield's appearance in town bothered Mercer a great deal more than it bothered him. But if it became necessary, this Schofield could easily join his brother in the cemetery.

He finished the milk, got up, washed the pan and the cup, then put them in the rack to dry. He returned to his bed, climbed in, and went directly to sleep.

⊗⊗⊗

In another part of the city, a nervous young negro called the number of his sister's house in the Bywater section. It rang four times, then a man answered.

"Johnny," the young man said. "It's Joe Earle."

"Hey, li'l brutha. "Where you at?" The name put cheer in Johnny's voice.

"Listen." Joe Earle Hope spoke in a low, tense voice. "Somethin' happened last night."

Johnny caught the note in his younger brother's voice immediately. "What is it, boy?"

"Hines brought this young brutha to the garage in St. Bernard, said he was in the hot car racket, lookin' for some cars to move. Only—"

"Only what?"

"Only Boxcars reco'nized him—he was a cop."

Johnny's voice fell to a dull whisper "Aw, shit. Does Mercer know?"

"Mercer was there. Boxcars tol' him right off, and Mercer took Hines aside to tell him. The cop musta smelled somethin', 'cause he lit outa there on foot. Mercer and Hines, they come out and took off after him. Mercer, he—he had that scattergun of his."

"They kill him?" Johnny asked in the same dull whisper.

"Reckon they did. But Mercer come back and had us break everything down and cart it all over to that place useta belong to Alex and Dom Mouton. Said we couldn't take no chances."

"Goddamn it to hell."

"Johnny, I seen Mercer kill a man five years ago. I only stuck with y'all 'cause you promised there wouldn't be no more rough stuff after the whiskey law expired. I'm scared. I'm thinkin' 'bout goin' over to Mobile or maybe Galveston and findin' a job of some kind."

"No." Johnny spoke forcefully. "Ain't no tellin' what Mercer might do if you was to take off. Just be cool, and do what the man tells you, and we'll see if anything happens."

"*Somethin'* done already happened, Johnny. I don't like it. I don't like it worth a cent."

"Do what I tell you, Joe Earle. I'll take care of you. Ain't I always taken good care of you?"

"Yeah, I reckon." Joe Earle's voice was shaky now, and he didn't sound all that certain.

"Go home. Go home and get some sleep. We gonna make out all right, you hear?"

"Yeah. I hear." Joe Earle Hope hung up the phone and walked away, not in the least comforted by his big brother's assurances.

Chapter 3

Sergeant Israel Daggett of the Negro Detective Squad stared out the passenger window of the squad car being driven slowly down Urquhart Street by Detective Sam Andrews, a burly, brown man with a heavy mustache.

Daggett was thirty-nine years old, a lean, lanky dark-brown man with a long oval face and large, intelligent eyes. He wore his hat tipped slightly back on his head as he scanned the house numbers of the shotgun cottages they passed. He drummed his fingers lightly on the open window ledge until he saw the house he wanted.

"It's that one, Sam—the white house with the pale green trim." Daggett pointed at a cottage two doors down from them. Andrews tapped the accelerator, then took the car out of gear and let it coast to the curb. As they drew to a stop, he cut the ignition.

Daggett got out of the car and stood on the sidewalk blotting the sweatband of his hat with a handkerchief. When Andrews joined him on the sidewalk, they walked up the steps to the front porch. As he pushed the button inset into the door frame, Daggett could smell the savory aroma of red beans and sausage and faintly heard the theme music for "Our Gal Sunday" coming from a radio. Presently, a stocky little light brown woman with a pleasant, round-featured face appeared at the screen door, wiping her hands on a dish towel.

"Mornin'. Can I do somethin' for you gen'lemen?"

Daggett smiled and took out his badge case, flipping it open so the badge was exposed. "I'm Sergeant Daggett, ma'am, and this is Detective Andrews. Is this the home of Mr. Johnny Hope?"

The woman managed to keep any show of alarm from her face, but her eyes registered the consternation of any Southern negro suddenly confronted by the police. "I'm his sister, Arthel Dandy. There ain't no trouble, is there, Mr. Sergeant?"

"No, ma'am, I don't believe so," Daggett replied in a kindly tone. "We just want to ask him a couple questions about a garage he used to run over in St. Bernard Parish. Is he in, by any chance?"

Daggett's mild tone and smile disarmed the woman, and she unlatched the screen door and beckoned for them to come inside. The interior of the front parlor was cool and a little dim. It had a small fireplace in the front room, now bricked up and equipped with a gas log. An oak mantle piece held an old clock flanked by ancient photos and tintypes of stern-looking black people dressed in stiff dark clothes.

"Y'all gen'lemen please sit down there," Arthel Dandy said, gesturing toward an old brown sofa, "and I'll go get my brother." She walked briskly through a door leading to the back of the house. Both men sat down, placing their hats on the coffee table in front of them.

"She look a little nervous to you, boss?" Andrews was perennially suspicious of everyone.

Daggett grinned. "No, I just think she's a little surprised to find two colored dicks on her front doorstep. I've never known a brutha or a sista, innocent or guilty, not to back up a few steps when the Man comes to call."

They heard footsteps coming, and each of them stood up. The woman emerged through the door, followed by a short, stocky man who somewhat resembled her. Thick muscles laced his exposed forearms, and scars covered his big-knuckled hands. Although his full, unlined face marked him as no older than thirty-five, his hair was woolly, and nearly white.

"I'm Johnny Hope," he said as he walked toward them. "Ya say y'all wanna know somethin' 'bout that old go-rage I used to run?" Unlike the woman, he was forthright and seemed not to be bothered by their presence.

Daggett nodded. "Yes, sir, Mr. Hope. Some other officers found a missing automobile there earlier today. We wondered if you knew of anyone who might be using it since you closed up shop a couple years ago."

Hope raked his blunt fingers through his thick mop of gray hair as he sat down in a Boston rocker on the other side of the coffee table. Daggett and Andrews resumed their seats, each regarding Hope's puzzled face intently.

"Well," Hope began, "I run plumb outa luck in nineteen and thoity-seven, and ended up sellin' most ever' thing I had. The gorage and the land it sits on I never could get shut of, so it's just sittin' there, I reckon."

"Know of anybody using it, with or without your permission?"

Hope's open face surveyed Daggett's, his eyes still wide and frank. "Law', mister, I ain't had no cause to go all the way out there, so I wouldn't know of nobody usin' it. Nawsuh, I wouldn't have no idea a-tall."

"Kind of a careless way to deal with an investment that size, ain't it, Mr. Hope?" Andrews asked casually. "I mean, somebody could'a been out there and burned the place down without you knowin' anything about it."

"Well." Hope raked his hair with his fingers again as he looked from Andrews to Daggett. "Weren't nothin' I could do nohow. I ain't gonna stir up no mess with nobody and likely get hurt. I ain't no fightin' man, nawsuh." He favored them with a quick, disarming grin as he spoke. He continued to shift his eyes back and forth between the two detectives. Daggett noted that he managed to look neither of them in the eye as he did so and Daggett felt a small smile grow on his lips.

"What've you been doing since your business went bust, Mr. Hope?" Andrews asked.

"Well, I pick up some odd jobs from some of the go-rages here in Bywater. I been puttin' some of the money aside, hopin' to build up a stake to open another bidness." He reached up with a thumb and forefinger and pulled on his nose a couple of times, then added, "It's slow goin'. Depression's liable to be over before I can get enough together." He laughed as though what he'd said was funny.

"How is it you had a garage all the way over in St. Bernard, Mr. Hope?" Daggett asked. "That's a good long ways from New Orleans. You live over there in those days?"

Hope scratched his head, and then his nose again, his bright, guileless eyes shifting from one detective to another. "Oh, reckon I can't claim to usin' much sense on that score. I took a chance that I could get some bidness and make a decent livin' over there, but it turned out to be a bad risk. The white folk over there got white go-rages they use, and the colored folk ain't got no money to get their cars worked on. They just run a car 'til it quit, then they leave it sit and walk 'til they kin scrape up the money to get another'n. I don't reckon I made enough to pay for grub and a roof over my head most weeks, nawsuh."

"That's tough." Andrews voice was devoid of sympathy.

Hope leaned forward in his chair. "If you don't mind my askin', how's come y'all so interested in my busted go-rage?"

Daggett studied his face for a minute. "A negro detective was killed over near Violet early this morning, and later in the day they found his car abandoned in the garage with the keys still in it. We were just tryin' to figure out who might've been using the property since you gave up on it."

At the mention of a dead cop, Hope leaned back in his chair and pulled thoughtfully at his nose again as his eyes shifted back and forth between them. Daggett watched him for any sign of surprise, but his face remained blank and his eyes open. He was a good actor, but not good enough. He should've looked frightened, or at least shocked, but he looked neither.

Daggett abruptly put his hands on his knees and stood up from the sofa. He bent to pick up his hat, and Andrews silently followed his lead.

"We appreciate your time, Mr. Hope. If we have another question to ask, are you likely to be here, or have you got a garage where you'd more likely be during the day?"

"Uh, well," Hope said, clearing his throat. "I reckon I'll be here with my sister, Arthel. And if I ain't, she'll know where to tell you I'm at."

"That's swell." Daggett held out his hand for the mechanic to take. "We sure appreciate all your cooperation, and I hope we don't have to bother you again." He turned and walked to the front door, holding the screen on his way out until Andrews was close enough to catch it.

As they reached their squad car, Andrews said, "I've heard some bullshit in my time, but he takes the cake. No colored mechanic I know is gonna leave New Orleans and risk everything he's got in a parish as poor as St. Bernard. Hell, most of the bruthas out there are lucky to have a mule, much less a car."

Daggett opened the door of the squad car and slid into the seat. After Andrews had situated himself under the wheel, he spoke. "There's plenty wrong with that story all right. Reckon we'd better look into his background before we get back to the Captain. I got an itch I can't scratch since we talked to Mr. Johnny Hope, and I can't sit down before I scratch it. Drive to that drugstore at the corner of Bienville and Mazant so's I can call the squad room. They can be checking on Hope while we run down a few people who can tell us what they know about his business."

⚬⚬⚬

Johnny Hope watched the two negro detectives get into their sedan and drive away, rubbing his hand over the lower part of his face. It had taken a lot out of him to sit there grinning like an ignorant darky as the cops had told him about the murder of the colored detective. When Joe Earle had called him and told him about the killing, he'd shaken his head in disbelief. It was the kind of dumb-ass thing that only a white crook would think he could get away with. He was going to have to talk to Mercer, and soon.

He'd been associated with Mercer since well before Prohibition ended, making good money. They'd met in prison, and had gotten out at approximately the same time. Mercer had contacts in the whiskey smuggling business, and soon was running his own operation, later joining forces with and eventually taking control of a bigger gang. Hope had driven trucks loaded with bootleg until Mercer realized how good a mechanic he was. After that, he'd reworked and repainted stolen cars that the gang used for whiskey smuggling or sold out of state for operating capital. After Prohibition ended, Mercer had reorganized the gang and car-stealing had made even more money than whiskey. It was the best money he'd ever earned, which almost made up for the fact that Mercer worried him plenty. He had seen from the beginning that this ofay was one bad motha-fuckah. It didn't surprise Hope a bit when he'd killed that sailor before Repeal. He'd always known about the sawed-off Model '97 Winchester pump in the trunk of Mercer's car, and knew from the look of it that the man didn't use it to hunt no quail or rabbit. That was a man-killin' gun, no lie.

He walked back into the shotgun cottage's second room, where his sister kept the telephone. He picked it up and asked the operator for a number. It rang twice before anybody answered.

"Yeah," a male voice said.

"This is Johnny Hope. I need to talk to Mercer."

"He ain't here."

"Then find him. The cops found out I own the place near Violet and they just been here givin' me the third degree." Hope's voice was low and urgent. "Put the word out to have him call me, and I mean damn quick."

The voice became suddenly alert and focused. "I hear you, man. Where you at?"

"I'm at my sister's place. He knows the number."

"Stay loose. I'll get the word to him."

Johnny hung up the telephone and stood there staring at the wall as he contemplated the world of grief that was rushing toward him like an avalanche.

"Johnny, what you doin' standin' there like that?" Arthel asked. "You sick or somethin'? And what'd those two po-licemen want with you?"

He turned and showed her the wide-eyed guileless look he'd shown Daggett and Andrews, smiling disarmingly at her. "Just some foolishness. Ain't nothin' to worry your li'l head about, sweetpea. You got any coffee on back there?" His sister liked to mother him, and he knew if he asked for food of any kind that she'd get right to serving some up for him.

"Yeah, you know I do," she said brightly. "Got some apple pie left over from yesterday, too. Want some with a li'l cheese on top?"

"You know it, li'l mama." He walked behind her as she scuttled back to the kitchen, feeling sweat collect at his hairline and on his upper lip. He hoped it was warm enough in the kitchen to account for it. He couldn't let his sister know a thing about this business.

❈❈❈

James Schofield knocked on the pebbled glass door with the legend CHIEF RESIDENT AGENT lettered on the glass. A voice responded and Schofield entered.

It was a medium-sized office with two windows behind a large dark oak desk. Two wooden chairs with green leather upholstery stood in front of the desk. The desk was empty but for three oak trays filled with neat stacks of paper.

The hard, fit-looking man behind the desk was somewhere in his middle forties. He had a lined, rugged face, a shock of dark blonde hair that fell over his brow, and eyes so black they seemed to have no irises.

"Agent James Schofield, sir. My supervisor in Washington told me to check in with you after I arrived."

"Paul Ewell. Have a seat." When Schofield was seated, Ewell spoke again.

"I expected you in here two days ago," he said pointedly. "Your boss in Washington said you were down here to investigate your brother's murder."

"Yes, sir. Nobody was ever arrested for the killing."

"I remember the case. Your brother was ambushed on Canal Street. There was shooting from at least two guns, and a man was seen running away from the scene, but that's all they ever found out. It was a long time ago." Ewell raised his left eyebrow at the younger agent.

"Yes, sir, I know that, but—"

"I'm sure you've already gotten the standard department lecture about not using your badge to pursue a personal agenda," Ewell interrupted. "So I won't harp on the fact that four different citizens have called in today asking why a young Treasury Agent has seen fit to visit and question them rather aggressively about things that they might or might not have done before Repeal."

Schofield paled under the disapproval in Ewell's voice. He cleared his throat nervously, and squirmed in his seat.

"I'll give you a different piece of advice instead," Ewell continued. "Washington has seen fit to let you perform your investigation, but I think all you'll find is what we already know— nothing. Treasury and FBI men working with the city police turned this town inside out when your brother was killed. All they got for their trouble was a handful of expended buckshot shells that could've come from anywhere. We were hot under the collar and motivated to get the killer, but whoever it was vanished off the face of the earth. My guess is that somebody around here imported a hit man to take your brother out. We could never even establish a motive, although we suspected it had something to do with his effectiveness in interdicting whiskey smuggling along the river. Your brother was an aggressive officer, and he'd made a reputation for himself. He was also a maverick. You might as well know that a few investigators privately advanced the opinion that maybe he'd had something going with a smuggler, got too big for his hat, and they killed him for it."

The young man's face flushed and his mouth got a hard, taut look to it. "Never. My brother was as straight as a die. He also loved the service. He'd never have betrayed it, not for any amount of money." As badly as he wanted to defend his brother, Schofield kept to himself that he'd discovered notes George Schofield had made before he died—notes indicating that he was conducting a private investigation that included some of his own men and people within the Treasury enforcement office. James Schofield didn't know who he could trust in New Orleans, so for now he was trusting no one—not even the chief resident agent.

"So what makes you think that five years later you can find out what sixty experienced agents couldn't do when the case was red-hot?" Ewell's weathered face was stern, his tone irritable.

"I'm not trying to take anything away from you and the other investigators, sir, but he was my brother. I want a crack at it, and this is the only time I've got."

"The department doesn't like mavericks, Agent Schofield. You're a private citizen while you're in New Orleans. Leave your service revolver in your valise, don't harass anyone without due and significant cause, and don't attempt to make an arrest until you've notified the proper authorities and have a local officer with you. Is that clear?"

"Yes, sir. Is that all?"

Ewell scowled at the younger man for a moment. "Yes. It won't do you or me any good in Washington if you get into trouble down here, you understand? In spite of what you think, we'd like to clear the ledger on this case, but it's got to be done by the book."

"Yes, sir." Schofield got up and left the room without another word, closing the door very gently behind him.

Ewell continued to stare at the door for another moment, then he removed the receiver from his private telephone line, dialed a number, and waited until he got an answer.

"This is Ewell. Agent Schofield finally checked in."

"I'm still on him," the other man said. "He's visited Agent Brackett, Agent Merrill's widow, and Janet Maxwell, that woman who was clerk of the evidence room. Merrill's widow slammed the door on him when he left."

Ewell's mouth stretched tight. "He's pretty clumsy, but it's possible his being here might make someone nervous. If anyone looks or acts the least bit scared or upset that Schofield's here, I want to hear about it, understand?"

"I hear you."

Ewell hung up the telephone and leaned back in the chair. He sat there frowning at the door until his secretary called and reminded him to go to lunch.

⊗≋⊗

Wesley Farrell eased his Packard to the curb across the street from a pool hall located on the east side of the Southern Railway tracks down near the river. A rusty sign on a bracket swung back and forth in the hot breeze. Whatever had been painted on it had long ago flaked away, leaving behind the impression that the business had no name. It was owned by a hustler named Nate Styles who'd bet his last dime on anything with four hooves but wouldn't give his right name unless there was a buck in it.

Farrell got out of his car and walked through the open door past a half dozen pool tables to the bar.

The room was dim and quiet, save for the muffled clicks of billiard balls on green felt. The bartender was idly pushing a soiled bar towel across the gleaming mahogany surface of the bar. He looked up at Farrell with a disinterested expression.

"Nate Styles in?" Farrell asked.

"Who's askin'?"

"Wesley Farrell."

"I'll check in the back." He turned and walked away soundlessly. In about a minute he was back, and jerked his chin over one shoulder. "Back there." His errand concluded, the bartender resumed polishing the bar.

Farrell nodded and followed the length of the bar until he reached a door, which he opened and walked through. On the other side he found a crummy room furnished with a desk, four file cabinets, a cracked leather sofa and a japanned radio bar that had some of the red enamel chipped off. Johnny Mercer crooned "You Must Have Been A Beautiful Baby" from the radio speaker.

A small man with slick black hair was talking on a two-piece telephone, making notes as he listened to whoever was at the other end. "Right, uh-huh, okay, babe. Put three Cees on Rocket's Red Glare in the first and six on Caliente Tomato in the second. That nag can run circles around everything else in that race. Sure, 'bye."

He hung up the telephone and stuck his pencil over his right ear as he leaned back in his chair to regard his visitor.

"Wes Farrell. It must be something big to bring you all the way down here. What's on your mind, podnah?"

Farrell tipped his hat back from his forehead and sat down on the leather sofa. He watched Styles intently. "Information."

The small man sat a bit straighter, his eyes flickering. The word 'information' made Styles smell money. "Spill it."

"Five years ago—a Coast Guard officer named Schofield was murdered on Canal Street. Remember it?"

Styles shrugged. "Sure. It ain't every day a Federal cop gets penciled out like that."

"What did the street say about it?"

"The street was awful quiet, Farrell. It ain't often that something happens in this town that scares people, but that had some knees knockin'."

"Whose?"

"Hell, most of the smugglers—the ones still in business, anyway. They was scared shitless the Feds would tear the roof off'a this town and make it impossible to do business."

"The killing happened when the Prohibition laws had only three months left to run. How much could anybody lose?" His question said, Farrell sat back and listened intently. Nobody knew street gossip like Nate Styles. He didn't look like much, but people of all stripes talked to him and he had a phenomenal memory.

Styles shook his head. "You ain't thinkin' straight. You were smart with your money—you saved it, sunk it into legit' businesses. Most of the others spent it faster than it came in, playin' the big shot. A lot of those boys needed those last few months to make a big enough score to tide them over until they could find another con to work."

Farrell nodded slowly. "So you're saying it was in nobody's interest to kill a Federal cop. To do that might gum up the works and shut off the flow of money prematurely."

Styles smiled wisely. "That's usin' the old coconut."

"So whoever killed Schofield didn't do it over whiskey trafficking. They had another reason, which was what?"

Styles shrugged elaborately. "If I knew that, I mighta been able to hand the killer over myself, collect the reward."

"There was a rumor I heard that somebody might've been tipping off a gang or gangs to the Coast Guard's movements up and down the river. Ever hear anything about that?"

Styles leaned back in his chair and tugged his lip thoughtfully with a thumb and forefinger. "No. But it wouldn't surprise me. They didn't pay those Federal guys beans. If somebody waved enough lettuce under their noses for a little information, I could sure as hell see somebody takin' 'em up on it. Hell, I could see Schofield takin' it. Then he gets greedy, tries to hold his connection up for more loot, and they send somebody to gun him out. Stuff like that happens in the rackets all the time."

Farrell knew that couldn't be the answer, but he refrained from saying so. "Maybe you're right. But if you are, which gang might've done it?"

Styles shrugged. "I wasn't payin' a lot of attention. What I remember was a lot of boys bitin' the dust." He held up a hand and began to tick names off on his fingers. "Big Tony Romero, caught by the Coast Guard down near Pilottown with a boatload of hooch the year before Repeal, and he's still in Leavenworth. Ike Gelhard's gang had already been wiped out by that rube sheriff, then the Feds caught Lefty Scheinbaum's gang up near Baton Rouge." He paused and searched his memory while his tongue probed a molar. "Hell, I don't know. I was mindin' my own business. Whiskey running was too damn dangerous, even to know about, much less have a hand in. You know me, Farrell—I'm a lover, not a fighter."

Farrell stood up and shoved a rolled-up twenty into the small man's shirt pocket. "Thanks, Styles. I appreciate the time."

Styles took out the bill and unrolled it, his eyes brightening. "What's your interest in all this ancient history, Farrell? You didn't say."

Farrell looked down on him and smiled. "No, I didn't. See you around, Styles." He turned and walked out of the office. Styles stared after him for a moment, then shrugged, picked up his telephone, and asked the operator for the number of another bookie.

⁂

Frank Casey parked his car across the street from 137 Rampart Street and got out. This was a negro shopping district, and, as usual, the sidewalks were teeming with foot traffic. A dark cloud swept in from the south as he stood there, while thunder rumbled and a freshening wind whipped at his hat and trouser legs. He walked past a large window with the letters "Connor Photographic Studio" painted across the top, pausing briefly to scan a display of photographic portraits of local negro celebrities. The thunder crashed nearby, lightning crackled in reply, and Casey felt hard droplets of rain battering the top of his hat. He ducked into the studio just ahead of the deluge.

"I'll be right out," a woman called in response to the bell which sounded as the door opened and closed.

"No hurry," Casey called. He took off his hat and looked out at the sheets of rain that were suddenly pelting everyone in sight. Lightning flashed again, and the lights in the studio flickered momentarily. As Casey looked around, an attractive, soft-featured woman with black hair and eyes came into the room. Florestine Paquet Connor was in her thirties, and in spite of her fair skin, a negro. She was also a noted photographer, respected for her portraiture. She smiled as she recognized Casey.

"It's Captain Casey, isn't it? I haven't seen you since Israel Daggett was sworn back onto the force. That was a big day for our people."

"It was that. I've still got that photograph you took of the two of us on my office wall. My secretary says it's the best anyone's ever done."

"How flattering. So what brings you here today?"

Casey reached into his pocket and withdrew an envelope. "I was hoping you could tell me who you gave this receipt to." He handed it to her, and she studied it, frowning.

"This was a little while ago, but I'll have a record. I have the negative, too, and you can get a look at them." She went to a desk and pulled out a ledger, then opened it and paged through until she found what she wanted. She jotted a note on a pad of paper, then got up and went into the back, where Casey heard a filing cabinet open. In a moment or two she was coming back into the room.

"I remember this now," she said, opening a file folder. "They were certainly a pair. Both a little tipsy. I wasn't certain they even knew what they were doing, but the man paid in advance. I think he was trying to please the woman, since the photo was clearly her idea." She pulled out a print and showed it to Casey.

He took it from her and looked at it, and saw a whipcord thin, narrow-skulled negro of thirty-five or so, with a pretty light-colored negro woman about ten years his junior. She was dressed in a cheap, flashy outfit that showed too much of her legs and cleavage, and a silly little bird-nest-shaped hat with a tiny veil perched on her dark curls.

"They sure look pleased with themselves. Who are they?"

"The woman gave her name as Lucinda Mayfield, and she asked me to send two copies of the print to this address on Dublin Street. The man didn't give a name, but I heard her call him 'Zootie,' a few times."

"Doesn't ring a bell with me, but maybe one of the Negro Squad detectives will recognize it. May I keep this?"

"Certainly," Mrs. Connor replied. "Can you tell me what it's about?"

Casey's mouth twisted. "I'm sorry to say that it's a homicide—another negro detective. I found that receipt near the murder scene. I don't know if it's related or not, but we have to track it down. I appreciate your help."

Florestine Connor put her hand to her mouth when Casey said "homicide." "I'm sorry I asked, but naturally I'll keep it to myself. Can you tell me who was killed?"

"Thomas Blanton. He left a wife and son."

Florestine Connor made a noise in her throat. "Dear God. I went to school with her. This is terrible. Do you think this man did it?" She pointed to the photograph.

"If I can find him, I'll ask, and you can be sure he'll tell me." Casey had a grim look on his face. "Thanks for everything, Mrs. Connor. I'll let you know what happens."

"Thank you. I'll say a prayer for all of you."

Casey turned to the window. The storm had passed as suddenly as it had begun, leaving the streets momentarily clean. He smiled at the photographer, put on his hat, and left the studio. As he got into his car, he heard his call sign on the radio. He keyed the mike and spoke into it.

"Detective Nick Delgado requests you call him at the lab on land line, over," the dispatcher said.

"Wilco." Casey saw a telephone booth on the corner, so he got back out and walked over to it. Dropping in his nickel, he soon had the police crime lab on the line.

"Just finished the analysis on the shotgun shell picked up at the Blanton murder scene, chief," Delgado said. "The ejector indentations suggest that it's probably from a Winchester model '97 pump."

"Pretty common. About half of our riot guns are model '97s. Winchester must've made a million of 'em."

"It's probably an ex-Army weapon or the riot model," Delgado continued. "The medical examiner called with a preliminary report and said the wide spread of the pellets in Blanton's face and neck suggests a short barrel. There's one thing about it that makes it unique."

"What's that?"

"There's a strange little half-moon shaped mark in the firing pin. Either a manufacturing flaw or a small chip knocked out of it through heavy use. I'll run a check against other shotgun homicides and see if I can find a previous use of this gun."

"Good work, Nick. I'll be back in the office later if you find anything."

"Right, skipper."

Casey hung up the telephone. He didn't expect a quick answer from Delgado. Shotguns were more common in the South than the Thompson submachine guns that got so much use in the Midwest and East Coast. They were easier to get, since there was no Federal law regulating their manufacture and sale. But still, there was that strange mark on the firing pin. Casey had a strange feeling that Nick would find something, eventually. He returned to his car and went back to work.

Chapter 4

As Farrell drove toward Lake Pontchartrain after leaving Nate Styles, he went through his memories of the last few years of Prohibition. Although he had been a significant player in the illegal import of booze to the city, he'd gotten into it rather late. Gangs had risen and fallen by the time he'd begun his operation about 1930. A prudent player, he'd scouted his major competition and taken pains not to poach on their territory or try to steal customers. There really hadn't been any need for it—New Orleans had uncountable speakeasies, not to mention the old line society clubs, Mardi Gras organizations, and negro social and pleasure clubs that had purchased liquor in large quantities for their members' private use. Still, rival gangs had killed each other off in order to get more and more territory, and even Farrell had occasionally found himself at war with those who coveted his action.

Law enforcement had been only a minor irritant to the better-organized gangs for a very special reason—most people wanted a drink once in a while, so few cooperated with the law, even those who considered themselves upstanding, law-abiding citizens. For straight-arrows like George Schofield, it must have been a frustrating time, particularly when one considered how many local cops and state prohibition officers had been on the take.

But Schofield's death was only tangentially connected to illegal whiskey. Nate Styles hadn't known what Farrell knew—that Schofield was trying to unmask a traitor. The question was, who was the mysterious traitor, and who was he working with? Farrell decided it might be easier to find the traitor by first discovering which gang he worked for, then working backwards.

Farrell continued Lakeward until he reached Southline Drive where he turned east, following it past Shushan airfield to a small cluster of houses known as Milneburg.

Near the back of the village, he found what he was looking for, a comfortable bungalow with a wide front porch covered with fine wire screen. He cut his engine, set the hand brake, and walked up to the porch. The screen door was unlocked, so he opened it and stepped into the cool, dim porch. The front door to the house was open, but he stood at the threshold and knocked on the door frame. "Hello, anybody home?"

He heard a slow, irregular tread, and eventually a slender old man with a crutch under his left arm hobbled out of the shadows. His left leg was missing below the knee, and the trouser leg was safety-pinned up near his waistband. His tanned face was furrowed with lines and covered with fine, white bristles, and pale blue eyes gleamed past high cheekbones. His hair was gray with a few streaks of dark brown remaining. He grinned broadly and held out his right hand. "I'll be damned—Wes Farrell. What the hell brings you all the way out here?"

Farrell took the hand and shook it warmly. "I got lonesome for your coffee, Dutch. How are you?"

The man shrugged elaborately. "Well, like the song says, I don't get around much anymore, but I've taken a fancy to this quiet, small-town life. Not to say I don't sometimes miss the old days. A car backfiring in the street still gets my blood up." He laughed in a soft, dry wheeze. "C'mon in the kitchen, son. I got some of that coffee on."

"Sounds good, Dutch. I miss your coffee as much as you miss the excitement." He followed as the older man hobbled toward the kitchen.

The kitchen, in contrast to the front room, was all windows and sunlight. The cabinetry was a gleaming white, and the sink counters were covered with alternating black and white hexagon-shaped ceramic tiles. Farrell sat down in a cane-bottomed kitchen chair and put his hat on the table while Dutch poured coffee into a pair of thick white china mugs, dumped in sugar and cream, then brought them to the table. When he was seated, he looked across at Farrell.

"I hear quite a bit about you. Every time I turn around, you're raisin' some kind of hell and gettin' your name in the papers. You used to be better at mindin' your own business."

Farrell shrugged. "You know me, Dutch. I never have to look for trouble—it just seems to find me. The nightclub and some of the other businesses keep me in the office a lot, which makes me a stationary target."

"With emphasis on the target. But I know all about that." He thumped the stump of his left leg with his hand, and for the briefest of seconds, his grin slipped.

"How's your memory?"

Dutch's grin came back. "About the old days, you mean? Pretty good. Fifteen years of dodging bullets sharpened it plenty. What about 'em?"

"You remember just before repeal a Coast Guard commander named Schofield was rubbed out, gangland style?"

Dutch nodded. "Never could figure that. Prohibition was almost over, and the Coast Guard wasn't hurtin' nobody but the small fry. None of them could've, or would've pulled off a hit that smooth. The few gangs of any size that were left by then wouldn't have done anything that stupid." He paused for a moment, his eyes flickering from some memory, then he looked over at Farrell. "What's all this to you, Wes? Prohibition's been over for nearly five years."

Farrell reached into his coat for his cigarette case and opened it, then pushed it across the table toward Dutch. "Cigarette?"

Dutch looked down at the white paper tubes with hooded eyes. "I guess you're not going to tell me, huh?"

"Let's just say it's a personal matter and let it go at that. I think Schofield was about to find out something—that there was a turncoat in his organization or in Treasury—and that whoever the turncoat was engineered the hit. But he didn't do it alone—whoever he sold out to helped him pull the trigger. I want to know whose pocket the turncoat was in—if I know that, I'll be able to find out the name of the man who set it up."

Dutch rubbed his hand over his unshaven chin, making a dry, whispery sound. "There were maybe five gangs, not counting us, who were bringing in enough booze to make it worth the risk by then. August Milton's gang was still operating, and there was Lou Prince, Old Man Morrison, Terry McShayne, and Archie Badeaux."

"I'd forgotten about Prince and McShayne."

"They're all still around, somewhere," Dutch replied. "Except Badeaux."

Farrell nodded. Badeaux had been killed in a gun battle with Farrell, Israel Daggett, and some gangsters the year before. "You know anything about where the others might be?"

Dutch picked up his cup and took a healthy swig of his coffee. "Like I said, I don't get around much, but once in a while I hear something from somebody passing this way. Lou Prince is running a trucking business now—strictly legit'. I knew him pretty well— he's not the type to kill anybody in cold blood, or help anybody else do it."

"Lou didn't like guns. Never knew him to carry one."

"Right. Now, Terry McShayne's a typical Irishman—loved to fight. But for all that, he was a half-way decent guy. Smart, too. He had pretty good street informants, and that kept him out of a lot of trouble." He shook his head. "Dealing with an informant in the Coast Guard would've been chancy—that would be another charge against him if he got caught. Terry never took long chances. That was the secret of his luck. He's livin' quiet and honest these days, too."

"So that leaves August Milton and Old Man Morrison."

Dutch nodded soberly. "If I was asked to make a guess for money, that would be the guess I'd make."

Farrell savored his coffee for a moment before speaking. "I haven't heard much of either of them since before Repeal. I wonder where they are?"

"Damned if I know. August Milton kind of stepped away from the rackets when his son and grandson died in a car accident not far from here. I heard a truck ran 'em off the road and they were both killed."

"I didn't know anything about that. Was his son in the rackets, too?"

"No. He was a lawyer, but strictly on the up-and-up from what I heard. The little boy was only six or so. This was seven or eight years ago. A hell of a thing." Dutch shook his head.

"I never even knew Milton had a family. He's been a racketeer of one kind or another since before I was old enough to know about such things."

"Yeah, and he was plenty savvy. He had cops on the pad all the time, so corrupting a Treasury or Coast Guard man wouldn't be anything special."

"Yeah," Farrell said. "Same with Old Man Morrison."

"Morrison—now he was a hustler. He probably brought the last boatload of illegal hooch into the city, right under the wire." Dutch grinned and scratched his chin. "He had plenty of jack at the end—he's probably livin' it up, for all I know. His right-hand man, Nose Morianos, is still around, though. He might talk to you. He might not, too. The Nose wasn't very sociable."

"Maybe I can find some kind of incentive for him."

Dutch grinned. "It must get dull in that office."

"It does, but that doesn't mean I don't like it." Farrell picked up his cup and finished his coffee.

"You need somebody to cover your back, I'm here, okay?"

Farrell reached across the table and gripped the older man's wrist. "You don't need to tell me that. If you hadn't always done that, I wouldn't be here now, and you—"

"And I wouldn't be hobblin' around on this stump," Dutch said without bitterness. "It was all worth it. We had a hell of a five years, didn't we?"

"Yeah, pardner. We sure as hell did."

⸎

It was nearing 4:00 P M when the 75-foot Coast Guard patrol vessel eased into the slip at the New Orleans Coast Guard Station. A well-built, blonde man in khaki with the collar devices of a lieutenant commander stood confidently at the helm, working the wheel and throttles as sailors in dungarees and chambray caught the bow and stern lines thrown to them by other seamen on the docks.

"All secure, Mr. Kelso," the seaman at the bow called. Kelso cut the engines and stood there, listening to the cries of the gulls and the sound of the ensign flapping in the stiff breeze.

"Very good. Hose the boat down, then go get chow. Starboard section gets liberty at 1630." Kelso jumped to the dock, pulling the bill of his cap down lower over his eyes as he walked to the administration building. He stared at the American flag and Coast Guard ensign snapping at the yardarm in front of the building, and calculated that he'd served twenty one years and eight months. It didn't seem that long since he'd joined up during the early years of the Great War. He'd only been sixteen and a half at the time, but he was big for his age, and the Chief Petty Officer in the enlistment office hadn't asked too many questions. It hadn't occurred to him at the time that he'd eventually work his way up to lieutenant commander with his own command. Even now it seemed unreal to him as he returned the salute of two petty officers in their undress whites.

He caught the pleasant aroma of ginger pot roast coming from the galley as he entered the building and walked to his office. "Any messages for me, Lowell?" he asked the second-class yeoman who served as his secretary.

"Just some routine radio traffic, Mr. Kelso, but this man has been waiting to see you." He indicated a tall, slender red-haired man who stood up from his visitor's chair. "Is that you, Jimmie? By God, it's been years. Let me look at you."

James Schofield walked over, holding out his hand. "It's been a long time, Emmett. You look good." He was grinning from ear to ear.

Kelso caught the offered hand in a warm grip. "So do you, kid. This is a big surprise. C'mon into the office." He led the young Treasury agent into his private office and closed the door. Schofield saw that the walls of the office were covered with photographs, correspondence school diplomas, and district commendation letters. He remembered that his old friend had been relentless in the pursuit of his own perfection, always chasing a new bit of knowledge, a new record, higher rank. Kelso gestured toward a couple of armchairs and the two men sat down across from each other.

"You down here on a vacation, Jimmie?"

Schofield leaned forward in his chair a little. "I'm down here to find out who killed George."

Kelso's eyes got wide. "After all these years? Man alive, that trail must be colder than leftover mashed potatoes by now."

"Maybe not. Six months ago, a man here in New Orleans that George rented from sent me a footlocker that had been overlooked in his basement when they cleaned out George's apartment five years ago. I went through it, and found a notebook with some interesting things in it. Notes that George made before he died."

Kelso raised his left eyebrow slightly. "About what?"

"It took me a little while to figure out what it was, but eventually I realized they were observations of men under his command and some people over at Treasury."

Kelso shrugged. "I don't see what that means. It's a funny thing, I grant you, but I don't know what you could make out of it."

"George never did anything without a reason. If he shadowed and recorded the movements of all these men, he must have suspected that something was wrong. You know how analytical George was—always playing with numbers, figuring percentages. He figured booze was getting past him, and for some reason began his own investigation to find out why."

Kelso tugged thoughtfully at his lower lip. "That's an interesting idea, kid. We'd made some real headway against the smaller gangs, and cooperation with state and Treasury people had put some of the big gangs out of business. But illegal booze flowed until the last day. He might've seen something going on. But why investigate his own people? Why not go to the brass or the chief Treasury agent?"

Schofield shook his head ruefully. "I wish I knew. He must have had some reason to believe that he couldn't completely trust them, or maybe he was just waiting until he had something solid to report. But somewhere along the line, the people he was investigating got wise to him—and they killed him." He looked at Kelso, his face twisted with anguish. "He never spoke of this to you, either, I guess."

Kelso leaned back in his chair and studied the younger man. "No, but that's nothing new. You know how by-the-book George was—he doled out information to his officers and CPOs strictly on a need-to-know basis. That even went for me, and I was his exec." He paused to shift to a more comfortable position in his chair. "Anything in the notes to tell you what he might've learned?"

Schofield grimaced. "I can't tell yet. There are names and bits of information he picked up here and there—I thought if I tracked down some of the people he investigated I could make sense of the rest of it."

Kelso frowned. "It's not very much to go on."

"I can't disagree with you, but I want to make a stab at it. Can you help me track down some of the officers and petty officers who are on George's list?"

Kelso considered for a moment. "I think most of them might still be around. There were some retirements and a death or two, but most of them are still on active duty or they settled down around here. We can find them."

Schofield looked across at the other man. Emmett Kelso had been like second brother to him when George was alive. "Thanks, Emmett. It means a lot to me."

"Knock it off before I bust out cryin'." Kelso flashed a wise-guy grin. "I'm where I am now because of your brother. Here's where I get to pay it back."

Schofield had a rush of memory to the days when his brother was alive, and Kelso would join them on their outings. "I was hoping you'd say that."

∞∞∞

Acting on a tip from an informant, Daggett and Andrews drove into Gentilly on Florida Avenue and pulled into a Sinclair gasoline station run by a negro named Bick Washington. Andrews parked the car beside the station and the two detectives walked into the office. Andrews got a little cellophane bag of peanuts out of a large jar and then selected a bottle of Coca-Cola from an ice-filled chest. Dropping a dime into a nearby collection can, he sat down in a chair and sipped the Coke while Daggett threw a hip over the corner of a scarred metal desk. They sat there quietly, Andrews shaking peanuts into his mouth and chewing them noisily until a long-legged, skinny negro walked in. He was wearing a suit of grease-smeared green coveralls with the name "Bick" stenciled over the breast pocket. His blue-black hair was chemically-straightened and slicked down with pomade. He stopped when he saw the two detectives and stood there uncertainly.

"'Lo, Bick," Daggett said. "How's tricks?"

"Long time, no see, Iz, Sam." Washington's smile had a lot of teeth, but little humor in it. "Need some work done on your car?"

"Tell us what Johnny Hope is into," Andrews said around a mouthful of peanuts.

Washington affected an air of casualness, and walked around the desk to sit in the battered swivel chair. "What makes you think I know any of his business? I got plenty of my own to worry about. You think it's easy runnin' a garage with this Depression on? Shee-it, I'm lucky to pay for the gas most weeks."

Daggett smiled. "Bick, you know we didn't drive all the way out here to listen to a lot of who-struck-John about how tough the gasoline business is. You and Johnny go way back, and if I'm not mistaken, your mothers are third cousins."

Bick Washington shook his head. "Iz, you know so much about everybody's business, why is it your head don't swell up and bust, huh?" His tone was light, but there was a dull anger lingering in the back of his eyes.

Andrews swallowed the rest of his peanuts, crumpled the bag, and threw it into a nearby wastebasket. "Don't make us take you Downtown, Bick. You know somethin', spit it out, you don't know anything, spend a little time convincin' us you don't." He took a long pull at the cola, then set the empty bottle on the floor near his feet.

Bick Washington's anger faded to a sullen frown. He knew he couldn't test Sam Andrews or Daggett, that they would make his life a living hell if he lied to them and they later found it out. "Last I heard, he was movin' some hot cars."

"Tell me something I don't already know," Daggett said.

"I don't know that much. The people he's with are keepin' it real quiet, stealin' a few cars here, a few there, makin' it look like a lot of small-timers at work 'stead of one big gang."

Daggett nodded. "I had a hunch in that direction. So who's calling the shots? Hope's a follower, not a leader."

Bick Washington grimaced. "I don't know, but I seen Johnny with another brutha. He ain't the boss, 'cause bossin' a lotta people ain't his specialty. He keeps people in line for whoever the boss is. Scary li'l mothah-fuckah."

"Who is this scary fella?" Andrews asked.

"Hines. Zootie Hines. He is one righteous bad sonofabitch. I believe he'd kill his mother if there was a dollar in it."

Daggett looked at Andrews. "Think I've heard of him before, but not in connection with car theft." He turned his gaze back to Bick Washington. "You got any idea where we might find this Zootie Hines?"

Washington favored him with a weary gaze. "Sergeant, I ain't been no angel, but even a devil gets sick of lookin' at the sun through a barred window. I try to make it a point to stay away from all the Zootie Hineses and tend to this gas station. I been straight for five years now, I got me a house with a flower garden and a woman who might marry me. I ain't gonna throw all that away for a fast buck on no stolen car."

Daggett nodded, and even Andrews looked less skeptical. "I believe you, man."

"I'll tell you this much, cause I heard it through the grapevine. It might be shit, but it might be sugar, too."

Daggett's eyes gleamed. "Tell it."

"This Zootie—he's a professional badman and a stone killer, but he ain't no perfessor. He hurts people, but somebody got to tell him who to hurt. Whoever that is got to be one big, mean, sonofabitch to keep Zootie on a leash."

"Uh, huh," Daggett said, just to keep Bick talking.

"Talk goin' round that Zootie's boss is a white man."

Andrews cocked an interested eyebrow. "You don't hear of that everyday. Boss, how many white men you ever known to used colored men to do their dirty work?"

Daggett laughed. "Plantation owners and prison guards." Daggett knew that last for a fact—he'd spent five years in Angola on a murder beef that his own cousin had framed him for. The cousin had been in the employ of a white gangster.

"Ought not to be too hard to find a white man like that," Andrews rejoined.

"Maybe." Daggett got up and pulled the brim of his hat down over his forehead. "Bick, I'm sorry if we leaned on you too hard. Far as I know, you've been straight, and I'm glad for you. Marry that gal and have some babies. There's too many of us getting killed. If you hear anything, you know how to get me, right?"

"Yep. And I *will* call you if I hear anything."

"Fair enough. Let's go, Sam."

Andrews got up, put his empty Coke bottle in the rack, and followed Daggett out into the afternoon sunshine.

❦

About that same time, Wesley Farrell stopped at the door to the Old Absinthe House on Bourbon Street and peered through the door into the silent, gleaming room of one of the oldest bars in the city. If its walls could talk, they'd have told many a tale of the Lafittes, of Dominique You, Basile Crokere, and James Bowie. Farrell had once spent a lot of time there, when the owners had been among his steadiest consumers of illegal whiskey. They'd even sold him drinks at a discount.

Farrell strode through the room, his feet making no noise on the ancient wooden boards. A handsome, clean-cut negro stood at the bar wiping glasses with a white bar towel. As he looked up a grin spread across his broad face.

"*Monsieur* Wesley Farrell. It has been a long time, no?" Armand was a Haitian by birth, and his accent still reflected his Afro-French background.

"That it has, Armand." Farrell offered his hand to the bartender. "I'm looking for someone I used to drink with in the old days. Maybe he still comes around now and then."

"*C'est possible.* I still see many old faces come in here. *Qui est?*"

"Remember Jake Broussard?"

"Haw!" Armand brayed. "*Mais oui!* Monsieur Jake, he is in the back room. I think he takes a little nap, yes?"

"Give me a bottle of Peter Dawson and a couple of glasses. It's time for him to wake up." When he had them in hand, Farrell grinned at the black man and walked through a short passage into a back room.

The back room at the Old Absinthe House was reserved for friends and regulars, many of whom were barflies that Armand felt some affection for. Several of the tables were occupied by faded malingerers. A frail-looking blonde woman who might've been any age from thirty-five to sixty, sat at an old piano where she worked her way desultorily through "Oh, Them Golden Slippers," pausing occasionally in mid-note to drink from a tall, misted glass resting near her right wrist.

Farrell stopped and tracked the room with his eyes. He'd made almost a complete circuit when he noticed a man slumped in a chair near the back of the room. His face was cradled on his folded arms, and his expensive Panama hat obscured his face. Farrell walked toward him, stopping at the table. He put the bottle of Peter Dawson and the glasses on the table and gently lifted the Panama hat until he could see the man underneath.

"Umph. Whazzat?"

"Jake, wake up. I want to ask you something."

"Go 'way. Busy," Jake mumbled, not bothering to lift his head.

"C'mon, help me drink this bottle of Peter Dawson." Farrell poured whiskey into the glasses, making sure to clink the neck of the bottle noisily against each glass.

As the melody of glass and gurgling liquid penetrated Jake's sleep-fogged brain, he pushed himself upright and rubbed his face vigorously with his hands. With some effort he peeled his eyelids back from his eyes and looked up. "Wes Farrell," he said with a lop-sided smile. "How are ya, you old hoss thief? Siddown and have a drink on me."

"Mighty generous of you, amigo." Farrell pulled up a chair. "I wondered where you'd got to."

"Business has been bad lately." Jake Broussard raised a glass to his lips. He drained it, licked his lips, then set the glass down and filled it again. "Not that I need any work. Ever since we inherited that money back in '33, I've been on a vacation."

Farrell smiled thinly. In 1933 Broussard had been a private detective looking for the wandering daughter of a wealthy man. He'd brought Farrell into the case to back him up, and when the dust was cleared they found themselves in possession of $50,000.00, the owner of which had most unfortunately gotten himself dead. Since there'd been no record of the money's existence, they'd simply appropriated it. Farrell later used his half to front a legitimate business and Broussard invested his in a couple of small office buildings, afterward taking up more-or-less permanent residence at the Old Absinthe House.

"So they tell me," Farrell said. "I've looked all over for you."

"Well, you found me, or at least what's left." He laughed heartily, then took a sip of his scotch.

Farrell smiled. Broussard was the same as ever. "I need your help."

Broussard caught the note in his friend's voice, and his face went through a startling transformation that took him from fun-loving drunk to sober and steely in five seconds. "Last time you said that to me, we shot a couple guys outside of Gretna." He grinned, and ran his fingers through his thinning black hair a few times. "What's up?"

Farrell offered Broussard a cigarette and lit it for him. "Remember the murder of a Coast Guard officer about mid-way through 1934?"

Broussard drew on his cigarette, and blew out a long plume of smoke. "Yeah. They never caught who did it. He was in command of a smuggler interdiction patrol or something, wasn't he?"

"Uh, huh. He'd been making a lot of headway against the smaller gangs, but some of the bigger ones were sliding past him over and over again. He'd come to the conclusion that somebody had been tipping those guys off as to when and where the Coast Guard would be patrolling so they could make an end run and get their shipments ashore. The night he was killed, he was hoping to meet a man who would tell him who that somebody was."

Broussard leaned back in his seat and crossed his legs, his face taking on a bemused expression. After a long pause, he said, "How is it that you happen to know what was on this joker's mind before he was rubbed out?"

Farrell lifted one corner of his mouth. "I was with him. We were both in the Honey Pot when a brawl blew up, and we ended up fighting our way out together. He knew my name, and we began a conversation. He was pretty green at gumshoeing and, I guess because I had an honest face, he explained why he was there. Right after that the shotgun squad turned up and blew him off the face of the earth."

"Uh, huh. That's interesting as all hell, but it doesn't explain why you're so interested after all these years."

"There's a good enough reason. Schofield's kid brother joined the Treasury Department, and he's here now trying to track down the killer. He's already been to my office, and he's made it plain he's going to take the town apart brick by brick until he finds out who killed his brother."

"And you're afraid that he'll eventually find out you were with his brother at the end, and might try to tag you for the murder."

"No wonder they used to call you the greatest private eye New Orleans ever had."

"Used to? That's a fine how-do-you-do. I'm not dead yet." He pushed his glass away from him and tapped his fingers on the table. Now that his mind was engaged with a problem, drinking held no interest for him. "By the time your friend was killed, there weren't many smugglers left who mattered. In fact, only two that I know of—August Milton and Old Man Morrison. They might've paid somebody a pile of cash to keep them clear of the Coast Guard patrols. So far as I know, they were the only two who thrived until the last, just like they were eating Wheaties and milk every morning."

Farrell smiled. "You might've been asleep for a few years, but you don't seem to have missed or forgotten anything. I don't know where to find those guys, but I thought you might."

"Hey, I'm touched. I'm gonna bust out cryin' cause you thought of your old pal, Jakie, the gossip monger." Broussard pretended to wipe a tear out of his eye. "Y'know, finding those guys will be a lot easier than getting them to admit they suborned a Federal officer and then connived at the murder of another."

"I'll worry about that later. Do you know where Milton and Morrison are?"

Broussard drummed his fingers on the table. "Nobody I know has seen Morrison in years. But Milton is around—in a manner of speaking."

"What's that mean?"

"It means he left behind his life of crime to become a gentleman of leisure."

"Yeah? What's the rest?"

"He's in a back yard across the river in Algiers. I'll give you the address."

⚬⚬⚬

Casey spent much of his time behind a desk lately, but he'd been one of the force's top investigators up until the day they'd placed him in charge of the Detective Bureau in the wake of the Emile Ganns/Gus Moroney scandal. It was therefore very little trouble for him to find the whereabouts of one Lucinda Mayfield, whose picture he held in his hand. There were white detectives who would have tried to avoid venturing into a negro neighborhood, and most of the Negro Squad were working on Blanton's murder, so Casey decided to continue on with the investigation himself.

Dublin Street was several streets over on the River side of Carrollton Avenue, and the Mayfield woman's address was in a rundown part of the neighborhood not far from the water treatment plant. Like virtually every other home in the neighborhood, Lucinda's house was half of a shotgun double, distinguished only by a fairly recent, and badly-applied coat of whitewash. In the flower bed, a few marigolds and begonias were locked in a death struggle with a host of various weeds, and a cheap tin mailbox hung askew on a single nail. He heard music coming from behind the door, so he knocked loudly a few times. Before long, the door opened and a young negro woman stood there behind the screen door. She looked at him insolently, a cigarette smoldering in the corner of her mouth.

"Lucinda Mayfield?"

"Who's askin'?" she demanded, not taking the cigarette from her mouth.

Casey held up his shield. "Police. I'd like to ask you a few questions.

Lucinda retained her insolent pose, but her dark eyes grew uncertain, and she shuffled her feet nervously. She took the cigarette from her mouth and flicked it with her thumb, careless of where the ashes went. "Uh—Lucinda ain't here right now. Maybe you could try back later."

Casey smiled kindly. He held up the photograph he'd gotten from Florestine Connors where the woman could see it. "You must be Lucinda's twin sister. I've seen twins before, but seldom such identical twins. Even down to that little mole on your temple."

Lucinda's eyes got large and she gulped audibly. "Whaadayou want with me?"

"For the moment, just a little talk. Do you want to let me come inside, or would you rather we talked Downtown?"

Without a word she held open the screen and he came inside. He heard the radio more clearly now, and he recognized Lee Wiley's voice singing "Let's Fly Away." Lucinda snapped the radio off and gestured awkwardly at a frayed sofa. Casey sat down while she sank into a white Boston rocker, watching him through haunted eyes.

"This man in the picture," Casey began. "Can you tell me who he is?"

"Zootie. Zootie Hines. Him and me, we used to have a few laughs every once in a while."

"Uh-huh. What does this Zootie do for a living?"

Lucinda took a jerky drag from her cigarette. "Hell, I don't ask a man what he does, long as he can pay for some fun. He could be a streetcar conductor for all I know."

"I doubt it. I'm looking for your friend Zootie in connection with a murder investigation."

"Murder!?" Lucinda's complexion became sickly gray, as her eyes protruded from their sockets.

"A copy of the sales receipt for this photograph was found out in St. Bernard Parish at an abandoned drop for stolen cars. A negro police officer named Tom Blanton was shot near there by the car thieves two days ago. Maybe Hines isn't responsible, but I want to talk to him. So where is he?"

Lucinda's mouth was open. In her eyes Casey could see her mind churning furiously as she tried to decide whether the truth or a lie would be more dangerous to her.

"I don't know nothin' about this."

"Nobody said you did, but you know where Hines is, and either you'll tell me, or I'm liable take you in for obstructing justice and let you sit in the Parish Prison while you make up your mind. Now what'll it be?" He stared at her, not unkindly, simply letting her know he meant business.

"I—I swear, Mister, I don't know where Zootie is. He ain't been over here in two months at least. He just stopped comin' around—I don't know why. Honest, I swear it."

"When you did see him, did he ever talk about what he did?" Casey's voice seemed to calm the frightened woman because she gradually regained her composure. Her cigarette had gone out, and she dropped it into an ashtray.

"I didn't know him long. Maybe five months. I met him in a bar down on Toledano Street, and after that he'd show up every few days, we'd get drunk and go hellin' around for a day or two. I didn't ask him much about himself, but he always had money. He was okay, but every once in a while he'd get to feelin' sorry for himself."

"What did he feel sorry for himself about?"

"He worked for this man and he was always worryin' about what the man was thinkin' 'bout him." She paused and pushed at a stray lock of hair. "It was a funny way for a guy to take on, but everybody's different, I reckon."

"Did he ever mention the man's name?"

"Uhn-uh. But he said they was in the car business once, and he laughed like that was funny. I tried to get him to tell me what he was laughin' about, but he was kinda drunk at the time, and just laughed some more." She half-smiled, looking away as though she could see him. After a moment, the smile left her, and she looked at Casey again. "There was one thing about him I found real strange, though."

Casey leaned a bit closer, intrigued by the girl's story. "What was that?"

She hadn't meant to talk about what had come into her mind, and she ducked her head a little, finding it difficult to look at Casey because she didn't know exactly how to tell this very personal thing to a man. "Well, I don't know the words to say it—I mean, sometimes, when we'd been—when we'd been together, like—he'd cry at the end. I never seen a man do that before. Maybe it was the liquor done it."

Casey nodded like he understood, but he didn't know what that particular piece of information meant or was worth. "I see. All right, Lucinda. I'm going to let you off the hook, but I'm leaving you a card. If you see or hear of Zootie Hines, I want you to call, day or night."

She took the card, relieved to know that she wasn't going to jail. "Yes, sir, I sure will."

Casey got up and half-turned to go, but Lucinda spoke again and he stopped to listen.

"He was a funny-lookin' li'l man, and talked real big, but there was somethin' almost sweet about him sometimes."

Casey nodded, then he left the house.

❦

Mercer was still asleep at the house his woman rented on Perdido Street when the call came that Johnny Hope needed to talk to him. The dark haired woman went to the bedroom and sat beside him on the bed.

"Bart—Bart—wake up. There's a guy on the phone—somethin' about Johnny Hope and the cops."

The word "cops" penetrated his unconsciousness, and he raised up on one elbow. "Who is it?"

"Says his name's Boxcars. Said it's real important."

Mercer got up and padded naked to the front room and picked up the phone. "What's this about cops?"

"Johnny said to tell you they been to his house," Boxcars replied. "Said to call him at his sister's."

"All right." Mercer broke the connection, then he got the operator and gave her the number of Johnny Hope's sister. Johnny must've been standing right beside the phone, because he picked up on the first ring.

"This is Mercer. Boxcars said the cops were there."

"They found out the place near Violet belonged to me," the burly negro said. "Iz Daggett and Sam Andrews come over. By now they done looked my record up and know I done time for car theft. I thought somebody was gonna get that dead cop's car away from there and make it disappear. The damn thing was layin' there waitin' when they come snoopin' around. This is some bad shit, Mercer." The words tumbled out of Johnny's mouth so fast that Mercer could not get a word in edgewise.

"Shut up a minute," he broke in. "I told Joe Earle and Oscar to get the Goddamn thing out of there. When I see those two they'll be sorry they didn't listen." His voice had dropped to a low snarl, and Johnny felt the hair on his neck stand straight up.

"Whippin' their heads ain't gonna help nothin'. I'm in a jam, Mercer. What you gonna do?" Johnny's fear, which had been on a low simmer all morning, began to boil over as his terror of Mercer was awakened. Mercer was the most frightening human Johnny had ever seen. He could pick up two ordinary men in his hands and shake them until their necks snapped. He had split the head of a rival gangster from crown to neck with one blow of a cane knife back in the '20s—Johnny had seen him do it, and the image haunted his nightmares all these years later.

"What am I gonna do?" Mercer asked in an incredulous growl. "I'm gonna lay low and button my lip, and you do the same. The cops got nothin' on you but the fact you own an abandoned garage. Nothin', you hear me? You go about your business and no matter how many times they come to you, you play dumb, get me?"

"Y-yeah, sure. What about the new drop?"

"I got enough boys there to do body work and paint jobs without you comin' in. Take some day work and act like a solid citizen. Sooner or later it'll die down, and you can get back on the job."

"You—you're sure? I mean, havin' Iz Daggett on your ass is bad trouble."

"A nigger cop bothers me like a quart of milk. You want to worry about somethin', Johnny—you worry about me, 'cause if you screw up and the cops come after us, I'll tear your fuckin' head right off your shoulders, you hear me?"

Johnny's insides had turned to water, and he pressed his thighs tightly together to keep from wetting himself. Mercer's contemptuous use of the word "nigger" was lost under the powerful image of his threat. "Y-yeah, sure. I get you. Keep calm. That's what I'll do." He paused for a moment, hardly daring to breath, frightened of what he had to say next. "About my brother—he didn't mean no harm. Don't—d-don't hurt h-him, okay?"

"You got yourself to worry about, Johnny. Let me worry about Joe Earle." Mercer slammed the telephone down, the sound of it in his ear almost enough to make Johnny faint.

Mercer turned around and saw the woman looking at him.

"What are you lookin' at?"

"Nothin'" Her face was empty of expression. "Just standin' here is all." Her hands, held behind her back, were tensed into fists to keep them from trembling.

"Make me some food then." He turned and stomped back into the bedroom.

Chapter 5

Frank Casey was an old cop, and an old cop knew from experience that you didn't find killers through clues and fingerprints. Seven times out of ten that stuff didn't exist, and when it did, it was good only for nailing the lid on an iron-bound coffin good and shut. Informants, stool-pigeons, back alley gossip mongers—they were the keys that opened the closets where the skeletons were hidden.

After leaving Lucinda Mayfield, Casey drove down Canal Street until he reached St. Anthony of Padua Catholic Church. At the corner he turned and drove two blocks behind the churchyard. Parking the car, he walked across the yard to the caretaker's cottage and knocked on the door. After a minute the door opened. A man of about sixty dressed in a pair of clean, pressed overalls and a black and green checked flannel shirt stood there. His face was bony and angular, with piercing gray-green eyes and a fringe of white hair surrounding a bald, sun-browned head.

"Frank Casey." His voice was flat and humorless. "Long time no see."

"Don't act so glad to see me, Meechum. I might get embarrassed that I didn't bring a cake." He paused for a second, then said, "It'll be easier if you invite me in and give me a chair to sit on."

Meechum's eyes roamed around Casey's features as he stood to one side and held the door so the red-haired detective could come in. As he shut the door, he gestured with his free hand to a couple of old, cracked leather club chairs. Casey took the one on the left, placing his hat on his knee as he leaned back.

"Nice place you got here. I heard through the grapevine that Father Tumborelli offered you a job after they let you out of 'Gola last year."

Meechum snorted. "He heard how good I got growing flowers up at the pen. Figured I'd be a natural at caring for a churchyard. I guess he's satisfied. He's not the kind of guy to let you skate on anything. So why the visit? I been out of the stir for eight months, three weeks, and four days. Kind of late for you to be delivering the keep-my-nose-clean-if-I-know-what's-good-for-me speech." Meechum's voice was even and steady, without bitterness in spite of his choice of words.

"You don't need me to tell you that, Bill. You were a smart crook—the smartest I ever went up against. If you'd had more luck than I did, you'd be riding high and I'd still be a detective sergeant." Casey paused to tug thoughtfully at his earlobe for a moment. "I want some help. I think you can give it to me."

"Me? Help you how?" Meechum's face was impassive, his eyes fixed unblinkingly on Casey's.

"A couple of days ago, one of my negro detectives—a young guy named Tom Blanton—was gunned down outside of Violet. He was working undercover on a hot car ring and had made contact with one of the gang. Something went wrong and Blanton was murdered. I think a negro named Zootie Hines may have been involved. This ring is big and well organized, which makes me think that even if this negro is part of it, there may be a well-connected white crook calling all or most of the shots."

"Yeah? What's that to me?"

"You know people. You can probably get me the name of anybody in the city with the savvy to deal in hot cars. If I've got a name, I've got a lever to wedge this gang wide open. I want the men who killed Blanton like a baby wants mother's milk—I want to put them in the electric chair and be there when they turn on the juice."

Meechum listened as he studied his work-roughened hands. He removed a small clasp knife from the bib pocket on his overalls, opened it, and used it to trim a ragged nail on his left hand. When he was finished, he blew the scrap of nail off the blade, closed it, and dropped it back into his pocket. "What makes you think I can help you? I never dealt in hot cars. I did banks. I also never had much truck with the nigger cons. They mostly had their own action and their own guys running it."

"But you spent ten years in Angola. While you were inside, you controlled more action there than Luciano does in New York City. A guy couldn't break wind in there unless you said it was okay." Casey leaned forward, his eyes very intent on Meechum's. "You know who the hot car people were up there, and you know how to get in touch with them if they're out."

Meechum examined Casey's face for a moment. "What's in it for me if I do?"

"Help me, and I'll go to bat with the parole board for you—get your parole time reduced. If I can crack the case, I'll ask them to consider a pardon."

Meechum stared at Casey. "You'd do that? For me?"

Casey nodded slowly. "I spent a year tracking you down and a lot of effort putting you away, Bill, but I never hated you. You never hurt anybody, and so far as I know never fired a gun in all the robberies you committed. You're no saint, but you're not a killer, either, and I don't think you have any sympathy for a killer. Play ball with me, and I'll go to the mat for you. You got my word."

Meechum considered for a moment. "I know a few people I can call. I might know something tomorrow or the day after."

Casey grinned. "I'll be waiting."

⚬⚬⚬

Near the St. Bernard Parish line, Zootie Hines was helping three other negroes wrestle equipment from the back of a large van into an abandoned garage that had once belonged to a pair of brothers named Mouton. The Moutons had met an untimely end the year before, and while they'd had no heirs to leave it to, neither had the bank held any liens on the property. The buildings and land had simply been left vacant after their demise—that is until Bart Mercer found out about them. There were few houses out this way, so Mercer was pretty certain they wouldn't be disturbed for a while. Hines had just finished wrestling a paint compressor into a corner when he heard a car outside. He turned, his head raised slightly, emphasizing the blade-like quality of his countenance. He reached inside his overalls for the .38 Colt Police Positive holstered there in a special pocket and peered around the corner of the open garage door. A new green De Soto pulled to a stop and Mercer crawled from behind the wheel. Hines tucked his roscoe away and went out to meet his boss.

"We near 'bout got everything in place. Didn't 'spect to see you before tonight." He looked at Mercer expectantly, wondering if he would say anything about how quickly Zootie had gotten things together. He hid his disappointment when the words did not come.

Mercer kept walking toward the office as Hines fell in beside him. "You need to keep out of sight for a while, Zootie."

"What gives?" Hines already knew from Mercer's expression that something was wrong.

"We got trouble. That knuckle-head Joe Earle Hope didn't get that dead cop's car away from the old drop like I told him, and the cops found it. That led them to Johnny, and he's about to shit in his pants."

"Goddamn," Zootie said. "You want I should break his neck?"

"You gotta lay low. I got word from a guy I know that the cops're lookin' for you, too. They been to see that pig you were shackin' with, too, and gave her the third degree."

"Huh? What pig you talkin' about?"

"Lucinda Mayfield, you dumbbell."

Zootie shrugged. "Well, that ain't no big thing. I ain't seen her in almost three months. 'Sides, she don't know nothin' 'bout us. She was just somebody to fuck is all." He smiled at Mercer, thinking that this was something Mercer, himself, might say.

"Maybe, but they got your name and they ain't lookin' for you 'cause they want your autograph. I don't like it."

Zootie's smile faded. "I'm sorry. I'll try to make it right some way, boss."

"Forget it. The main thing is for the cops not to find you. If they don't find you, they can't find the rest of us."

Zootie looked up at him with a frown. "Johnny knows how to lie and crawfish, but he's soft. If the cops keep after him, he'll crack and sing like a fuckin' sparrow."

"I told him to steer clear of this place and take some odd jobs. If he plays it cool, they'll stop payin' attention to him and look for another patsy."

Zootie shook his head. "What if they don't?"

Mercer shrugged. "Then we'll make him disappear. I can always find another mechanic."

Zootie took on a serious expression. "Let me take care of it, boss. I caused you some grief. If I take care of Johnny, it'll be right again."

Mercer considered him for a long moment. "I'll give him a little while, but we'll watch him. If it looks like he's gonna cave in, you can do the job. That satisfy you?"

Zootie nodded earnestly.

Mercer nodded back. "Okay then. Tell the other boys to go home, and then let's throw some grub on the table. I'm starved."

Mercer's words warmed Zootie's insides in much the same way Violetta's caresses did. With a renewed sense of purpose, he yelled at the other negroes to knock off and go home. He turned, and saw Mercer grinning at him, and he grinned back before he walked to the house to open some cans for dinner.

⬥⬥⬥

Wesley Farrell drove his Packard over the bumpy gangway of the Canal Street ferry onto Delaronde Street in the borough of Algiers and turned right at Pelican. It was a quiet respectable street in New Orleans' most remote and respectable borough. Lined with majestic old oaks that formed a shady canopy over the avenue, it was not at all the kind of a place one would expect to find a retired master criminal.

Thanks to Broussard's instructions, Farrell found the address without any difficulty. It was an interesting design, having a wing that came out from the rest of the house at a ninety-degree angle, with a rounded glassed-in room at the end nearest the sidewalk. From the street he could see that the room was lined with bookcases. There was a tall poplar tree in the center of the yard. Its flower beds were full of marigolds, cosmos, and cyclamen which still bloomed in spite of the weather turning warm. Farrell eased the car to the curb and cut the engine.

Following Broussard's instructions, he started up the walk, turning at the front porch and continuing around the side to the rear of the dwelling.

"Keep your hands in plain sight," Broussard had advised. "August won't be expecting you and you don't want to scare him."

Broussard's face had worn a strange grin as he gave this advice, but Farrell hadn't questioned him.

As is customary in many New Orleans neighborhoods, the back yard of August Milton's address was far larger than the front, and was shaded by pear trees. There was a carriage house with a small porch, and on the porch a white-haired man sat in a rocker with a little girl in his lap. He was reading to her from a child's picture book, but when he spotted Farrell, he spoke gently to the little girl. She slid off his lap and ran past a luxuriant bed of red, pink, and white carnations to the back door of the main house.

The man reached casually to the table beside him and moved a folded newspaper to his lap, his long legs stretched comfortably before him. As he drew closer to Milton, Farrell saw the man inspecting him with piercing steel-blue eyes that never blinked. Although his posture was languid, Farrell noticed that his right hand was now hidden in the folds of the newspaper. In spite of the white hair, there was a sharpness and a decided air of danger about him.

Milton smiled mirthlessly. "Whoever you are, don't let the hair fool you. I can still shoot faster than you can move. Who are you?"

Farrell paused and pushed his Borsalino off his forehead. "The name's Farrell. We were kind of in the same line of business once."

Milton studied Farrell's face, then nodded. "I thought you looked familiar. I don't think we ever crossed paths before. Correct me if I'm wrong." The white-haired man didn't move a muscle as he spoke, and his right hand remained rigid under the newspaper. The skin of his face was taut and surprisingly free of lines. He might've been no older than fifty.

"You're not wrong, Mr. Milton." Farrell let his hands hang empty at his sides. "And you don't need the gun. I'm just here to talk."

Milton's smile widened, but his eyes remained hard and bright. "Sit where I can see you, Farrell. I've heard too often of people you didn't like suddenly growing knives between their ribs." He took his hand from under the paper, revealing a nickel-plated .45 Colt automatic with checked ivory grips. He held it negligently, but no one who had seen his eyes would ever suspect him of carelessness. Farrell sat down and took off his hat. "What do you want?"

"Mr. Milton, I'm kind of interested in some things that went on near the end of Prohibition. Your gang and Old Man Morrison's were the only big players left in the smuggling trade when the Volstead law expired in '34."

Milton's eyes flickered, and the corners of his mouth turned up slightly. "There's no need to pretend. Even the T-Men knew— but they could never prove anything."

Farrell nodded. "You were one of the smart ones—you had to be, since you're one of the few left alive and not in prison."

"So you came to compliment me on my sagacity. How kind of you. Is that all?"

Farrell leaned forward, propping an elbow on one knee. "Mr. Milton, Treasury agents and Coast Guard people cleaned up most of the small action and several of the big gangs by the middle of 1934. Your gang was the biggest and probably the most successful. I've got a theory about how that might have come about."

"So, you want to try out your theory on me—are you writing a book?"

Farrell ignored the gibe. "I think it's possible you had some help—maybe a ringer within the Coast Guard or Treasury Department who kept you informed where the patrols would be when you had shipments come through."

Milton rubbed his chin reflectively. "What of it? Even if I did, and I'm not saying for a moment that it's so, who would care after all these years about a Federal man being on the pad to a smuggler? Whoever he might be, he's probably gone on to better things with the payoff money he made, wouldn't you think?"

"If he had any sense, he might well have. But people have a funny way of getting comfortable, Mr. Milton. After all this time, he might be feeling the wool's been pulled so good and tight over the government's eyes that he can pretend to himself that what he did never even happened. But today, he ought to be a little worried."

A tension had grown in Milton as Farrell talked. It was there to see in the way he had unconsciously drawn his legs under his chair and the way his thumb had hooked around the hammer of his Colt. "Why today, of all days?"

"Do you recall the murder of a Coast Guard commander just before Repeal? Schofield was his name."

Milton's face was rigid. "I don't remember, if it matters to you."

"Let me refresh your memory. He was responsible for intercepting smuggling operations along the river. He was good at it—he'd knocked off a lot of shipments and put quite a few people in jail. But there was a fly in the ointment—he was convinced somebody was double-crossing him and tipping off one or more of the larger gangs as to where the patrols would be on given nights. He was on his way to find out who that was when he was shotgunned in his car." Farrell leaned forward, his pale eyes colder than the grave. "I think he was set up. Somehow the traitor or the people he'd sold out to discovered Schofield was on their trail and they decided to eliminate him before he learned too much."

Milton blinked, and he shifted uncomfortably in his chair. "I don't see what any of that has to do with me."

"Tell that to Schofield's brother when he gets to you. He's a Treasury agent, and he's in town investigating his brother's murder. I've talked to him, Mr. Milton. He's young and he's mad, and he's going to break a lot of crockery the way he's bulling around in this particular china shop. If you know who set Commander Schofield up to be killed, then tell me his name."

Milton's carefully constructed facade was crumbling, and he was looking away from Farrell like a man searching for the exit from a burning building.

"Dad, I saw you had a visitor, so I brought some lemonade." It was a woman's voice, coming from behind.

Farrell and Milton both stood as a slender woman of about thirty walked toward them from the back door of the main house. She held a tray with a pitcher of lemonade and two glasses filled with chipped ice. She placed it on the table, and poured the lemonade into the glasses. When she was finished, she took the glasses and handed them to Farrell and Milton.

"I'm Sally Milton," she said. "I'm Mr. Milton's daughter-in-law." Farrell noticed that Milton's gun had disappeared back into his newspaper

Her face was round-cheeked and pretty in a girl-next-door way, with dark brown hair that fell in waves to her shoulders. Her fingers around the glasses were long and strong looking, and she looked at Farrell through penetrating black eyes that went oddly with her soft features.

"I'm Wesley Farrell. It's very kind of you, but I was about to leave."

"Dad doesn't get many visitors, Mr. Farrell. Her voice was almost chiding. "There's no need to run off yet." She paused for a moment. "Your name is familiar to me for some reason. I don't think we've met, but…"

"Mr. Farrell manages to get his name into the newspapers from time to time, my dear," Milton said dryly.

"Yes." She turned back to Farrell with a smile. "That's right. You've had quite a career helping people—like the police."

"I was doing something else entirely, and it just happened that the police benefited from it. I'm not a cop, and you couldn't precisely call me a friend to the cops, Mrs. Milton."

"Well, I've held you up long enough. I'll leave you to what you were doing, Dad. We'll have lunch in about a half hour."

"That would be fine, my dear."

The woman walked back into the house with her tray. When the door had closed, Milton turned back to Farrell.

"I don't have anything to say to you, Farrell. I've been over here minding my own business for quite a while now, and I aim to keep on doing it."

"That would be fine," Farrell said. "But for reasons of my own, I want to know who the killer is, too. If I were you, Milton, I'd rather do my talking to a friend than to a young cop with a mission."

Milton allowed a wintery smile to grow on his face. "How did you and I get to be friends, Farrell? A long time ago you and I made a lot of dirty money and both of us killed people doing it. Competitors would more accurately describe us, but even that is in the past. Friends? No, never. Young Schofield has his ax to grind, and you have yours. Neither of you can do me any good, even if I could help you. Now, I think I'll wash up for lunch. So sorry you can't join us this visit." He stood there, looking Farrell in the eye, and he had the Colt automatic clenched in his fist again. Farrell cast a brief glance down at the gun, then he put his lemonade glass on the table, turned, and walked away. He paused at the car and took out his cigarette case. As he selected and lit one, he considered how close he'd come to getting something useful out of Milton, and wondered if he'd get another opportunity.

Farrell walked to the driver's side, opened the door, and paused for a moment to look into the rounded library windows. Sallie Milton stood there looking out at him. She held his gaze for a moment, then turned and walked deeper into the house. Farrell got into the car, cranked the engine, and drove away from the house.

The only other name he had to work with was Old Man Morrison. He didn't know where he was, but there was an associate of Morrison's he could talk to, if only he could get the man to open up to him. Unfortunately, this was a man who would once have cheerfully emptied a gun into him.

⌗

Sheriff Paul Chauchaut had been busy since his visit from Frank Casey earlier in the day. He'd detailed Luke Peters to go out to the abandoned garage and had other deputies calling at various places along State Route 1 in an attempt to find someone who'd seen anything that might lead to the capture of the murderers. It was the biggest manhunt the St. Bernard Sheriff's Department had ever conducted, and his men all knew the sheriff meant business.

The sheriff, thinking ahead to the gubernatorial election, went to the Parish's weekly newspaper, *The Gazette*, to give the editor an in-depth report of the crime, and state his intention of bringing the criminals to justice. Editor Jack Trosclair, who had supported the sheriff in all three elections, promised to give it front-page exposure.

He accompanied Trosclair to a luncheon sponsored by the state Rotary Club, where he was the guest of honor. As the dessert course was being served, Chauchaut mounted the podium in his white suit, his steel-rimmed spectacles catching glints of light from the banquet hall chandelier as he nodded to the applauding assemblage. He stood there, for a long moment, drinking in the clapping and whistling and shouts of encouragement, wanting to burst from it, but not wanting to appear too vain of his popularity. When he thought it prudent to do so, he spread his legs wide and raised his hands to call a halt to the applause. When it was dead silent, he gripped the sides of the podium and fixed the audience with a steely, earnest look.

"Fellow Louisianians, I appreciate the friendship and support you've given me in these past years. It shows that you consider the choice of your next governor a matter of considerable importance. I agree with all my heart.

"We've been through some hard times in this state. The Depression has smashed many of our farmers into the dirt, and some of them are still there in spite of Mr. Roosevelt's alphabet soup of welfare-style programs."

There were mutters of agreement to this. Many did not think much of Roosevelt, and even less of his so-called work programs. Paying artists and writers from the public coffers for badly painted murals and guidebooks for tourists was anathema. Reading their minds, the sheriff rolled on.

"We've also got rampant crime in this state—not as bad as during Prohibition, but bad enough." He blotted his high forehead with a handkerchief, then favored his listeners with a grim smile. "Crime at high levels and low continues to dog this state, drain its natural resources, and frustrate the citizens who try to raise families here. I know what my opponent says to that—we know where his sympathies lie, gentlemen. We know who deposits money into his campaign coffers. The same people who would make this state friendly to criminals and unscrupulous businessmen—the same people who made this state such a dark and bloody ground during the term of the Volstead Act."

This was strong stuff to some of his listeners. Some of them suspected that Terry Hobby, former Mayor of New Orleans and Democratic candidate for the governorship, was on the take, but no one had any real proof. Chauchaut was going out on a limb here—or he knew something that he was saving to blast Hobby out of the running. The audience murmured with curiosity.

The sheriff removed his glasses and leaned over the podium to be nearer to his listeners, and his voice got low and thick. "Well, we knew how to take care of such people in those days, didn't we? Didn't we? And we can do it again!"

Those who remembered his courageous stand against bootleggers, rum runners, and other hoodlums began to clap, and others joined in, chanting "Chauchaut, Chauchaut," building in force and speed until the room sounded like an powerful and invincible railroad locomotive bearing down on an obstacle that needed smashing. It was a thing that Chauchaut's campaign manager had hit upon several months ago, and now his stronger supporters always managed to work it in anytime he gave a speech. It was a good image, the kind Chauchaut relished. It continued for several more minutes, while various business and elected officials came from the floor to reach up and shake his hand. His life had never seemed as glorious to him as it did now. He beamed like a boy with a new bicycle.

He didn't need to say anymore, so he discarded the rest of his speech, which he admitted to himself was nothing more than standard bromides. The people were afraid of crime, and he was giving them what they wanted—a crime-buster. People in his cabinet could tend to other state problems while he polished his role as an anti-crime crusader. Eventually he sat down to savor a dish of his favorite dessert—vanilla ice cream with caramel sauce— while he listened to the energized crowd's approving murmur.

Driving back with Trosclair, he relaxed in the car, feeling pleasantly fatigued.

"Paul, you got this election sewed up," the editor declared. "You got Governor Bastrop's endorsement, and you've captured the loyalty of the most important people in the state. That ain't no small accomplishment."

Chauchaut glanced at his friend and smiled thinly. "We're doing pretty well, but we lack support in Orleans. I'm trying to get a police captain over there interested in the campaign. He's got a reputation as a crime buster, too, and that'd really help me out."

The editor shrugged. "You know how politics works. You just gotta find out what he wants and give it to him."

Chauchaut nodded. "Well, I know what that is—he wants the killers of his colored detective. And I'm going to give them to him. Dead or alive."

❈❈❈

In Algiers, lunch at the Milton home was over, and Milton's granddaughter, Clemmie, had been excused and put down for her afternoon nap. Milton remained at the table drinking tea with English malt biscuits, trying not to think about Wesley Farrell's visit. It had upset him more than he was willing to admit even to himself. He had allowed himself to feel safe here in this peaceful neighborhood, but the pale-eyed gambler had shattered the calm he had lived in for the past several years.

Once August Milton had ruled part of New Orleans like a pitiless despot, but now he was a lion in winter. The deaths of his son and grandson had shattered him, and taken from him much of the strength and power he had so effortlessly exercised. He could, as he did today, call up that remembered identity for a while, but it was a sham.

He was staring at the wall, unconsciously nibbling a biscuit, when Sallie returned to the dining room.

"August, what did Wesley Farrell want?"

The question shocked him out of his reverie, and he turned to face her. Lately, in their quieter moments together, she had begun calling him by his first name. It pleased him in some way he didn't quite understand. "It was nothing, my dear. Just an old acquaintance stopping by."

Sallie smiled, and sat down beside him. She placed a smooth, warm hand on his arm and said, "Don't try to kid a kidder, August. Wesley Farrell is a dangerous man. He was a rum runner during Prohibition and a dozen other things, most of them illegal." She paused, squeezing his wrist tenderly. "I saw the look on your face when I came out. What he wanted—it had to do with the bad time, didn't it?"

Milton gave her a brittle smile. "You were a good match for Billy—your mind is every bit as sharp as his. But there's nothing to be gained by telling you what Farrell wanted. I couldn't help him and I told him so. He was on his way out when you came with the lemonade."

She shook her head slowly. "After everything that's happened, don't you think it's better that I know everything? You and Clemmie and I have a pretty nice life here—better than I ever thought possible after—" She broke off for a moment and looked away from him. He saw it and took her hand in both of his, murmuring softly to her. For a brief moment, tenderness flowed between them like a cool mountain brook.

When she had composed herself, she looked up at him again. "Don't forget all that I already know. It's too late to pretend that I'm the innocent little girl your son brought home. I can never be that again."

"No. No, of course not." He spoke dully, and his throat felt dry and tight. He picked up his cup and drained the remains of his tea, licking his dry lips. "Farrell wants to dig into some trouble that happened before Repeal."

"Trouble?"

"He said there's a Treasury agent in town looking for the killer of a Coast Guard officer—Schofield he said the name was."

"What did you tell him?" She was looking down at their hands on the table cloth, her voice subdued.

"That I knew nothing, of course. There was nothing else I could tell him."

"Yes, of course. Did he ask anything else?"

Milton heard the tension in Sallie's voice, and felt miserable. "No. Nothing else."

Chapter 6

Israel Daggett and Sam Andrews returned to police headquarters in the early afternoon. While Andrews made phone calls about other cases they had in progress, Daggett went to Frank Casey's office. Mrs. Longley sent Daggett in.

"Afternoon, Captain. I just got some information I wanted to pass along to you."

"Same here. Let's hear yours first."

"Sam and I tracked down a known associate of Johnny Hope's earlier today, name of Bick Washington. He runs a gasoline filling station in Gentilly. He'd heard rumors that Hope was mixed up in a car theft ring. From what he understood, it was a good-sized gang that operated in such a way to seem like several smaller gangs."

Casey nodded. "That bears out Blanton's hunch."

"Yes, sir. He also said that he'd seen Hope in the company of a colored hood named Zootie Hines. I haven't pulled his record yet—"

"Don't bother. I followed up another lead and got to Hines that way. He's got a record going back to when he was fourteen—has a reputation as a rough customer."

"That's what Bick Washington said, too. There was something else, though—he heard the car ring was being bossed by a white man."

Casey raised an eyebrow. "He have a name?"

"No, sir. But how many white hoods have you known who used negroes as key members of their gangs?"

"Not many—which means that somewhere, somebody knows about this guy. I've got some men beating the bushes on that. They're also looking into the background of this Hines character. I talked to his ex-girlfriend a little while ago, but she couldn't tell me much, other than that he seemed anxious to do a good job for his boss. Interesting wrinkle in a gun punk, isn't it?"

"Want me and Sam to interrogate her?"

Casey shook his head. "My gut tells me that she doesn't know anything. What's your next move?"

"Sam and I have a few more places to go, but I want to go to Mama Lester's and brace Harvey Prado. He knows half the thieves and killers in this town, and I think Harvey'll give me something about Hines if we lean on him a little."

"Good luck. Keep in contact with me."

Daggett got up from his chair. "Right." He paused for a moment. "You seen Tom's wife yet?"

Casey nodded, his eyes bleak. "Yesterday afternoon. We had to get a doctor to sedate her—he took her in an ambulance to Flint-Goodrich Hospital. The little boy's at his grandmother's house. I don't think he understands completely yet."

Daggett stood up. "He's only four years old. He'll have the rest of his life to understand it." He picked up his hat and walked out of the office, leaving Casey sitting behind the desk staring at nothing.

⧉

It took some patient looking, but Farrell eventually ran into a gambler who went by the name of Reno Eddy. Eddy had just come from a crap game in the middle of the warehouse district where Morianos had been. Farrell took a cab to the address near Magazine and Gravier Streets.

Leaving the cab, Farrell headed into an alley between two buildings. About halfway in, a man stopped him.

"You lost, bud?" The man was about a yard across and had a jaw you could build a skyscraper on.

"You've got an awfully short memory, Morphy. The last time I saw you, you were losing your shirt in a crap game and were about to take off your pants to bet them. I buttoned them up and gave you a sawbuck to get home on."

"Oh. 'Zat you, Mr. Farrell? Jeeze, sorry, I didn't reco'nize you at first." Pete Morphy's face had reddened, and his gruff voice had become contrite. "Glad I run into you, on account of I never paid you back." He thrust a hand into a pocket, rummaged around in there, and brought out a crumpled twenty-dollar note. "Here's what I owe you, with interest, on account of me bein' so late payin' you back."

Farrell reached out and took the twenty and put it in his own pocket. "Thanks, Pete. I'd forgotten all about it. Not every man pays his debts, much less the interest."

Morphy blushed. "It ain't nothin', Mr. Farrell."

"I'm looking for the Nose. He around?"

"Sure, he's up there cleanin' half them guys out, like usual. I heard once he had a home, but I ain't never seen him go there. Go on up the fire escape and then down the hall. You'll see 'em."

"Thanks, Pete. I appreciate the help." He left the big man and mounted a rusting iron fire escape, listening to his shoe leather ring against the metal steps. At the top he walked through an open door and down a dimly lit hallway until he reached a larger room filled with noisy men. They were grouped around a banked felt-covered table, all of them kibitzing or calling on their luck as a dark-haired string-bean of a man rattled the dice in his hand.

People referred to him as "The Nose," or just "Nose." He was dressed in a well-cut dark suit and wore a gray felt hat perched on the back of his head. His face was sallow and of a narrow cast, with dark eyes and black curly hair that fell in a disorderly lock across his forehead. His nose was a high, arched beak that would have done a Cyrano proud.

Farrell stood a little apart from the table, watching the big-nosed man's technique with a professional interest. Unlike other dice shooters, The Nose didn't croon to his dice, cajole them, or talk about baby needing new shoes. He simply rattled them in his fist and listened. When he heard the right sound, he flung them at the end of the table to a chorus of cries and groans. He said nothing, as though the winning combination of spots was no more than he expected. He picked up a thick wad of bills, riffled them into a neat packet, and slipped them into his pocket as he bade the others farewell. "Always quit a winner, friends. Thanks for the dough." He ambled toward the bar, ignoring the grumbling and grousing behind him. Farrell followed.

"You're hotter than an old maid on Valentine's Day, Nose."

Morianos turned around, his eyes wary. He saw Farrell's face and wary recognition flared in his eyes. "Farrell, right?"

"You've got a good memory. Drink?"

"Why not?"

Farrell snapped his fingers at the bartender, and the man walked silently over and filled two glasses with I. W. Harper. They picked up the glasses, raised them in a silent toast, and drank. Morianos put his glass back down on the bar and looked at Farrell. "This dump is kinda out of your class, ain't it?"

"I didn't come to gamble, I came here to talk."

"Talk? About what?"

"About the Old Man's action during Prohibition."

Morianos's face gave nothing away. "That's deader than last Christmas."

"Humor me a little. Tell me how it was you boys managed to keep out of the Coast Guard's way the last two or three years the pipeline was open."

Morianos's eyes grew hot and smoky. "What the hell's it to you?"

"I got reasons. I'm not out to hurt you or the Old Man."

Morianos glared at Farrell for a long moment, then he snapped his fingers imperiously to the bartender again. He stood there looking at Farrell until the glasses were filled and the barman had retreated to the opposite end of the bar.

"We had a deal with August Milton." His voice dripped hatred. "Until the bastard tried a double-cross."

"What kind of a deal?"

The Nose's face was still dark with suffused blood, but in the back of his eyes Farrell could see a gleam of curiosity. "Those last few years, Milton and the Old Man had a kind of loose partnership. He had information about where the Coast Guard patrols would be, and what times they'd be there. We had more boats than Milton did, so we pooled our resources and brought in larger loads. We each got a percentage of the profits according to what we put in. We'd been makin' plenty before that, but with the partnership we made plenty more. It was a good arrangement—while it lasted."

"So what queered things?"

Morianos clenched his jaw. "Milton got greedy. He sent some boys to hit the old man—they used buckshot on him. I was with him. Me and a couple of boys got him to a doctor in time, but he lost a leg and the use of one arm." His teeth were showing and there were points of harsh light in his eyes. One of his hands gripped the edge of the bar so hard that Farrell waited for it to snap off in his fingers. "We hit back—we tried to keep things goin', but losin' the Old Man like that took the sand outa the boys. We kept on for a while, but our shipments got hijacked, some of us got killed—finally we cut our losses and found another grift."

At the mention of a shotgun, Farrell felt a ripple in his spine. He nodded sympathetically. "That's tough. I never heard about any of that."

Morianos had calmed down a little with the telling of his story. "There's a good reason. We kept it quiet. I figured if we let Milton think the Old Man was dead, they wouldn't come looking for him. We put him in a house out by the Lake with round-the-clock nurses and guards."

"Did Milton or his men ever name their informant?"

Nose shook his head. "That was their action, and so long as they shared the information, we didn't need to know the name. Afterward, it didn't matter."

Farrell fingered his empty glass for a moment, thinking. "Tell me, Nose. Did your boys have anything to do with killing Milton's son and grandson?"

Morianos stiffened. "What the hell you talkin' about?"

"Milton's son was run off the road and killed a few years before Repeal. His kid was in the car with him."

"Listen, Farrell, and listen good. I might be a sonofabitch, but I ain't a fuckin' sonofabitch. I don't make war on kids or women, no matter what happens. I didn't even know Milton had any family."

"Can you vouch for the Old Man on that, too?"

"I'm what the Old Man made me. I did what he did and didn't do what he didn't. Anybody says different is a liar."

Farrell saw it was time to change the subject. "When Morrison made his deal with Milton, did Milton do his own talking, or did somebody do it for him?"

Farrell's question was so abrupt that it took The Nose a moment to shift gears. "Well, I wasn't there, but the Old Man told me later that Milton had some new blood in his organization—people he didn't know. Milton did the talkin', but he had these new people backin' him up."

"You know anything about them?"

"This goes back a ways, and some of it's gossip, but I heard a new gang had formed up out of one that Pascal DeLatte ran back in the late '20s. From what I heard, new guys came in as partners— later they got rid of Pascal."

"Who were these new guys? Out of town talent or what?"

Morianos shook his head. "Never really got the straight of it. Couple'a my boys happened to be in a 'speak' one night, keepin' an ear to the ground, and they overheard some guys. They were low-level talent of Pascal's who'd gotten out when Pascal got hit. They talked about it some, mentioned a big scar-faced man they called 'Mercy.' This guy wasn't the big boss, but he called a lot of the shots. My boys said these guys talked about him like he was a *loup-garou*—a monster. They was scared shitless of him."

Farrell almost smiled. The *loup-garou* was a Cajun bogie man— a werewolf of the swamps. "Mercy, huh? I don't recollect hearing that name before. I always wondered what happened to Pascal."

"Pascal was a punk—him gettin' rubbed out didn't bother me at all. But these guys later hooked up with Milton, this Mercy and the others. He's the kind of a guy who'd use a shotgun on somebody. Common low-life bastard." Morianos shook his head, then reached inside his coat for a package of Lucky Strike. He offered one to Farrell and took one for himself, lighting both of them off a kitchen match he struck on his thumbnail. He inhaled a lot of smoke and then let it feather slowly out of his nostrils. "Farrell, there's somethin' I wanna tell you. It's kind of ancient history, but I want to clear it up."

Farrell looked at the big-nosed gambler. "Yeah?"

"Back in '32, the Old Man told me to hit some of your trucks over toward Morgan city. You were cuttin' into our profits and he wanted it stopped. He said he wouldn't care if you got in the way of a bullet, either."

"Uh, huh."

"I want you to know it was just business—nothin' personal."

Farrell smiled. "Sure, Nose. See you around, hear?"

"Yeah. See you around."

⧁⧁⧁

A long, green streetcar clanged as it passed the Plymouth coupe' driven by Emmett Kelso on St. Charles Avenue. As the streetcar went by, Kelso made a left turn across the median and entered an enclave called Rosa Park. The enclosed circle was filled with tall, majestic Victorian homes, all with morning sunlight glinting off faceted glass doorways and turreted windows.

"Nice neighborhood," Schofield said. "A man could live a nice life here, with a little luck."

Kelso laughed. "When you find out how to get any of that luck, call me up. I'd like to get a few shovelfuls of it." He laughed softly again. "I know that house is along here somewhere." As he spoke, he saw the address he was looking for. He pulled to a stop in front of a three-story peach-and-white frame house. The house had turrets on each front corner and a gallery that wound around the right-hand side. Schofield stared at it, awed.

"Jesus. It's a mansion."

"Yeah, that's what I said when I saw it a few years ago." There was an unaccustomed note of envy in Kelso's voice that made Schofield shoot a look at him.

"What kind of a guy is he?"

Kelso shrugged. "A punk. A sea lawyer. A guy who put the uniform on, then didn't know what to do with it."

"You didn't like him?"

Kelso shrugged again. "He just wasn't ship-shape. Your brother had him on the carpet quite a few times—inattention to detail, poor seamanship—stuff like that. When he resigned, I figured the service was better off without him. I never figured him to have the savvy to put all this together—or the money to get it started." A layer of manly contempt was thick in Kelso's voice.

The two men got out of the car and walked across the street. Kelso opened a wrought-iron gate and the two men mounted the stairs to the porch. Schofield pushed the doorbell button and in a moment a plump man in his early 30s opened the door. He was in his shirtsleeves with his vest unbuttoned and his hair tousled. He peered at them owlishly through spectacles with thick Bakelite rims. "Mr. Kelso, is that you?" He seemed genuinely surprised. "You're a lieutenant commander now."

"That's right. This is Treasury Agent James Schofield."

"Schofield? Why you must be the late commander's brother. You're the spit image of him. Won't you come in?"

The sailor and the Federal agent removed their hats and walked into a spacious foyer as Fuller closed the door. He led them into a book-lined study and gestured toward two comfortable-looking leather armchairs that faced a broad mahogany desk. On the desk were neat piles of paper and the leavings of sandwiches and a glass of milk.

"Pardon the mess," Fuller said. "My wife and little boy went to spend part of the summer at Grand Isle, and I'm 'batching'. Can I offer you a drink or a cigar?"

"Actually, we're here on business," Kelso began. "You might recall that Agent Schofield's brother was murdered, and that the killers were never caught."

Fuller's face took on a stricken look, and he shook his head. "I've never known anything as tragic as that, Agent Schofield. Every man in the command looked up to him."

"Somebody didn't. I've been privy to notes he made that dealt with his activities before his death. Your name was mentioned several times, mostly in regard to minor disciplinary actions."

Fuller's eyes got round. "You must be joking."

"I wish I were. Someone had hard feelings against him—hard enough that they connived at his death."

Fuller looked confused for a moment, then, slowly, understanding crept over his face. "Are you suggesting that I might want to harm him? That's utterly ridiculous." He turned to Kelso. "Commander Kelso, you can't think this."

"Is it?" Schofield snapped. "Kelso had copies of your records sent over from Coast Guard Personnel and we checked them. Before his death, George had recommended against your promotion to full lieutenant. Twice."

Fuller wagged a hand dismissively. "Let me correct an impression for you, Agent Schofield. I wasn't a very good officer, even I knew that. The truth is, I never wanted a military career. My father was a distinguished naval captain during the Great War. I was his only son, and it was a mandate that I would follow him into the service. I managed to get an appointment to the Coast Guard Academy, but my heart was never in it. When my father died, the only reason I had to continue in uniform was gone."

"Come on, Fuller," Kelso said. "You'd been passed over for promotion twice. Are you telling me you didn't feel any resentment? I remember you looking pretty cut up about it. Even sounding angry."

Fuller leaned back in his chair, looking sad and a bit weary. "Mr. Kelso, I don't know what you saw or heard—I may have been upset, but not to the point of committing a crime." He turned to Schofield, extending a hand in supplication. "Agent Schofield, as a sailor, I stank. I had no more business commanding a crew of sailors under fire than a dog has riding a bicycle. Your brother did me a favor. I was already planning to leave the service when my enlistment was up. When he was killed, I recognized that he'd probably be replaced by someone who'd be a great deal less sympathetic toward me than your brother was. A few months later I resigned from the service. I went into maritime insurance with the inheritance my father left, and I've made a success of it. I married a lovely girl who gave me a wonderful little boy. I'm a lot happier as an insurance man than as a sailor, and that's gospel truth."

Kelso's face was hard. "That's a good story, Fuller. I don't know if I believe it or not. I'm curious about this inheritance, though, and I'm going to look into it."

Schofield examined the plump man's face minutely, but if he was lying, he was good at it. On the other hand, the grand scale of Fuller's civilian life suggested a success that Schofield couldn't imagine in such a short span of years. When the other man said nothing else, he got up from his chair. "I'm only just beginning my investigation, Fuller, so I suggest that you not leave town. If I find any discrepancy in your story, I'll be back."

Fuller looked more hurt than frightened, but he got up and offered his hand. "I'm sure you're only doing your job, so no offense is taken. I want you to know that I admired your brother, as most of the men in the command did. I did my best to be like him, but I never could have been in a million years. For what it's worth, you've got my sympathy."

"It's worth something, Fuller. Thank you." Schofield took the insurance man's hand. "C'mon, Emmett. I think we're done here."

"Okay, if you're sure." Kelso's voice still held a note of skepticism.

Fuller led them to the front door and watched them down the porch and out to the street. When he'd closed the door, Kelso turned to the younger man.

"He's pretty slick, isn't he? I almost believed him myself there for a couple of minutes."

"He seemed sincere enough. If he was lying, I couldn't tell. I'll look into his finances, but my gut says he's clean."

"Well, you're the man-hunter, kid." Kelso laid a hand on his shoulder. "But I don't know of a guy who had more reason to hate your brother than he did, no matter what he says now. I wouldn't write him off so easy."

"Don't worry. I'm just getting started. Let's get out of here."

"Aye, aye, Mr. Schofield." He laughed and slapped the younger man on the back, then they got back into Kelso's Plymouth and left the neighborhood.

They'd driven a few blocks when Schofield said, "What do you know about a man named August Milton?"

Kelso cut his eyes at him. "Rum runner, but too big for us to nail. Had a fleet of fast boats, well-armed crews, plenty of money. What about him?"

"George made quite a few notes on him based on waterfront gossip and other sources. He still around?"

Kelso shrugged. "Who knows? He might be."

"I think I'm going to look him up. A big-time rum runner who'd been hurt by George's tactics stood to gain a lot from having him out of the way."

"Could be you've got something, but Milton was no cream puff—he won't bust out crying because you call him a murderer. You'll need something solid to tackle him."

Schofield nodded slowly. "Yes, I know."

⊱⊰

After Farrell left Nose Morianos, he walked back into the Quarter thinking about what he knew so far. It was plain from talking to Morianos that Milton had held out on him. There had been an allegiance between the two largest gangs in the city and Milton had been the pipeline to the Coast Guard traitor. It had been a match made in heaven up until the time Milton decided to double-cross Morrison.

There was something about that part of the story that bothered Farrell. Why would a man ruthless enough to assassinate his partner now be living on a small town back street, seemingly afraid to leave home?

The key might be this "Mercy" that Morianos had mentioned. The attempted murder by shotgun was too close to the way Schofield was murdered to be brushed aside. This same man had already eliminated Pascal DeLatte, himself a criminal to be reckoned with. Farrell needed to know more.

The deaths of Milton's son and grandson also intrigued him. There was a connection there, Farrell was sure of it.

If you were a cop, he thought, you could simply call the records department and have the case file sent up. That made him smile. His father wouldn't be very pleased with him right now. But how pleased would he be if he knew you were the only witness to a five-year-old murder and had never came forward? Farrell grimaced. Being the son of a cop was pretty complicated, even when you didn't advertise it.

He was nearing Basin Street when an idea struck him. The cops weren't the only people with records of old crimes. He turned a corner and headed back in the direction of the offices of the *New Orleans States-Item.*

Fifteen minutes later he reached the newspaper building. He walked in and asked to speak to Art Frizzell, a crime reporter and occasional poker buddy.

Frizzell was at his desk eating a corned beef on rye with a big sour pickle when Farrell found him.

"Farrell, what the hell you doin' here? Hey, you want half of this sandwich? They make these things so Goddamn big it takes two guys to eat one, anyway." Frizzell was in his shirt sleeves, and his tie had a splotch of mustard he hadn't yet discovered. He was a slender man of medium height with a long, bony face, sharp nose, and curly brown hair. He spoke in a nasal Ozark twang.

"Thanks anyway—corned beef gives me gas," Farrell said with a grin. "You can give me some information, though."

"Gives you gas, huh? Jeeze, that's tough. I love corned beef, myself. What kinda questions you got, pal?"

"You know who August Milton is?"

"I guess I do. He was suspected of bringing in over half the smuggled hooch this town drank before Repeal. A hell of a big operator. Haven't heard much about him since Repeal, though."

"I understand that his son got killed about three years before Repeal, and that his little boy was with him."

Frizzell shook his head. "Jeeze, that was sickening. Bill Milton—he was a lawyer of some kind—was ridin' down Lakeshore Drive with his five-year-old kid and there was a wreck. Both of them killed."

"Any information on how it happened? Any witnesses?"

Frizzell made a shaky gesture with his hand. "The cops wrote it off as an accident. Then this couple'a guys who were out in a fishing boat that day came in and said how they saw it happen. Blue Pontiac sedan forced them off the road—the car rolled. Hell of a mess. I almost heaved."

"A blue Pontiac, you said." It was too much to be a coincidence. He recalled with exquisite sharpness the blue Pontiac sedan carrying the men who had shot up Schofield's Marmon five years before.

"You don't look so hot, Farrell. You keepin' too many late nights again?"

Farrell looked at the reporter. "Tell me, you ever hear of a guy called 'Mercy' connected with the rackets?"

Frizzell ruminated for a moment, then shook his head. "Doesn't ring a bell. Think he's connected to the Milton kills?"

"I don't know—maybe. If you dig anything up, let me know, okay?"

Frizzell for once didn't crack wise. He'd known Farrell a long time, and had seen that look on his face before. "You got a bee in your bonnet about something, don't you, boy? Is there a story in it?"

"Maybe. If I can pull all the strands together."

"Do I get the exclusive?"

"If I can give it to you and stay out of jail afterward. I'll see you later, Art."

"Yeah, later, kiddo."

Farrell got up and walked out of the newsroom. Frizzell watched him, thinking of all the stories they told about the bronze-skinned man, wondering if somebody out there was about to get a very unpleasant visit from a man who wouldn't take no for an answer. He shook his head and went to paw through his old files. Mercy was an unusual name—a nickname, maybe?

∞∞∞

The special line on Paul Ewell's desk rang and he snatched it from the cradle. "Ewell."

"It's me. Schofield hooked up with Commander Emmett Kelso and they've begun to visit Coast Guard guys now."

"Anybody we know?"

"They visited a retired chief quartermaster named Dunning and an ex-lieutenant named Fuller so far."

Ewell's eyes were flickering as he noted the names. "Kelso was Schofield's executive officer, wasn't he?"

"Yeah. In charge of New Orleans Coast Guard Station and the four seventy-five footers there now. It figured Schofield would hook up with him."

Ewell rubbed his face tiredly. "I'm surprised it took him so long. Kelso's been around here long enough to know where everybody is. Stick with them."

"Right."

Chapter 7

Sam Andrews cut the engine of the police cruiser and set the hand brake. Daggett remained in his seat, drumming his fingers on the open window ledge. He was tired, but he had a feeling they were close to a breakthrough of some kind. If they could lay hands on Zootie Hines, Daggett was certain they could get the identity of Blanton's killer.

Since they'd released him from prison, there had been nothing else Daggett had wanted quite as badly as putting handcuffs on this particular murderer. Negroes lived an uncertain existence, oppressed by bigoted whites and preyed upon by criminals of their own color. Sometimes all that stood between a colored victim and those who would misuse him was a negro police officer. Killing a negro cop was a crime deserving the ultimate punishment in Daggett's book.

"Been a long couple of days, ain't it?" Andrews commented. "We keep on like this and I might be too tired to arrest anybody if we do find 'em."

"Yeah. He's not in here, but odds are he has been. We might be able to squeeze something out of Harvey. Let's go." They left the car and strolled into the honkey-tonk.

Mama Lester's Homestyle Bar and Grill had been a hangout for hustlers, pocket-edition badmen, and hookers since the turn of the century, but it was not unusual for negro *bourgeoisie* to come there on slumming expeditions. There were always a few people in evening clothes hoping to sneak a look at a real-live gangster.

As the detectives opened the door and stepped into the dimly lit interior, they heard Maggie Jones, "the Texas Nightingale," singing "Temptation" on the juke box. Many of the tables in the joint were occupied. A few unescorted women looked up hopefully when Daggett and Andrews entered, but when the women saw their hard eyes and stern mouths, they quickly buried their noses back into their glasses.

Daggett saw the manager, Harvey Prado, chatting up a hot-bodied banana-skinned chick with hair so red it must have come bottled by Tabasco. The barman's eyes were full of hopes for the night until he saw the two tall dark brown men coming toward him. He straightened up convulsively, shoving his hands into his pockets. That was a dead giveaway right there—Harvey's hands always tended to sweat when he was nervous. Harvey's movement made the high-yellow chick turn. When she saw Daggett's expression, she slid off her stool and made tracks for the ladies' room.

"'Lo, Harvey," Daggett said softly. "Kinda quiet in here, eh?"

"Well, it's kinda early yet. Real action in here don't start until about 8:00. Get y'all a glass of beer or somethin', Sergeant?" Harvey smiled hopefully at them.

"What I want is Zootie Hines. You know him?"

Prado's eyes examined the ceiling thoughtfully as his tongue probed the inside of his cheek. "Hines, you said?"

Andrews grinned. "He wants to play patty-cake. Reckon he wants to go in the back room so we can play in private?"

Sweat beads had collected in the bartender's Duke Ellington mustache and in his hairline. Daggett leaned an elbow on the bar and glared at Harvey. "We been all over town looking for this Hines, Harvey. We're tired, hungry, and frustrated. Neither of us is in the mood to waste time, so start talking before we decide to close you down."

Harvey looked indignant. "Ain't nothin' wrong goin' on around here. What right you got to shut me down?"

Daggett smiled way back in his jaws. "Listen, punk. There's two women I know are hookers sittin' over there with two men— that's soliciting. I see another guy back in the corner who bears a certain resemblance to a bunco artist we been lookin' for. If that ain't enough, Sam can start shakin' people down and I'll bet he'll find a wheelbarrow load of shivs and unlicensed gats."

"Shhh! For God's sake." Harvey made a pushing motion with his hands. "You want every nigger in here to hear you? I won't have a customer left in this damn place."

"So talk straight to us, Harvey, and we'll leave you alone," Andrew said, trying not to laugh.

"Awright, awright. The brutha ain't no friend of mine, but I don't wanna get on his bad side, neither."

Andrews nodded. "We know he's some kind of tough egg."

"Too tough for his own good," Daggett cut in. "We think he helped kill a negro cop. That means we want Hines about six times as bad as we want anybody else, you dig?"

Harvey's eyes got big and he swallowed hard. "Killed a cop? Listen, I don't know nothin' 'bout—"

"We didn't say you did. We want a line on him. You know half the two-bit punks in this town, and I figure you know where to start lookin', so give and we'll scram."

Harvey took out a silk handkerchief and blotted the perspiration on his face. "I can't tell you much. He had a young chick named Mayfield—"

"She ain't seen him in three months. Dig deeper."

Harvey was sweating again, and his eyes were blinking rapidly as his mind raced to find something to get him off the hook. Suddenly, he recalled a piece of gossip. "Wait a minute—this is somethin' I heard the other day, and I ain't had time to check the truth of it. He's supposed to've hooked up with a new woman in town—I don't know where she lives, but they say she is one hot mama. Goes by the name of Violetta."

Andrews looked at Daggett. "That's a new one on me. You heard of her, boss?"

Daggett shook his head. "She's not from around here, huh?"

Harvey shook his head. "Don't think so. Word is she's from over in Pass Christian, although that ain't a place you normally think of as a breedin' ground for sexy women."

"What's she looks like?"

"Man told me about her said she was small—maybe five-foot-two, real dark brown skin, and light brown hair."

"She got a last name?"

Harvey shrugged. "All's I got was Violetta. I ain't never known a Violetta before. She sounds, real—real, uh—"

"Exotic?" Daggett supplied.

"Yeah, man, exotic. That's it. I'd like to get a look at her." He licked his lips, and his eyes gleamed.

Andrews put his notebook away. "Careful there, Harvey. You're liable to drool on your shirt."

Daggett laughed as the two men turned and left the bar.

Harvey watched them go, wiping his face with his silk handkerchief. Every time they come in here, he complained to himself, I sweat off twenty pounds. He saw the women's powder room door open, and the beautiful red-head emerged. Harvey straightened his tie and turned his attention to more important things. Violetta was, for the moment, forgotten.

∞∞

Emmett Kelso had not known the whereabouts of August Milton, so Schofield consulted a retired Treasury agent named McGivern, whose name he had been given before leaving Washington. McGivern continued to keep tabs on what was left of the smuggling fraternity and was able to provide minute instructions on how to locate Milton.

It was past 6:00 when Schofield, in Kelso's car, disembarked from the Canal Street Ferry and negotiated the streets of Algiers. The bucolic nature of the borough surprised and fascinated the young agent. He'd expected an ex-booze kingpin to be living in flashier surroundings with a coterie of bodyguards.

He found the house without trouble and walked through the alley to the back yard, where he saw the carriage house. He removed his badge case from his coat as he approached the small house and had it open when he knocked on the door. It opened immediately, as though Milton had been waiting for him. He held up his shield as the light fell on him.

"Treasury Agent James Schofield, Mr. Milton. I'd like to talk to you for a few minutes.

Milton's steel blue eyes bored into the young man. "Suppose I say no, and tell you to beat it?"

"That's your privilege, but I'll keep coming back. It'll be easier if you just let me get it over with."

"I suppose you're right," Milton replied in a voice curiously devoid of hostility. He stepped to one side and held the door. "Come in and have a seat."

Schofield pocketed his badge and entered the small living room. It was comfortably furnished, but there was little that couldn't be purchased in an average department store, save for a collection of sailing ship models occupying a tall bookcase. As he turned to face Milton, he found the older man had already seated himself in a platform rocker upholstered in red leather. Milton spoke first.

"I know why you're here, but I can already say that I can't help you."

Schofield scowled as he sat down. "You mean you won't—isn't that closer to the truth?"

Milton regarded him through half-closed lids. "What you want is beyond your reach."

"How do you know what I want?"

Milton smiled thinly. "You've been in town for a few days, young man, and it's a small town. People talk—particularly people who had ties to whiskey smuggling. You came to get the man who killed your brother. The killer was undoubtedly a torpedo working for someone else. That someone else—"

"Is just as guilty as the trigger man," Schofield interrupted. "He's the one I really want. If I can get him, I can get the others."

Milton crossed his legs, his eyes locked on the younger man's. "Your brother was an effective deterrent while he was alive. Many of the smaller gangs were put out of operation by his men, or had to quit because they kept hitting so close to home." He shook his head solemnly. "Any number of people could have killed your brother. My guess is that someone with more luck than brains staged the hit, and thanks to that luck they got away with it."

Schofield frowned. Milton's logic was compelling. He'd expected the man to be defensive and hostile, but instead he was cold, calm, and analytical. "My brother left notes behind that came to light just a few months ago. They make it plain that he was conducting a private investigation, because there are a number of names along with descriptions of their backgrounds, movements, and habits. Your name was chief among them, which suggests to me that he'd figured out you were the key to it all."

Milton raised his left eyebrow. "How flattering. It was no secret that I was head of a gang, but I was careful to make sure that no incriminating evidence could ever be brought to bear on me. My reputation alone was probably sufficient to draw your brother's attention to me. However, an army of federal agents weren't able to arrest me, so his lone efforts could not have been much use." Milton bridged his fingers and rested his chin on them. "You said your brother's investigation was private. May I venture that he did not share whatever his suspicions were with his superiors or the Prohibition enforcement people?"

Schofield felt his face flush, and he fought to keep from losing control of himself. "Unfortunately, that is true. I don't know George's reasons, but it was clear that he had reservations about sharing his information."

Milton allowed a small smile to grow on his lips. "Then you should go home. Nothing you can do can bring your brother back to life, and it is unlikely that you'll ever find anything to connect me to his murder, since I, in fact, had nothing to do with it."

Schofield stood up, his body trembling. "You think you're pretty smart, don't you, Milton? Just remember this—Capone thought he was invincible, too, and so did a lot of others. I'll hound you to kingdom come if that's what it takes to find out why my brother was killed and who did it." When Milton offered no reply, the young agent jammed his hat on his head and left, slamming the door behind him.

Milton waited for a while, waiting for the pounding in his chest to subside, then he got up heavily and walked across to the telephone. He picked up the receiver, gave the operator a number, then waited as the number rang. On the fourth ring, a familiar voice spoke.

"Treasury Agent Schofield was just here," Milton said. "He's a very angry and determined young man."

"So far that's no reason to get shaky knees," the voice replied. "He can only do so much, since he has no official backing."

Milton nodded imperceptibly. "You've spoken to our friend, then."

"Mercer wised him up, and he's been paying close attention. He's a good man."

"You'd say that about Judas Iscariot, wouldn't you? Well, if you won't worry about Schofield, perhaps you'll worry about Wesley Farrell."

"Farrell? What's he got to do with this?" Milton enjoyed an instant of malicious glee as he detected a small note of anxiety in the man's voice.

"It sounded to me as though the elder Schofield was a friend of his, although I don't understand how that could be. He may be looking to hand Mercer and our friend over to Schofield just to keep the authorities from digging around in his own past history."

"Farrell's only one man. What could he do?"

"Your ignorance surprises me sometimes. Do you know who Emile Ganns and Joe Dante were?"

"They were big-time mobsters. Why?"

"Several years ago, each of those gentlemen went up against Farrell. They're both very dead now, their organizations blown away like dust. Farrell is poison. What's more, he's somehow gained the friendship of the chief of the Detective Bureau. Are you getting my drift yet?"

Silence, then, "Yeah, I do. I remember now why I hooked up with you—you never overlook the small details. I better take care of Farrell before he gets any nosier."

Milton laughed dryly. "Make certain you don't miss. I can promise you that he won't."

"Farrell won't stand a chance against Mercer."

Milton felt a cold chill through him. Mercer was little better than an animal, but he killed with a ruthless efficiency. "I hope you're right. We can't afford any more mistakes."

The other man's voice was sober. "You're right. I'll tell Mercer to do it quietly—no shotguns. He'll hit Farrell like a ton of bricks—just like he did Pascal Delatte. I'll call you when it's done." Then the line went dead.

Milton hung up the telephone, then went to the kitchen and opened a cabinet. He took down from a shelf a quart bottle of Bacardi, and poured three fingers of the dark rum into tall glass. As he stood there, staring at nothing while he sipped the drink, he began thinking about how much he missed his grandson. He hadn't been much of a father, and he regretted that now. His only son was dead, and he'd died almost a stranger in the car crash that killed the beloved grandson.

Money had been Milton's God all his life. He had made it honestly a few times, but most of his considerable fortune had been made by breaking one law or another. As a young man he had rustled cattle and stolen horses along the Texas-Mexican border. Later, he had run guns to several groups of Central American revolutionaries. He had hired out as a mercenary soldier a few times, and, upon returning to the States, he had even robbed some banks.

His wife had been the prettiest girl he'd ever seen, and he had tried to make an honest living in order to enjoy what he thought was a normal life. He'd had no clue as to how unutterably dull such a life could be to a man like himself, even alongside the prettiest girl in the world.

When she'd become pregnant, his strongest feeling had been panic. He suddenly felt tied down. He began going away on business trips, and with each trip he stayed away a little longer. The trips were never about business—they were a way for him to recapture the footloose feelings he'd had before marrying. And they were a way for him to do what he felt he was best at, which was stealing. He built a respectable fortune, always knowing when to pull back, or leave a place, or bail out of something that smelled wrong. He never served a day in any jail throughout those years.

He'd come home one day to find his wife and son gone to live with her mother and father. She also left him an ultimatum— remain at home or give her a divorce. Well, that was an easy choice. He gave her the divorce and never saw her again. She died in the influenza epidemic of 1917.

He eventually found his son living in New Orleans. Bill had a successful career, a wife, and a little boy. Upon seeing that boy, Milton was flooded with an emotion so foreign that it took him a while to understand what it was—love for a child.

It was difficult at first. Bill wasn't receptive to his overtures, naturally resenting the way he'd abandoned his mother. His wife, Sallie, was somewhat more understanding, recognizing in Milton the same kind of love she felt for her son. Gradually, Bill had relented, although he was never more than polite to his father. As time went on, Bill seemed to thaw a bit, and Milton began to see a ray of hope that they might be reconciled. Even if that reconciliation had never come to pass, Bill still allowed his father to become a grandfather, and Milton reveled in the role. The boy returned his love, and for once, Milton felt complete.

Then had come the accident. Milton felt as though his heart had been torn out by the roots. He had never known grief until now, and it took all his will not to burst into tears in public. He felt it was a holy judgment on him for the kind of life he'd led, and he wrestled with that night and day.

Although he couldn't prove it, he became certain that some enemy of his had killed his son and grandson. He was eventually led to believe that his partner, Old Man Morrison, had done it to put him off balance long enough to take over their combined gangs. Milton knew how to deal with that—he had Morrison killed and his gang destroyed.

After Bill's death, Sallie discovered she was pregnant with another child. Milton was assailed with conflicting emotions—happy at the prospect, but terrified that another enemy would try to strike at him through what was left of his family. He gave the responsibility of running his bootlegging empire to subordinates, and took up residence in the carriage house, watching over Sallie and Clemmie day and night. Although it was a confining existence, he accepted it as a kind of penance. His affection for Sallie, which had begun as respect and admiration, had grown beyond that into something as yet undefined. His love for the little girl was the equal of his feelings for his dead grandson.

Now, after all these years, his sins were back to haunt him. He had put up a brave front to Farrell, but the nightclub owner had shaken him. He hadn't ordered the hit on Commander Schofield, but he'd allowed it to happen. He could have said no and stopped it with force if necessary, but the old argument was there—remove the threat and let the money keep flowing in. What was another dead man after all the others he'd killed or caused to be killed?

August Milton had shaken hands with the Devil a long time ago, convinced that he was a match for him. But he now knew that the Devil always demanded a reckoning. Wesley Farrell was the harbinger of that reckoning, and for the first time in his life, August Milton was really afraid.

He finished his drink, rinsed the glass, then turned and went to his bed feeling terribly old, weak, and alone.

⊗⊗⊗

At his sister's house, Johnny Hope was fretting. He hadn't heard from Joe Earle, and he was more and more afraid that Mercer would find the boy and kill him. Johnny was afraid for himself, too. He had the cops breathing down his neck and Mercer standing over him like the Damoclean sword. He felt like his nerves were crawling with ants.

His sister was listening to the Jack Benny program, snickering as, once again, Rochester made a fool of his tight-fisted boss. Ordinarily, Johnny enjoyed that program, too, but tonight it was an irritant to him. He got up and stared through the screen door at the back yard. When he tired of that, he walked back to the front of the house.

He went to the telephone, and began calling people he knew, asking if they'd seen or heard from Joe Earle. With each one, he left the message that his brother was to call him immediately. When he'd called everyone he could think of, he sank down in a chair and picked up the issue of *Collier's Magazine* that had come in the mail that day, and began leafing through it, barely paying attention to the colorful advertisements or the stories inside.

Time passed slowly. At 9:00 his sister said she was tired and going to bed. He told her good night, and said he would stay up a little longer. At 10:00, the telephone rang, and Johnny snatched it before it could ring again.

"Johnny, it's Joe Earle."

"Where you at?"

"Why you want to know?"

"Listen, Mercer's real sore about you not gettin' rid of that policeman's car. You need to lay low—at least 'til I can square it with him."

Joe Earle was silent for a long moment. "Oscar and me went back to get it, but there was a New Orleans cop there. If we'd tried to do anything, we'd of been arrested sure."

"I can tell Mercer that. He'll understand." Johnny was relieved there was an explanation—if he crawfished enough, Mercer would let them off the hook.

"Get this straight, I ain't goin' back to work with y'all. Killin' a cop is where I draw the line. I been thinkin' about it all day, and I made up my mind."

"Joe Earle, please—we got to stick this out. We can't be crossin' Mercer. Ain't no tellin' what he might do."

Joe Earle sighed, the sound of it traveling over the lines to Johnny's ear. "Don't you get it, big brother? I know just what he'll do. Things is gonna start fallin' apart now the cops are snoopin' around, and when they get too close to Mercer, anybody who can squeal to the cops about him is gonna die. And the bad thing is, you prob'ly gonna be the first—you and him go back such a long way."

"Where you gonna go?" Johnny asked in a dry, hollow voice. "How are we ever gonna find you again?"

"I don't know, I just don't know. I'll have to figure that out later. First thing to do is get as far away from Mercer as I can get." He paused, and when he spoke again, his voice was sad and heavy. "I'm gonna miss you, big brother. I hope you're gonna be all right."

Johnny put the telephone receiver back on the hook. He buried his face in his brawny forearms, and cried silently until there was nothing left in him.

Chapter 8

Finding a prostitute in New Orleans was as easy as asking the right cab driver, but finding a particular girl when all you had was a first name was a needle-in-a haystack job. Daggett and Andrews had gone on searches with even less. They headed to Erato Street at the edge of Downtown and parked near a tavern called The Fat Man Lounge. Inside they found the owner, Big Boy Jenkins, leaning on the bar, listening to Fats Waller sing "Georgia On My Mind" on the juke box. Daggett gave the barman a two finger salute.

"Hey, Big Boy."

"Hey, Iz, Sam. What you fellas prowlin' after?"

"Seen Longboy?"

"Yeah, he's in the side lounge countin' the money he made today. You gonna roust him?"

Andrews grinned. "Why—you want us to roust him?"

"I wisht you'd slap the sucker sideways, but I owe his cousin money, so don't hurt him too bad—less'n you take him outside." Big Boy grinned as they left for the side lounge.

Arthur Meekins was a pimp, no other way to describe him. It was a fact that he was tall and skinny, but he began calling himself "Longboy" because he thought a pimp should have a name suggesting sexual prowess. Everybody but his girls laughed at him. They knew he'd jerk them baldheaded for disrespecting him.

They found him in a corner booth with a red-skinned gal named Lola and a bleached-blonde high-yellow who called herself Bette. The detectives stopped at the table and glared at the girls.

"You two—go powder your noses. We want to talk to Mr. Longboy there." Daggett jerked his chin at the two women.

When the girls looked at Longboy, Andrews leaned over the table and growled like a dog. The girls leaped up and went missing. The detectives slid in on either side of the pimp and boxed him in.

Longboy looked sick. "I swear, whatever you want, I ain't got it, and whatever it is, I ain't done it."

Andrews reached down and grabbed his upper thigh where the skin was tender and pinched it, hard, with his big hand. Longboy lurched in the seat and his breath whistled through his teeth. His eyes resembled a pair of boiled eggs about to pop out of his skull.

"Listen, you walkin' pile of rat dung, you keep your mouth shut until the sergeant asks you a question, and when he does, you give him a civil, truthful answer, understand?"

"Yeah, yeah, yeah," Longboy grunted. "Please, yeah."

Daggett nodded and Andrews let Longboy go. The pimp began to massage his leg, and he scooted as far away from Andrews as Daggett would let him get.

"Heard some talk today about a new gal in town. Goes by the name of Violetta. You know her?"

Longboy nodded, keeping a wary eye on Andrews. "Yeah, I heard of her."

"You know where she lives?"

"Nope. Word is she come over from some wagon crossin' in Mississippi, and she specializes in French."

"She got a pimp?"

He shook his head. "Free-lance—for now, but somebody gonna scoop her up before long. Gals workin' alone—sooner or later they all gotta get somebody to take care of 'em."

"What if she's already got somebody takin' care of her? Say, Zootie Hines?" Daggett watched Longboy's face and saw a flicker of recognition in the other man's eyes.

"He's for damn sure a bad enough mothah-fuckah,. Only—"

"Only what?"

Longboy shrugged. "Just talk. Some of the gals say he ain't very good at it—if you know what I mean."

Andrews raised his eyebrow. "No lead in his pencil?"

Longboy shrugged again. "Like I say, just some talk. He slapped a couple gals around—maybe they just spreadin' shit to get even with him. You know what women's like."

"Listen to me, Longboy. It would do you some good if you could come up with an address on this woman. Sooner or later your ass is gonna be in the fire and you're gonna want a friend to help you drag it out. You understand what I'm sayin'?"

Longboy looked at Daggett, then shot a glance over his shoulder at Andrews before he returned to the sergeant. "You wanna hang around, I'll make some calls."

Daggett winked at him. "That'd be real fine. There's a phone booth yonder. We'll wait right here for you."

❈

It was getting dusk when Farrell left the offices of the *States-Item*. Not seeing a cab, he began walking in the direction of the Café Tristesse. He was beginning to get a picture of things now. Milton and Morrison had been partners but there'd been a falling out. The deaths of Milton's son and grandson seemed to have happened before, but near the time of the attack that had incapacitated Morrison. There had to be a connection there—but why would Morrison hit Milton's family? Suppose Nose Morianos had lied to him, and there had there been no falling out—had Morrison somehow intuited that hurting Milton's family would weaken him enough that he could usurp Milton's power? If that were true, then Morrison had badly miscalculated.

The man known as Mercy was the key to unlocking the puzzle because he seemed to be connected to the Schofield murder and the attack on Morrison. Mercy—his name seemed like some kind of macabre joke, given the things Farrell believed he had done. He stopped in the long shadow of a building and looked up and down the street, plagued with indecision, wondering why he seemed to be making such slow progress. Maybe, he thought, it's because you're being so methodical—maybe it's because you're so damn busy worrying about exposing yourself that you've forgotten how to work this town to get what you want from it. He left the shadow and began walking into the Quarter.

All he knew was that Mercy was a big man with a scar on his face. That might not seem like much to go on in a place visited by fight-scarred merchant seamen from all over the world, a city inhabited by a host of hard-living dock workers—but enough if you knew as many people as Farrell.

He passed through the Quarter to the edge of the river, and prowled southwest into a region populated by warehouses, loud, rough-edged taverns, and bawdy houses catering to men who liked quantity and not quality. Over a period of a couple of hours he passed through a half-dozen establishments, examining and inspecting everything and everyone in them. In each he spotted one or two people he knew from the past; each remembered him with striking clarity. Some he had befriended—others were in his debt for some significant favor. All knew that no matter what he asked, or when he got around to asking, they had to give what he required. To each he conveyed his curiosity about the man called Mercy and his interest in talking to anyone who might know him.

He made a strange sight, moving among these denizens of a subterranean New Orleans unknown to the tourist and genteel visitor. His expensive clothes drew occasional stares from those who took him for an easy mark, but the way he carried himself and the glitter in his pale eyes never failed to quell any violent impulse they might consider.

It was past the hour of 9:00 when he came to a warehouse that no longer warehoused tangible goods, but instead served as home to a bordello with a reputation said to reach as far away as Singapore and Madagascar. It was run by a small, delicate-looking woman called Sparrow. Farrell found her in a room with wallpaper of maroon silk and incense burning in a brass bowl. The walls were incongruously decorated with a group of nineteenth-century steel engravings from the Waverly novels, all framed in elaborate gold leaf. They clashed wildly with the exotic furnishings and wall coverings, but Sparrow didn't care. It was her room, and in there, she called the tune.

"Hello, Sparrow. Business seems good."

"As long as men want women, business will always be good." Sparrow wore a tight-fitting black silk dress that was common in China, with a short skirt and sleeves and red piping, and red shoes with very high heels. She was sensitive about her stature, Farrell knew. Rich black hair cut short in the Chinese style framed a fine-featured face with an olive complexion. Her eyes were like pools of oil, reflecting very little of her emotions. Farrell had always believed she was of Jewish or Arab extraction, but he had never heard her called anything but Sparrow. Her past was as mysterious as his own.

"You want something, Farrell. What is it?"

Without waiting for an invitation, Farrell sat in a tall chair with elaborately carved arms and legs and a seat of woven cane. He put his Borsalino on the table beside him. "I'm looking for a man."

One corner of her mouth curved upward. For Sparrow, that was a landslide of emotion. "This is the wrong place."

Farrell returned her half-smile with interest. "Don't fence with me, Sparrow. The man I want is like all men—he wants a woman when he feels the itch, and he doesn't go looking for one at ice cream socials. He's a big man with a scar on his face—they call him Mercy. I heard that he's not gentle—he takes what he wants."

Sparrow's face relaxed into its normal cast of indifference. "No man takes anything here unless I say so. Men who like things rough don't last long in my place."

"One of your girls might know him, or know of him. Even whores tell their girlfriends things about men. It's worth something to me to get a line on this man."

"How much?"

"You know me, Sparrow. I don't haggle over price."

"What's he done?" Farrell detected something like curiosity in her voice.

"You don't need to know that."

"Call it part of my price. I'm intrigued."

Farrell was silent for a moment, then he nodded. "A long time ago he killed a man. I want to see him pay."

"A friend of yours?"

"Let's say I owed him—let it go at that. Will you help me?"

"Are you still running that glitter palace on Basin?"

"Still."

"I'll see what I can find out. You're right about whores—they all talk. They talk if a man is a good lay and they talk if he's a vicious brute—but they talk. And someone always hears."

Farrell smiled. "Thanks. I'll be in your debt."

"Yes," Sparrow said, smiling broadly for the first time. "I'll enjoy that very much. Goodnight, Farrell."

Farrell knew when he was being dismissed. "Goodnight, Sparrow. A pleasure, as always." He got up, retrieved his Borsalino, and left the maroon silk walls for the street that brought him there.

Once outside, he hugged the shadows again. By now a hundred people knew he was looking for the man named Mercy. He was taking a big risk—Mercy might discover Farrell was searching for him before Farrell could uncover who and where he was. Such men attacked when they felt threatened—that was how they survived. He would have to be careful now.

He looked at his watch and saw it was nearing 11:00. He'd been away from the club all day long. He retraced his steps through the warehouse area until he found a telephone booth. He went inside, dropped in his nickel, and asked the operator for the club. Harry picked up within two rings.

"Harry, it's Farrell. Is anyone looking for me?"

"Hiya, boss. No business calls, but Captain Casey called earlier in the evening. Said he was going home and you could call him there."

"Thanks, Harry. I'll be in before closing."

"Right, boss. Bye."

Farrell felt guilty for not having called his father. Without realizing it, he had begun to look forward to, and to cherish, the time they spent together. He looked at his watch again, and figured his father might still be up listening to a late radio program. He dropped in another nickel and asked for Casey's number.

"Hello?"

"Hey, Frank, it's me. Harry said you called earlier."

"I was hoping to catch dinner with you, but you were somewhere gallivanting, Harry said. Everything okay?"

"Sure," Farrell said carefully. "How about with you?"

"It's been a hell of a few days. One of my negro detectives was murdered in St. Bernard two days ago—shotgun job."

Farrell felt a chill collect in his middle. "Oh, yeah? You get the guy who did it yet?"

"No. It's a hot car ring we've been trying to get a line on for some time. We think our man made contact with them through a negro hard-case named Zootie Hines. When they got to the hideout, something went wrong."

"Damn, that's tough. The guy have a family?"

"Yeah. Wife's taking it pretty hard."

"This Hines—you make him for the shooter?"

"Could be," Casey replied. "But the case has a funny wrinkle. We heard from two contacts that the boss of the gang might be a white man who goes by the name of 'Mercy.' We don't know if that's a nickname or an alias yet."

Farrell felt weak in the knees. A minute ago he'd been looking for something more than five years old, but now, thanks to Frank, it had attained a sudden immediacy. "Doesn't ring any bells with me," he heard himself say.

"We don't have a line on the guy yet, either, but I'm feeling lucky about this for some reason. Listen, we haven't seen one another in a couple of weeks. How about dinner one night this week?"

"Yeah, sure. I'd like that. I wish we saw each other more often."

"Well, maybe we should work on it a little harder. Tell Savanna hello for me when you see her."

"Thanks, Frank. I will. I'll try to call you tomorrow and see if you're free."

"Great. G'night, kid."

"'Night." They broke the connection simultaneously. Farrell looked at the telephone with mingled feelings of warmth and regret. Although they'd been separated for over thirty years, in the past four years a relationship—something beyond mere friendship—had grown up between them.

And you just lied to him, he thought. No matter how much time passes, you still see him as a cop and you on the other side. When are you going to let that go?

But now he had something else to work on—a negro named Zootie Hines who had a connection to the mysterious Mercy. There was somewhere he could go with that name. He left the booth and headed back to the Quarter.

⊗⊗⊗

Mercer entered the house on Castiglione Street to the sound of the telephone ringing. He walked through the darkened house with the quick, sure strides of a feral cat, never hesitating, never touching anything but the floor. He picked up the receiver, knowing from the persistent ringing who it was. "Don't you have anything else to do but call me? You need to get yourself a woman."

He began to laugh, but the silence in the receiver made him wonder if he'd misjudged the caller.

"You've got trouble no woman can fix," the familiar voice said finally. "Wesley Farrell's looking for you."

The name stopped Mercer cold for a brief span of seconds. "Never heard of him. I don't even know what he looks like." His attempt at nonchalance fell flat. That anyone could know him and be on his trail was disquieting. He'd believed himself virtually invisible, having relied on people like Hope and Hines to do most of his dirty work.

"Then you'd better find out. He's been to Milton, and a man on the waterfront who tells me things called to say Farrell's been combing the taverns and whorehouses over that way asking for a scar-faced man called 'Mercy.' Somehow he's connected you to the Schofield killing."

"How could that be?" Mercer could not quite keep the shock from his voice. "Only four people know about that hit—you, me, Milton, and the driver. Milton didn't even know until afterward, you said."

"Didn't you tell me you took a colored boy along as back-up? Somebody you were grooming to be your top-kick?"

Mercer caught his breath. Joe Earle. He'd forgotten about him. "Oh, yeah. Joe Earle Hope. He was no good at the rough stuff. I took Hines on after that."

"So what about him? Are you so sure he didn't talk?"

Mercer felt a tremor go through him. But no, he was sure. It couldn't be. "That kid is so scared of me that he almost shits his pants when I walk into the room. He wouldn't dare rat on me."

"I wish I was as sure as you are, Mercer. You're good at what you do, but I don't know as I believe in your ability to size up men. You were wrong about him once—maybe you were wrong all the way."

Mercer felt anger rising in him now. "What about the driver? What makes you so sure he's not selling us out?"

"Like I said, I don't have that much confidence in your judgment where other men are concerned. Our friend had a very specific goal in mind, and he got everything he wanted and then some. For him to stir up something that's been buried for five years would go against his grain. No, the Hope kid's your problem—fix Farrell, then fix Joe Earle."

Mercer's lip curled. He'd never liked the way this sonofabitch talked down to him—like he was some snot-nosed know-nothing. "Ain't you the smart guy was givin' me all the grief about 'fixing' the nigger cop the other day? And now you want me to go and 'fix' two other guys."

The voice at the other end of the line had been relatively passive and matter-of-fact up until now, but when the man spoke this time, his voice was hard, with muscle behind it. "Listen, you thick-necked palooka. You got careless the other day, and your solution was to kill a man. Now we've got the Saint Bernard cops, the New Orleans police, and Farrell all looking in our direction. That might not seem like much trouble to you, but if we don't screw the lid down on this, we're liable to have the State Police and maybe T-Men breathing down our necks. You getting a good, clear picture now, smart guy?"

Mercer was still furious, but he could not deny his partner's logic. His reply was grudging, but in the affirmative. "How do you want things handled—just so we ain't got any misunderstandings between us."

"Leave the shotgun at home. Killing like that calls too much attention to you. I want this done quiet. You'll have to take Farrell by surprise, and get in the first lick—good and hard. You can't make any mistakes with him—if he finds you, he's half-way to me. I can't afford that."

Mercer hadn't heard uncertainty in the other man's voice before, and it was so close to fear that it intrigued him. "I hear this Farrell thinks he's a knife man. I'll show him a knife he won't forget. Joe Earle will be a cinch." Mercer was grinning now, the other man's insult nearly forgotten. Using a knife was something he knew, something he enjoyed.

"Just so there are no more mistakes." The other man sounded a bit calmer now, the anger and uncertainty both gone. Even he had respect for Mercer and his big knife.

"Where does Farrell live?"

"He's got an apartment on the second story of the Café Tristesse on Basin Street. If you move fast, you might be able to get in place before he makes it back there."

Mercer's large yellow teeth made a pale, evil crescent in the darkened room. "I'm leaving now."

∞∞∞

Joe Earle Hope put the telephone down and left the booth at the rear of a juke joint on Toledano Street. Outside the booth the sound of Charlie Christian's electric guitar and Goodman's Sextette doing "Flying Home" washed over him. He would have appreciated the song a little more if he'd had a home to fly to just then. Right now he felt like an outcast. He'd left most of his stuff at his shack in Arabi, taking with him only his supply of ready cash—about $1,800.00—plus his German steel spring-blade knife, and a .32 Owl's Head five-shooter he'd bought in a hock shop for three dollars. It was in his mind to leave town through the most expeditious, but unobtrusive, route. He had rejected the train as too expensive and the bus as too slow, and was torn between the choices of buying an old car from someone or catching a ride with a negro trucker heading north to Chicago or west toward Los Angeles. Each destination had a sizable negro community where he could lose himself. Later, he figured, he could contact his sister, Arthel, and find out how and where his brother was.

He moved slowly through the crowded tables to the bar, where he caught the eye of the bartender, a middle-aged ex-fighter named Tubby Pauger. The barman grinned and moved his still-muscular body down the bar with a languid grace. "What say, my man? Ain't seen you for a while."

"Hey, Tubby. Tryin' to make a livin' over in St. Bernard—don't get over here much these days."

Tubby shook his large head. "Must be hard. Ain't much one of us can do for money, poor as it is over there."

"Yeah, reckon that's so. Fact is, I thought I'd move on somewheres else. Maybe you can help me. You know of anybody, a trucker or travelin' man who might be headin' Chicago way or maybe to the west? I can pay my share of the gas and help drive."

As a bartender, Tubby Pauger had heard many things, and had listened to them long enough to tell when something in a story didn't jibe. "Hell, why not take the bus, man? That way all you got to do is lay back and sleep the whole way."

Joe Earle shrugged. "Didn't feel like makin' all them stops. That's why I was hopin' to hook up with somebody who wants to high-ball it." Joe Earle wasn't used to lying, and he knew his eyelids were blinking too much as he vainly strove to keep looking Tubby in the eye.

Tubby cleared his throat and leaned a bit closer to the younger man. "Listen, brutha—if you got trouble, you ain't got to tell me about it, but if you want to, maybe I can help you some. You dodgin' the law?"

Joe Earle's heart pounded, and he swallowed hard, trying not to vomit. "N-no, no I ain't. But—"

Tubby put a huge hand on his shoulder. "You ain't got to say no more. But you are tryin' to stay outa somebody's way, ain't you?"

Unable to speak, Joe Earle nodded quickly.

"Okay. Listen, you go and sit over in that corner—it's kinda dark and nobody's likely to notice you. You had anything to eat?"

Joe Earle shook his head.

"I'll have the cook make you up a plate while you have a drink—couple of them and your nerves'll settle down a mite, and you'll be able to think straight again. Okay?"

"T-thanks, Tubby. I-I'll be okay in a minute. Just a-ain't had much p-p-practice at this."

"You're young yet, son. A negro gets looked at and chased after plenty unless he's luckier than most. I know a few people I can call—they'll keep their mouths shut—and maybe I can find you a ride out of here tonight, or tomorrow at the latest. You can bunk with me if it takes a li'l while. Awright?"

"Awright. Awright."

Chapter 9

Blood was humming in Sheriff Chauchaut's veins. It had been some time since there had been any real excitement in his parish. Keeping his parish free of crime had made things dull. He realized that he missed creeping through the bayous with a rifle to surprise a gang of bootleggers.

Captain Luke Peters seemed to read his mind. "Like old times, eh, Sheriff?"

"You know me too well, Luke. I've missed this."

"Think you'll be able to forget sheriffing after you're in the governor's mansion?"

"It'll be hard, but you'll be commander of the State Police. Every now and again you can take me out so I can keep my hand in. I won't be governor forever."

"No, sir, I reckon you'll go on to Washington in the Senate or some such."

Chauchaut smiled. "What did your informant tell you about this boy?"

"Well, the man said Oscar Boulet worked for Johnny Hope the whole time he was in business over here. Also said Boulet didn't seem to have no regular job but was living mighty fat. I reckon we lay hands on this boy, we can learn a whole lot from him." Chauchaut heard the steel in Peters' voice lying just beneath the words. It made him proud to know he was commanding men like Peters.

They arrived at their destination, a house in a sparsely-settled negro neighborhood in the village of Arabi. Peters stopped across the road from the house and both men got out. Chauchaut, dressed in his white shirt and cowboy hat, stood out like a ghost in the darkness. He loosened the pistol in his holster. "I'll take the front, Luke."

"Good idea, sheriff. I'll take the rifle and go around back." Peters reached into the car and removed a Winchester rifle.

Chauchaut gave his deputy a chance to get around the back, then he walked slowly toward the front porch. When he was about fifteen yards from it he cupped his hands around his mouth and called out, "Oscar Boulet. This is Sheriff Chauchaut. Come on out."

There was a dim light burning in the front room and the windows were open, the curtains billowing from a slight breeze. Chauchaut heard crickets and tree frogs chirping all around him, and little else. He cupped his hands around his mouth again and called out. "Boulet, this is the sheriff. Come out or I'm coming in."

The door opened and a young negro dressed in denim trousers and a white cotton undershirt came out on the porch, his movements slow and wary. "I'm Oscar Boulet. What you want with me, sheriff?"

Chauchaut's attention was riveted to Boulet. "I want to talk to you about Johnny Hope."

Boulet stiffened. "I ain't worked for Johnny since he went broke. Ain't even seen him in a while." There was a quiver in the man's voice that put Chauchaut on guard. He put his hand on the butt of his ivory-handled Colt revolver.

"Then you don't have anything to worry about, do you?" Chauchaut said, still walking toward him. Then the lights in the house blinked out. Chauchaut stopped, trying to keep an eye on Boulet while watching the darkened house. As he stood there, a jet of fire exploded from the front window and something slapped him hard on the right thigh. Chauchaut felt no more than that, but the leg became weak and wouldn't support him. He drew his .38 as he fell and began firing wildly at the house. He saw Boulet grab his chest and collapse to the porch floor. Supporting himself on one elbow, he kept firing until his gun was empty. The repeated roar of Peters' Winchester sounded from behind the house, silencing the hidden crickets and frogs.

The numbness from the bullet's impact was slowly replaced by sharp, lancing pain. Chauchaut could hear himself groaning, but he forced himself to eject the empty cartridge cases from his .38 and replace them with fresh loads from his belt. "Luke," he cried. "Luke, I'm hit." There was more firing, then, as suddenly as it began, the gunfire ended and silence fell over the scene like a pall. Chauchaut covered the house, trying not to pass out.

After what seemed an eternity, Luke Peters appeared at the side of the cottage. He saw Chauchaut on the ground, Boulet lying on the porch. He ran to the sheriff first.

"How bad is it?" Peters voice was tense.

"My leg," Chauchaut gasped. "My leg."

Peters took out a handkerchief and tied it tightly around the wound, then went over to Boulet. He came back almost immediately. "He's hit in the chest but still breathin'. I'll call for an ambulance." He ran to the patrol car and Chauchaut could hear him talking excitedly. After a moment he came back. "They'll be here in a couple minutes, Paul. What happened out here?"

"I was talking to Boulet," Chauchaut said, his teeth clenched against the pain. "Somebody inside—killed the lights—started s-shootin'. I got—I got h-hit, started shootin' b-back. Boulet got hit. Don't know after t-that."

"Whoever it was came out the back after you started firing," Peters said. "I traded shots with him, but he got away into the woods. That's when I came out here."

"That was good…information you g-got, Luke. Boulet—hope he don't d-die—before we can—question him."

"Don't talk anymore, Paul. The doctor'll be here soon."

Chauchaut tried to reply, but the sound of the ambulance siren distracted him, and before he could find the energy to speak again, he passed out in Peters' arms.

⊗⊗⊗

When he reached the edge of the central business district, Farrell caught a streetcar that took him into the Downtown area and over to Rampart Street. They might as well have called the famous street Music Avenue, because the blare of trumpets, the chirp of clarinets, and the moan of saxophones, backed up with bass, guitar, or harmonica, came from every door. Particularly at night, when a host of flickering neon signs held back the darkness, the air had a sharp hum that quickened the pulse. Farrell had lived in the midst of it for much of his life, and even preoccupied as he was, he was glad to be alive in it.

He was bound for a juke joint identified only by a neon sign of a red, top-hatted crayfish leaning against a martini glass with two olives. Although it had no official name, it was known throughout the city as "The Happy Crawdad." The owner was a huge negro called Little Head Lucas. He was one of Farrell's closest friends, and a man who could always impart some wisdom about the negro underworld.

The joint was, as usual, crowded with men and women playing the game of love as they drank and danced to the big, neon-lit juke box sitting just off the dance floor on a small raised stage. Count Basie's rendition of "One O'Clock Jump" blared from the speaker.

Farrell skirted the dance floor, ignoring the curious stares from some of the clientele as he threaded his way through a cluster of tables. Little Head, as usual played chess with himself, oblivious to the din. An area of calm and quiet surrounded the big man as he stared at the black and white chessmen and sipped a Tom Collins from a tall glass. Lucas sensed Farrell's approach before he arrived and he spoke without looking up. "Evenin', Mr. Farrell. Drag up a chair and light down."

Farrell pulled out the chair on the opposite side of the table and seated himself. "How do you do it?"

"What?"

"Sit here in all this racket and figure out chess moves. Anybody else would've been driven nuts by now."

Lucas turned up one corner of his mouth. "Maybe I'm crazy already. Look at how many years I been doin' it."

Farrell smiled and nodded. He and Lucas had known each other since Prohibition days when the big man operated a speakeasy and Farrell had been his main source of supply.

Farrell pushed his cigarette case over to the big man, and Lucas took one, leaning over the chess board for the light. He inhaled and then expelled enough smoke to engulf a Cadillac limousine. "Tell me what's goin' on," he said.

"Trouble."

"I think you like trouble better than I like chess, much of it as you get into. Who you lookin' for?"

"Zootie Hines. Know him?"

"In a small way. He cut up in the speak' I used to run. Pulled a knife on me and I knocked him through a wall. He ain't come around me since then."

Farrell grinned. "He's supposed to be tough. He never tried you again?"

A soft laugh came from the big man's throat. "He's tough, sure, but he's li'l. Them li'l guys hit the deck awful hard. They ain't usually spry enough to come back for a second helpin' no time soon." Lucas inhaled more of the cigarette. "But don't turn your back on the mean li'l bastard. He'll back-shoot you in a pair of seconds."

"I need to get my hands on him. He's supposed to be partnered up with a white man they call 'Mercy.' I need Hines to lead me to him."

Lucas cut his eyes at Farrell. "I heard a li'l somethin' about this Mercy. They say he's a giant—that he lives in the dark and eats other men's souls."

Farrell nodded slowly. "He sounds like a bogey man, all right, but one thing is the truth—he kills people. I know of three people he's shotgunned, and I heard today that he killed Pascal DeLatte with a cane knife."

Little Head's eyes got big, the whites almost glowing in his dark face. "Damn, that's enough to make your marbles shrivel up. What's this bogey man done to you?"

"A long time ago, he killed a man I knew, and did his best to kill me. There's a Treasury agent in town trying to reopen the case. For personal reasons, it would be better if I could hand Mercy to him and prove he was the shooter."

Little Head Lucas cocked an eyebrow. "You don't want much. Why don't you ask God to turn all us black folks white while you're at it?"

Farrell laughed. "I've broken too many laws to ask God for anything. Besides, my Aunt Willie Mae was fond of saying that God helps those who help themselves."

Now Little Head laughed. "Well, I wish he'd get to helpin' us. We been on our own since they brought the first boatload of us here 300 years ago. But you didn't come to listen to theology. You want that li'l weasel, Hines."

"I'm not alone—I just got word the police are looking for him in connection with the murder of a negro cop."

Little Head sighed heavily. "Damn. Ain't there enough white folks killin' us without us killin' each other?" He put his hand on a black pawn and moved it within striking distance of the white king.

"You know anything about where he might be found? There must be a woman or two he might visit."

Little Head nodded. "With most punks like him, that would be the best guess. Trouble is, he ain't like most punks—that way, anyhow."

Farrell caught something in Little Head's tone that intrigued him. "How is he different?"

Little Head scratched the tip of his ear. "Woman I happen to know—JoNelle Johnston—she ain't no Sunday school teacher. Mostly been makin' a livin' off of men's weaknesses. She told me a story 'bout meetin' this Zootie Hines at a bar on St. Claude. Said he was a li'l drunk, makin' jokes and laughin' like a fool. He flirted with her a li'l bit, bought her some drinks. One thing led to another—as it always does in those situations. Anyhow, JoNelle took the li'l fella home and they had some more whiskey, then got down to business. Well, seems like Zootie couldn't get his motor outa neutral."

Farrell shrugged. "Some guys take on a load of booze, nothing works. Working girls tell me it's pretty common."

Little Head nodded. "She told me that he started cryin'—kind of took her by surprise, since he'd been such a confident li'l rooster. She said she tried to make him feel better about it, and he flipped his cork. Knocked her off the bed and begun whippin' on her head, yellin' and callin' her names. When she was about half cock-eyed from the whippin', he—well, she didn't go into a lot of detail, only said beatin' on her seemed to help his problem—he took his pleasure in a way that didn't help her much."

Farrell grimaced. "Has she seen him since?"

"I don't think so, 'cause she promised she'd kill him if she did. She carries a .38 now and never takes it off."

"So he's a sadist, and not just a thug."

"Since I heard that story from JoNelle, I made some inquiries, and heard stories from other women he's beat up on. He's left a world of trouble behind him."

"Any of those women know where he could be found?"

Little Head smiled sourly. "Most of 'em makin' it a point *not* to find him. But he's a fella who don't light long in one place. He might stay where his boss is, or maybe he found himself a woman who likes bein' beat on."

"I've got to find Mercy, and soon," Farrell said. "Hines is the only key I've got to his whereabouts."

Little Head nodded. "I hear you. I'll put the word out tonight." He looked at the clock on the wall. "You oughta go on home, get some sleep. You lookin' a li'l frayed around the edges, my friend."

Farrell gave him a tired grin. "Thanks for the help. One of these days, I'll be able to do something for you."

"You got kind of a short memory. Las' year, you helped get my cousin, Gladiola, away from Archie Badeaux. If it wasn't for you, she might be as dead as Archie. A favor that big'll carry you for quite a spell on my books."

"Thanks. Guess it's time to make tracks. I'll be back soon, and you can try to explain this game to me again."

"You know how—you just like listenin' to me tell it." As he laughed again, Farrell got up, gripped his shoulder for a moment, then walked out the way he'd come.

※

It was well past 11:00 when a dark-haired, full-figured white woman of thirty entered a diner on South Solomon Street. She was wearing a thin cotton dress and a tattered woolen sweater. She was shivering, and her face was pale except for a fresh bruise on the left side. Her eyes had the raw, red look that follows a fit of hard crying. She went to the last stool at the counter and sat there, resting her elbows on the chipped linoleum surface.

The proprietor, a rugged-looking man in his late forties saw her and the hard, cynical look in his dark eyes turned to one of pity. He straightened the white sailor hat on his bald crown and limped over to her. He'd been a merchant seaman until a shipboard accident had cost him a leg. After his recovery he'd taken his savings and pension and used it to open this diner.

"'Lo, Dolores. What's the good word?"

"I wish there was one," she said bitterly. Her lip trembled as she spoke, and a tear escaped her left eye, tracing a watery line over the curve of her bruised cheek.

The ex-sailor looked around the diner, and when he saw no one was looking, he poured some whiskey into a coffee cup from a pint flask he kept under the counter, then filled it up with coffee and threw in a few cubes of sugar. He stirred it with rapid, shallow strokes, then put it down in front of Dolores. She looked at him gratefully, then took the cup and drank about half of it in a single draught.

"Thanks, Pete," she said in a soft voice, wiping her lips with the back of her hand.

"The new man's givin' you a hard time again, huh?"

She shook her head from side to side, her eyes large and blank. "I'm scared to death of him. He seemed like a nice guy when I hooked up with him, but the longer I'm with him, the meaner he gets. All he does is wear me out—" she looked at the older man quickly, slightly embarrassed for letting that slip—"or he's screamin' for me to get him food, or whiskey, or just 'cause he's meaner'n sin."

He looked down at his work-roughened hands. "You could leave him, y'know. There's other ways to get along." He wanted more than anything to tell her that he thought she was beautiful, and that he'd like to marry her. He imagined she'd laugh at the idea that a bald, gimpy-legged man ten years her senior could be taken seriously as a suitor. "I could use some help in here, and I know of a room that's available—six bits a week. You could eat your meals here and—"

"Gosh, Pete, that's real sweet of you." She drank some more of the whiskey-spiked coffee, then touched the bruise tenderly with her fingertips. "I don't know what he'd do if I walked out. He's got a terrible temper. He might—"

"You could let me worry about that, Dolores. He might be big and he might be mean, but after twenty years as a bos'n on more tramp steamers than I can count, I learned a thing or two about dealin' with tough guys." He leaned a bit closer to her, and gently laid one of his big, scarred hands on her wrist. "You gotta do somethin', kid. He's liable to kill you one day."

She looked directly into his face as he said this, and her eyes got large and round before she looked down at his hand. "It ain't that bad. He's just got some troubles these days. Mercy ain't a bad guy most of the time."

"Mercy? That his name?"

"It's really Bart Mercer. Mercy is like a nickname."

"Hummph. Mercy's a funny kind of nickname for a guy who goes around beltin' helpless women. Look, are you sure you won't take what I'm offerin'? It ain't no way to become a millionaire, but you'll make enough to feed and clothe yourself, take in a movie once in a while, even go down to Ponchartrain Beach on Sunday. It's a better livin' than a lotta people got." He was making it sound a lot better than it really was. He hadn't been to a movie in four years, and he couldn't remember ever going to the beach. If she were in the picture, however, he knew he'd make the effort.

She was still shivering, and was rubbing her hands up and down the insides of her upper arms. Her nose had begun to run and she wiped it with a paper napkin Pete had given her with the coffee. Talking to Pete was making her feel a little better, but what she really needed was a fix. She'd been after Mercer for money, and that was the reason he'd knocked her around. She'd come to Pete because she was pretty sure he'd give her the two dollars she needed to make the connection with her dealer.

"You don't look so good, kid. You comin' down with a cold, or somethin'?"

"Maybe you're right. I need some medicine to fix me up." She felt like she was coming apart, and hoped she could hold out long enough to get the money and leave.

"You need a little money to get something?" he asked solicitously. "Would a couple of bucks help?"

"Yeah. Yeah, it sure would. You're one in a million, Pete." She gave him the best smile she could muster as she took the two crumpled bills. She slid off the stool, trying not to rush.

"Please, Dolores. Think about the job. I know things'd get better for you if you'd get away from that palooka. I'd hate to see you get hurt."

"I'll think about it, Pete. I promise." She gave him one more wan smile, then walked out into the darkness.

Pete looked sadly at the diner door for a few moments, then he hobbled back to the center of the counter, filling coffee cups and taking orders for pie or seconds on the chili. He took no notice of a man in a dark shirt and knit watch cap who had been intently reading a newspaper in a booth not far from where Pete and Dolores had been talking. He put a half-dollar on the table, folded his newspaper, then left the diner, walking directly to a telephone booth across the street. He put in his nickel, asked the operator for a number, then waited as the number rang.

"This is Sparrow," a woman's voice said in his ear.

"This is Stubbs. I heard something you want to know."

⊗⊗⊗

Somewhat earlier in the evening, after waiting for Longboy to make several calls, Daggett and Andrews left the Fat Man Lounge and drove across town to a small, poverty-stricken neighborhood known as Gerttown. Although there were a number of hard-working negroes there struggling to feed and educate their children, it was also the kind of place where you could bet on a horse on Long Island, score enough morphine to stun the Fighting Irish football team, or hire the services of a 14-year-old whore. It was as hard and cruel as New Orleans could get.

Daggett and Andrews skirted the edge of Gerttown on Earhart Avenue until they found the street they were looking for. As they turned into the area, each detective used a searchlight to scan the addresses.

"Here it is," Daggett said. Andrews quickly applied the brakes, then shifted into reverse and eased the car next to the dirt path that served as a sidewalk on this street. He killed the engine and the lights with a single motion.

"What do you think, boss? Do we need a shotgun?"

Daggett looked around. "You see anything around here that looks like Hines's blue Chevrolet?"

"Uh-uh. Most of these cars lucky to have any paint at all, much less blue. Unless Vehicle Identification is wrong about his wheels, he's probably not here."

Daggett looked at the radium dial on his wristwatch and made a face. "We've hunted all over Hell's half-acre for this woman, so we might as well knock on the door." The pair got out of the car, and each loosened a revolver under his coat. Daggett had recently retired his matched set of .41 Colts for a .38-44 Smith & Wesson Super Police with a five-inch barrel. Andrews favored a .38 Detective Special that he carried in a suede-lined hip-pocket holster.

They walked up on the porch of a nondescript shotgun cottage, keeping clear of the door and the large, full-length window. Andrews knocked loudly, then stood to the side, waiting. After a moment or so, they heard a feminine voice from within. "Who's there?"

"New Orleans Police, Miss Dalton. Open up, please." Daggett had his badge case in one hand, and his .38-44 held down alongside his right leg.

The door opened wide and a delicate-looking brown woman with light-brown hair stood framed in the opening. Neither detective could see anything threatening behind her.

"What do you want?" the woman asked. She was dressed in a rose-colored bed gown and her hair had the look of being fresh from the pillow.

"We understand you're acquainted with a man named Zootie Hines," Daggett said, replacing his badge and gun.

"Well, what of it? Is it a crime?"

"Knowing him, no," Andrews replied. "Concealing his whereabouts, yes. He's wanted in connection with a homicide."

That made no more impression than a fist bouncing off Popeye's jaw. "Can we come in?" Daggett finally asked.

"You'll just push yourselves in anyway if I say no." She stood to the side and let the two detectives into her small house. The lights were on, clear back to the kitchen. It was the work of less than forty-five seconds for Andrews to walk back and check each of the three rooms. He returned, shaking his head.

Daggett turned his eyes on the woman, searching her face for any deception lingering there. Hers was an off-beat prettiness unusual in a prostitute—she was almost beautiful in some ways. She had a feature that was unusual in colored people: blue eyes that had to have come from the same white ancestor as her light brown hair. Her skin was a deep, but not dark, brown and except for her lips her features were not especially negroid. She looked at the detectives without any particular fear or dread—no doubt she had talked to police before, a number of times. In spite of the frank gaze, something about her, Daggett thought, did not seem quite right.

"Can you tell us where Zootie Hines is?"

"No. And I prob'ly wouldn't tell you if I could." She spoke without any particularly hostility. "He's a crook and y'all are the cops. I know how it goes."

"Have you seen him lately?"

"He was here earlier tonight. Now I s'pose I'll have to tell him not to come here no more, 'cause y'all will be watchin' this place, won't you?"

"If you won't cooperate, I suspect we will." Daggett pushed his hat off his forehead and regarded her frankly. "It looks like Zootie might mean something to you, Miss Dalton. If that's true, the best thing you can do is ask him to come into the station voluntarily. There's a dead policeman to answer for—a dead negro policeman—and the evidence points to him being involved. If he comes in and makes a statement as to what he knows, he'll come out of this with his skin. If he doesn't—"

"You'll bring him in tied to the fender of your car like a gutted deer carcass. That's what happens to people who kill policemen, ain't it?" Hostility had crept into her voice now, and her pale eyes flashed fire.

Daggett responded with bluntness. "What do you expect? If he won't come in, we have to figure he'll take a shot at the next cop he sees. If he makes it a war, we'll shoot back. That's a fact. If you care about him, you'd rather see him in prison still alive, than dead, wouldn't you?"

"You talkin' that jive to the wrong person. I had a cousin who got sent to the chain gang, and he died in the hot-box 'cause he dared talk back to the cap'n. You know how they treat us down here. Would you want that for somebody you cared about?" Her voice had gotten husky, almost a growl, as she made her case.

Daggett's face was bleak. He couldn't argue with her. Zootie would be sent to a chain gang—if he was lucky. He could very well be executed as an accessory to murder. "I can't talk to you about what I'd want. It's Zootie—and you—who're in this situation. This white man he's workin' for is a cold-blooded killer—if it comes down to him or Zootie, Zootie'll be the one he sacrifices. He's a career criminal and a multiple murderer. He won't be taken alive."

As he spoke, her face started to break apart and she pressed her hands up to her mouth. "You think I ain't told him all that? You think I ain't tried to get him away from that crazy animal? He thinks that man, Mercer, is some kinda hero, and that he's his hero's right-hand-man. He's like a li'l boy, talkin' about it." She burst into tears then, the sobs coming from her open mouth like the cries of a wounded animal. Daggett had seen loved ones in this position before. It never failed to wring his heart.

But he had heard one thing that made his ears perk. "Mercer? Is that the man's name?"

"Yes, Mercer. I don't know his other name. Zootie calls him 'Mercy,' like it's a nickname or somethin'."

"I don't know what else to say, ma'am. If you can do anything to help, I hope you'll do it, because he's marked for death the way it stands now."

She looked at him, still crying. The huge tears made muddy tracks across her brown complexion. Her anguish was as real as a knife cut.

After a moment, Daggett couldn't stand it anymore, and he walked out, Andrews behind him. They walked down the two steps and out to the street. As Daggett got ready to get in, Andrews looked at him over the top of the squad car.

"Don't let it get you, Iz. You can't do nothin' but what they pays you to do."

"Maybe that's true, but I don't always have to like it." He got into the car, and after a brief pause, Andrews slid behind the wheel. A half-minute later, they left Gerttown for their homes in Carrollton.

Chapter 10

There was no facility in St. Bernard Parish capable of dealing with two medical emergencies at once, so the ambulance carried Chauchaut and Boulet into New Orleans Charity Hospital. The emergency room entrance was lit up like day for the white-clad nurses, interns, and orderlies who hurriedly dealt with the victims of various big-city mishaps. Two teams, alerted to expect the wounded men, were waiting when the sheriff's ambulance arrived.

Captain Luke Peters, following behind in his squad car, jumped out to help the first team gently remove the still unconscious sheriff and wheel him into the operating room. A second team bore Boulet to another operating theater.

Art Frizzell, the crime reporter for the *New Orleans States-Item* hurried after Peters. "Hey—Captain Peters. Art Frizzell with the *States-Item*. What happened here?"

Peters turned to the reporter. He was perfectly composed, his eyes steely. "Sheriff Paul Chauchaut was shot trying to apprehend a suspect in the murder of a New Orleans detective. As usual, the sheriff confronted the suspect while I covered the rear exit. Shots were exchanged with an unknown assailant, and the sheriff was hit in the leg. The suspect, Oscar Boulet, was also hit, and he's in surgery."

"Hot damn." Frizzell scribbled furiously in his notebook. "The stuff about the New Orleans cop is news to me, Captain. What can you tell me about that?"

"It was a man from the Negro Squad."

"Oh?" Frizzell was puzzled. "Why was this New Orleans cop in your parish, Captain?"

"You'll have to ask the New Orleans police, Art. They're treating it hush-hush."

"Well, excuse me, Captain, before you go. If y'all suspected this man was involved in the murder of a New Orleans officer, wouldn't it have been in line for some New Orleans cops to be with you?"

Peters' boyish face was taut with strain, the skin around his eyes and mouth pale and hard looking. "We got a tip from an informant in our parish. We followed up on it. If we'd had a chance to question the suspect, we'd have brought in the New Orleans police in due course. As it was, we were attacked and we shot back, as any policeman would. Now if there are no other questions, Art…"

Frizzell saw he was losing his subject's attention, and quickly changed the thrust of his questions. "You think the way this arrest went will affect the sheriff's run for the governorship? Nobody's closer to the campaign than you."

"Ridiculous notion. Paul Chauchaut's a lawman's lawman. You notice it's *him* in there with a bullet and not me—he's always been first in the fight for law and order, and, not for the first time, he's taken the big risks. If anything, this'll improve his chances in the election."

Frizzell stepped in front of Peters to prevent his escape. "Can we expect any further arrests in this case?"

Peters nodded. "We know the names of other gang members, and you can count on arrests very soon. Now if you'll excuse me, I've got to check on the sheriff." He pushed past Frizzell and disappeared around a corner.

Frizzell frowned and closed his notebook. A negro killing wasn't big news in the South, but the murder of a member of the New Orleans Police's Negro Squad was—even more so since it occurred in St. Bernard. So why hadn't it been reported? What kind of angle were the local police playing?

Frizzel walked through the hospital into the main lobby where he entered one of a bank of telephone booths and called the copy desk at the *States-Item.*

"Hello, Malloy, this is Frizzel. Get ready. Tonight Paul Chauchaut, crime-busting sheriff of St. Bernard Parish and leading candidate for governor, was badly wounded in a shoot-out with members of a gang believed to be responsible for the murder of an as-yet unidentified member of the New Orleans Police Negro Squad. The sheriff and a suspect, also unidentified, were brought into Charity Hospital's emergency room at 10:45 PM this date. Details are sketchy, but Chauchaut's chief deputy, Captain Luke Peters, says other suspects have been identified and arrests are imminent. Got all that? Swell. No, I didn't know anything about the colored dick, but I'll be back with you later. Check." Frizzel hung up and left for Police Headquarters.

⣿

It was nearing 1:00 when Farrell reached Basin Street. He was dog tired, having trod several miles of concrete in his quest to identify Mercy and get a line on Zootie Hines. He was close to something, and knew that with a nickel's worth of luck he could locate both men and get out from under this mess.

When he came in sight of the neon lights bathing the street in front of the Café Tristesse, he realized that if he entered the front door, someone or something would claim his attention. Tonight, he was having none of that. He cut down the alley which led to his private entrance, tugging his tie away from his neck in anticipation of a hot shower and a tall drink. He was thinking how good it would be to get his shoes off when the hair stood up on the back of his neck. The split-second warning of a shadow falling over him activated reflexes honed by thirty years in the underworld. Farrell threw his body into a long forward roll as he felt something cut the air above him.

Farrell landed in a crouch, facing the mouth of the alley, his German steel straight razor open in his hand and his breath roaring in his ears as he fought the shock of fear coursing through him. As he bounced on the balls of his feet, a huge figure lunged at him with a glittering, broad-bladed implement raised high above his head.

The man was at least a head taller than Farrell and perhaps fifty pounds heavier, yet he moved with the quiet grace of a cat, forcing Farrell back away from the lights of the street. As Farrell shifted from side to side, looking for an opening, Nose Morianos's voice returned to him—"a *loup-garou*"—a ravening beast, an animal in the shape of a man—the same man who'd split Pascal Delatte's head to his shoulders. Panic tore at the edges of Farrell's mind, and in that split-second of indecision and hesitancy, Mercy struck. The heavy blade whizzed through the night air with a distinctive whistle toward Farrell's head.

There was no time to plot strategy or even to run. Farrell pivoted right just as the blade swept past, leaving the other man's left side exposed to the cold steel flashing in Farrell's hand.

A bellow of rage and pain echoed off the damp bricks as the razor bit into soft flesh, gouging a bloody trench as Farrell's hand followed through and across Mercer's unguarded face. Mercer's free hand struck out blindly, instinctively, knocking Farrell into a pile of garbage cans. As he struggled to gain a purchase and find his feet, Farrell saw the big man staggering toward the street, the cane knife dangling uselessly from his right hand as he clutched at his wounded face with his left.

In the precious seconds it took for Farrell to regain his footing and sprint to the mouth of the alley, Mercer disappeared from view. Farrell heard an engine stutter into life, an impatient foot kicking it into a snarl. He reached the sidewalk in time to see a late model De Soto careen past him, the license plate shrouded in the early-morning darkness. Farrell looked after him, fury bubbling in him like hot oil in a steel caldron. He was no longer tracking an unsuspecting quarry—the prey had turned.

"Boss! Boss!" a voice shouted behind him. He turned and saw Harry and Pete Zuckerman, the chef, each running up to him with a weapon held high. Harry was armed with a baseball bat and a flashlight while Zuckerman held a cleaver. "Boss—you all right? What the hell happened?"

Farrell's breathing was labored and he fought an almost overwhelming desire to vomit. He felt around his body for bleeding wounds, finding a few scratches from his tumble.

"Man, you fetched somebody a lick." Harry played the flashlight beam down at Farrell's right hand. Farrell looked down and saw the mirrored sheen of the razor clouded with thick, red blood that had also spattered his hand and the cuff of his jacket. He felt an irrational desire to drop the bloody blade and tear the jacket from his body.

"Who was that?" Harry's voice was pitched high and very persistent. "You want I should call the cops?"

His voice snapped. "No. The last thing we need is cops crawling all over this place, upsetting the guests. Get inside—make like everything's normal. I'm all right."

Harry looked down dubiously at his employer's blood-spattered hand, but knew better than to argue. He'd been with Farrell a long time, and this wasn't the first time he'd seen his boss in this alley wearing the marks of violence. He said a quiet word to the chef, and the two of them disappeared inside. Farrell stood there for another moment until he'd mastered his fear, then he turned, picked up his hat, and walked to his apartment, careless of the blood that dripped from the bone-handled razor to the pavement behind him.

❧

Mercer had been hurt before. Over the past twenty years he'd been shot three times, been beaten with ax handles, and stabbed, not to mention the attack that had given him the scar through his eyebrow. The man who had produced that scar had been a rival smuggler who'd tried to kill him with a weapon Mercer had never seen before—a type of broad-bladed machete known as a cane knife. It resembled a hideously large cleaver more than it did a traditional machete, but the weight and shape of it made a fatal blow possible when wielded by a strong arm. Mercer had killed that man with his own weapon, and had taken it with him—had made it part of his persona. In later years, the mere sight of him entering a room with the cane knife in his hand was sufficient to silence any commotion.

But now the tables had been turned. Farrell was every bit as deadly as his reputation suggested. He had moved so quickly that he had been inside Mercer's reach before Mercer could recover and change his angle of attack. Mercer hadn't even seen the blade in Farrell's hand before it hit him.

The cut burned like it had been etched in his skin with acid. He felt warm blood soaking into his jacket and his shirt, but he ignored it, his breath hissing through his teeth as he fought going into shock and wrecking the car. He knew he couldn't go to the hospital with a wound like this. Policemen would immediately appear at his side with their questions, and before long he'd be in custody, where his record would come to light.

He knew doctors in New Orleans who would stitch him up with no questions asked, but he knew he'd never get to one of them in the shape he was in now. He examined the signs at the intersection as he cruised through it, quickly realizing he was closer to Dolores Rogers' house than his own. He gunned the engine and headed in that direction.

Earlier in the evening, he and Dolores had had an argument over money and he'd slapped her. He'd seen that look in her eye, the one warning him to watch her. Just a pig, and an addict at that, but she'd be looking for a chance to even the score, just like they all did.

Mercer pulled up in front of her house and managed to get out of the car and up to the front door, his head swimming. He pounded on the door with the flat of his hand until she opened it. He heard her gasp as he pushed past her, but he paid no heed as he went to the kitchen.

"Ice. Get—me—ice," came through his clenched teeth. He went to the kitchen sink, turned on the cold water, and stuck his bleeding face under the faucet. The cold water stung the wound, but it felt good, too. He knew he was taking a chance, leaving his back to her this way, but he had to get some relief. He felt something being pressed against his face, and he straightened up, taking the cloth bundle of ice from her. He sat down on one of her kitchen chairs, gasping for breath.

"Call—Poe—Dr. Poe. Lake-seven-four-eight-two. Tell him Mercer needs him. Tell him." He looked at her, his teeth bared, and saw that she looked back at him calmly. She'd gotten her speedball somehow, he thought distractedly. She went away, and not much later he lost consciousness.

He awoke flat on his back in a bed. His bloody clothes had been stripped off and a fat, pale-skinned man with greasy hair stood over him in his shirtsleeves.

"Welcome back to the land of the living, Mercer," Dr. Poe said. "It's a nice clean cut. You can thank the boy what cut you that he at least keeps his blades honed nice and sharp. Took twenty stitches at that."

Mercer touched his face and felt gauze beneath his fingers. His face was numb, and he was grateful.

"Shot you full of morphine, boy. You're lucky you didn't die of shock before I got here. You owe me three Cees for the house call, by the way." He looked at his watch and winced at the time.

"Money in my pocket." The morphine had made Mercer's mouth numb on the left side, so talking was a chore.

Dr. Poe smiled at him genially. "I found it already, and even washed off the blood. If I were you, I'd stay on my back for a few days, let the cut begin to close. I'll leave you enough morphine tablets to help the pain, but you better keep 'em away from your dolly. She's got a hell of a monkey on her back and might get ideas."

"Gimme." Mercer held out his hand.

Poe smiled and put the bottle of morphine tablets in his outstretched palm. "I'll be seeing you, Mercer. Hope you have better luck next time. I can sew a head up, but I can't sew one back on." He let loose a strangled-sounding wheeze that passed for his laugh, then left the room.

Mercer lay there for some time, his body a lead weight that seemed to have little to do with his head. He felt helpless, and he didn't like the feeling at all. Using all of his strength, he managed to sit up and swing his legs over the edge of the bed. His blood-stained clothing lay on the floor around him and he rooted through it until he found the .38 Smith & Wesson in his pants pocket. He assured himself that it was still loaded before lying back down, holding the gun in his right fist.

He knew he couldn't lie here for very long. Not only had he bungled the job with Farrell, he still had to find and silence Joe Earle. His partner had told him to get Farrell first, but clearly he would not be able to do that now. Farrell had bested him—taking him on again would have to wait until he could get Zootie's help.

Joe Earle would not be difficult to find, but he would need to get Zootie busy. What was the name of that whore he was shacking with? He had dumped Lucinda. But there was somebody else—Daisy? Iris? Some kind of a flower. Violets—no, Violetta. What the hell kind of a name was that?

Zootie was like some kind of a puppy, always looking up at you with his tail wagging, waiting for you to smile, pat his head, and tell him he was a good boy. It was Zootie's constant need for approval that made him ideal. He would kick any ass that Mercer could point to and look back happily for Mercer's grin or nod. Mercer had seen men like Zootie before. They wanted you to think they were strong, but inside they were mush. If Zootie ever met up with somebody strong enough, he would melt like candle wax. Sometimes Mercer wanted to do it himself. He used Zootie but was repelled by him at the same time. His neediness was sickening. It reminded Mercer of some women he'd known—hell, all of the women he'd known. They all wanted you to say you loved 'em, then you had to show 'em how much you loved 'em, over and over again. They never got enough of it. A Goddamned pain in the ass, all of them. He lay there clutching the gun, clenching his teeth against the oncoming pain, hating the world just because it was there.

✖

Frank Casey arrived at his office a half-hour earlier than usual the next morning, carrying with him a cardboard container of coffee bought at the diner across the street from police headquarters. He was settled in at his desk, getting ready to open a report that had come in during the night, when his secretary, Brigid Longley, arrived.

"Wow, you got a new alarm clock or something, boss? Some of the chickens are still asleep." She was a widow in her middle 40s, and but for a streak of white through the center of her dark brown hair, she could have passed for ten years younger. She and Casey had been carrying on a low-level flirtation for the past year or so, but so far, neither had figured out how to carry it to the next stage.

"I must've been working in my dreams," he replied. "I woke up and couldn't go back to sleep so I came in early."

She shook her head at him from the doorway. "You think too much, boss. It's not good for you." She smiled and turned back to her desk.

Maybe, he thought, but not when I'm thinking about you. Before he could turn back to the report, she stuck her head back inside. "Nick Delgado to see you, boss."

Casey sat up a bit straighter. Nick Delgado was the best crime lab man in the state. When he came to visit, enlightenment was sure to follow. "Send him in."

Brigid stood to one side and the bespectacled police scientist came through the door with a thick manila envelope in his hands. "Morning, Captain. I've been up all night, but I discovered some things. It's hard to know exactly how to interpret them, though."

Casey's nose was almost twitching from the scent of information that seemed to emanate from Delgado's person. "Sit down and clue me in, Nick."

Delgado pulled up a chair and drew it closer to Casey's desk. When he was settled, he opened the manila envelope and drew out some photographs which he laid on the desk in three piles so Casey could see them clearly. He pointed to the photos on Casey's left. "Here's the shell we picked up from the Blanton murder scene—a Western brand twelve-gauge double-ought buckshot shell. Here's the microscopic photo of the base so you can see the striker pin indentation."

Casey looked a the photo. "I remember your telling me that some flaw in the firing pin produced that little half-moon-shaped mark in the primer."

Delgado nodded. "I discovered upon further study that there's some kind of burr on the ejector that leaves a peculiar mark on the base, too. I also made a check of several Model '97 Winchesters we have in the lab, and although the burr is distinctive, the general shape of the marks is similar enough that we can assume that the murder weapon was the same type."

"Uh, huh. You were going to check this against some other shotgun murders."

Delgado smiled back. It was a smile Casey had seen before when the crime lab man had found something he considered particularly interesting. "And I did. Surprisingly enough, there haven't been all that many—less than fifteen in the last twenty years."

"Go on." Casey knew that Delgado preferred to explain very carefully, ignoring not even the slightest detail.

Delgado frowned. "What I found doesn't enlighten us much on the Blanton murder, but it's of interest all the same. Do you recall the murder of a Coast Guard officer about five years ago?"

Now it was Casey's turn to frown. "Yeah, as a matter of fact I do. We worked with the Treasury Department on it but we never found anything to identify the killer."

Delgado nodded. "Here are some photos of the striker indentations on several shotgun shells picked up at that scene. It's a different brand of shell—a Remington Nitro Club—but the striker indentations are the same. And see here, where the ejector caught each shell as it was ejecting it? The ejector's got the same burr and left that same distinctive nick in the brass. They're identical on all four shells from the Schofield murder."

Casey looked at the second group of photos and whistled. "I'll be damned. Two murders, five years apart." He rubbed the side of his face unconsciously as his mind raced. It wasn't impossible that the shotgun had changed hands, but for some reason Casey didn't believe it. But how to connect the two cases? Casey looked up from the photos. "There's no doubt—it's the same gun?"

"No doubt at all, chief. I checked the striker and ejector marks under a comparison microscope, and then took photos and superimposed one negative over the other. Perfect match."

Casey nodded. He laced his fingers behind his neck and leaned back in his chair. "Shotguns and Tommy guns went out with Prohibition, and even at that they were both rare in these parts. That's strictly Chicago stuff."

"That's right," Delgago replied. "And I had a feeling you'd think along those lines. You probably know that most of the surrounding parish sheriff's departments don't have crime lab facilities, so they usually send their stuff to us. I checked back to see what else we had in the way of shotgun killings in those parishes over the past two decades. There weren't that many."

Casey cocked an eyebrow. "What else did you find?"

"There were a total of thirteen homicides." Nick paused to clean his spectacles with a handkerchief. "Five were domestic killings—somebody came home, found the husband or wife in bed with the wrong person, and a double-barreled shotgun was the handiest implement to settle the score. Two more were perpetrated during bank holdups by the same man who was subsequently killed in a police shoot-out. He used a sixteen-gauge Ithaca Featherlight pump, by the way.

"That's seven," Casey said.

"The eighth, ninth, and tenth were done by a man out of work who couldn't feed his family," Delgado continued. "He killed his wife and kids, then turned the gun on himself. A twenty-gauge Remington repeater that time."

"And he makes eleven. What's left?"

Nick's lips curved into a half-smile. "This is the one that's really got my brain stewing. In 1927, the town constable of the village of Violet and his deputy were shotgunned outside of town and their bodies left near a fallow sugar cane field. Once again, the shells were Remington Nitro Club, and they were both fired by the same gun that killed Schofield and Blanton."

Casey came bolt upright, his eyes blaring. "Wait a minute. Ike Gelhard's gang was fingered for those killings—Sheriff Paul Chauchaut's deputies wiped them out."

Delgado held up a palm in a mildly dismissive gesture. "That leaves us with two possible theories. One, after the gang was killed their guns fell into other hands, or—"

"Chauchaut's posse didn't kill the right men."

Nick nodded. "Uh, huh. There's one other thing I wanted to mention. I found a partial print on one of those shells that you found in St. Bernard."

Casey's head snapped up. "How partial?"

"A third to a half, maybe, but probably enough to make an identification—if we can come up with some prints to compare it to."

"Okay. Damn fine work, Nick. Go get some sleep. I've got a feeling I'm going to need you again soon."

Delgado looked at his wrist watch and smiled ruefully. "Then I better just go and catch some sleep on my cot in the lab." He got up, gathered his photos, and left the office.

As he passed through, Brigid Longley poked her head through the door once again. "Phone call for you, Captain. A Mr. Bill Meechum. He said you'd know what it was about."

Casey felt a strange humming in the air. "Put him on." The phone buzzed and he picked it up. "Casey."

"I got something for you," Meechum said. "I looked up an old-time car thief named Carp Doheny. Remember him?"

"Sure, he got that nickname because his eyes bug out like a fish's. What's he doing now?"

"He's got a custodian's job over at the Audubon Park Zoo now. He had the names of two different guys he's seen lately that he knew from the old days. The first guy is Walt Zimmer—he's kinda small time, not into rough stuff. I don't think he's the guy you want."

"No, doesn't sound like it."

"The other guy is somebody he remembers from Angola. Name of Bart Mercer." Casey heard some tension in the old bank robber's voice.

"What's special about this guy?"

"He's something more than just a run-of-the-mill car thief. He came down here from Chi-town back in the early '20s—got smacked down for a five-spot at 'Gola. I remember when he came in. He got noticed plenty. Remember Mike Littlejohn?"

"I should—I put him there for contracting a hit on a judge."

Meechum laughed. "Well, you were flattering me a little when you said I controlled a lot of action up there. Littlejohn was the real boss turkey. This Mercer became Littlejohn's enforcer. There were four cons who crossed Littlejohn while I was there—Mercer shanked all four of them, but the screws were never able to trace it back to him. He's a born killer. I heard he hooked up with one of the big bootlegging gangs here in the city when he got out. But he knew cars—with Prohibition over, he probably went back to what he knew."

"I like the sound of this Mercer. I like him a lot. Thanks, Bill. I won't forget my promise. I'll let you know when we've wrapped this up."

"I'll be around. I got a lot of flowers to tend."

Casey laughed and told him goodbye, then he buzzed Brigid Longley. "Get me Sergeant Mulwray in Records and Identification." There was a pause of perhaps a minute.

"R and I, Sergeant Mulwray."

"This is Casey. I want you to send up the records on an ex-con named Bart Mercer. And get his prints to Nick Delgado—he's got a partial print to compare them to."

"Consider it done, Captain."

Casey put down his telephone and stared at the wall. This was the way an investigation often went. You blundered around in the dark until something you didn't expect jumped up and smacked you in the face. He looked down at the blotter and saw Daggett's report, and he opened it. A quick scan of the words was enough to confirm what Bill Meechum had just told him—that Mercer was Zootie Hines's boss. Mercy—the nickname of a cold-blooded killer—could be no one but Bart Mercer.

But it nagged at him that perhaps the killer of the Violet town constable had not been part of Ike Gelhard's gang—that he had been someone else with other motives in killing Constable Valdez and his deputy. What had the rural lawmen learned that the killer had not wanted discovered?

That brought up some uncomfortable conjectures. One, that Chauchaut made an unconscionable blunder in blaming the killings on the Gelhard gang; two, that he knew Gelhard's gang wasn't responsible but used the murders as an excuse to attack him and wipe his gang out—either for political reasons or something worse; or three, Chauchaut himself might be complicit in the murders of Valdez and his deputy.

Casey knew that all through Prohibition there had been lawmen on the local, state, and even federal levels who made deals with smugglers and illegal producers. Chauchaut had been a moderately successful businessman before running for parish sheriff—curious that he lived high on the hog even today, years after he'd given up his business interests.

Casey placed his elbows on the desk and propped his chin in his cupped hands. He was faced with the inescapable fact that Chauchaut was either a criminal or criminally incompetent. It was the first choice that troubled him the most. If Chauchaut was in league with a criminal gang, then he was an accessory to the murder of Tom Blanton.

He knew he had options to consider. He could go to the State Police with his findings and ask them to initiate an investigation. He could go to Ewell at Treasury and see if they'd cooperate with him. But he really didn't have anything yet but some matching shotgun shells and the name of a known felon behind them. It was enough to convict Bart Mercer, but not enough to arrest Paul Chauchaut. No, it was too early to ask for warrants. He decided the next step was to talk with Chauchaut to see what he could get out of the man before he did anything rash. But deep within, Casey knew something was wrong in the sheriff's office, something that would rock the state when he found out what it was.

In spite of his late night and hair-raising close call with Mercer, Farrell had risen early and was paying bills when Harry called to tell him Mrs. Sallie Milton was asking to see him. He frowned for a moment, then told Harry to send her up. He was waiting at the door to the stairs when her knock came. He found her standing there in a dark blue sleeveless dress, a matching saucer-shaped hat, and white gloves. She had a blue leather bag on a slender strap that she held in front of her like a shield.

Farrell stepped to the side. "Won't you come in? I've got some fresh coffee made. Would you like to have some?"

"Yes. Black, no sugar."

He took her to his living room and offered her a seat on the sofa, then went to get the coffee. When he had arranged the coffee things on the table, he sat down across from her in an armchair.

"What may I do for you?" Farrell asked, running his fingers through his tousled hair.

"I—" she hesitated, her eyes cast down. "I came because I hoped you could tell me something."

"What?"

"I—I wondered why you came to see August yesterday." She busied her hands pouring coffee into both cups, somehow managing not to look directly into his eyes.

"Why not ask him?" Farrell watched her closely. He had the feeling she knew more than she was letting on.

She finally looked directly at him. Her eyes were not the nervous eyes of an innocent, unworldly young widow. There was a hint of calculation in them. "Mr. Farrell, let us not fence with one another. You and I both know that August is a criminal. At various times, you've been a criminal, too. Lately you've been helpful to the police, but that's a relatively recent role for you, isn't it?" The words came out in a sardonic tone—she wanted to let him know that she was no woolly little lamb, that she'd been around.

Farrell's mouth leered at her. "Don't be so sure I'm as big a crook as some people say. Maybe I encourage that reputation to keep some people away and lure other people in. What's your game, Mrs. Milton?"

She smiled. "I deserved that, I suppose. I also suppose you know my husband and son were killed years ago."

Farrell nodded. "It came to my attention. It must have been a terrible loss."

She turned her eyes from him quickly, and a shaky laugh came from her. "It was nearly the end of everything. If I hadn't been expecting Clemmie, I might have killed myself." She leveled her gaze on Farrell again. "No, that's not true. August helped me stay alive. He was there all the time, getting me to eat, to take care of myself, and he was in the waiting room when it came time for Clemmie to be born. Since then, he's—he's been like a partner in my domestic life." Her voice had changed as she talked about her life with August Milton. It had lost the business-like quality it had earlier, and now had an almost elegiac tone. She seemed to hear herself, because she stopped suddenly, and looked at him, her eyes full of guilt.

"You're in love with him, aren't you?" Farrell asked.

She colored and looked down at her cup. "Is it that obvious?"

"Only to someone who's looking. I watched your act with the lemonade the other day. It was too much like watching a movie with William Powell and Myrna Loy to have been a man and his daughter-in-law. Does he know?"

"He might, but he's more concerned with protecting us than in consummating a romance." She put her cup carefully on the table and touched her lips with the napkin. He saw that she was trembling. "You—you think I'm terrible, don't you? That a woman should feel that way about her father-in-law—a man over twenty years her senior and a criminal?"

Farrell put his coffee cup on the table. "He's a strong man, and still very much a man. The years don't matter. As for his being a criminal—who am I to judge? But you've got bigger problems than that, Mrs. Milton."

"Wh-what do you mean?"

"A man I knew was killed five years ago. Your father-in-law was connected to it—indirectly, maybe. And it gets worse. I don't think your husband's death was simply the result of a drunk or a hit-and-run driver, Mrs. Milton."

She'd been doing pretty well until he said that. The words rocked her like a blow to the chin, and her face turned the color of bone. "What? Wh—what are you saying?"

"It's kind of a complicated story. That man I told you about—he was shotgunned by someone driving a blue Pontiac sedan with Mississippi plates. I heard from a reporter yesterday that witnesses to the crash of your husband's car said he was run off the road by a man driving a blue Pontiac sedan—with Mississippi plates."

She laughed, but it was a bit off-key. "Surely that means nothing. There must be hundreds of blue Pontiacs in this city and the outlying parishes."

Farrell nodded. "If that's all there was, I'd be inclined to dismiss it as a coincidence. But there are other things. The man who killed Commander Schofield used a shotgun. Schofield was murdered because he was trying to find out who was betraying the whereabouts of Coast Guard patrols to your father-in-law's gang."

"I don't see—"

"And there's more. A man with a shotgun attempted to kill a partner of your father-in-law's—a man named Morrison. The man with the shotgun also likes knives. He killed a rival gangster named DeLatte about ten years ago as an entré to your father-in-law. Last night that same man tried to kill me outside with a machete—the same way he killed Pascal Delatte."

"Please—please—" She couldn't talk. One of her white-gloved hands was pressed up to her mouth, the other held out clumsily in front of her as if to ward him off. His catalog of murder and deception had driven her helpless onto the ropes.

"Mrs. Milton, I know this is a lot to take at a single bite, but things are coming to a head and it's going to be ugly at the end. I got into this because I was trying to save myself some grief and pay off a debt I owe to a dead man, but it's gone past that now. Somebody's afraid I know too much—maybe it's your father-in-law, or maybe it's just the men who work for him—I don't know that yet. What I do know is that now they've shown their hand, and I've got to draw some heavy cards or fold. There's no choice now."

Her mouth had crumpled and her expression was blurred, as though every emotion she had was at war with her will. "Can't—can't you leave all this alone? You can't bring any of those men back to life."

"I know who pulled the trigger on Commander Schofield, but I want to know who gave the order, Mrs. Milton. Don't you want to know the name and face of the men responsible for your husband and son's death? The same man has just killed again—killing is what he does, and he's good at it. He'll kill again and keep on killing until somebody stops him." Farrell paused, and leveled his pale eyes at Sallie Milton. "August Milton knows that man's name, and where he is. He knows who gives him his orders, too."

She stood up quickly. "I—I shouldn't have come. Forgive for intruding on you."

Farrell stood up, too, and went to her side. "Come on, Mrs. Milton, don't you want to know who, and why?"

Her back of her gloved hand was pressed to her mouth. "I've lost too much already. To you, August Milton is just a criminal. To me he's half of my family—he's someone I love and want to go on loving, even if it's all unsaid. Don't take away what little I have left, please." She was near hysteria now, her words desperate, pleading.

Farrell looked at her, the pity rising in him. "I'm sorry, Mrs. Milton. I didn't deal the cards in this game—all I can do now is play them to win. If I can get the answers I want without hurting August Milton, I'll do it—but I'll get the answers, one way or another."

She couldn't talk anymore. She pushed past him and left the room. In a second or two, he heard the door to the stairs open and close sharply, and then there was silence.

Chapter 11

At Kelso's suggestion, Schofield moved from the hotel to Kelso's house, a two-story cottage with a long gallery across the front. It was a comfortable, masculine place that showed ample evidence of Kelso's nautical background. The stair banisters, rails, and slats were meticulously covered in coxcombing, French hitches, Turk's head knots, and decorative rope mats. Prints and photographs of ships covered the walls, along with wind-tattered ensigns and pennants. In the front hall were two photos of Kelso standing arm-in-arm with George Schofield. They were in their dress blues, laughing happily.

Schofield came downstairs, knotting his tie around his neck as he followed food smells to the kitchen, or galley, as Kelso preferred to call it.

Kelso looked up from the stove as his friend entered. "I bet I woke you up blundering around down here."

Schofield waved a dismissive hand. "No, I didn't sleep all that much." He paused to accept a cup of thick black coffee before he sat down at the kitchen table. The coffee was steaming hot and impenetrable as tar. He took a healthy sip and the caffeine hit his nerves like an exploding shell. "Wow—is this coffee or battery acid?"

Kelso grinned. "Engineer's coffee, kid. Just like we brew it in the engine room." As he stirred eggs around in a skillet, he asked, "You see Milton yesterday evening?"

Schofield winced. "Yeah. For all the good it did. It was like trying to crack marble with a tack hammer. I'll need something solid to force an admission out of him—and yet I'm sure he knows. He was almost mocking me."

Kelso shrugged as he stirred his eggs with deft, sure strokes. "He was the biggest smuggler around here before Repeal. And pretty slick—nobody ever got anything on him. You can believe the Treasury boys tried."

"Emmett, tell me something. How tough would it have been for someone to get mission orders before the patrols were launched in those days?"

Kelso's attention was on his pan of eggs, which he took from the stove and divided evenly between two plates of bacon and toast. "Pretty tough. Your brother would coordinate with the district intelligence officer and Prohibition enforcement at Treasury, then wait until the last minute to brief the boat commanders."

Schofield sipped more of the strong coffee. "That would put the ball in the laps of the intelligence officer or the Treasury people if there was a leak."

Kelso put the plates on the table, added silverware, ketchup, butter and jam, then sat down and picked up a fork.

"I don't know, kid. I was just a snotty lieutenant. When you wear a uniform, you do what you're told and don't ask any questions—not if you want to collect your pension." He winked and shoveled some egg and bacon into his mouth.

Schofield nodded, ate for a while, then said, "You know a Chief Petty Officer named Tom Harrigan?"

Kelso looked up from his plate, his eyes hard. "Ex-Chief, you mean. Yeah, I knew him. He on your list?"

Schofield nodded.

"I can guess why. Finish up, and I'll take you to him—or at least to what's left of him."

They left the Uptown area, then took Canal Street past the Odd Fellows Rest and Greenwood cemeteries, and on out to Lake Pontchartrain. Jim took out his cigarettes and held them out to Kelso.

"No, thanks, kid. I never caught the habit." Kelso was cheerful, grinning at Jim. There was a youthfulness about him that made Schofield think of his brother. Kelso must be at least forty, but life on the water had kept him boyish. Jim realized how precious his friendship with Emmett was now that George was gone.

"Maybe you're right." Schofield put his cigarettes back inside his coat. When he withdrew his hand, he held a .32 Colt automatic. He worked the magazine release, examined the magazine, then re-inserted it into the butt.

Kelso eyed him. "I thought the high-muckety-muck at Treasury told you to leave your gun at home."

"He told me to leave my *service revolver* in my valise, which I did. This is a personal gun." Schofield colored a bit. "I'm splitting hairs, but I'd hate to need a gun and not have one." He put the gun back under his arm, then said, "Think there'll be someplace to get more coffee at Bucktown?"

"Yeah. There's a café in Bucktown. I was stationed at the lighthouse on Lake Pontchartrain years ago, and we'd hike over there once in a while for something to do."

"Tell me about this retired chief we're going to see."

"Yeah, Harrigan." Kelso's mood slipped a bit, and the skin around the mouth whitened. "He's a drinker. I can't stand that. A chief's got a lot of responsibility, and when you're half-boiled all the time, you're taking risks with your equipment, your, men—hell your reputation."

"Sounds like you don't like him."

"I didn't like trusting him with a boat and men. Oh, I don't mean he didn't have a good record otherwise. He followed orders and did what he was told—but he was just a lousy drunk. You can't trust them."

"But why do you think he might've sold out?"

"He had another problem. He gambled, and he lost all the time. A chief doesn't make enough money to be at a crap game every night, or the race track every weekend."

"George knew about that. There were notes about it under Harrigan's name. How long did you know?"

"I didn't find out about it until after George was killed. I wondered then how long it had been going on—and where he got the money in the first place. It didn't occur to me until later that he might've been in somebody's pocket—by then he was retired and time had gone by."

"Well, we'll talk to him. I've dealt with criminals who were drunks. They break easy."

"Yeah." Kelso's voice was harsh. "Just like glass."

Bucktown wasn't much more than a docking area for a number of commercial fishing boats, a café that specialized in seafood, a marine gasoline station, a general store that doubled as a post office, and a cluster of shanties off the Old Hammond Highway. Kelso parked his sedan and they got out and looked around. Gulls were shrieking in the hard blue sky, and dock pilings were occupied by fierce-eyed brown pelicans who stared at them suspiciously.

There was a fence with a long row of rusted, tired-looking mailboxes mounted on it, their front flaps yawning like open mouths. All had names painted on the sides, but none pointed to a particular house. Kelso began walking to the café, Schofield following him.

The interior of the café was dim and cool and smelled faintly of bread baking and coffee brewing. A pretty woman with platinum-blonde hair eyed them from behind the counter where she'd been reading the newspaper. "Coffee, gents?"

"Sure," Schofield said. The two men sat as the woman put cups on the counter and filled with them with black, fragrant coffee and chicory. She put two doughnuts on a plate and slid them between the coffee. "You're my first customers, and they're fresh. On the house."

"Thank you, ma'am." Schofield took a sip of his coffee. "Great coffee."

"Thanks." The woman favored him with a grin. "You must be from out of town. I haven't seen you in here before."

"No, we're looking for a man named Harrigan who lives around here. I don't suppose you know him?"

"Tom Harrigan? Sure I know him. Every village has to have a village drunk, and Tom's it." She smiled ruefully. "Looks like he was a good-looking guy before the booze got to him. He was a chief in the Coast Guard or something."

Kelso nodded. "You know where to find him?"

She shrugged. "No big secret. There's an old scabby green houseboat moored at the end of the dock. Only time he ever leaves there is to come up this way for a pint. Poor guy looks like he's on his last legs." She shrugged again.

Schofield washed a bite of doughnut down with the remainder of his coffee. "Not hungry?" He pointed at the untouched second doughnut.

Kelso shook his head. "Doughnuts are the undoing of many a middle-aged sailor. Got to keep in trim." He patted his flat stomach and grinned at the younger man. "Ready?"

"I guess." He brought a half-dollar out of his pocket, which he slid along the counter. "Much obliged, ma'am."

She took the half-dollar and flipped it high before catching it. "The name's Doris. Don't make me out to be older than I am, sweetie."

Schofield smiled and tipped his hat, then he and Kelso walked outside and down toward the dock.

Most of the fishing fleet was out, and the dock was quiet save for the lapping of Lake Pontchartrain against the dock pilings. A few minutes walk brought them to the dilapidated green houseboat Doris had mentioned. It was low in the water, as though the bilges were long overdue for a pumping. The two men gingerly mounted the slimy wood gangplank connecting the listing boat to the dock, and stepped to the deck. Schofield listened for a moment, then called out. "Hello, Mr. Harrigan? Are you aboard?"

"Sing out, Harrigan," Kelso barked. "I know you're aboard this scow."

The cabin hatch flew open with a crash, and a ruin of a man stood in it, a steel marlin spike in his hand. "What the hell you doin' on my boat? I didn't invite no company." He raised the spike menacingly, and advanced halfway out of the hatch.

Schofield held up his badge in his left hand and had his automatic in his right. "Federal Agent, Harrigan. Put it down so we can talk."

"Talk? Talk about what? I got nothin' to talk about." He glared at the two men, but he half-lowered the weapon.

"Sure you do, Tom." Kelso spoke in a soft, dry voice. He reached out and snatched the pointed steel from the drunk's hand and shoved him roughly against the bulkhead. "So be good if you know what's good for you." He threw the weapon into the scuppers where it landed with a clang.

The voice startled Harrigan, and he shifted his gaze to the lieutenant commander. "Kelso." He said the name like it was something vile on the back of his tongue.

Kelso smiled. "Glad your memory's still working. This is Jim Schofield—he's the commander's kid brother."

The name jarred the drunken man. He turned back to Schofield and examined his face for a full minute before speaking again. "Goddamn. It's like lookin' into his face again." He half-fell back into the cabin, and the two men followed him inside. Schofield almost gagged at the stench. Harrigan flopped down behind a small wooden table covered with coffee rings and other stains and began pouring rye whiskey from a brown pint flask into a tin cup. He lifted it to his lips and drank it, his face lit with a strange ecstasy as the rye went down his throat. Swallowing his disgust, Schofield grabbed a wooden chair and straddled it. Kelso followed suit.

Harrigan glared at them. "Whatever it is, get it over with and get out." He poured another drink into his cup.

Schofield glared at him across the table. "I want to know who killed my brother."

Harrigan's hand froze halfway to his mouth as his red eyes snapped open, looking first at Schofield, then at Kelso. He emptied the second drink, then pounded the empty cup on the table. "Why come to me?"

"I'll tell you why. My brother was conducting a private investigation into the activities of several smugglers and a selection of Treasury and Coast Guard men. He believed somebody was selling information on Coast Guard patrols to the smugglers. I think he was assassinated because whoever he was investigating got wise."

"That's nothing to do with me." Harrigan spoke belligerently, but there was a tremor in his voice and his eyes rolled wildly.

"My brother knew about the gambling, about the heavy losses you were incurring at the track and the places where you played cards and dice." Schofield's tone was hard and bitter. "He tailed you, checked up on you, and you or your bosses found out. You set him up for the hit, didn't you? Didn't you!" Schofield screamed in the other man's face.

Harrigan's gaping mouth revealed yellowed, rotting teeth. His smell was thick and gamy, like an animal penned up too long. "No, no, it ain't true, it ain't." His voice cracked, his emotions teetering on a razor's edge.

"Like hell," Kelso said. "There was only one way for you to get the money—you sold out. You leaked information about where our patrols would be." Kelso was smiling horribly at the other man, his voice insinuating, almost mocking. "Get it off your chest, Tom. Tell us and we'll let you alone. We'll even get you a fresh quart of rye."

"You son of a bitch." Harrigan stared helplessly at Kelso. "You never let a man get up before you kick him in the teeth. That was always the way you was. You'd suck up to Schofield, makin' sure he knew about every patch of rust or slack piece of line even if you had to crawl through the bilges to do it. I wish it was you that they'd killed instead of Schofield. I wish to Christ it had been you." With a shaking hand he grabbed the pint and put the neck to his lips. He drank and drank, his throat working like a pump until Schofield reached out, grabbed it away from him and put it on his side of the table.

"Talk, Harrigan. Talk or I'll make you wish you'd never been born."

Harrigan looked at him bleakly. "You're too late."

"This is your last chance, Harrigan. Talk or I'll take you downtown. There won't be any bottles down there, and before long you'll be climbing the walls for a drink."

"I never sold your brother out. I never sold nobody out. Sure, I'm a drunk, and I gambled, but I ain't no killer and I never sold nobody out."

"So where'd you get the money you gambled with?"

Harrigan's face fell apart like wet cardboard. "I—I stole." The words were like a whimper from a whipped dog.

"What, from where?"

"Anything. Everything. I prowled the docks—stole copper pipe, cordage, lumber. If that wasn't enough, I'd ride into town and break into houses. I got so good at it that I almost considered gettin' out of the service and doin' it full time." He leered, trying to appear smug, but the gesture was as empty as the man who made it.

"How many years did this go on?"

The old man's wasted face took on a strange smile. "I lost count. Anyways, after a while I burned the gamblin' out of me. When I retired, I come here and bought this dump. My pension's enough to keep me in whiskey." He bowed his head and ran his fingers through his grizzled hair.

Kelso laughed derisively. "Don't let him soft soap you. He's slicker than oil. Otherwise he'd have been drummed out of the service before he could retire."

Harrigan's withered lips drew back over his yellowed teeth. "You rotten fuck. You make out like you're such a plaster saint— like you worked your way up through the ranks 'cause you're some kinda choir boy. You got them commander's leaves by standin' on better men's shoulders—that and lickin' Schofield's boots until they sparkled."

Kelso stood up, then bent over the table, bracing himself with his arms as he shoved his face down close to Harrigan's. "You lousy bum—you were a disgrace to the uniform. We're gonna find out that you're lyin', and when we do, I'm gonna be standing there when they drop the trap from under you." Kelso's smile was almost fiendish, and his eyes gave off a peculiar light that made Schofield shiver.

Kelso stood up, then walked straight-backed out of the cabin without another word.

Schofield looked down at Harrigan, who now had his head in his hands. "Chief Harrigan, as far as I'm concerned, you're a prime suspect. I intend to have Treasury look into your background to see if they can substantiate any of your story, which I personally doubt."

Harrigan looked up with red eyes. "What do you think you can do to me, boy? Put me in prison? Just shoot me now—you'd be doin' me a favor."

Shofield looked down at the man with revulsion, then he turned and left the stinking cabin. He found Kelso on the dock with his back to the houseboat. The muscles in his back were so tight you could have bounced quarters off them. Schofield put a hand on his shoulder and spoke to him in a soft voice. "He said some lousy things in there. George was close to you, he depended on you. Only a weakling like Harrigan would try to make something dirty out of it."

Kelso turned to him, the skin around his mouth and eyes still hard and white. The confrontation had awakened something unpleasant that still writhed inside him. His face worked, and eventually something resembling a smile took hold on his face. "Yeah, I guess I shouldn't of let him get my goat like that."

"I'm going to call Ewell and ask if he'll detail an agent to investigate Harrigan. I can see him as a conduit or a go-between, but he was only a chief. He needed a connection to get any secret information."

"Who else was on your brother's list?"

"There's a Commander Charles Bracken. George didn't have time to get much about him, although there was a note that he was posted to District Intelligence."

Kelso's eyes brightened and he nodded. "That job would've given him access to Treasury intelligence field reports. He'd have known where to go and who to talk to in order to make the deals." He paused, licked his lips, and his face took on a look of barely suppressed excitement. "He and Harrigan knew each other. I can think of several times he asked for Harrigan to act as coxswain of a patrol boat he used to get photographic intelligence of one kind or another. It's possible they got to know each other well enough that Harrigan began to act as a go-between for him."

"What's he doing now?"

"He's in charge of Marine Inspection. He has an office in the Customs House on Canal Street."

"I think I want to look him up next," Schofield said.

"Let's get to a telephone, and I'll check to see if he's in the office today. I heard he'd taken leave recently—he might still be at home."

The young Treasury man nodded. "Even better, from a tactical standpoint. He won't be able to use his office to dominate the interview."

Kelso grinned at him. "They taught you a few things up in the big city, didn't they, kid?"

∞∞∞

Johnny Hope had taken work at Hogge's Richfield station on St. Claude in order to get out of the house. He felt nervous as a cat, worrying about Israel Daggett on the one hand and Mercer on the other. Daggett was somebody to fear, because he was persistent and knew how to make people talk to him. Mercer was more terrifying, because he was mercurial and tended to react with his gut. There was no telling what he was thinking or doing right now.

Johnny had just broken loose a nut on the cover of a universal joint when the station owner called into the bay to tell him he had a phone call. He yelled that he was coming, and crawled out of the pit, wiping his greasy hands on a rag. Just as he got into the office, a bell sounded, alerting Hogge to a gasoline customer rolling onto the apron. He left Johnny to take care of it.

"Yeah?" he said into the mouthpiece.

"It's Boxcars. You hear about Oscar?"

"No, what about him?"

"The Saint Bernard sheriff went out to his place last night and called him out. Some way or other, the sheriff got shot and so did Oscar. He's in Charity Hospital, bad off they's tellin' me."

"Oh, no." Johnny reeled from the news. "Why'd they go after Oscar? Hell, he don't even carry a gun."

"His cousin, Alfred, said the sheriff had some tip-off that Oscar was part of the gang that kilt that colored dick. This captain who works for the sheriff said he don't know for certain who shot the sheriff, but right now Oscar's gettin' the blame. Oscar dyin' anyhow—he got a bullet in the chest."

"Aw, man." Johnny gripped the phone harder. "Listen, I gotta get in touch with Mercer. If they found out about Oscar, they might find out everything else. Where you at?"

"I got the hell outa my shack and went to Ada Jack's. I can't stay here long, but I wanted to tell you, 'case you didn't know." He paused, and Johnny heard a tremor in his voice. "Johnny, I didn't get into this to do no killin', and I sure as hell don't wanna die. What we gonna do?"

As Johnny stood there, listening to the hiss and crackle of static over the line, he heard Joe Earle's voice in his head, his predictions and warnings. Panic welled up in him and he tasted bile in the back of his throat. "Listen, stay where you at. Nobody knows any of our names yet or there'd be a dragnet out for us right now."

"How you know there ain't?"

"Cause the cops been to see me already, They know where to put their hands on me whenever they want, and I'm still free as a jaybird. Whoever tipped off the law about Oscar didn't tell the law 'bout the rest of us. You stay at Ada Jack's until you hear from me. I'm gonna find Mercer and get the straight of this."

"You ask me, Mercer's the one got us into this shit. We shoulda got away from him a long time ago." Boxcars' voice was bleak and despair oozed from him like oil around a defective head gasket.

"Keep your head, boy, and do like I tell you. I'll be back with you soon as I can." He hung up and stood there with sweat pouring out of his hairline. He couldn't remember when he felt as hopeless as he did at this moment.

Johnny looked out the window and saw Hogge coming back with money in his hand. He stepped to the door to meet him.

"Mr. Hogge, you mind if I take lunch a li'l early? I got me a kind of emergency to deal with."

Hogge nodded his head. "Sure, Johnny. I got everything taken care of here."

"Thank you a whole lot." Johnny went back into the bay to get his coat. Within seconds, he was in his car driving away from the gasoline station. Six blocks away, he stopped in front of a neighborhood pharmacy and went directly to the telephone booth outside. As he dropped in the nickel, he mopped his face on his sleeve as he asked the operator for Mercer's number on Castiglioni Street. It rang and rang but no one answered. He hung up the telephone and waited for his nickel to drop into the coin return. As he stood there, he tried to think where Mercer might be. Mercer couldn't be ignorant of the trouble in St. Bernard. He might have decided to come to Orleans Parish to hole up until he thought it was safe to return to the old Mouton place. But he wasn't at home—where else might he be? It was then that Johnny thought of the woman. What was her name? Dolly? Dorothy? No, Dolores. Dolores Rogers, that was it. He pulled the directory out of the shelf and looked her up. There were at least fifteen Rogers—but only one D. Rogers. He had heard that single women sometimes listed themselves that way to protect themselves from masher calls.

He got his nickel from the slot and started to put it back into the telephone, but he stopped at the last second. If he called Mercer on the telephone, he might just give Johnny a lot of guff about having everything under control and not to worry. Johnny was in no mood to be put off. He made a mental note of the address, then got back into his car and drove into the city. The woman lived on South Perdido Street, a few blocks off Broad, a working-class neighborhood of small narrow houses. He saw Mercer's De Soto before he saw the address. He parked behind the sedan, got out, and walked up to the driver's door. He was stunned by the sight of bloody hand prints all over the door panel. He looked through the open window and saw blood all over the steering wheel and seat cover. He began breathing in quick, rapid pants. His hands were shaking so badly that he dropped his car key on the street. Not even bothering to pick it up, he almost ran to the front door of the house, where he saw even more blood. He knocked several times, trying all the while to see past the shade. When he least expected it, the door opened and a young, dark-haired white woman stood there, her face expressionless.

"Who are you?" she asked.

"Mercer—I work for Mercer. Is—is he here?"

Her demeanor was sluggish, but she understood what he was saying. "He ain't so good. He got hurt last night."

"Listen, I gotta see him, and we gotta get the blood cleaned up 'for somebody sees it and calls the cops. You got some rags and a bucket of hot soapy water?"

"Yeah." She nodded calmly.

"Then get 'em." Trying with all his might not to lose patience with the woman, he nevertheless pushed past her and closed the door. He continued through the house until he came to a bedroom, where he found Mercer.

Mercer's huge body was naked and a large bandage covered most of the left side of his face. His yellow eyes gleamed dully but the short-barreled revolver in his fist was leveled at Johnny's gut.

"Mercer, what the hell happened to you?"

"What are you doin' here?"

"I just heard from Boxcars that the sheriff went to Oscar Boulet's house last night and there was shootin'. Oscar's bad off in the hospital and so's the sheriff." Johnny realized he was wringing his hands, afraid to move for fear Mercer's gun might go off.

Mercer took in his story with an impassive face, but his eyes flickered, and he frowned. "Where's your brother?"

"He called last night to say he was lightin' out. Might be he had the right idea."

"Where'd he call from, Johnny?"

"A bar someplace—I dunno. Mercer, what we gonna do?"

Mercer turned his head slightly on the pillow and called out. "Zootie." Zootie emerged from the kitchen. He had a leather blackjack in his right hand and a revolver in his left. His eyes were large with shock and uncertainty, as though seeing Mercer badly wounded had altered his view of the world in some tragic and elemental way.

"Hit him," Mercer said.

Before Johnny could move, Zootie swung the sap in a short arc to a spot just behind Johnny's ear. The mechanic grunted and collapsed to the floor.

"Tie him up and gag him," Mercer ordered. Wordlessly, Zootie moved to obey.

Dolores came into the room as Zootie tied Johnny with his belt and shoelaces. She seemed only dimly aware of it, not caring one way or another.

Mercer fixed her with a hard eye. "What was he sayin' to you out there?"

"He said there was blood everywhere. He told me to get some hot water and rags and clean it up." She spoke in a disinterested monotone.

Mercer's eyes widened. He had forgotten that he'd bled all over himself. "He was right. Hurry it up and get it done. We're lucky nobody spotted it and called a cop."

"Nobody notices nothin' in this neighborhood." But she moved to obey, knowing better than to argue with Mercer, even in his weakened state.

Zootie stood up and looked at Mercer expectantly. "What we gonna do with Johnny?"

"We're gonna use him. He said Joe Earle's tryin' to skip town. The boss thinks Joe Earle handed my name to Wes Farrell for killin' that sailor five years ago. He wants Joe Earle shut up before he tells anybody anything else."

Zootie grinned knowingly. "So we gonna use Johnny to get Joe Earle to come to us, right?"

Mercer grinned with the side of his face that still worked. "You're a good little doggie, you know that, Zootie? That's just what we're gonna do, then the two of us are gonna go and pay Mr. Farrell back for this." He jerked a thumb at his ruined face. "Now get goin'. You know all the joints Joe Earle went to in this town. Get to them and put out the word that Joe Earle's brother's in a lot of trouble and needs him real bad—get me?"

"Yeah, yeah, I get you. I get you real good." With a big grin on his face, Zootie turned and left the house.

As he walked away, Mercer could almost see a whippy little puppy tail wagging behind him. "You're a good little doggie, all right. A real good little doggie."

❦

Not long after Casey spoke to Sergeant Mulwray, a call came from Nick Delgado that the partial print on the shotgun shell matched the left middle finger print on Bart Mercer's print record. He immediately called down to the dispatcher.

"Take all of this down, sergeant. The suspect is Bart Warren Mercer, age, 37, height, six feet, five inches, weight, two-oh-five, hair light brown, complexion ruddy, eyes hazel. Identifying marks, knife scar running diagonally through right eyebrow. Subject is believed to be armed with a shotgun and should be considered extremely dangerous. He's wanted in conjunction with at least two and possibly five murders, so approach with caution. Got that?"

"Right, Captain. It'll go out over the wire now."

Casey had no sooner replaced his phone in the cradle when it rang again. This time is was Sergeant Snedegar.

"Skipper, did you know the St. Bernard sheriff was over in Charity hospital?"

"No, what happened?"

"From what I can gather, he and one of his men went to talk to a suspect in the Blanton murder. There was shooting and the sheriff caught one in the leg. The suspect was hit in the chest—he's still in critical condition."

"Was the suspect Zootie Hines?"

"No, some other colored kid named Boulet."

Casey frowned. "Thanks, Ray. I think I'll go over and see him." He hung up his telephone and went to get his jacket and hat. He felt like the world was spinning around him at 78 rpms while he was stuck in a lower speed. He was shrugging into his jacket as he passed his secretary's desk. "I'm going over to Charity to look in on Sheriff Chauchaut."

"Right, boss."

He stopped short, turned and looked at her. "Look, there's a lot going on right now, and I'm liable to be running in six different directions. I don't want to take anything for granted, and maybe you'll think I'm out of line, but—would you like to have dinner tonight?"

"Sure." She looked up at him with her hands folded on her desk, as though nothing extraordinary had happened.

"Oh. You didn't need to think about that, huh?"

"Nope. I'm glad you asked. Any instructions for anyone before you go? And when will you be back? Just in case somebody asks."

He was trying not to smile, but he was almost overcome with a wholly childish elation. "No—no instructions. I'm not sure when I'll be back. If anything big comes up, have the dispatcher radio me in my car."

"Right, Captain. I'll take care of it."

"One more thing."

"Yes, sir?"

"Why don't you call me Frank? We've known each other long enough."

"I think we have."

"Great. Bye." Casey left the office, feeling as though his feet weren't quite touching the ground. By the time he reached his car, he was almost back to earth again.

He parked near the emergency room ramp when he reached the hospital, leaving the placard on the dashboard which identified the car as a police vehicle on departmental business before he left to enter the hospital.

After stopping to ask directions, he found the sheriff on the seventh floor. There, he discovered from the ward nurse that the operation had been successful, and that no permanent damage had been sustained. Casey walked to the door, peeked in, and saw the sheriff lying recumbent, his hands clasped on his chest. Casey knocked lightly, and Chauchaut raised up, straightening his glasses.

"Is that Captain Casey?"

"Yes it is, sheriff. I just heard about the shooting and came over to see how you were."

"Well, it looks like we're making some progress," Chauchaut said proudly. "We went to pick this boy, Boulet, up for questioning, but an accomplice in his house opened fire on me and hit me in the leg. I returned fire, but he ran out the back of the house. Peters was back there, and he traded shots with whoever it was, but the man got away."

"He get a description, at least?"

"Just a colored male. I reckon once this Boulet regains consciousness, we can get from him who the man was."

Casey frowned. "How did Boulet get shot?"

Chauchaut looked a bit flustered and he coughed once or twice. "Well, he was in the crossfire, and I guess he caught a round from one side or the other. Don't know yet."

"Uh, huh. You're a lucky man, sheriff. Was the hidden gunman using a shotgun, by any chance?"

"Doesn't look like it. The slug they dug out of me was a .44 or .45."

"Uh, huh." Casey fingered his chin. "Sheriff, we've been developing a case over here based on some fingerprint evidence I found at Johnny Hope's garage. The fingerprint, which we found on a twelve-gauge buckshot shell, belongs to an ex-con named Bart Mercer. He's a white man, and he's got a penchant for using a shotgun."

Chauchaut blinked. "You don't say."

"I do." Casey paused a moment, drew up a chair, and straddled it so he and the sheriff would be at eye level. "Mercer's criminal history goes back to before Prohibition. Based on more ballistic evidence, there's a strong probability Mercer might've also killed Violet Town Constable Robert Valdez and his deputy."

The sheriff stiffened. "You're mistaken. It was the Gelhard bunch who killed Valdez and his deputy. And we cleared every last one of them out."

"Let me ask you a question, sheriff. On what evidence were you able to determine that Valdez and his assistant were killed by the Gelhard gang? Did you have ballistic evidence, or perhaps a witness?"

The sheriff's face was red, and he'd balled his fists on top of the sheet. "Look here, Casey—"

"No, you look here, Sheriff. For almost ten years you've been making political hay out of wiping out Gelhard and avenging the death of a brother officer—that part doesn't bother me so much. What does bother me is that by insisting that Gelhard was the killer, you've left the real murderer free for almost ten years. All that time, he's been killing other people, among them a Coast Guard officer who was busting smugglers without getting his name in the paper once."

"You mean—"

"Yeah, that's what I mean. Mercer killed him, too, with the same shotgun he used on Valdez and on my man, Blanton. Now I don't give a happy Goddamn whether you get elected governor or not, but I do care about murder. Something stinks in your parish, Sheriff. Either you help me find out what it is, or I'll go to the commander of the State Police and ask him to help me figure this out."

Casey heard the low murmur of voices behind him, and turned to see several nurses clustered in the door. He got up from his chair and went to them with a sweeping motion of his arms. "Sorry about the noise, ladies. But I've got police business that won't wait." When he had the door closed, he turned back to the sheriff, who now lay back on the pillows, his face chalky and his hands like claws on the sheet.

"Now, Sheriff. As I was saying."

Chapter 12

Joe Earle Hope awoke in the rooms above Tubby's bar, and for several agonizing seconds could not remember where he was. The dregs of some disquieting dream lingered in his mind, and he felt sweat on his face and under his arms. He sat up and saw that it was daylight and rubbed his face vigorously to wake himself up.

He swung his legs over the side of the bed where he'd slept, then got up to rummage in his trousers for his Ingraham pocket watch. It was nearly 3:00, which meant the sun would soon set on another day with him still in New Orleans. He'd stayed up late, hoping Tubby could help him make a connection, but had been forced to give up in the small hours of the morning and had gone to bed in Tubby's extra room. He was jittery and unhappy.

He replaced the watch in his fob pocket, then pulled the slacks on. When he was covered, he walked all through the small apartment before realizing that Tubby was probably downstairs minding the bar. As Joe Earle entered the small kitchen, he saw a telephone.

He hadn't said anything to his sister, Arthel, and knew in his heart that it would be cruel and indecent for him to leave New Orleans without at least telling her goodbye. Slowly, hesitantly, he reached for the receiver, picked it up, then gave the operator his sister's number. He was pretty sure that this was one of the three days a week when she wasn't cleaning and cooking at the white woman's home on Versailles Boulevard. He listened impatiently as the telephone rang four, then five times. He was about to hang up when his sister answered.

"It's Joe Earle, Arthel."

"Oh, Joe Earle." Her voice was pitched high, and on the verge of hysterics. "H-have you seen your brother?"

The question was like a knell of doom. "No. No, I ain't, Arthel. Why, is somethin' the matter?" With a supreme effort of will, he kept his voice steady, betraying none of the torrent of emotion surging through him.

"He was workin' for Mr. Hogge over on St. Claude, and he left work about 10:30. Said he had an emergency and would be back. But he ain't back, Mr. Hogge said. He called here a li'l while ago askin' if he could do anything to help."

"But there wasn't no emergency?"

"That's what I'm tryin' to tell you, boy. I done talked to everybody I can think of, and nobody knows nothin' 'bout no emergency. It's like Johnny dropped off the earth. And where are you, anyhow?"

Joe Earle was fighting to make his brain work. His instincts told him that the emergency had something to do with Mercer. "I—I'm over at a friend's place, Arthel. I was talkin' to somebody about a new job, and ended up stayin' the night." Joe Earle was no hand at lying, so he stuck as close to the truth as he could to keep from upsetting his sister further.

"Well, for the Good Lord's sake, please see if you can find Johnny. I'm worried to death about him. And come home as soon as you can. I want one of you where I can see you 'til this mess gets straightened out, you hear?"

"Okay, Arthel, okay. Let me see what I can find out and I'll talk to you presently." He stood there patiently as his sister nattered at him for a few moments more, hardly breathing until she hung up the telephone.

Joe Earle put the receiver back on the hook, then went to see about some coffee. Finding a percolator on the stove with cold coffee in it, he lit the fire under it. As he performed these humdrum activities, the rest of his brain was trying to make sense of what his sister had told him. He was pouring the warmed-over coffee into a cup when Tubby came from downstairs with the afternoon paper in his hand.

"Joe Earle, ain't you got a friend named Oscar Boulet?"

The same portent Joe Earle had felt talking to Arthel hit him again as he turned to look at his friend. Tubby showed him the *New Orleans States-Item*, folded back to the lead story on the front page. The headline read ST. BERNARD SHERIFF SHOT IN BATTLE WITH MURDER SUSPECT. Joe Earle put down his coffee cup and took the paper from Tubby with a shaking hand. He read the story through twice, then sank into one of the kitchen chairs.

"Boy, you all right?" Tubby's voice was anxious. "You don't look too good. Joe Earle? I'm talkin' to you, son."

Joe Earle looked up into his friend's worried expression. "Tubby, can you lend me your car?"

"Yeah. Yeah, I reckon so. What you gonna do?"

"Johnny's missin'. I gotta go find him."

"What you mean, he's missin?"

Joe Earle got back up again. "I mean he's in trouble. We're all in it up to our necks and we don't look much like gettin' out." He walked back to the room he had slept in and quickly pulled on the rest of his clothing. As he checked the Owl's Head .32, he felt Tubby's presence and looked up to see him standing in the door, his eyes large and shocked at the sight of the gun.

"What you gonna do, Joe Earle?"

"Take the next train to Hell." He shoved the cheap, nickel-plated revolver into his pants pocket. "I'll try to leave your car somewhere you can find it later, in case I can't bring it back." He took the keys from Tubby's hand, and before his friend could respond, he walked down the stairs and out of the tavern.

Tubby had taken good care of his old Model A Ford sedan, and it started readily. Joe Earle turned out of the back yard into the alley and followed it to the street. He wasn't sure where he was going, only that he had to find Johnny before Mercer did something to him.

∞

After Sallie Milton's visit, Farrell spent a lot of time on the telephone talking to contacts in the negro underworld about Zootie Hines and mostly getting nowhere. The small negro gunman was as elusive as his white boss—many people knew him, but few had seen him lately. As the morning came to a close, Farrell's frustration was mounting. He had never known a time when his vast network of informants had failed to produce, and he wondered what he could do that he hadn't already done.

He was pacing the floor, smoking one cigarette after the other when the telephone rang. He went to it, crushing his cigarette in the ashtray. "Hello."

"This is Sparrow."

Farrell gripped the receiver tightly, hardly daring to breathe. "You got something for me?"

She laughed softly. "You sound like a child on his birthday, Farrell. Yes, I have something—I don't know what it's worth, but here it is. A man who works for me was in a diner last night and he heard a woman talking to the cook. It seems she is shacking with a brute named Bart Mercer, whose nickname is Mercy. Apparently, he's been mistreating her, and she's frightened of him."

"That sounds like the man. You got a location?"

"It took a little doing—the cook at the diner has something of a case on the woman, but I've noticed that when a man is lovelorn, all he needs is a sympathetic ear to get him to talk. The woman's name is Dolores Rogers. She lives at 8315 South Perdido Street, a few blocks west of the Broad Street intersection."

"Thanks, Sparrow. What's the payment to be?"

Sparrow laughed softly again, sounding almost like a girl. "When I decide, I'll call you."

Farrell grimaced, knowing that whatever she eventually wanted, it wouldn't come cheap. "A deal's a deal. I'll hold up my end."

"Of course, Farrell. You're a man of honor, in all things. Oh, there's one more thing about this Rogers girl."

"What?"

"My man discovered that she's a morphine addict. That may be useful to you."

"It might at that. Thanks again, Sparrow."

"*Shalom*, Farrell. Until we meet again."

Farrell put down the telephone and went into his office, his face settling into blunt, hard planes. He would not let Mercy escape him this time. He opened his desk and took out the Italian spring blade stiletto and strapped it to his left forearm. The old .38 Colt automatic he clipped to his waistband over the right hipbone and a spare loaded magazine went into his hip pocket. He also removed a Luger automatic and laid that on the desk blotter.

He left the room for his coat and hat, then he placed the Luger into his left-hand coat pocket. His razor, freshly cleaned and honed, rested in the special pocket within the lining of his suit. He left the apartment through the back door and walked down the iron stairs to his personal parking space. Seconds later he drove the Packard Marlin out Basin Street and headed across Downtown to Dolores Rogers's neighborhood.

Less than twenty minutes later, he eased the car to a stop a half-block from the house. The neighborhood was quiet—no children on the streets and no one on any of the front porches nearby. There was no car parked anywhere near the house, but he knew better than to take anything for granted.

He reached the front of the house without incident, then took the right-hand alley to the rear. As was true of many neighborhoods of shotgun houses, the alley was barely wide enough to accommodate a grown man, and the walls were thin enough that he fancied he could hear voices from inside.

He reached the back and made a quick survey. The yard was unkempt and overgrown with weeds, with only a dilapidated storage shed at the extreme rear.

Farrell crept under the kitchen window and up on the small back porch. A rusty screen door sat, off its hinges, propped against the wall, leaving his way clear to the kitchen door. He gingerly grasped the knob and tried it, finding it locked. Seeing that it was a common skeleton-style lock, he took out a ring of keys and tried three before he found one that would open it. Seconds later, he eased the door open, his Colt cocked in his right fist.

The kitchen was empty, save for a sink full of dirty dishes— blood was splashed all over the sink and the dishes. He felt a grim satisfaction as he saw how much blood there was. He advanced further into the house, moving the muzzle of the gun from side to side as he inspected each room. He now heard a radio going near the front, and realized with chagrin that those were the voices he'd heard. The house was empty—but wait. A woman's voice was singing along with the radio. In the front room, he found the woman sitting in a rocking chair beside the radio. On the table beside the radio was a syringe, a candle, and a spoon. She watched his approach indifferently.

"Where's Mercer? Answer me!" He reached down and slapped her, twice. It bothered her like a flea bite.

He used every foul word he knew. She was the one person who could tell him what he needed to know, and she was under the influence of a fresh fix. He shoved his gun inside his waistband, then took off his hat and coat and hung them over a chair. He got the woman under the arms and pulled her upright. She felt like a sack of Portland cement.

He dragged her into the bathroom, pulled her dress over her head, then made her step over into the big, footed tub. She sat down willingly enough, leaning back in the tub like it was a comfortable armchair. Leaving her there, Farrell went into the kitchen and found a saucepan which he took back to the bathroom. Rolling up his sleeves, he turned the cold water on and began pouring pans of it over the woman's head. He went on like that for quite a while, filling and dumping, filling and dumping. Eventually the chilly water began to make an impression on her numbed mind, and she began to fuss and hold her hands over her face. Soon she began to cry. Farrell let her. He'd left his pity behind in the empty drawer of his desk.

When she was sober enough to cry harder, he went into her bedroom and found a blanket. He got her out of the tub, wrapped the blanket around her, then he took her to the kitchen. After placing her into a chair, he found a cheap tin percolator and a can of coffee, and proceeded to brew up the strongest coffee he could. By the time it was boiling, her crying fit had subsided into a piteous sniveling.

"Here." He shoved a cup into her hands. "Drink it."

She tried to put it on the table, but he forced it back up to her mouth. "Drink it, or I'll pour it down your throat." His pale eyes were like something out of a nightmare, and the woman took the cup from him, trying not to look into his face.

She drank it, and he gave her another cup, and then another. After four cups, she could talk to him.

"You make me drink any more of that, I'll puke it back up," she said petulantly.

"Fine. Tell me where Mercer is."

"I don't know where the bum is."

"How bad hurt was he?"

She looked at him now, really seeing him for the first time. "Are you the one?"

"What one?" Farrell's voice was sharp and irritable.

"The one who cut his face open. Lord, mister, I ain't never seen nobody cut up like that before."

"I'm the one. How bad was it?"

"Bad enough for Doc Poe to come over here and put twenty stitches into him. He had to give him a lot of morphine, too. But Bart's tough. He was able to get up this morning, and after they cold-cocked Johnny—"

"Who's Johnny?"

"Johnny Hope. He's a colored man who works for Bart. He come here all in a swivet, and when he wouldn't tell Bart where Joe Earle was—"

"Who's Joe Earle?"

She frowned at him. "You ain't makin' it very easy to tell this story. He's Johnny's kid brother. Bart said he had to be the one told you that Bart killed some sailor years ago. So when Johnny wouldn't tell, Zootie knocked Johnny into the middle of next week."

"Where are they now?"

"Bart sent Zootie out to find Joe Earle—I reckon they aim to kill him before he tells anybody else. Said when he'd done that they'd go and kill you, too."

"He tried already. He won't do any better the next time. Do you know where they've gone now?"

She shrugged. "After Zootie left, Bart rolled Johnny up in an old rug of mine, then he put him into the trunk of his car. He gave me some money and then he left."

"And you took the money and went on a toot. Do you know how long ago all this happened?"

"Hell, I don't even know what day it is." Her petulance was growing as the fix wore off.

"It's around 1:00 in the afternoon. You didn't go on that big a toot."

"Johnny come before noon—that's all I know." She wiped her nose on the back of her hand, then leaned over and squeezed water out of her hair. It dribbled down to the floor, creating little rivulets among the scars and scratches in the wood.

Farrell walked to the kitchen window. All that effort, only to run into a dead end. You're some detective, he thought. He turned and walked back to the bedraggled woman. She saw the look on his face and shrank back from him.

"Wh-what are you gonna do with me?"

"I'm gonna do what I should have done a long time ago. I'm going to call a cop."

She made an effort to stand up, and he pushed her back into the chair. "Not on your life. I might need you."

He went to the telephone and asked the operator for his father's office. Mrs. Longley answered on the second ring.

"Captain Casey's Office. May I help you?"

"Mrs. Longley, it's Wesley Farrell. Is the Captain in?"

"No, Mr. Farrell. He went to talk to the St. Bernard sheriff, who was wounded in a shoot-out last night with one of Detective Blanton's killers—according to the newspaper."

"It's urgent that I speak with him. Can you help me?"

She caught the note in his voice, and became instantly alert. She didn't completely understand the relationship between her boss and this nightclub owner with the shady past, but she knew there was a strong affection and respect between them. "I think I can. Where are you, Mr. Farrell?"

I'm at 8315 South Perdido—about two blocks west of the Broad Street intersection. The telephone here is—"

"Just stay on the line. I'll be able to tell you something in just a moment."

He heard her shift to another telephone and call down to the dispatcher. It was the work of only a moment to have the dispatcher radio Casey's call sign. When Casey responded, Brigid Longley relayed Farrell's location to the dispatcher, who relayed it in turn to Casey. Casey radioed that he'd go directly to the address.

"He'll be there in less than ten minutes, Mr. Farrell."

"Does he have any idea what a treasure he has in you, Mrs. Longley?"

As she remembered Casey's clumsy and quite charming dinner invitation a few hours before, she replied, "I think he might, Mr. Farrell. I'll have to ask him one day."

Farrell was waiting at the door when Casey's squad car rolled up to the Perdido Street house. He waved, and Casey trotted across the street.

"If this is some new piece of property you're thinking of buying, it doesn't really look very much like you, kid."

Farrell's mouth smiled, but Casey saw in his eyes that haunted look that he had only seen a very few times before. "Come in, Frank. I've got a story to tell you."

Casey realized then that Farrell was mixed up in something again, but admitted to himself that this was a first—Farrell had never talked to him before there were several bodies to account for.

Casey came into the living room, sparing a look for the half-drowned woman who remained swaddled in a blanket. Cocking a quizzical eye at his son, he took off his hat, sat down, and began to listen. It took Farrell about a half-hour to relate all he knew, and more than once Casey marveled at what Farrell alone had gleaned from the city's streets and back rooms. It often took dozens of men to uncover similar information over weeks of concerted effort.

"Well, we seem to have ended up more or less in the same place," Casey observed. "I've got all points bulletins out on both Mercer and Hines, but we still don't know where the hell they are. We also don't know who betrayed Commander Schofield, but maybe that'll come." He paused a moment, then looked at his son. "Tell me something, Wes. You were going off on your own and making progress—but you decided to come to me. You've been up against tougher things than this, and you kept everything to yourself up until the bodies had been counted and the survivors carted off to jail. This time, it was different. Why?"

Farrell leaned back in his chair, suddenly feeling tired. "I almost told you yesterday evening, but I didn't want to admit that I concealed knowledge of a crime five years ago or that I was getting mixed up in police business again. I didn't know how to tell you that I wasn't doing what I'd promised you a year ago—to mind my own business and keep my nose out of police investigations. I should have told you as soon as Schofield left my office, but I couldn't do it. Later, when you tipped me off in your phone call that we were looking for the same man and that he had killed again, it seemed too late to come to you."

"It wasn't. You could have told me. And you did tell me—before it got to be a big mess. You were a little slow, but you did the right thing."

Those few comforting words warmed Farrell, and he looked at the red-haired captain with gratitude. He had the revelation that Casey's affection for him was no small thing, that it would survive quite a bit of knocking around. "So what are we going to do now?"

Casey grinned at the "we." "Well, thanks to what you've told me, we know a lot more than we did, even if we don't have anybody in jail yet. I'm going to take this young woman into custody for her own safety, and you can go about your business. If you hear anything, get in touch with me as soon as you can—and try not to break any more laws if you can help it."

"That doesn't seem like very much to do under the circumstances," Farrell complained.

"Welcome to the world of police work—sixty-five percent mind-numbing routine, thirty percent boredom, and five percent stark terror." Casey put a hand on Farrell's shoulders. "I've got half the force looking for these men—there's nothing you can do that they can't do better. Go home and leave the rest to us. I'll keep you posted, and if you get anything from one of your sources, you let me know."

"Okay. You win." Farrell shoved his hands into his pockets, trying not to look dejected. Casey grinned and slapped him on the shoulder, then turned to tell Dolores Rogers to get dressed.

⊗⊗⊗

It was early afternoon when Schofield and Kelso arrived at Commander Charles Bracken's house on Second Street in the Garden District. Schofield had seen some pretty grand homes on St. Charles Avenue, but even by those standards Bracken's house was palatial. The yard was large and green, surrounded by an elaborate wrought-iron fence, and on the other side of the fence, Schofield could see water running from a fountain into a rock-lined pond full of water lilies.

"Does anybody in this town live in a small house?"

"Only us poor folks, kid," Kelso said. "Bracken married money." They walked through the gate and on up to the front porch. Kelso leaned on the bell, then stood back, almost at attention.

A languid, beautiful woman of thirty-five answered the door. Her clothes—a print skirt, crisp white blouse, and a peach-colored silk scarf—were tasteful and obviously expensive. She wore a diamond solitaire around her neck on a gold chain and a diamond-studded Longines watch on her left wrist. "Yes?" She stared a trifle haughtily.

Schofield held up his badge. "Treasury Agent James Schofield, ma'am. And this is Lieutenant Commander Kelso. We're here to see Commander Bracken."

She raised an eyebrow. "Is it terribly important? Charles is on leave, after all."

"If it weren't, we wouldn't be here." Schofield's voice was coldly polite.

She didn't like that. Displeasure put small lines in her brow and around her mouth. "Very well. Come in." She held the door for them, and each man entered, removing his hat as he did so. The house was as quiet as a funeral parlor, and was similarly furnished in heavy, subdued furniture and wall hangings. She led the pair down a hall to a set of tall mahogany doors. The smells of tobacco and good whiskey came to them faintly as they entered.

"Charles, this is Treasury Agent Schofield and Lieutenant Commander Kelso. They insisted on seeing you." The small note of impatience in her voice made it clear the pair had invaded their home against her strong objections. She turned and left, closing the doors behind her.

Bracken, a man of perhaps forty with a thick head of dark, curly hair shot with gray, got up from a leather armchair and put the crystal tumbler he was drinking from on the coffee table. "Kelso? What are you doing here? And you say this man is a Treasury Agent?"

"That's right," Schofield said. "I'm down here investigating the death of my brother, George Schofield. I've got some questions to ask you, if you don't mind."

Bracken frowned. "Why should I mind? But I don't know anything. For Christ's sake, that was five years ago."

"There's no statute of limitations on murder, Commander. I understand that you commanded the District Intelligence office in those days."

"Kelso could have told you that much."

"The reason I'm here is that not long ago I discovered a list of names and a set of detailed notes my brother made before his death. It was obvious that he was investigating those men for some reason. There were known smugglers on the list, along with the names of both Treasury Department and Coast Guard personnel. Your name was on that list."

"What are you saying? That he suspected me?" Bracken's handsome face was dark with outrage. "I've never heard of anything so absurd."

"Why? My brother was assassinated because he obviously suspected collusion between rum runners and people assigned to fight them. You ran the Intelligence section—who would be in a better position to compromise secret patrol orders?" Schofield knew he was going too far, but he felt certain he was close to finding what he needed to make the case.

Bracken's teeth drew back over his lips in a snarl. "You son of a bitch—you dare to come into my house and make accusations like that." He turned his head to Kelso. "I guess I have you to thank for this. You were George Schofield's Number One—the two of you were always cooking something up, looking for some way to cover yourselves in glory—a pair of mavericks, both of you. Schofield got himself killed and you lost your ace-in-the-hole. And you've been scheming ever since to get back on top."

Schofield responded sharply. "That's enough, Bracken. Casting blame on other people won't get you anywhere."

"Unless you've got a warrant for my arrest, I suggest you get the hell out of here, and take that sea lawyer with you." Bracken pointed a finger at Kelso. "I'm not going to answer any more of these ridiculous charges, and you can be sure I'm going to report all this to the District Commander and the chief resident Treasury agent tomorrow."

"Go ahead. But I won't turn loose of this. My brother obviously had reasons to suspect you of something, and I'm going to find out what that is."

Bracken's temper snapped. He balled his right fist and threw a punch at Schofield's head. The young Treasury man easily blocked the punch and knocked the other man down, upsetting the coffee table.

The noise must have carried out to the hall, because Bracken's wife threw open the door and stared at them in horror. "What in the name of God are you doing? Let him alone—let him alone, I say." She stormed into the room and went to her husband, who sat on the floor holding his head.

She looked up at the two of them, her eyes snapping with rage. "My lawyers will call on your superiors as soon as I can get them on the telephone. You'll find out you can't come into my house and assault my husband."

"He assaulted me first, lady." Schofield was in no mood to be conciliatory. "I'm not through with you, Bracken." He grabbed his hat and strode from the room, Kelso on his heels.

When they were back in the car, Schofield blew his breath out. "Whew. I didn't expect anything like that. I hope I didn't get you in any trouble in there, Emmett."

Kelso shrugged. "Don't worry about it, kid. I can retire if they decide to play rough with me. You handled yourself good in there. You rattled his cage plenty."

"Yeah, I thought so, too, but I can't make an arrest just because a guy blows his top."

"When people start blowing their tops, that's when they make mistakes. "My guess is he'll get in touch with Milton before he squawks to the brass. He'll try to make trouble for me, maybe get you called back to Washington—but not immediately. As long as you're free to operate—"

"They'll both know the pressure's on."

Kelso nodded sagely. "Why don't I drop you off at my place, and I'll check back in at my station?"

"Sounds good. I've got some calls to make. Some way or another, I'm going to bust Bracken wide open."

"I'll drink to that, kid."

Chapter 13

Zootie had never been friendly with the other men who worked for Mercer, but as Mercer's watchdog, he had paid close attention to their conversations about where they hung out, the names of their girls, even the brands of cigarettes and beer they liked. He knew that sooner or later, the information would be worth something to Mercer.

Zootie was, in his unique way, something of a street-corner psychologist. He knew instinctively that Joe Earle Hope would not try to escape town in the normal way. Taking a train or a bus would get him seen, and his name would be passed to whoever wrote the ticket. Zootie also knew that all it took to get information was money or a kick in the face. Zootie never paid for anything he could take.

Joe Earle didn't have a car, so his most likely strategy would be to get a ride out of town with somebody else. For that, he needed a contact of some kind. So Zootie went on a small odyssey that took him through ten service station garages, four waitresses, two beauty parlor employees, and six bars, the last of which was Tubby's. Any other man might have felt frustrated by then, but Zootie was a methodical man. He enjoyed this game because it was something he was good at and felt pride in.

Tubby's bar had been open throughout the afternoon, but business was slow. Only two men and a woman were in the place when Zootie came through the open door. He stood there with his nose in the air, taking the measure of the place and its occupants until he spotted Tubby behind the bar. From Tubby's expression,

Zootie knew he'd finally found the right place. He walked to the bar with a casual stride, his hands swinging loosely at his sides.

"Hey, brutha. I could sure do with a cold beer. You got any Pabst?"

"Yeah." Tubby reached into his ice chest and brought out a bottle. It had chips of ice clinging to it, and when he popped the cap, frosty vapor escaped the neck.

Zootie licked his lips, took the open bottle, and put it to his lips. His Adam's apple worked like a fishing bobber with a catfish at the other end until the beer was gone, then he wiped his lips.

"Ahhhhh. Damn, that was good. Tell me, brutha, you seen a cat named Joe Earle Hope in here lately?

"Never heard of him."

Zootie grabbed Tubby's shirt, jerked him half-way over the bar, then hit him on the jaw with the bottle. Tubby grunted and went limp as the bottle smashed into a hundred shards. The people who'd been sharing the afternoon with Tubby disappeared like smoke, leaving Zootie and Tubby all alone.

"Brutha," Zootie said in a soft, sweet voice. "Ain't nothin' works me up like somebody lyin' to me. You know Joe Earle as well as you know your own lyin' ass. Now you tell me where he is, else I'm gonna beat you until you can't get up, then I'm gonna beat you some more. You gonna be cryin' for your mama and daddy before I'm through, you dig?"

Tubby's jaw felt as though it might be broken, and, hurt as badly as he was, he knew he didn't stand a chance against Zootie. "He—he took my car—three hours ago. S-said he was go—goin' to h-hell."

Zootie laughed at that. "He said that? Damn, that's funny." He tightened his grip on Tubby's collar and pulled him a little closer. "Now tell me where he's really gone, mothah-fuckah, 'fore I kill you."

"Swear—he read—'bout Oscar Boule—in newspaper. Real— real shook up. Borrowed—m-my car—had gun. All I know— swear it." Between the broken jaw and the stranglehold Zootie had on him, Tubby could barely speak.

"A gun, huh? I'll be damn'. He's a reg'lar banty rooster, ain't he?" Zootie let go of Tubby's collar, and the badly beaten bar owner slid to the floor behind the bar.

So, he's got a gun and a car, and he knows about Oscar. Could be he don't know about Johnny, but he's figurin' Mercer for a double-cross, anyway, the little man mused.

He walked to a pay telephone on the wall, and gave the operator a number. Mercer answered in a hoarse voice.

"Yeah?"

"It's Zootie, boss. Joe Earle was figurin' on lammin' outa town, but he found out about Oscar. He's got him a car and a gun—I'm bettin' he's comin' to you, one way or another, and he don't even know you got Johnny."

Mercer sounded pleased. "You better get over here then. I wanna make good and damn sure he don't get away."

"Okay, boss. Be there soon." He hung up and turned to go, but before he reached the door, he retraced his steps to the bar. Stepping over Tubby, he reached into the ice chest and took out another Pabst, knocking the cap off on the edge of the cooler. He stepped back over the unconscious bartender, then walked out sipping the beer like he hadn't a care in the world.

◈◈◈

Johnny Hope awoke on a hard floor in a dark room. His head ached like a sore tooth and his arms and legs were numb from being tied so tightly. He shifted to ease a cramp, but managed only to make his head ache a little worse.

It came back to him little by little—Mercer lying naked on a blood-stained bed, his face half-obscured by a bandage. He couldn't imagine another human being powerful enough to hurt Mercer that much. It had diminished Mercer, but not enough. He was still powerful, still meant to kill Joe Earle, and Johnny could do nothing to stop him.

A door opened and a shaft of light came into the room, blinding him momentarily. Frightened by the suddenness of it, he cried out. "M-mercer? Mercer? That you?"

The bulky shape in the door laughed mirthlessly. "Sure, Johnny. How's your head?"

"L-listen, they's been a mistake. Joe Earle ain't told nobody nothin'. I swear it. Joe Earle's a good boy. He ain't after makin' no trouble for nobody. Please—let him go...let me go. Ain't none of us gonna hurt you."

"It's gone too far, Johnny. People know me now—they know my name, know my face. There's a police dragnet out for me—did you know that?"

"Mercer—you gotta listen to me. Ain't none of us tried to sell you out. I don't know how they got your name, but it wasn't from none of us. Hell, we was all makin' good money—why would we want to queer that, huh? Huh? Think about it, for God's sake."

"God's got nothin' to do with it. It'll all be over soon, Johnny. You won't have no worries where you're goin'."

Mercer turned and closed the door, leaving Johnny once again in darkness. The mechanic groaned aloud as he thrashed, trying to break the bonds that held him. After a while, he gave up, exhausted, and in more pain than ever. As he stared up into the darkness, he started to pray. He told God that he'd been a no-account, sinful sonofabitch, and he knew he deserved to go straight to Hell. He accepted that there was no likelihood he would be delivered from his own predicament, but he prayed that Joe Earle could get away safe. It was all he knew to ask.

Violetta Dalton had known many and varied sufferings, but few compared to learning that Zootie was being tracked by the police. She had kept watch all day, but if there were policemen outside, she couldn't see them. They were likely hidden in another dwelling, watching with binoculars for Zootie to walk into a trap.

As the afternoon wore on and darkness began to fall, Violetta could stand the isolation no longer. She dressed in a black skirt and blouse, draped a black shawl over her shoulders, then gathered fifteen dollars and a straight razor into a small purse. She was no fighter, but in her line of work, it paid to have a weapon.

Leaving the lights on in the front, she slipped through the back yard to a place in the fence with a loose slat. Swinging it to one side on a single nail, she squeezed through to an alley, which she followed to the next street.

Gerttown was dark and seemingly deserted. The decent were locked inside their hovels and the indecent were prowling for something to steal, someone to mug, or some kind of debauchery to enjoy. She headed cautiously for a place where she knew a negro taxi driver named Redding often stopped for a couple of beers between fares.

She came to the open door of an evil-looking tavern. From inside the voice of Robert L. Johnson sang "Thirty-Eight Special Blues" on a radio full of static. Peeking inside, she saw Redding at his usual spot, his head propped in one hand. He wore a foolish grin as he nodded his head in time to Johnson's mournful tune. She entered on cat feet, hoping to get to him without being noticed. Her hopes were doomed—it was a place few women frequented.

"Hey, li'l mama," a rough voice said. A hand reached out and caught her shoulder, pulling her toward the bar.

"Get that hand off me or I'll cut it off." Her hand was in her bag, and her eyes flashed. The joker drew his hand back like she was a leper.

The other men mumbled and cursed to themselves about her as she went by them. Her face wore a hard scowl as she faced down each set of eyes that dared to look at her. When she reached the taxi driver, he was already watching her.

"Mr. Red, I need a ride."

"Where to, baby sister?"

"Over near the Fairground—Castiglione Street."

"Hell, that's almost five bucks—you got that much?"

"I got it. Can we go now?"

He looked at her with new respect. "Let's go." He slid off his stool and led her out of the tavern. Some of the men continued to give her dirty looks, which she repaid with interest. When she was finally in Aaron Redding's taxi, she began to tremble and had to bite her lip to keep from crying. It was always like this—always having to live among animals and somehow not yourself become one.

Violetta had left Pass Christian because she was different, and knew there was no place for her in such a small town. She'd hoped that New Orleans would be better, but it wasn't. Or, at least it hadn't been until Zootie. In the beginning, she'd thought he was just another crude loafer looking to cop a feel or get her into a dark corner. It was only later, when they were alone, that she discovered how much alike they were—how they'd both been looking for the same thing, never thinking they'd find it.

She knew she was taking a terrible risk going to this Mercer's house. Everything Zootie had told her about Mercer repelled and frightened her. He sounded more like a monster from a child's nightmares than a man. Only someone as lost and pitiful as Zootie could ever see anything admirable in such a person. It made Violetta sad to contemplate that side of Zootie, so she pushed it away.

It took almost an hour to reach the neighborhood where Mercer's house was located. She saw when they arrived that the house was mostly dark. She got out, handed Redding $4.50 for the cab ride, and added a fifty cent tip.

He looked at her doubtfully. "You sure you want to be left here, Miss Violetta? It sure looks dark and lonesome."

She worked a grin onto her face and nodded. "It's fine, Mr. Red. My friend works in that house yonder."

Redding glanced dubiously at the dark house. "I reckon you're old enough to know what you're doin'. G'night, now."

"'Night." She stood there as he let in the clutch and drove out of sight. When he was gone, she looked at the house and shivered. Zootie's car was nowhere in sight, but Mercer's De Soto was in the carport. Knowing that she couldn't wait on the street, she decided to sit in the shadows on the running board of the De Soto. When Zootie showed up, she'd be able to reach him before he entered.

She lost track of the time as she sat there in the dark. Memories of her mother and grandparents, and of a school teacher who had taken a special interest in her floated through Violetta's mind. She dwelt for some time on the pleasure she'd gotten finger painting with the teacher—creating lavish landscapes with trees and birds and fish leaping from brooks. The world of those pictures was what she had wished for, and hoped yet to find. No luck, so far, she thought. Here you are riskin' your ass for a boy so dumb he thinks a racist killer is a knight on a white horse.

She had fallen into a doze when the sound of a car door closing awakened her. She rubbed her eyes, and saw Zootie. Standing up, she gathered her skirts and ran across the grass to him. "Zootie," she whispered. "Zootie."

He saw her and a smile of pleasure lightened his face. "Violetta. What you doin' here?"

"I had to see you. Some colored detectives come to the house lookin' for you today. I'm sure they got the house staked out, but I slipped out without them seein' me. I remembered you tellin' me about this house and where it was, and I got Mr. Red to ride me over in his cab."

He put his arms around her waist and kissed her. She kissed him back, and for a moment, she forgot what a mess everything was and basked in his tenderness. It soon passed.

"Come on. Mercer's waitin' for me, and Joe Earle Hope's liable to show up here before long. We got to get ready for him." He snickered like a boy up to a prank.

"Zootie, let's just go. Forget Mercer and Joe Earle. Let's go someplace where there ain't all this trouble. Where the cops don't even know you're alive. Stayin' here's gonna end up bad for us, I know it." Violetta put all of her persuasive power into her plea, all of her pent-up longing for a normal life with somebody she could love.

"Don't be talkin' silly, honey. Mercer needs me—I can't let him down." He caught her by the hand and dragged her to the door. He knocked and it opened. The biggest man Violetta had ever seen stood there, made all the more menacing by the bandage covering the left side of his face. His yellow eyes burned like those of an animal as they swept over Zootie and Violetta.

"What the hell's this?" Mercer demanded as Zootie led Violetta into the living room.

"This here is Violetta, Mercer." Zootie's demeanor was that of a boy introducing his girl to his father.

"You dumbbell. Outsiders ain't supposed to know about this place—I told you that over and over." Mercer stared at Violetta like she was something filthy tracked on the rug.

"Listen, it's all right. Violetta come here to warn me about the cops."

"I know. The cops are lookin' for both of us. We're gonna have to take care of Johnny, Joe Earle, and the others. If they're all dead, they can't say a word against us. You'll have to get rid of her."

Zootie was abashed. "Okay, I'll get a cab."

Mercer grabbed his shoulder and shoved him against the wall. "You stupid black shit—I said get rid of her."

Zootie looked at Mercer, his eyes full of shock. "You don't mean—?"

"Let him alone." Violetta's voice cut the air between them like a hot wind. She had the razor in her right hand, ready to strike. She felt the odds were in her favor—Mercer thought she was just another helpless victim.

He turned and leered at her. "I guess I'll have to do it myself." He advanced with a speed that was shocking in such a large man. Her hand flew up, the blade of the razor whisking out of the handle, glinting in the pale lamplight as she struck down with all her might. Maybe because Farrell had caught him like that before, Mercer was primed for it. He blocked the blow with one huge arm, snagging her wrist and twisting until the razor dropped from her nerveless fingers. She screamed, kicking at his legs.

Mercer slapped her, forehand and back, knocking her almost senseless, then he grabbed her by the front of the blouse and ripped it open—and stopped. There were no breasts—not even buds. Violetta's chest was flat, with the undeveloped pectoral muscles of a boy.

Mercer held what he'd thought was a woman out at arm's length, and started to laugh. "So this is what you've been doin'. My little pupdog's got a taste for something beside meat and potatoes." He laughed again, shaking Violetta like a rag doll.

Zootie stared with disbelieving eyes. The person he'd finally found some happiness with, the person who'd awakened in him the possibilities of physical love—was being manhandled by the man he'd loved from afar for so long.

"Stop. Stop—don't hurt him no more." He ran up to Mercer and began pounding him on the back with his fists. In his hurt and rage, he forgot all he knew about street fighting, and attacked Mercer with the same mindless fury as he had once attacked the childhood bullies who had mistreated him. He screamed and cursed, pounding with futile blows against a giant who shrugged him off.

"So, you wanna fight, huh?" Mercer caught the smaller man around the throat, balled up one fist and smashed Zootie in the temple. Zootie's eyes rolled up in his head and he dropped lifeless to the floor. "Get up, you queer little bastard. Get up." Mercer shouted and cursed as he kicked Zootie in the ribs, but Zootie was past feeling anything. Mercer's single blow had fractured his skull and killed him.

Violetta, whose real name was Jeremiah Dalton, formerly of Pass Christian, Mississippi, lay on the floor, knocked almost senseless. He heard Mercer shouting and the sound of blows, but it seemed to be happening in another world. Jeremiah sent message after message to his arms and legs, but nothing worked.

He gradually became aware that the curses and blows to Zootie's lifeless body ceased, but Mercer's presence was apparent in his stentorian breathing and muffled oaths. He's going to kill me now, Jeremiah thought. He didn't care to live anymore anyway. Zootie was gone, taking with him the cherished hopes for the life they could have lived. Jeremiah felt Mercer grab him, felt the skirt and step-ins being torn from his lower body. Mercer was laughing now, the laugh of a scavenging hyena. Jeremiah instinctively knew what would happen next. He tried to scream, but his mouth wouldn't work. As Mercer brutally penetrated him, Jeremiah's mind shut off and then there came blessed, unfeeling darkness.

⊗⊗⊗

Earlier that afternoon, Frank Casey was thinking about only two things. One was that it was nearly time to go home. The other was where he and Brigid might go for dinner. He had almost made up his mind to take her to Kolb's German Tavern when he heard the telephone ring in her office. Five seconds later she had buzzed his line.

"I'm here." He was grinning foolishly.

"Frank, Inspector Grebb's on the line. There's been a shooting near the Coast Guard docks."

"Put him on." He heard the line clicking and then the faint sound of a siren. "Casey here. What's up Grebb?"

"Looks like attempted murder, chief. "We've got a Coast Guard commander named Bracken, shot in the head near the Coast Guard docks."

Something about this sent a ripple of excited anticipation through Casey. With the murder of George Schofield so fresh in his mind, he knew he had to go over there. "He's still alive?"

"Yeah, but I don't know for how long. Ambulance just took him to Charity—the intern didn't know if he'd make it."

"Call in all the men you can to seal off the area, and see who's on call in the crime lab. I'll be over there in ten minutes." Without waiting for Grebb to reply, he broke the connection and dialed the number for Treasury Enforcement. When he got a reply he asked for Paul Ewell.

"Don't talk, Paul. Just listen. They've discovered a Coast Guard officer named Bracken shot near the Coast Guard docks. I'm on my way over there."

Ewell was silent for a long moment. "That's not far from my office. I'll meet you there." Ewell broke the connection without another word.

Casey got up quickly and grabbed his coat near the door. "Brigid, I'm going to the Coast Guard docks. You might as well lock up and go home." He shrugged into his jacket and put on his hat. "I'll call you at home later."

"Slow down, Frank." As he paused, she went up to him and turned down the collar of his jacket which he had twisted in his hurry. She was so close he could smell her perfume, and he could not quite ignore the flawless quality of her skin or the alluring shape of her lips.

"Thanks." His voice was a little husky. "Uh, I'll—I'll see you in a little—I'll see you later."

"Good. I'm looking forward to the dinner and the story. Be careful, okay?"

He nodded solemnly. "I promise."

Still dazzled, he left the building and was in the car with the siren blaring before he knew it. Part of him was still preoccupied with her beautiful lips and her perfume.

When he reached the dock area, he pulled his car to the curb and got out his badge case, holding it up so the uniformed officers could see, following their pointing fingers. He found Grebb, a thick-set gray-haired man in his early forties, a baby-faced blonde detective named Mart, and Paul Ewell standing at the open passenger door of a dark blue Lincoln sedan. Blood was spattered everywhere.

"Tell me what you've got."

"Nobody heard the shot," Grebb began, "But considering all the noise around here, that's no surprise. Pretty good-sized entry wound but no exit wound. Probably a .38 revolver. I already looked around for a spent shell and couldn't find one, so it's good odds it wasn't an automatic. Whoever it was walked right up on him and popped him— might've been somebody he knew."

"A Coast Guard enlisted man found him, skipper," Mart said. "He was on his way to the Customs House when he saw the car idling and the man slumped behind the wheel. After he saw the blood, he got to a phone and called the Shore Patrol, and they called us."

"What do we know about the victim?"

"Not much just now," Grebb replied. "His Coast Guard identification card said he's Commander Charles Bracken, and his car registration has a Garden District address."

Ewell glanced at Casey, then drew the red-haired detective to the side. "I got a complaint in my office earlier today from this man's lawyers."

Casey looked at him with interest. "What about?"

"There's a young Treasury agent from Washington down here conducting an unofficial investigation into the murder of his brother—Commander George Schofield—he was killed a few months before Repeal. The kid's gone all over town leaning on people and making a nuisance out of himself. I've been looking for him so I could chew him out and send him home."

"So this young agent had been to Bracken's house?"

Ewell nodded. "He got into a fight with Bracken and knocked him down. Bracken's wife wants to sue us."

"And a few hours later, Bracken turns up shot. That's not too good, is it?"

Ewell's eyes were hooded, his mouth drawn down. "I warned him to walk easy around here, but he's obsessed with his brother's murder. He must have split down the middle after the fight and decided to be his own judge, jury, and executioner."

"You want me to have him picked up?" Casey asked because he was obligated to, but in Ewell's shoes, he'd have wanted to handle it another way until they knew more.

"We've got to find him, if for no other reason than to establish his whereabouts since he was at Bracken's house. He checked out of his hotel yesterday, so I'm not even sure where he's staying now." Ewell turned to look at the automobile and massaged his neck for a moment. "Yeah, you better pick him up. His name is

James Schofield. He's about 26 years old, six feet even, maybe 175 pounds, wiry, slender build. Reddish-brown hair, aquiline features, blue eyes."

"Let me get some men started canvassing the docks and I'll get his description out."

"Right." He fell in step with Casey, his hands shoved deeply into his pockets. Casey shot a quick glance at him.

"What do you suppose the odds are of a man coming to town to investigate the five-year-old murder of a Coast Guardsman, and within days another one is shot in his car?"

"I'm no mathematician, but I'd figure about one in ten million." Ewell's mouth was brittle and his eyes had a cloudy look.

Casey stopped at the murder car and called the other detectives around him. "We need to nail down when this happened as quickly as we can. Mart, go to Bracken's house and break the news to his wife. Find out if he's had any trouble with anyone lately." Casey decided not to share the news about Schofield's visit—better for Mart to go in with no preconceived notions.

"I'm gone, skipper."

"Grebb, get some detectives and some uniformed men started up and down this vicinity and see if anyone saw anything out of the way, or if they remember seeing Bracken drive in here. See, in particular, if anyone noticed a white male in his middle twenties, six feet, one-seventy-five, reddish brown hair, blue eyes, aquiline features. Where's the Shore Patrol?"

"Here." A solid-looking blonde man wearing dress khakis, a sidearm, and a shore patrol brassard on his left arm stepped forward. "Lieutenant Oliva, sir. I've got a dozen men with me."

"Can you get them to talk to everybody in uniform up and down the docks to see if anybody remembers seeing Bracken talk to someone in the last hour?"

"Can do," the Lieutenant replied.

"Go to it." When everyone had scattered, Casey went to his squad car, got the microphone from its dashboard clip, then gave the pick-up order for Schofield and his description to the dispatcher. When he was finished, he turned back to the senior Treasury agent and found him staring at the victim's car, gnawing his lip.

"I don't think there's much else we can do, Paul. We've got plenty of men out and Grebb's a capable investigator. If there's anything to find, he'll find it."

Ewell shook his head regretfully. "I put a man on him the first day he came to town and passed the word to my street sources to keep their ears open, just in case Schofield's blundering around would make somebody scared enough to make a move of some kind. He lost my man earlier today and we haven't relocated him."

"Maybe he did scare somebody. I admit, it looks bad for the kid right now, but we also don't know whether or not Bracken knew more than he claimed."

"He was never under suspicion."

"Maybe not. But if the gunman wasn't somebody trying to shut his mouth, maybe they figured that by killing him, we'd be throw off the real scent. Let's do it by the numbers, and see what happens, okay?"

Ewell's eyes narrowed. "It's too close to home for me, I guess. You're right. I'm going back to work on this from my end."

Casey nodded. "I'll get in touch when we know something. Good night."

"'Night." Ewell turned and walked toward the Customs House, and the gloom quickly swallowed his lanky form.

Casey's mind was spinning with possibilities. Thanks to his conversation with Farrell, he knew things what Ewell didn't— that August Milton was high on the young agent's list, and that the retired criminal could not help but be nervous with both Schofield and Farrell sniffing around his ankles. Casey well knew that Milton had killed and ordered men killed in his career— another Coast Guard officer more or less wouldn't cost him any sleep. Casey looked at his watch. He could catch the ferry to Algiers, interview Milton, then get back in plenty of time to make his dinner date. After leaving word of his evening plans with Grebb, he got back into his squad car and drove in the direction of the Canal Street Ferry slip.

Chapter 14

Joe Earle Hope watched the house on Castiglione Street from the back seat of Tubby's sedan, hoping no one could see him. If a cop found him lurking in a white neighborhood with a gun, and in a car that didn't belong to him, Mercer would be the least of his troubles.

The resolve with which he'd left Tubby's had evaporated upon reaching Mercer's house. Joe Earle had experienced his share of adolescent fights, but he'd never been in a gun battle in his life. Fighting someone like Mercer required a kind of experience that he'd deliberately avoided. He looked down at his small pistol, which now looked as puny and ineffectual as he felt.

As he sat there, a taxicab pulled up near the house, and a girl got out. Soon the cab drove away, the girl watching until it was out of sight. She cast a furtive look around, then walked across the grass to Mercer's carport and disappeared into the shadows. His indecision grew as he pondered her puzzling actions.

Perhaps forty-five minutes passed before a Chevrolet coupe slowly rounded the corner and pulled to a stop in front of Mercer's house. A small, slender man emerged whom Joe Earle immediately recognized as Zootie Hines. The girl came from the darkened carport and ran into Zootie's arms. They kissed passionately, then talked quietly for a moment or two before Zootie caught the girl's wrist and pulled her into the house.

Joe Earle rolled the rear window down to get some air, and as he leaned toward the opening, he heard muffled shouting and sounds of a struggle come from inside the house. He put his hand on the door handle, but the noises stopped as suddenly as they began. Paralyzed with terror, he saw the lights in the front wink out.

He drew back, realizing that someone might be coming out. If it was Mercer, this might be the chance to take the big man by surprise and kill him. He quietly unlatched the door, shivering as cold sweat ran down his face.

Eventually the front door opened, and two figures came out. One was large—it was easy to make him out as Mercer. But the other person was too bulky to be either Zootie or the girl. As Mercer dragged the other man toward the carport, there was just enough moonlight for Joe Earle to distinguish Johnny's features. Mercer dragged Johnny to the rear of the De Soto, opened the trunk, and brutally shoved him inside.

As Mercer slammed the trunk lid, Joe Earle climbed quickly over the front seat and slid behind the wheel. Waiting until he heard the De Soto's motor crank, Joe Earle started the Ford, then watched until Mercer drove into the street and away from the house. Joe Earle gave his quarry a half-block lead, then he followed, leaving his headlights off until they reached St. Bernard Avenue.

Mercer handled the De Soto skillfully, keeping within the flow of traffic, never exceeding the speed limit, switching lanes only when it was prudent to do so. Together, they traveled almost the entire length of the street, finally turning east on St. Claude Avenue. It became apparent to Joe Earle that Mercer was returning to the Mouton Brother's garage, which gave him a slim hope. There he might be able to catch Mercer off guard and rescue his brother.

The young man took some comfort from the fact that Tubby's old Ford was one of a hundred such on the city streets. There was small likelihood that Mercer would spot a tail in this traffic. As they neared the St. Bernard Parish line, however, traffic thinned rapidly, forcing Joe Earle to quickly drop behind.

They crossed the Intracoastal Waterway bridge over the Inner Harbor Navigation Canal, and continued past the parade grounds of Jackson Barracks. Clusters of small houses and businesses gave way to farmland and undeveloped property, and Joe Earle realized he was practically alone on the road with Mercer. He cut his speed even further and doused his lights, praying Mercer was too intent on his destination to notice a pursuer.

Just as he passed a landmark that alerted him to the nearness of the road leading to the garage, Joe Earle saw Mercer's red tail light disappear. Slowing almost to a crawl, he continued the last half mile before cutting his wheels to the left and heading down the dark road. The marl-covered surface crunched and popped beneath his wheels like English bones ground between a giant's teeth.

There was no sign of Mercer at all now, and in the enveloping darkness, his motor sounded unnaturally loud. He realized he would have to cover the rest of the ground on foot or lose the element of surprise he was counting on. Pulling onto the grassy shoulder, he cut his engine and got out, his damp fingers caught around the butt of his gun.

The darkness around him was heavy and still. Even the frogs and crickets who celebrated the night were oddly silent. Joe Earle had an irrational desire to scream just so he'd know he was still in the world.

He reached the edge of a clearing, and in the gloom saw the hulking shape of the barn and house that had belonged to the Mouton brothers. As he pondered an angle of attack, he heard something, a low, muttering sound that made the hair stand up on the back of his neck. He turned his head in a slow circuit, trying to place the direction from which the noise was coming. He gradually recognized it as the idling of a well-tuned car engine. As he turned back toward the garage, a pair of powerful headlights suddenly nailed him to the spot. He threw up a hand to shield his eyes, and jumped to the side just as the engine rose to a snarl and the headlights leaped at him. He was still moving when the car hit him broadside and knocked him spinning into the undergrowth.

☡☡☡

Casey reached the Canal Street ferry as it prepared to leave for the west bank of the river. Thanks to Farrell, he had precise directions to August Milton's lair at the back of his daughter-in-law's house.

Casey pulled to a stop in the warm glow of bright lights inside the big house. He got out, and walked silently to the back yard. The front window of the carriage house, too, was flooded with light, and through the open curtains, Casey saw August Milton standing at the mantle, lost in though. He seemed to be looking at something far, far away as he stroked his chin. Casey's knock brought his head up sharply. He appeared at the window, looked out, then came to the door and opened it. "Well, well. Captain Casey, isn't it? I've half been expecting you." He gestured grandly for Casey to enter.

"You've got a good memory. It's been a long time since we saw each other—I was only a sergeant in those days."

"Yes, but you've moved up in the world since then. Now you're an assistant chief and Wesley Farrell's friend and apologist. I'm surprised you didn't come here when he did."

Casey ignored the sardonic tone in Milton's voice and took a seat directly across from the retired smuggler. "If I'd known some of the things Farrell just told me, I might have. In fact, I decided to come to see if I could get a little cooperation."

"Ha! First Farrell and his 'one friend to another' speech, then the boy Treasury agent tries to scare me into a murder confession, and now here you are with your folksy charm. I don't know when I've had a more amusing week." He laughed bitterly, sitting tall in his chair, perfectly relaxed.

Casey smiled at him and wagged his head. "I suppose we look pretty silly to a smooth operator like you, Milton. But maybe you're too smooth for your own good."

"Meaning what?"

"I've already got enough ballistic and fingerprint evidence for the district attorney to indict Bart Mercer for first degree murder in the deaths of Lieutenant Commander George Schofield, Violet Town Constable Robert Valdez and Deputy Salvatore Maggio, as well as Negro Squad Detective Tom Blanton. But I think he's guilty of two more murders—two that are a lot closer to home than you'll like."

"I don't know what you're talking about." Milton's steel blue eyes were commanding, his sardonic smile still intact.

"When Mercer and his pals murdered Commander Schofield, Wes Farrell was in the car with him. Since Mercer was shooting at him, too, he recalls quite a few details—the main item being that Mercer's car was a blue Pontiac with Mississippi plates."

Milton said nothing, his bearing almost regal.

"Farrell also tipped me to something else. At his suggestion, I went over some eyewitness reports to a certain accident that happened a few years before, Milton. An accident that you'll remember—the day your son and grandson were killed."

Milton did not move, but something in his eyes changed.

"You and I both know that was no accident," Casey went on. "They were murdered, and you knew it at the time. Farrell figured out that you believed Old Man Morrison was responsible. You and Morrison had a loose alliance during the last years of Prohibition, and you did pretty well together. Unfortunately, both of you were greedy, and it was only a matter of time before the partnership broke up—one way or another. When the *accident* happened, you either figured or were convinced by others that Morrison had staged the hit to weaken you enough to hit you and wipe you out. So you sent Mercer after him. For once, though, Mercer slipped up with his trusty shotgun. He wounded Morrison badly, but not so badly that his men didn't have time to spirit him to a hideout and save his life. He's been in hiding somewhere in the city ever since. The few of his men that Mercer and his thugs left alive swear that he had nothing to do with the murder of your son and grandson. They're a pack of Godless thieves, but I believe them."

Milton's look of sardonic amusement had faded, and he squinted at Casey with unfeigned interest. "So who did?"

"Farrell tracked down some information that was reported at the time, but hadn't meant anything to us. It seems that when your son's car was run off the road on Lakeshore Drive, there were a couple of fellows just offshore fishing. They saw the whole thing—it wasn't an accident or the result of a near collision with a drunk. Someone in a blue Pontiac with Mississippi plates deliberately ran them off the road. A blue Pontiac in all likelihood driven by your favorite murderer, Bart Mercer."

Milton's eyes widened, as though a bright light had suddenly lit up a dark, forgotten corner.

Casey took out his bulldog briar and tobacco pouch and began to pack the pipe with his special mixture. He did it slowly and methodically, keeping his hands busy as he continued to talk. "I don't know where you found Mercer, Milton, but he hasn't been your friend. It's well known that after the death of your son and grandson, you backed away from the business and let someone else run it. I doubt that man was Mercer—he's strictly a killer, a man who carries out orders and keeps other people in line. You had a silent partner—maybe somebody in the Treasury Department or the Coast Guard—maybe somebody else. Whoever it was has kept your old gang clear of the police, allowed them to switch from smuggling booze to stealing cars on a grand scale, and no doubt rake in a hefty share of the profits. How much of a percentage are you getting now that you're no longer calling the shots, Milton? Forty percent—thirty? Or maybe less than that? It probably isn't much—you've been too busy standing guard over what's left of your family to worry about money. And your partner's been counting on that."

"Are you finished, Casey?" Milton's face had paled and the sharp edges of his teeth were just visible through the slit of his mouth. His eyes had flattened and lost any resemblance to those of a man—Casey saw that no matter how old he had grown, no matter how deceived and cheated he had been, Milton still harbored a tough, dangerous character inside.

"Pretty much." Casey paused to light his pipe. "I don't really care about you, Milton. Your own greed has already hurt you more than the law can. If I can manage it, I'll try to have you brought before the grand jury to answer questions about your connection to the Schofield and Blanton murders, but you might slide out from under those charges. But once I get my hands on Mercer and the man he kills for, I'll know everything, and I'll give it all to the United States Attorney. Your goose is cooked, pal." He got up and picked up his hat. Puffs of sweet, aromatic smoke billowed from the bowl of the pipe, and Casey looked quite contented. He gave the ex-smuggler a single, amused glance, then he turned and left the house.

Milton was frozen in his chair. The Devil had finally come to take his due—the men he'd thought under his control had driven a stake through his heart. That they had killed his son and grandson was bad enough, but the blow to his towering ego was devastating. They'd pulled the wool over his eyes, just as though he were a useless, doddering old man. Outside, a long roll of thunder sounded in the distance. He stirred, seemingly in response, but the movement was sluggish, unsure.

Marshaling his strength, he got up and went to the telephone. He looked at it with a sinking heart, wondering if he still possessed the savvy to outsmart a consummate liar. He picked up the receiver and gave the operator a number. As he stood there waiting, listening to the ringing under the static in the line, his right hand flexed until the knuckles were white and his fist was quivering.

"Hello?"

"This is Milton. I need to see you."

"I thought we agreed we should keep our meetings to an absolute minimum—we can't afford to be seen together."

"I've thought of that," Milton said. "There'll be no one to speak of at the Governor Nicholls Street Wharf this time of night. I can catch the Third District Ferry and meet you. I'll come on foot to keep from attracting any attention."

"This must be important." He sounded intrigued.

"If it weren't," Milton said silkily, "I wouldn't have called."

There was a pause at the other end of the line, then, "It's almost 9:00. I can be there in about an hour."

"Fine. I'll reach the other side about that time."

"See you then." The other man broke the connection.

Milton went to his desk and unlocked the kneehole drawer. He took out the nickel-plated .45 automatic, checked the magazine, then jacked a cartridge into the breech. The clash of metal-on-metal was drowned out by a long peal of thunder that signaled the arrival of the storm. A crooked finger of electricity lit up the yard outside Milton's window as the thunder died.

Milton went to his bedroom where he changed his white shirt for one of charcoal gray. He selected and knotted a dark wine-colored tie around his neck, then got a spring-clip shoulder harness from a hook in the closet and strapped it around his shoulders. When he was satisfied with the fit, he put on a dark jacket and returned to the living room to pick up the ivory-handled Colt. He placed it carefully in the spring clip, letting the jacket fall naturally over it.

As he went to get his hat, he was arrested by his image in a tall mirror. The features were familiar to him, but something was different. The cold, ruthless August Milton who had flouted law and crushed enemies was gone; someone far less capable had taken his place. He felt something like despair flood his chest, forcing him away from the image.

A violent wind lashed his window with rain as he put on a dark felt hat with a pinched crown and a heavy army raincoat with a shoulder cape and belt. He looked around the room, as though trying to imprint it on his memory, then he turned out the lights and left the carriage house.

Jagged blades of light were discharging over the River, and intermittent sheets of rain slashed at the trees and homes along the pleasant street. Milton pulled his hat down low over his face and walked in the direction of the River, his tall, powerful body straight and unbowed before the wind.

When Milton was well on his way, another figure left the protection of a tree and followed along in Milton's wake. He matched his pace to Milton's, his face lost in the shadow of his hat brim, his hands shoved deeply into the pockets of his overcoat.

It wasn't a long walk through Algiers to the ferry slip, but Milton seemed to be timing his stride in order to meet exactly the sailing time. He looked neither to the left nor right, but kept his face headed directly into the wind and occasional bursts of rain. The ferry slip's lights became visible in the distance, but Milton's purposeful strides neither quickened nor slackened.

His pursuer realized that the closer they got to the docks, the greater was the likelihood that he might be spotted, so he slowed his own pace to allow Milton time to board the ferry well ahead of him.

Milton walked across the ramp, then went amidships to climb the ladder that would take him to the passenger cabin on the upper deck. As Milton entered the cabin, James Schofield crossed the ramp, then moved to a place of concealment between the ladder and an open locker.

The gloom concealed the desperation in the young agent's face. This late night foray was a last-ditch attempt to uncover evidence that would keep his investigation alive and his badge in his pocket. He well knew that he was grasping at any straw the stormy winds might blow his way.

Despite Kelso's encouragement, Schofield was certain the incident at Bracken's would wreck everything he'd worked for. Without something concrete to justify his actions, he fully expected be sent back to Washington to face dismissal from the department. He was hoping against hope that he had shaken

Bracken enough to contact Milton, and he had staked himself out in the rain on the slight chance that Milton would break cover and meet with his henchman.

Two automobiles came aboard the ferry, their wheels clattering as they crossed the heavy steel ramp, and not long after that came the rattling of chains that signaled the crew was pulling in the gangplank and preparing the boat for departure.

The mournful hoot of the boat's whistle sounded twice, heralding a furious thrashing as the screws fought to gain a purchase in the brown water, then a shudder as the squat, flat-bottomed boat lumbered away from the dock. Schofield spread his legs and grabbed the ladder until the vibrations eased.

In the middle of the River, wind-whipped water broke over the gunwhales and ran in frothy streams across the deck as blue-white slashes of electricity bathed the lower deck in a baleful light. Schofield had never seen such violent water, even as a Coast Guard Academy cadet; several times his stomach flipped as the ferry broke through boiling waves and crashed back to the River's surface.

After an interminable fifteen minutes, the boat began to slow for the approach to the eastern dock. Again the boat shuddered as the pilot threw the engines into reverse, the crew whistling and shouting as they made the boat fast and let down the heavy ramp.

The few cars aboard started their engines and left the boat quickly. A moment or two later, Schofield shrank back into the darkness as he heard the hollow click of leather heels on the steel ladder. Milton passed so close that Schofield could have grabbed him, then he turned and walked slowly across the gangway.

Schofield waited for him to make the street, then he left his hiding place and followed, keeping to the shadows, ducking into doorways when Milton paused to look behind him. Somewhere near the Governor Nicholls Street Wharf, Schofield saw Milton fade into a doorway. Schofield quickly found a hiding place of his own and waited.

For fifteen or twenty minutes, the street was deserted save for a driving rain and a howling wind. Schofield shivered from nerves and cold rain that ran down his collar. Another ten minutes passed, and the Treasury agent began to fear that Milton had spotted, and somehow managed to lose him. He was considering a very short list of options when a Chrysler station wagon rounded a corner with its parking lights burning. The rain had slackened to a light drizzle as the station wagon passed Schofield's hiding place and continued on.

As the vehicle approached Milton's position, the tall, gray-haired man stepped out and held up a hand. The wagon eased to a stop and Milton entered the passenger door.

Schofield's heart raced as he realized his proximity to the man for whom he'd been searching. Moving with agonizing caution, he crept from his hiding place, and closed with the rear of the parked car.

Reaching the automobile without detection, Schofield was rewarded with the sound of voices clearly emanating from the open passenger window.

"Milton, I don't know what you're going on about. Why don't you talk a little straighter, so I can go home."

"How's this for straight? Who told me that Morrison was responsible for the deaths of my son and grandson."

The other man spoke in a casual, reasonable tone. "I seem to remember it was me. What of it?"

"I've been getting a lot of visitors lately. People are suddenly looking very closely at me and our operation. We've got that trigger-happy goon of yours to thank for it. By killing that negro cop, he gave them enough ballistic evidence to tie him to the Valdez and Schofield killings."

"They might have some ballistic evidence that ties his *gun* to the killings, but not necessarily him."

"Wrong. He left a fingerprint, and that's how they identified him. He's good at killing, but he's a little sloppy with the small details. That's what gets you hung."

"Get to the point."

"Here it is—thanks to Farrell, they know about the Pontiac Mercer used in the Schofield kill—a car that he also seems to have been used to run my son's car off the road." Those words were punctuated with the sound of a gun being cocked.

Schofield was incredulous to hear soft laughter. "Put the gun down, Milton. That won't get you anything."

"It'll get me something. After I blast your guts out, I'll find Mercer and shoot little pieces out of him until there's nothing left. You were the one who came up with the idea to get together with Morrison in the first place—I'd forgotten that until today. Were you already planning to start a gang war with him when you suggested the alliance, or did that bright idea come later?"

"Later. We needed his boats and his contacts during those final years of Prohibition. Once we had all that, we didn't need Morrison anymore—he was taking too big a cut. I was smart enough to see long before Prohibition ended that they'd sooner or later repeal the law—I planned in advance for that, so there'd be plenty of money to live fat and find a new grift. Mercer helped with that—he'd been stealing cars for years before Prohibition. It's come in real handy for little things like supporting Chauchaut's candidacy for governor. Governor Chauchaut—what a free ride it'll be with that hick in the governor's mansion." He laughed.

"If I were you, I'd forget about all that. Your time to play politics and kill people is about up." Milton's voice had become thick and coarse.

"Put the gun away, August. If I don't come back, Mercer will use his machete on your daughter-in-law and the little girl." The man sounded calm and matter-of-fact, very much in control.

"You're a liar. I put my granddaughter to bed hours ago."

"Yes, hours ago. You're a lousy poker player, August. When I heard your voice, I knew you'd found out things I didn't want you to know, and it occurred to me how hot-headed you used to be. I figured you to try this stunt. Mercer contacted me a little while ago. He's got Johnny Hope out at the Mouton brothers' place, and he managed to snag Joe Earle Hope, too. He was on the verge of killing both of them, but I told him to go to your place first—put the arm on the woman and the kid. You know Mercer—he likes to hurt things, particularly little, weak things. If he doesn't hear from me in the next thirty minutes or so, he starts chopping them into cutlets. And thirty minutes isn't enough time for you to get there and stop him."

"You filthy, double-crossing bastard!" Milton's hatred erupted like molten lava from the open window. Schofield knew he had to stop it now or there'd be nothing to take to his superiors.

"Federal officer!" he shouted, training his Colt automatic at Milton's open window. "Give me the gun, Milton. *Now, Goddamnit.*" He snatched Milton's .45 from his hand and then covered the car with both guns. "Both of you, get out of the car and keep your hands where I can see them. *Do* it or I'll shoot both of you." Schofield bounced lightly on the balls of his feet, shifting the guns to cover both men.

Milton cautiously unlatched the door, kicking it open. With his hands raised, he eased himself out of the car. His mouth was a bitter slash across the bottom of his face. Schofield covered him with his left-hand gun as he kept an eye and the other gun on the driver. He heard the driver's door latch, saw the door open. A man's head and right hand became visible above the roof line— too late Schofield saw the gun in his left hand.

An explosive lance of yellow fire leaped past Milton's shoulder. The bullet hit Schofield's side like a charging rhino. He tried to get his gun up, but a second shot struck him in the upper chest. He fell to the ground, fighting to stay conscious. As he stared up into the storm-tossed sky, he saw a face he didn't know, a boyish face that spoke in a voice with an east Texas twang. He held a long .44 Smith & Wesson in his hand, pointed across Schofield's body at Milton.

"Go home, August," Captain Luke Peters said. "With any luck, we can bluff our way out of this. After all, the only people who can hurt us are dead—or are about to be. I'll take this kid along and Mercer can get rid of him, too."

"Peters, let them go. You can take me in their place." Milton's voice, so strong before, now sounded weak and insubstantial, even to Schofield's failing ears.

"No, August," Peters said, wagging his gun. "I'm leaving you loose for the same reason I don't kill you. They're all watching you right now. If you disappear or turn up dead, they'll start wondering why, and start looking everywhere to find out. I don't want them looking in my direction, not when everything's about to fall into place. So go home—and wait until I call you. I'll take care of the woman and the girl until things die down—and you come back to your senses."

As Schofield listened, he exerted every ounce of his will to stay conscious, and to fight. His searching hand brushed the butt of the .45, but as his fingers sought a purchase, something hard struck his temple and a fury of red and yellow lights erupted inside his skull.

Chapter 15

Jeremiah, who had for a time been Violetta, came back to consciousness on the living room floor of Mercer's house. He was clothed in only a few rags, and the wetness and pain below his waist let him know that he'd been used like a piece of meat, then cast aside like scraps. He didn't ask himself why he was still alive. An animal like Mercer left his prey alive to know what had been done to it. Killing would have been merciful, and that was something the man called Mercy never was.

Hot charges of electricity briefly lit the dark room, illuminating the sight of Zootie's body across the room. Using his elbows to propel himself, the boy managed to crawl to where Zootie lay. The dead man's eyes were open. His face wore a look of complete surprise. Jeremiah cupped Zootie's face in his hand and stroked the skin for a little while, feeling the heat already slipping away from his lover's body. Jeremiah laid his face on Zootie's chest, and wept silently, grieving for Zootie and his own dead dreams.

After a while, it occurred to Jeremiah that he couldn't remain there. Mercer would eventually return. Using the coffee table for support, Jeremiah managed to get to his knees, then to his feet. His legs were wobbly, and he hurt all over. He felt his way through the room and down the hall until he found a bathroom. When he switched on the light, he flinched at the bruised and bleeding face that stared back at him from the mirror. He looked down at his legs and saw strings of dried blood running to his ankles.

The tub was rigged with a shower head and curtain, for which he was thankful. He needed to get Mercer's smell off of him, but he was in no shape to sit in the tub. He managed to lean over far enough to turn on the hot water tap, and when the stream grew warm enough, he activated the shower and climbed painfully over the wall of the tub.

He began to tremble as the hot water hit his face and cascaded down his body. He put his hands on the wall, afraid his legs would buckle. As he stood there with his head spinning, it came to him that nobody would care about Zootie's death. To the police he would just be another punk who got what was coming to him. They wanted Mercer for other reasons, and if they found him, he'd be punished for those reasons, alone. Zootie would be shoveled into a hole and forgotten.

After a few minutes under the shower, some strength returned to Jeremiah's limbs. He found a sliver of soap in the soap dish, and used it to methodically wash his body. When he had washed himself twice over, Jeremiah turned off the water and dried himself with a threadbare towel that hung on the wall beside the tub. Walking was still painful, but it was a pain he could endure. He was still oozing blood, so he used some frayed washcloths for absorbent padding, and tore strips from the towel to tie them into place. As he bandaged himself, an idea began to form in his mind.

He returned to the living room, listening to the thunder outside. As a bright flash briefly lit the room, Jeremiah knelt beside Zootie and began removing his clothing. He and Zootie were close enough in size that he knew the clothes would fit.

As he removed Zootie's trousers, Jeremiah heard a thump, and saw the black shape of a revolver lying on the rug. He picked it up and caressed it with his small, delicate hands. A few moments later, he stood there dressed in Zootie's clothing and shoes. He tucked the pistol into his waistband, then pulled on Zootie's jacket and picked up the cap. As he put on the cap and tucked his hair under it, he knelt down beside Zootie, touched his face again. Jeremiah found that he didn't have any more tears to shed. He stood up and left the house.

The rain had lessened to a hard drizzle as he walked across the yard to Zootie's Chevrolet. The clothes were still warm from Zootie's body, and he did not begin shivering as he feared he might.

Jeremiah hadn't driven in a long time, but the skill returned to him quickly. He had once been a delivery boy for a general store in Pass Christian—the only job his frail physique permitted. He had tried farm work and had worked for a time in a fish cannery on the Gulf coast, but the former had been too taxing, and the other left him stinking of fish. His private life had been difficult. There were few people like him in such a small town and those few guarded their secret assiduously. One he found who would confide in him made it plain that if he remained in rural Mississippi, he had little to look forward to. If his secret got out, he could be ostracized, beaten, or even harassed out of the vicinity by the Ku Klux Klan.

He eventually made the decision to let his hair grow out, then move to the city in the disguise of a woman. He quickly discovered that he felt more comfortable in this role, and although he was eventually forced into prostitution to keep a roof over his head, he at least began to discover more people like himself. The feeling that he was less alone in the world somehow made up for what he was forced to do in order to survive.

Zootie had been drawn to him by some magic that neither of them understood. Jeremiah had gradually helped him accept what he was, and for a short time, they had known some happiness with each other. Jeremiah had tried to get Zootie away from Mercer, but he now understood that Zootie's devotion to Mercer had masked a strong, if misunderstood, attraction to Mercer's cruel virility.

Jeremiah had no idea of how to get to the Mouton brothers' garage in St. Bernard Parish. He had not been out of New Orleans since arriving there two years before, and had been advised by other negroes that remnants of the Ku Klux Klan still flourished in the outlying rural parishes. That didn't matter now. He had accepted that he was going to die before this night was over, but he planned to take Mercer with him.

⊗≋⊗

Sallie Milton had begun her evening worrying. Since she had first admitted to herself the love she felt for her dead husband's father, she had always dreaded the possibility of his criminal past coming back to haunt them. She sometimes tried to find the line that separated August Milton, the criminal, from August Milton, the doting grandfather, the devoted and affectionate helpmate, but she had never been able to do it.

She wanted to talk to him about his past, to get him to help her understand what he had been and why—it was really all that stood between them. The age difference didn't matter to her. She was 32 to his 54, but the death of her husband and son had aged her far beyond her years. Yet Milton's past remained like a stone monolith—impenetrable and incomprehensible. She couldn't break through it, and he hadn't opened the door that would lead her inside.

She thought she heard a whimper from Clemmie's room, and she got up to check. At the door to the room, she saw in the shaft of light from the hall that the child was sound asleep. If some dream had made her cry out, the frightening part must have quickly passed. Her breathing was easy and her expression placid. Sallie smiled down at the little girl, and returned to the living room.

She was standing at the taboret, pouring herself a glass of sherry, when another sound startled her. She turned to confront a man of monstrous proportions. He dripped rain water, and half of his face was covered with a huge bandage that showed rusty spots of dried blood. He had the yellow eyes of a wolf, and they burned with a strange hunger.

The glass fell from her hand and shattered at her feet. "Who— Who are you? What are you doing in my house?" She struggled to keep the panic out of her voice, to do nothing that would wake Clemmie up. No matter what happened to her, the child had to be protected. "Get out of here this instant, or I'll call my father-in-law. He's got a gun."

The yellow-eyed demon's mouth opened, and a hollow, mocking noise came out, a noise so hideous that it took all her strength not to scream and keep on screaming.

"He can't help you, because he ain't here, pretty lady. Now you get your raincoat and bundle up that sweet li'l gal, and we'll take a nice ride in the country." As he spoke, he moved his right arm from away from his body, and she saw a bright, wicked blade in his hand, glinting and winking in the lamp light. "Don't scream, pretty lady. I ain't supposed to hurt you, but if you scream, all bets are off." He laughed again, as though what he'd said was a huge joke.

She fought to keep her composure, to keep from running, but this was too much, more than she could fight. She grabbed at the taboret as her head began to swim, but a black pool opened at her feet and she slid down into it.

⧇

It was the middle of the evening when Daggett and Andrews returned to Violetta's neighborhood to check with the stake-out team. They reported nothing unusual, so Daggett and Andrews crossed the street to talk to her again. Rain was falling heavily, and the wind tore at their hats and raincoat tails.

They knocked on the door, waited, then knocked again. "Miss Dalton, it's Sergeant Daggett from the police. Open up, we want to talk to you again. Miss Dalton?"

Andrews looked at him with a grimace. "That li'l gal's pulled one over on us, boss."

"Go around the back and check the door," Daggett said. He knocked again, calling Violetta's name while Andrews made his way through the alley. He was still knocking and rattling the knob when Andrews opened the door.

"She ain't here, Iz. It's as empty as a hobo's purse."

"Sonofa*bitch*." Daggett tore off his rain-soaked hat and slapped it against his thigh. "Where the hell could she go on a night like this?"

"Hard to say, but she couldn't get very far on foot—she ain't got a car."

Daggett walked to the edge of the porch and turned on his flashlight, sweeping the beam in a circle. As he did so, he put two fingers against his lips and emitted a piercing whistle. The surveillance car's headlights came on and it tore up the street, skidding to a stop in front of the house. Daggett went down to it as the driver rolled his window down.

"She's gone. Must've gotten through the fence back there somehow."

"Damn." The uniformed negro officer grimaced. "That li'l thing couldn't reach high enough to climb that fence. How'd she get out?"

"Never mind that now. Check the alley behind here, and go up and down the neighborhood, stop anybody you see and question them. The weather's been bad all night, but there are taverns, a café, and a pool hall within walking distance of here. She's a good-looking female—some man noticed her."

The officer pulled down the bill of his cap, and the car moved away briskly.

Cursing to himself, Daggett returned to the inside of the house, finding Andrews waiting for him.

"Found a loose board back there," he reported. Swings to the side on a nail. I couldn't make it through there, but a li'l slip of a thing like her wouldn't have no trouble."

Daggett scowled in disgust. "Well, it's done now. Let's search the place while the uniformed men canvass the neighborhood. Somebody drove her away from here—maybe Hines, maybe somebody else. God damn it to hell."

Andrews retreated to the kitchen and began to work from that end, leaving Daggett to begin in the living room. Because they had nothing else to work with, each detective sifted everything that came to hand. Violetta's life seemed to have no beginning before New Orleans. There was a savings bank book in Violetta's name that showed a total of $767.83 with regular deposits of five and ten and twenty dollars—Daggett had never known a prostitute with a regular savings habit and was intrigued by it.

In a bureau drawer, Daggett found a collection of women's step-ins, slips, and blouses, but no brassieres, which he found interesting. He didn't remember Violetta being particularly voluptuous, but even small-breasted women still wore brassieres, he knew. There were some handkerchiefs, and a tattered and dog-eared manila envelope, which he opened. It was an old photograph of a group of school children with their teacher. At the bottom the photographer had printed the name of every child there. Daggett looked at the names, then at the faces. There was no Violetta Dalton, but there was a boy, Jeremiah. As he studied the face, Daggett fancied he could see a resemblance—her brother, maybe, he thought. He put the picture and envelope on top of the bureau.

The bathroom was between the second and third rooms, just off a small hallway. As he arrived at the door, Andrews turned and held out his hands. In them were a shaving mug and a good-quality badger hair shaving brush. "First time I ever known a woman to use these things. There's a straight razor on the sink, too."

"Hmmmm. Hines's, maybe."

"You find anything else of his here?"

"No. Nothing but women's things and a school picture."

"Who's in the picture?"

"Looks like she might have a brother—Jeremiah, I think the name was."

Andrews gave Daggett a quizzical look, then put the shaving things back on the shelf. They walked back into the next room, and Andrews bent to take a peek at the school photograph. He stared at it for a long time, and a grin began to spread across his face. "Boss, you're gonna think I'm crazy."

"I know you're crazy. Only a crazy man would be a cop and work these kinds of hours."

"No, I mean it. This boy in the photograph—either he's Miss Violetta's twin, or he *is* Miss Violetta." He straightened up, his face earnest. "Think about it—ain't nothin' here that belongs to a man but shaving things, is there? And remember what Longboy told us about Hines—how he couldn't seem to do nothing with any of his gals? I think our boy Zootie has a secret, and only Violetta knows it."

Daggett nodded. "I've heard stranger things in my life. When we catch up to Violetta, we'll have to ask her—or him."

Daggett saw the lights of the stake-out car sweep across the yard, and he went to the door to see if they'd found anything. He did it automatically, without hope.

The burly officer who'd done the driving walked through the rain with a middle-aged negro who wore a heavy coat and cloth cap. Daggett met them as they walked up the porch steps.

"Sergeant, this is Mr. Redding. He drives a cab, but he likes to hole up in a joint about six blocks from here. Tell him, Mr. Red."

Redding didn't look all that alert, and Daggett guessed from the blood-shot vessels in his eyes and the general unsteadiness of his posture that he'd done more drinking than driving this night.

"Yeah, was a couple hours ago, this li'l woman goes by the name Violetta come into the joint. Said she needed to go over to Castiglione Street real bad. But she had the money—paid hard cash and a fifty-cent tip, by golly."

Daggett's heart leapt at this news. "Do you remember the address?"

"Not the number, but I can tell you where it is. Big, two-story stucco place, near the corner of Rendon—got one of them carport things along the side. Only place like it on the block."

Daggett was moving before Redding was finished. "Get this man's name, address, and telephone number. Andrews and I are going over there now."

"Done and done, Sergeant."

Daggett jerked his chin at Andrews and the pair of them left the house at a trot. Seconds later, Andrews revved up the Dodge police cruiser and they headed out of Gerttown at a fast clip. As they drove, Daggett took the microphone from the dash and began talking into it.

"Dispatch, this is Inspector Nineteen."

"Go ahead, Nineteen."

"Requesting backup at a house near the corner of Castiglione and Rendon. We'll be running silent, so warn them to do the same and to be on the lookout for two plainclothes officers. The objects of the call are Bart Mercer and Zootie Hines, over."

"Roger, Castiglione and Rendon, run silent." The dispatcher relayed the information to the relevant district, and Daggett heard a car roger the message.

It took them twenty minutes, running flat out to make it through the rain-slick streets to the Fairgrounds neighborhood. As they rolled up the street with their lights out, they saw two marked police cars approach from the opposite direction. Andrews blinked the parking lights at them once, and they responded.

The negro detectives got out of the car, Andrews pulling a twelve-gauge Winchester shotgun from the back seat, and they walked quickly to where the four uniformed men waited.

"Sergeant Daggett from Headquarters," he said softly, showing his badge. "I think Zootie Hines and Bart Mercer might be in here. They're both killers, so don't take any chances. Andrews and I are going in the front, so keep close watch on the back."

"Will do." The senior officer, his partner, and the other two men split up and fanned out across both sides of the yard and soon were out of sight.

Daggett drew his revolver and started across the yard to the front door. There were no lights inside, but that meant nothing. A few yards from the house, Andrews faded to the left, leaving the right to Daggett. As they neared the entrance, Daggett noticed that the door was ajar. He held up a hand to Andrews, who checked himself and brought the shotgun to his shoulder.

Daggett tiptoed to the porch and eased up alongside the door. With his foot he pushed the door open a bit wider. When nothing happened, he dropped almost to his knees, then dove in through the opening. Andrews advanced, keeping clear of the opening. When the lights came up suddenly, he stopped short, his finger hard against the trigger.

"Sam—come on in. There's nobody home." Daggett's voice reached Andrews plainly, and he moved quickly to obey. He stepped through the opening and saw his partner standing over the corpse of Zootie Hines.

"What the hell?"

"Dead—looks like somebody cracked his skull. There's a big bruise on the temple, and he's hemorrhaged from the ears and nose."

"Where are his clothes?"

Daggett said nothing, his eyes tracking the room. He saw rags on the floor and went to them. As he picked them up, it was clear that it was a woman's blouse, ripped almost in half. Andrews spotted a skirt and step-ins and held them up. The step-ins were smeared with blood. He held it up so Daggett could see, his eyes shocked.

Daggett stared for a long moment. "Something bad's happened here. Ask the uniformed men to call for the crime lab and the coroner's wagon. Tell them not to come in the house, but to search the yard and exterior of the house for whatever they can find."

"Right." Andrews dropped the bloody underpants on the floor and walked through to the back, flipping on the light switches as he went.

Daggett moved carefully through the house, glancing in each room as he went. Eventually he found the bathroom, and saw that the floor was wet. The tub was wet, too, and there were flecks of dried blood clinging to the sides and bottom of the tub. As he recalled the suggestions that Andrews had made back at Violetta's house, his imagination began to work. The things he saw there were too ugly to contemplate for long. Andrews' return spared him any further speculation.

"I got a hunch that Violetta came here to find Zootie. It looks like she found him."

"Yeah, but what the hell happened after that?" Andrews asked.

"Mercer killed Zootie, that much we can guess. After that, something else happened—I'm guessing from all the blood a rape—a mean one. After that I think Violetta took Zootie's clothes, and his car—probably a gun, too."

"After Mercer?"

"I could only tell two things about Violetta in the short time I spoke to her—she loved Zootie and she had some guts. When a man decides to live like a woman, he takes a big step—leaving behind one kind of a life and going into one that depends on taking big risks and keeping a secret from everybody he meets. I expect this boy's had a long, tough road."

"Jesus, boss. You sure gettin' philosophical over a damn queer."

Daggett looked up at his friend. "Do me a favor, Sam. Don't call him that in front of me. I was in prison for five years—I learned that people got to do all kinds of things to survive—to stay alive. I can't judge him for it—don't you, either, you hear?"

Andrews shrugged, a little embarrassed to be called down by his partner, but he took it. "What do we do now?"

"We got this far by searching the last place. Let's turn this place upside down and wait for the coroner and the lab men. Maybe we can figure out where Violetta went."

"Damn. We're lookin' for a miracle."

Daggett looked down at Hines's dead face. "Living's a miracle, but we do it every day, if we're lucky."

❧

Farrell sat at his private table at the Café Tristesse tapping his foot to the sound of Bones Melancon's Sextette as they performed an up-tempo version of "I've Got You Under My Skin." They were a good group—one of the best in the city—and the audience was dancing to their music with abandon. Farrell watched them, envying them. He and Savanna had never danced, except once in her apartment, to some records. In spite of her imposing height, she was light on her feet and moved with him like they'd been born from the same egg. He hadn't seen her all week, and looked forward to meeting her later. They'd talked on the telephone earlier, and he'd been glad to know she wasn't hurt by his neglect. He'd given her a little of the story. She'd agreed that he was probably doing the right thing.

But now it was over so far as he was concerned. He was content to let his father take it from here—or at least that was what he was telling himself. It bothered him that Mercer was still running loose, and that he still didn't know the name of Mercer's betrayer.

A waiter had just brought him bourbon on the rocks in a tall glass when he saw August Milton standing at the entrance to the main floor. Farrell told the waiter to bring him to the table. Two minutes later, Milton was standing in front of him. He didn't offer to shake hands.

"What brings you here?" Even before Milton replied, Farrell sensed a palpable aura of dread surrounding him, like the subtle odor of decay that comes from a dying man.

"I need help. I didn't know where else to come." Milton's voice was strong as ever, but there was desperation in his eyes, and his shoulders slumped imperceptibly.

Farrell motioned for him to sit. "You made a point of telling me not long ago that we weren't friends, Milton. Normally a man can ask for help only from a friend."

"Don't hold my feet to the fire, Farrell. I'm in trouble. I'll give you anything if you'll help me."

"I'm listening." Farrell took out his cigarette case, took one for himself, then slid the open case to Milton. Milton took one, leaning over for Farrell's light. The first lung full of smoke seemed to do him a lot of good.

"It's Sallie and Clemmie. Mercer's got them."

Farrell held his surprise in check. "Mercer works for you. Why has he taken your family?"

"Frank Casey was over to see me earlier today. He told me about the blue Pontiac. He told me about the way I'd been taken in about Morrison. The more he talked, the more I realized that the people I'd been in league with had simply used me. There came a time when they wanted me out of the way, but still needed my name, my backing. They achieved that end by attacking my family, realizing I'd draw away from the business to protect them."

"The people you were in league with—who are they, besides Mercer?"

"Since the end of the 1920s, I had the help of Luke Peters, the chief deputy of the St. Bernard Parish Sheriff's Department. Thanks to his manipulation of the sheriff, we were able to clear every other smuggler out of the parish and use it as a safe haven. We brought thousands of barrels and bottles of liquor ashore along that part of the river. The only people who ever got close to knowing about it were Constable Valdez and his deputy. Peters set them up for Mercer and he killed both of them. Between us, we killed, caused to be killed, or ran out of the parish every other gang, large or small, well before Prohibition expired."

"And then what?"

"Mercer had experience in stealing cars, changing their appearance, and then selling them out of state. We had plenty of money from smuggling to set up in a different line of thievery, so that's what we decided to do. By then I'd drawn back enough so that I was always around to take care of Sallie and the child, and Peters had taken over much of the work of managing our men and finding buyers for the cars. Mercer and a crew of negro mechanics handled the theft, body work, painting, and what have you. He liked using negroes, he said, because they were invisible and they did what you told them."

"And they gave you a cut just because they were nice guys."

"I didn't care about the money, but I suppose they figured that if they gave me what looked like a reasonable cut, I wouldn't ask any questions—and they were right. I suspect I've only been getting a pittance. If they hadn't started killing again—"

Farrell interrupted him. "Were you in on killing Schofield? For five years I've wanted to know who set him up, Milton. If you want my help, you'd better come clean on that." Farrell had dropped his voice to almost a whisper, but the threat in his words was as real as a bullet.

"Why should you believe me, one way or the other?"

"Because I know you—I know what kind of man you are. You're in a weak position right now, pal. If I tell you to go to hell, you'll walk out of here with nothing, so give."

Milton's face looked flabby and tired. "If it matters, I didn't have anything to do with it. We discovered that Schofield was snooping around, investigating on his own. We had a source of information that, if compromised, would have cost us a great deal of money and perhaps sent some of us to jail. No, I didn't give the order to kill him, but my men did it, and I profited by it."

"The name, Milton."

"I don't know the name—I never did."

"You're a Goddamned liar." Farrell's harsh voice reached out like a blade and sliced at the older man.

"Peters took care of all that. He had law enforcement contacts— I don't even know if it was a Coast Guard man or a Treasury agent he corrupted."

Farrell straightened in his chair, his eyes like glass shards. "Get out. I'm sick of your lies. Get out, or I'll have the waiters throw you into the street."

Milton's hands came up in supplication, his face sick with desperation. "You've got to believe me, Farrell. Peters wanted control over that part of the operation, and I let him. What did I care who the traitor was, so long as the money came in? I swear to you, I don't know the name and never did."

Farrell stared at the older man. What he wanted was to knock him down and throw him out into the street, but he realized that Milton could help him exact some payment for George Schofield while putting Mercer out of business at the same time. He made up his mind quickly. "All right, Milton. Where have they got your family?"

"There's only one place they could go. There's an abandoned garage with a house out in St. Bernard Parish not far from the River. It used to belong to a pair of brothers named Mouton. I think you knew them."

Farrell took in smoke and let it feather out of his nose. "Why didn't you go to the police with this, Milton?"

Milton's grave, slack face gave way to his sardonic smile. "If you were me, Farrell, would you trust the police?"

It was Farrell's turn to smile. "Touché, Milton."

Chapter 16

James Schofield was in such a deep, dark place that he began to fear he was in Hell. Around him he could hear the moans of the damned, something that intensified the fear until he gradually recognized the moaning voice as his own. The feel of cool water on his brow gradually brought him back to consciousness. As his eyes fluttered open, he saw the face of a stocky, gray-haired negro looking down on him. The man's face had fresh bruises and cuts on it.

"Man, I was afraid you was gonna die on me, mister."

"Where—where am I?"

"We locked up on the second floor of an old commercial garage. You been shot twice mister—you in a pretty bad way, but I reckon we's all in a pretty bad way just now. Mercer's gonna kill us, sure, just as soon as the boss gives him the word. I figured to be dead already, but Mercer left after the big boss showed up with you in the trunk of his car. Figured to die again, but Mercer went off somewheres else. He's back, but I don't know what to think now."

The burly negro was talking rapidly in a soft voice, and his hands were steady, but his eyes screamed for help. "My name's Johnny Hope. I used to be a mechanic with this gang, but they kilt a cop the other day, and so much fuss got raised, I reckon they figured it'd be simpler to get rid of anybody knowed about it and start over from scratch later."

Schofield's right arm was bound tightly to his side, but he found his left arm would work. He reached up a hand and felt his head. It felt pulpy on the side. He remembered getting shot, but he nothing about his head. "Is—is there water?"

Johnny Hope filled a tin cup from a bucket and held it clumsily in bound hands so Schofield could drink. Some spilled on his face and neck, but the young Treasury agent managed to drink most of it. "Thanks, Mr. Hope. I'm Jim Schofield. I'm a Treasury agent."

Johnny Hope's eyes rolled. "Lord have mercy. If they're up to killin' T-Men, things is a lot worse than I figured."

Schofield could not help but smile. "I—I wish I could d-disagree with you, Mr. Hope. I've...never been in this much...trouble before." He felt a pressure in his chest, and found it hard to breath. He guessed that a sucking chest wound was causing the sensation. If he didn't get help soon, he would surely die. He heard a low moaning from elsewhere in the dimly-lit room, and he stirred. "Who's that?"

"My brother, Joe Earle. I don't know what Mercer done to him, but he looks all busted up. Mercer ain't got many brains, but he sure knows how to hurt people. Reckon my brother was tryin' to help me, which is a shame. I ain't worth a hair on that boy's head."

Schofield felt surrounded by death, his hope trickling away like his blood. A wave of pain and nausea swept over him, and he passed out again.

Hope rested his elbows on his knees and then put his head into the cup of his bound hands.

※※※

Peters was waiting in the house when Mercer showed up with Milton's women. He stood at the door, watching as Mercer opened the trunk of his car and took out the limp form of a woman, bound hand and foot. He carried her to the open door, where Peters saw that she was also gagged and blindfolded.

"Any trouble?"

"Nope. Duck soup, Luke. All's I had to do was show her my pretty smile and she conked right out."

"Where's the kid?"

"In the trunk. Want I should leave her in there?'

Peters made a disgusted face. Mercer had his uses, but there was nothing about him a normal man could like. Crudity and violence were the major facets of his personality. "No, you fool. Put the woman into the back bedroom, then get the kid and put her with her mother. Close the door and lock it, and leave the lights out."

Mercer did as he was told, but Peters could see from the look in his eyes that he was appraising Sallie Milton's body, imagining what it would be like to use it. Peters wondered if he would end up having to kill Mercer, too, before he degenerated into nothing more than a mad dog. But that's all he's ever been, he thought. That's why you hooked up with him. His throat felt dry, and he badly wanted a drink.

Mercer returned and went back to the car. He scooped up the still sleeping child in one arm, closed the trunk with the other, then walked silently past Peters to complete his mission. When he returned to the big front room, Peters was sitting at the table, smoking a cigarette. His boyish face was expressionless, his demeanor patient. There was an open bottle of liquor and a glass in front of him. The glass had only a thin film of whiskey in the bottom.

"What now?" Mercer asked.

Peters looked at him. "Now? Now we figure out how to make the most of this mess. Milton can't trouble us anymore, because he knows we'll pay him back through his family. The New Orleans cops will soon think, if they don't already, that Schofield shot Bracken, and when they can't find him, they'll assume he got away somewhere. I checked with the hospital not long ago—Boulet isn't expected to last the night. The sheriff's .38 nicked his aorta, and they can't stop the internal bleeding."

Mercer showed his big yellow teeth. "And we got the Hope boys next door, ready for the Grim Reaper. I'll cut all their throats and put them in the river before sunup."

"And Zootie—tell me again how it was that Zootie got killed?" Peters' eyes narrowed as he watched Mercer.

Mercer's face took on a sly look. "That little faggot. He got a little bit cute, bringin' his 'girlfriend' to the house, and we had some words about it."

Peters caught the word "faggot" and the heavy emphasis on the word "girlfriend," and he watched Mercer closely, his hand on the butt of his revolver. "What do you mean, 'you had words'?"

"Well, he come back from lookin' for Joe Earle, and he had this twist with him."

"What happened, Mercer?" Peters saw that strange light in Mercer's eyes as he spoke. He was grinning at Peters—he hadn't liked the tone of Peters' voice, but he was minding his manners—for now.

"Like I said, he brought this twist to the hideout. He knew Goddamned well that nobody outside the gang was supposed to know about the hideout. I told him to get rid of her, and he wouldn't, so I grabbed her to do it myself—only her shirt tore off, and it wasn't a twist at all. Just a skinny kid dressed up in girl clothes." He reached over for the bottle and Peters' glass, poured himself a full tumbler of the whiskey, then picked up the glass and drank half of it in a single draught. He put it down and met Peters' eyes with an insolent yellow stare.

"Anyhow, Zootie come unglued once I seen he was a queer and had touched his playmate. He come at me, and I hit him—just once." Mercer shrugged elaborately. "He fell down and didn't get up again." He picked up the glass and drank the rest of the liquor.

"What about the girl—Zootie's friend?"

Mercer smiled and ran his tongue obscenely along his big yellow teeth. "I left the sweet li'l thing with something to remember me by." He laughed again, a loud, high-pitched bark that rose goose flesh on Peters' skin.

Every fiber of Peters' being told him to shoot Mercer under the table without another moment's hesitation. The pistol was in his hand and his finger was tight to the trigger. He had the trigger half-way depressed when both of them heard something.

Mercer reacted with an animal's instinct. He killed the lights and leaped to the window, his huge body making no more sound than a leaf falling. As he peered through the filthy window, Peters came to his elbow.

"What is it?"

"I don't know." Mercer spoke in a hoarse whisper. "Thought I heard a motor quit out there. Maybe Milton's come to try and rescue his gals."

"Milton's not that big a fool," Peters hissed. "It must be somebody else." Then the thought came to him. "Farrell. It can only be Farrell. Somehow he found us."

"Farrell." Mercer said the word and it seemed thickly layered with his hate and his desire for revenge. "Okay. I'm ready for him this time. He won't get past me." He slipped away from the window and disappeared from the room.

Peters was concerned rather than worried. If Farrell had come alone, there was no great likelihood he could both best Mercer and escape Peters' gun. Peters decided to find a vantage point to wait out the confrontation. He'd take care of the victor—no matter who it was.

⊗⊠⊗

Farrell took Milton upstairs to his apartment where he went to his desk and took out the tools he knew he'd need for the night. As he slid the .38 Colt into his waistband he removed the Luger from the drawer. "Have you got a gun?" he asked the ex-smuggler.

"Peters took it." Milton held out his hand and accepted the Luger, checking the magazine before feeding a cartridge into the breech.

Farrell picked up the telephone and dialed his father's number. It rang and rang without an answer. Frowning, he called police headquarters, identified himself, and asked for Captain Casey. A moment later, Sergeant Ray Snedegar answered.

"The skipper's out for the evening, Farrell. What can I do for you?"

"Listen, Snedegar, this is an emergency—life and death. There's a woman and child who've been kidnapped, and I need to tell him where I'm going. Can you get a message to him?"

"What? What woman?"

"Look, I don't have a lot of time. There are complications and it'll take his authority to deal with them. Please don't ask a lot of questions, just help me reach Casey."

Snedegar was silent for a moment. He wasn't one of Farrell's fans. "He left word where he'd be. I'll try to reach him there— where are you?"

"I'm in my office, but you can tell him I'm going to be gone in another ten minutes." He hung up without waiting for Snedegar to reply.

Milton paced the room, looking at his watch as they waited. Farrell went to a closet and took out something that looked vaguely like a boomerang covered with black leather. He laid it on the desk while he waited.

"What's that?" Milton asked.

"The last time I met up with your boy, Mercer, he came at me with a cane knife. He came off second best, but that was mostly because I was lucky. When I see him the next time, it'll be on even terms." He took the object by one end and drew it out for Milton to see. It was a short sword, about two feet long, but curved out and down from the handle. The concave edge was honed razor sharp. "A friend brought it to me from India—it's a weapon called a *kukri* that's carried by a tribe of warriors called Ghurkas."

Milton nodded, saying nothing. He walked out of the office and sat down in the living room. Five minutes later, the call from Casey came.

"You've really got Snedegar in an uproar. What's up?"

"Listen—Milton's with me. He's been in cahoots with Captain Peters of the St. Bernard Sheriff's Department all these years. Peters engineered Chauchaut's clean-up of the parish so Milton's gang could operate there unmolested. When you visited Milton to tell him how his son was killed, he went after Peters, but Peters beat him to the punch. They've kidnapped his daughter-in-law and grandchild, and they're holding them out at the old Mouton brother's garage. I'm getting ready to go out there now, but you'll need to get some cops out there who won't take orders from Peters."

"Listen to me, Wes, you can't go out there. This is police business and police have to handle it. I can start for there now and ask for some State Police from Troop B to meet me there. Please, son, don't take the chance. You've already had one near miss with this Mercer."

Farrell heard the entreaty in the word "son" and wished that he could heed it. "I've got to go. I owe something to George Schofield yet. I can probably get there before you or the State Police."

"Damn you, can't you just for once not stick your neck out? Can't you wait and let the people who're getting paid for it take the chances?" His father's harsh words went oddly with the tender tone in his voice.

"I'm too much like you, Dad." The sound of the word shocked him—he hadn't actually meant to say it, but it had come out anyway. He only wished he could have said it to Casey's face.

After a long pause, Casey said, "Good luck, son. I'll be with you as soon as I can." He broke the connection before Farrell could reply. Farrell gently put the telephone down, picked up the big knife and went to the living room where Milton waited. "Let's go." He led Milton out the back door down to where the Packard sat waiting.

Lightning flashed as they entered Basin Street, and with the sound of thunder blasting overhead, Farrell pushed the accelerator to the floor. They made Rampart in a matter of minutes and soon after, St. Claude. As they sped to the parish line, rain lashed the road in sheets, wind buffeting the car as though it were made of cotton.

Farrell said nothing—his attention was focused on the road and the fight he knew was coming. Mercer wouldn't be easy to take this time. He was like an animal—cunning, quick to learn from a painful mistake. He would not give Farrell an easy opportunity to get inside his long reach.

Milton broke the long silence. "Farrell—Farrell."

"I'm listening."

"What was Schofield to you?"

"I'd never met him before the night he was killed. He came into a bar, a brawl started, and we fought our way out together. We got away in his car just before the cops came to break it up. For some reason he started talking to me about why he was there. He knew somebody in the Coast Guard or at Treasury had sold out to you, and he was trying to find out. He'd been lured there with the promise of a name."

"So why are you so anxious to risk your life to expose his betrayer? You're no saint, Farrell. You've made money off liquor, women, gambling, and quite a few other things. What do you care about a dead man who was just another cop?"

Farrell cut his eyes at Milton. "Maybe I liked him, and I don't like the way he was set up. He was a babe in the woods where we were concerned—he didn't stand a chance. It sticks in my craw, and I'm sick of choking on it."

"Who would ever have guessed you had any sentiment or ideals?" Milton murmured, almost to himself.

"Anybody can surprise you, Milton. Take your daughter-in-law. She loves you. She'd marry you if you asked her. She couldn't feel that way unless you showed her there was something decent in you."

Milton's bowed his head and ran his fingers through his thick gray hair. "I know she would. Sometimes, when I've allowed myself to dream, I've thought about what it would be like to have a home with a woman like her and a child to raise. But I threw all of that away, long, long ago. It's too late now. I'll belong to the law before this night's over—if I'm still alive."

"I don't have any intention of dying, Milton, and if you do what I tell you, maybe you won't, either." He paused a moment as he held the wheel against a gust of wind. "I'll tell you something I learned a few years ago. Anybody can get another chance—if he wants it."

Milton looked over at Farrell, searching the shadowy contours of his face for a moment before turning his gaze back to the rain-streaked windshield.

As they passed Jackson Barracks, Farrell began to slow down. He knew the road he wanted was not far ahead. The rain had slackened, but intermittent flares of lightning still lit the landscape while thunder rolled ominously overhead. A parish road marker warned him in plenty of time to make the turn, and with only his parking lights, he began to creep along the marl road. He had not been here since just after the fight in which the Mouton brothers had died, but he remembered that the garage had been about five miles down this particular road. When the odometer told him that they'd made four miles, he cut the parking lights and crept forward at five miles per hour.

As they reached a bend in the road, a tremendous flash of lightning back-lit the barn-like garage and house that adjoined it. Farrell shut off the engine and they both got out of the car.

"What do you plan to do?" Milton asked.

"My guess is that Sallie and Clemmie are locked up somewhere in the house. You take the front of the house, but keep out of sight. I'm going to make a circle and come in from behind. With luck, I'll be able to get inside without anyone hearing or seeing me."

"And then what?"

"I'm just playing this by ear, Milton. You'll have to do the same. If we're really lucky, Captain Frank Casey and some State Policemen will be here soon. Peters will have enough sense not to fight them, but Mercer won't go down without taking as many people with him as he can. I'm going to try to get between him and your family."

"He's barely human." Milton spoke with a tremor. Farrell could feel the chill of his fear.

"Go on," Farrell ordered. He went back to the car and opened the trunk. He removed the Ghurka *kukri*, drew it from the sheath, then turned and disappeared in the darkness.

Farrell was grateful for the bad weather—it was the only thing in their favor. He hoped it had masked their movements, but he had lived this kind of life too long to invest in such a hope. Like so many times in the past, he knew only his luck and skill stood between him and disaster.

As he neared the rear of the cavernous garage, lightning flashed again, briefly outlining the huge shape of Bart Mercer against the building. Farrell paused as the light died, just long enough for Mercer to disappear. He looked about, certain that the big man had seen him, too. He approached the garage with the short sword raised to shoulder level. As he reached the corner, Mercer leapt out at him with the cane knife, a hideous cry erupting from him. Farrell checked his stride, bringing the *kukri* up to parry the cut. His blade met Mercer's with an incredible ring of steel, and the force of the blow shook Farrell to his ankles.

Farrell twisted away, swinging down at Mercer's body. Mercer's knife parried his with extraordinary speed, but the curious angle of Farrell's knife gave it an added power on the down stroke. Farrell's blow actually knocked Mercer's blade aside, narrowly missing the big man's leg. Mercer danced nimbly away and slipped around the corner from where he'd launched his attack.

A blast of thunder shook the ground that Farrell stood on as a furious gust of wind tore his hat from his head and blew the tails of his coat behind him. Mustering his courage and his energy, he went wide around the same corner, and saw an opening yawn, the wooden door beating against the wall. Farrell felt a sickening dread grow inside him. Mercer had undoubtedly gone inside to wait for him.

Casting a last look about, he crept toward the opening, his weapon loose in his hand. He flattened himself against the barn as the wind tore at his hair and clothes, gathering his strength. When he could stand the wait no longer, he launched himself headlong through the doorway, rolling over until he came to his feet again.

Flattened against a wall, he willed himself to remain still, to bring his breathing and heartbeat under control. It was a trick he had always known, and it did not fail him now. Safe in the darkness, now he could make the rules.

As he stared into the pitch black, he saw there were gaps where the weather boards on the outside had shrunken, cracked, or rotted away over time. Through each of them, the lightning outside erratically poured brief spurts of illumination, allowing him quick glimpses of his surroundings. Not enough to see an entire picture, perhaps, but enough to provide an impression of shapes or movement.

As his ears began to grow used to the thrashing of the storm outside, he began to register other sounds. There was a scraping sound that could only be the soft slide of a leather sole across concrete. There was the sound of mouth breathing, slow, regular, but rough. But to hear it was not enough. He had to pinpoint its direction.

The wind outside was dying, and along with it the illuminating flashes grew fewer and farther between. The man-sounds grew more audible. Farrell watched the walls as he listened, and finally he was rewarded. A sudden crackle in the gloomy heavens gave him at least three seconds of illumination, and in that brief space a long shadow slid toward him. Farrell smiled, and for the first time felt the odds turning in his favor. He moved toward the shadow, holding his heavy blade across his chest.

Farrell's rubber soles made no more impact on the dusty concrete than the footsteps of a spider. By inches he moved, his breath nearly stopped. He could hear Mercer ahead of him now, and then came his smell—a rank smell, more pungent than the earthy odor of men who earn their smells through hard, honest work. This was like something foreign and unclean, something that no soap and water could dispel.

Farrell never knew what tipped the man off to his proximity, but he felt, rather than heard, something moving through the dark, musty air at him. He pulled back instinctively, tucking his head between his shoulders just as Mercer's heavy cane knife hit the wall in front of him. Before the big man could recover, Farrell raised his weapon and brought it down. It met steel and bounced away, but Farrell recovered and attacked again and again, each time striking the invisible blade in the other man's hand.

Mercer's breathing had become a thick growl of hatred and blood lust, and he slashed at Farrell. Their violent ballet moved them inevitably into a small area in the middle of the vacant barn, where a ray of light shot through the ceiling each time lightning ripped the sky. No longer content to skulk in the darkness, both men flailed wildly at each other, neither giving quarter, each of them determined to destroy what was in front of him.

Mercer's strength and power were beyond anything Farrell had ever seen, but his own speed and agility kept him even with the big man as they cut and parried and thrust and chopped. Sparks flew in the darkness between them, the blades meeting like they had some eldritch life of their own. Mercer was bellowing curses, chopping at Farrell with an inhuman strength and rage.

Farrell's arm and the *kukri* had melded into a machine, his own fury keeping fatigue and fear at bay. There would be no second place in this contest, and that knowledge edged his spirit with a keenness that matched the edge of his weapon. His knife clashed on Mercer's again and again, and as he felt the big man's blade slide from his own, a bright light flashed through the space in the roof. In that split second, Farrell brought the *kukri* up and struck down at the muscle between Mercer's neck and shoulder, burying the great knife to the heel.

The shock of the wound convulsed Mercer's body with such force that it jerked the weapon from Farrell's grasp. The big man screamed, screamed until nothing but strangled breaths escaped him. In the pale light Farrell could see him grasping at the handle of the knife, struggling to tear it out of his body. Farrell could only stand there, transfixed by the sight of the man struggling against the object that was killing him.

Mercer felt his strength leaving him. As great as it was, he knew he was dying. He let go the handle of the knife, stretched out his huge hands, and advanced on Farrell, his yellow eyes protruding from their sockets, a single purpose reflecting from them.

There was nowhere to go. Farrell had come here to kill a man, and it wasn't finished. His right hand flew to his waist and came back up with the automatic. He fanned back the hammer with the flat of his left hand and squeezed the trigger, firing again and again until the hammer struck on the empty chamber. The slugs hit Mercer in the center of his body, staggering him. His mouth opened and one last strangled sound was torn out of him as he fell backward, hitting the concrete floor with such force that clouds of dust rose all about his corpse.

Farrell stood there, his lungs laboring and his heart battering his ribs. He looked down at Mercer, knowing he was dead, but not quite believing it. No one had ever fought him harder or longer. He looked down at the empty gun and saw his hand shaking like a leaf in a high wind. With clumsy fingers, he ejected the spent magazine, shoved a fresh one into the butt, then turned. He heard noises above him, sounds like cries for help. He saw the dim form of stairs across the barn from where he stood. Crossing quickly, he climbed the steps two at a time.

"Who's in there?"

"Johnny Hope. I got a Treasury man and my brother in here, both hurt real bad. Get us out, get us out."

Farrell saw there was no key in the lock. "Stand away from the door." He fired twice into the lock and kicked at the door. It swung open and he saw the gray shapes of men in there.

"Where's Mercer?" Johnny Hope asked.

"Down there. Dead."

"You sure?" Disbelief was heavy in Johnny's voice.

Farrell removed his razor from inside his coat and slashed Johnny's bonds with a single deft stroke. "Dead sure. You'd better stay here. Luke Peters is probably still around. After we've secured the grounds somebody'll be up for you."

"Praise Jesus. I thought I was a dead man tonight."

"Stay put." Farrell's voice was blunt. "The night's not over yet."

Chapter 17

Jeremiah hunched over the wheel of Zootie's Chevrolet, struggling to see the landmarks he'd been told to watch for. He had already gone several miles in the wrong direction before deciding to stop at a Texaco station and ask the negro mechanic if he knew of the Mouton brothers. The craggy-faced mechanic looked at his bruised face a bit strangely until he explained that he'd fallen down a flight of stairs.

"What for you wanna go out there on a night like this, boy? Ain't nobody there?"

"I know that," Jeremiah replied. "But I didn't have to work tonight, and I've been thinkin' of buyin' it."

"Man, you sure pickin' a hell of a night to go lookin' at property," the man said, shaking his head. "You liable to run off the road into a ditch, and they ain't many places over there that're gonna send out a wrecker tonight."

"Maybe you're right. But I still need to know how to get there. Tomorrow'll be soon enough, I reckon."

"Now you're usin' your head, brutha." The mechanic proceeded to explain in detail how to reach the part of the parish where the abandoned garage was located, all of which Jeremiah copied on a scrap of paper with a pencil stub he'd found in Zootie's glove compartment. Thanking the man, he got back into the Chevrolet and departed for the garage.

Jeremiah felt a heaviness in his spirit that he couldn't shake. He was glad the drive was taking so much physical energy and attention, because he could not stand to think about all that had happened to him.

By the time he reached the vicinity of the garage, the rain had slackened to a hard drizzle, but violent discharges of lightning continued to provide him with brief glimpses of the most forbidding landscape he'd ever seen. He was in bayou country where tall stands of waving grass and trees draped in heavy veils of Spanish moss provoked an eerie feeling in the young man.

Not having thought to switch off his head lamps, he saw clearly the Model A Ford abandoned on the shoulder of the unpaved road. He had a brief moment to wonder why it was parked in this uninhabited area before a brilliant blade of lightning slashed the sky over the house and garage some two hundred yards ahead. Belatedly, he cut the lights and switched off the engine. Taking a moment to pull down the brim of his cap and button his jacket to the neck, he picked up the revolver and got out of the car.

He had no idea what he was doing, but since he'd already given up the idea of living, he proceeded directly toward the house, planning to simply walk in and shoot the first person he saw. When he was less than fifty yards from the buildings, he heard a tormented, soul-splitting scream, followed by a fusillade of gunshots that stopped him in his tracks. At another time, he might have turned and fled, but not tonight. As Jeremiah drew nearer, he saw a man in dark clothes crouched beside a wrecked car. Suddenly, another man ran headlong toward them from the house.

⁜

When Peters heard Mercer's death scream and the shots that followed it, he knew that Farrell had bested his killer. The incredible fact of Mercer's death destroyed any confidence Peters had that he might stand up to Farrell and come out on top. He opened a window and jumped to the wet ground with his gun in his fist. Throwing a quick glance around him, he began running from the house.

He'd only gone a few yards when a man rose in front of him. In a split second, he recognized Milton, saw his gun, and fired. Milton went down hard. Without breaking stride, the lanky deputy vaulted the body and continued his headlong rush for freedom. Adrenaline was pumping through him, lending him strength and speed. He cast a backward glance—no one was following him. As he faced front, he was startled by the sight of a slight figure in dark work clothes ahead of him. He had time only to think Zootie? before fire erupted from the other man's fist. Peters felt a hard blow on his chest. He tried to keep running, to raise his own gun to fire, but as he moved, he felt himself slow down, felt his strength flowing out of him. He was vaguely aware of the revolver slipping from his fingers before his legs collapsed under him and darkness closed in.

⊗⊗⊗

Jeremiah didn't know why the stranger was running toward him, but he'd seen him shoot down the other man. For Jeremiah, the act of naked aggression combined with the headlong flight from the house spelled only one thing to him—the man was in some way connected to Mercer. Instinctively he fired. The man collapsed, then lay there, his eyes fixed at the flickering sky.

Jeremiah had never killed before. A part of him wanted to drop the gun and run away—but he hadn't seen Mercer yet. He reached the house and pushed open the door, the gun level in his fist. Nerves were jumping in his face, but he kept going, heedless of what lurked in the unlit rooms.

Finding no one on the ground floor, he took what remained of his courage and mounted the stairs, his eyes searching above him. By the time he'd made the head of the stairs, his heart was pounding and his breath was coming in ragged pants. There were three doors up here, all of them closed. He went to the first one and threw it open with all his might. Nothing. He went to the second and found it locked. This time he heard a whimpering that startled him. He saw a key in the lock, turned it, and kicked the door open. Shoving the gun out in front of him, he advanced toward the bed. As lightning flared outside, he saw a white woman bound, blindfolded, and gagged on the bed, and a small whimpering girl in Mickey Mouse pajamas clinging to her. Sticking the pistol into his waistband, Jeremiah removed the blindfold and gag. The woman looked at him, her mouth and eyes wide with terror.

"Who are you?"

"My name is Sallie Milton," the woman said in a rush. "A horrible man kidnapped me and my little girl. Please help us, please."

Jeremiah was startled by this new responsibility. He hadn't come to save anybody, only to avenge Zootie and find a cleansing death of his own. "Do you know where he is? His name is Mercer."

"No. I fainted and woke up here tied up and unable to see or speak. I don't even know where we are. Please, untie me, please."

He found that the ropes were bound so tightly that untying them was beyond his strength. He remembered Zootie having a knife, quickly searched his pockets, and found a long thin clasp knife with mother-of-pearl handles. He opened one of the blades and began sawing at the ropes.

As the ropes parted, Sallie pulled the little girl to her as both of them broke into long, racking sobs.

He looked down on them with tremendous pity. "I got to find Mercer and kill him. Stay here." It was useless advice, and he knew it, but he could not cope with another responsibility until he'd done what he came to do.

He left the room and went down the stairs quickly, all pretense of stealth abandoned. He exited the house and saw an open passage yawning in the side of the garage. He was vaguely aware of the distant sound of sirens. Had he been less involved with his own personal mission, he might have remarked to himself how strange it was to hear those city noises out here in the bayou. He continued to the passage and went through it without hesitation.

It was dark in there, but he'd been in darkness so long that it took no time for his eyes to adjust to the deeper gloom. The flickering of light through the holes in the walls and ceiling drew his attention to a heap on the floor. When Jeremiah recognized the face of his dead enemy, he felt an overpowering sense of defeat. He could not avenge his lover, nor join him in death. Jeremiah began to cry, and as he wept, he kicked the corpse, over and over, as he cursed the man in every way he knew. He didn't hear the approach of footsteps behind him.

"Put the gun down, Zootie." It was a voice Jeremiah didn't recognize.

"Zootie's dead. He's dead and this bastard killed him." He dropped his revolver on Mercer's body and collapsed to his knees.

As the man removed Jeremiah's cap, his long, light-brown hair fell in waves around his face.

"He can't hurt anybody now. He can't hurt anybody ever again." Farrell shoved his gun into his waistband and walked out of the garage toward the flashing lights of the police cars arriving on the property.

He hadn't gone very far when he saw the bodies—first Milton and then Peters—each of them dead. Farrell stood there for a moment, consumed with disappointment. He had gotten some measure of revenge for George Schofield, but he still didn't know the name of the man who'd betrayed him. And the only man who could have told him—Luke Peters—lay at his feet with a bullet in his chest. He wanted to curse, but he lacked the strength.

"Wes." It was his father's voice. "Wes, are you all right?"

He felt Frank Casey's strong hands on his arm and shoulder, smelled the familiar aromas of Old Spice and molasses-soaked pipe tobacco, and put his hand over his father's. "I'm okay, Dad. I'm okay."

"Thank God."

"Listen, there's three men in the attic of the garage. One of them is that kid Treasury agent, and the other two are negroes who were members of the gang. The T-Man's got two bullets in him and he looks pretty bad. The younger of the two negroes looks like he got hit by a car or something."

"I got two ambulances directly behind me," Casey said. "I'll make sure they get the word. What about the woman you said was kidnapped?"

"She and her little girl are unhurt so far as I can see. There's somebody else, too."

"Who?"

"A young girl dressed up in a man's clothes. She's in the garage. I found her there a few minutes ago kicking Mercer's corpse. I think she came to kill him."

"He's dead, then."

"Yeah, Dad. It wasn't easy, but he's finished."

Casey's hand was still in his, and neither of them seemed to want to let go.

"There's one more thing," Farrell said. "Milton claimed he didn't know the name of the man who set Schofield up. I didn't get the name, and Luke Peters is lying over there, dead—he can't tell us a Goddamned thing."

Casey sighed. He knew what this failure meant to his son. He squeezed his hand again, then said, "Let me get the ambulance people and the State Police up to speed. If you need to go and sit down, my car's over there, and there's a flask in the glove compartment."

Farrell exhaled a long, shuddering breath, then let his father go. "Thanks. I think I'll take you up on that after I tell Sallie about Milton. I don't want her to come out here and find him—like that."

Casey walked toward the lead State Police car and began shouting instructions. As the men got out and began scattering across the landscape, Casey looked up at the sky and saw that the storm had passed. A three-quarter moon bathed the bayou in a soft glow as stars dotted the sky for the first time that night. Farrell had done the best he could, but Casey knew he wasn't satisfied. He wondered if he ever would be.

Farrell reentered the house and found Sallie Milton coming down the stairs, holding the little girl protectively in her arms. Sallie's eyes were wide with shock, and her face was pale. As she got to the foot of the staircase, she met Farrell's eyes, and saw the somber cast of his face.

"August—is he—?"

Farrell shook his head. "He didn't make it."

She sank down on the steps, clutching the child in her lap, her face twitching as she tried not to give in to the tears. Farrell knelt and put his hand on her shoulder.

"On the way out here, he told me he loved you. He said that more than anything in the world, he'd liked to have settled down with you and helped you raise Clemmie."

"He—he said that?" Her breath was catching in her throat as she fought to keep the sobs down, but the ghost of a smile traced itself across her lips.

"Yes. But he also said that he'd thrown the chance for that away long ago, and didn't expect to get it back. He came out here to give you the chance to live again. He bought that for you with the only thing he had left."

She nodded dumbly, as the realization hit her. She hugged the child a bit tighter and closed her eyes. After a long moment, Farrell got up and went back outside.

⊗⊗⊗

Israel Daggett and Sam Andrews found Jeremiah sitting on the floor beside Mercer's body. His knees were drawn up to his chest and his face was cradled in his arms.

Daggett knelt beside him. "Jeremiah?"

"Yeah, what do you want?"

"It's all over now. You need to come on out of here."

"Let me alone. Let me die."

Daggett hesitated, then put a hand lightly on the boy's shoulder. "Killing him wouldn't have helped. Zootie would still be gone. You can't quit living, either. He wouldn't want you to."

"What the hell you know about it, man? What in the world can you know 'bout what this feels like?" Jeremiah raised his head from his arms and stared into Daggett's face, his soft features blurred with emotion.

"Quite a bit." Daggett bowed his head, and his voice went soft. "Some years ago, I was framed into prison on a murder beef— I spent five years in there, knowing every day that I didn't deserve it. When I got out, I found out the woman I loved and wanted to marry had been murdered, and then later found out it was my own best friend had done it. Sure, I wanted to die, and I wanted somebody to pay, but in the end, I had to find a way to live in a world that'd been ripped apart. It wasn't easy."

"How? How am I gonna live after all this piece of trash took from me?" Jeremiah turned his face toward the black detective. In the glow of Andrews' flashlight beam, Daggett could see the bruises and cuts on the boy's face that Mercer had put there while he was raping him.

"It stabs you like a hot iron every day for a while," he replied. "Then it gets to be a dull ache. It never really goes away, but after a while, it's like a clock ticking on the wall. You don't notice it anymore."

Jeremiah put his face back on his arms. "I wish I could just cut out my heart and stop it beatin'."

Daggett stood up, and lifted the boy up by his arm. "Come on. I know a doctor who'll treat you and not ask you any questions you don't want to answer. I'll take you there." He led the frail, wounded boy out of the garage and down to his squad car, where he helped Jeremiah lie down across the back seat while he covered him with a blanket.

Andrews remained beside Mercer's body on his haunches, marveling at the size of the man, at all that it had taken to kill him. After a while, he shivered, shook himself, and left the body with nothing but the dust to keep it company.

⊗⊗⊗

In the week after the fight at the garage, facts came to light in small pieces that eventually presented a more-or-less complete picture of Milton's criminal activities over a period of nearly twenty years. He'd left a lengthy letter to his daughter-in-law in which he explained his Prohibition-era smuggling operation, the car theft ring that had grown out of it, and most importantly, the collusion with Captain Luke Peters. There was, however, nothing about the Schofield murder, or evidence of collusion with anyone in the Coast Guard command or the Treasury enforcement arm.

The ballistic evidence that connected Bart Mercer with the murders of Schofield, Valdez, and Detective Blanton was confirmed by the discovery of Mercer's Winchester Model '97 shotgun, a special model that had been designed for use by the U. S. Army in the trenches of France. His fingerprints all over it, and fingerprints were found on shells similar to the one used to kill Detective Blanton.

Crime Lab Chief Nick Delgado, on Casey's orders, had also visited the scene of the Oscar Boulet incident and conducted a thorough investigation there. Behind the house were a quantity of .44-40 cartridges and several spent bullets in the back wall of the house, itself. The bullets taken from the wall of the house were found to be a positive match with the slug taken from Sheriff Chauchaut's leg. The weapon, a lever-action Winchester repeater, was later found in the trunk of Luke Peters' station wagon. During an interview with Sheriff Chauchaut, it became clear that Peters had lured the sheriff out to Boulet's house with a story about information from a non-existent stool pigeon. Once there, he went to the rear of the house, ostensibly to cut off any retreat, waited until he heard the Sheriff call Boulet out onto the porch, then entered the house and fired at Chauchaut from the front window. This action precipitated the gunfire that had mortally wounded Boulet. A cartridge case matching those found behind the house was discovered under a chair in Boulet's front room.

Although Sheriff Paul Chauchaut had lost a good deal of blood, Peters' bullet had passed through without breaking his leg. As the full truth of Luke Peters' treachery became front-page news, Chauchaut checked himself out of the hospital and returned to his office in Chalmette, where he shut himself away from the hoard or newspaper reporters who clamored for his comment.

Having experienced the support of newspaper editors and politicians across the state, Chauchaut now found himself almost completely alone as, one by one, his former supporters distanced themselves from his listing campaign. He had a cot brought into his office and hot meals were ordered in from a nearby restaurant, and he communicated with the outside world with his personal secretary. After two days of looking at the sheriff's haunted face, the deputy requested a transfer to patrol duty.

Chauchaut's disappearance was so abrupt and complete that it gave the newspapers more ammunition to use against him. When no statement came from his campaign manager, newspapers across the state began asking questions in their headlines. The negro weeklies in New Orleans, Baton Rouge, and Shreveport declared that the death of Oscar Boulet was a cold-blooded murder, and called for Chauchat's ouster.

After facing journalistic hostility and skepticism by himself for two days, campaign manager Arthur Foy finally discovered Chauchaut's whereabouts. When he entered Chauchaut's office, Foy almost didn't recognize him. Chauchaut seemed physically diminished, his earnest demeanor and piercing gaze evaporated. He'd never seen Chauchaut take a drink, but a bottle of cheap bourbon and a filmy glass sat on his desk beside his ivory-handled revolver.

"For the love of God, Paul—you've got to make a statement of some kind if you expect to save your skin." Foy's eyes were bloodshot, and his skin was grainy from lack of sleep.

"What can I say? My best friend—a man I raised up from sergeant to chief deputy—betrayed me to criminals. I'm the victim here, Arthur." Chauchaut's jaw jutted defiantly, but he was clearly frightened.

Foy shook his head in wonder. "Are you insane? The papers have got a confession from this bootlegger that says Peters was on the pad to him for about fifteen years—where the hell were you all that time? Asleep?"

"Don't talk to me like that. My reputation is spotless—I brought criminal gangs to justice—I shot it out with Ike Gelhard myself."

Foy pursed his lips in disgust. "The information they're giving out is that Gelhard didn't even kill Constable Valdez—you made your reputation killing the wrong man." He shook his head. "Don't you see how this looks? Either you knew Peters was involved with Milton and turned a blind eye to it, or you were too damn stupid to see it. Either way you're washed up."

Chauchaut looked up, shocked. That his climb to glory could be over had never occured to him. "Don't talk nonsense, Arthur. Governor Bastrop just endorsed me. I can't lose. I just can't."

Foy stood up, removing an envelope from his pocket. He very solemnly placed it on the sheriff's desk beside the open bottle of bourbon. "The governor's calling a press conference in a half hour. You know what he's going to tell 'em, Paul? That he was deceived. By tomorrow he won't even know your name."

"No. He wouldn't do that—he wouldn't."

Foy's mouth curled cynically. "The voters like a winner, Paul. Right now you smell like rotting fish. That's my resignation I just handed you. If I were you, I'd just bow out quietly."

Chauchaut's mouth hung open. He didn't even hear the door open and close as Foy left his office. He swept the letter and the bottle off his desk, not hearing the crash at it hit the floor. He looked at the gun, had an image of putting it into his mouth, but he gagged at the thought.

The phone at his elbow rang, but it continued for a minute or more before he came sufficiently to his senses to pick it up. "H-hello?"

"It's Jack Trosclair, Paul. Paul, are you there?"

"Y-yeah, Jack. I'm—I'm still here."

"The governor's just repudiated you, Paul. What are you going to do?"

Something between a laugh and a sob escaped Chauchaut's mouth. "Got your pencil, Jack?"

"Yeah. What do you want to say?"

"Say I just retired. I retired and I'm goin' on a trip."

The editor's voice was carefully controlled and modulated, as though he very much feared saying the wrong thing. "Going where?"

"Just goin'. No forwarding address."

∞

Special Agent James Schofield survived the surgery for his gunshot wounds, but was in critical condition and remained under guard in a private room. His service revolver had been found in a storm drain several blocks from the scene of the attempt on Commander Bracken's life, and ballistics tests verified that it was the weapon used. Bracken was in a coma, and it was too early to say if he would survive the attack.

Because Schofield himself had not yet regained consciousness, no formal charges had been filed, but Frank Casey reluctantly conceded that unless some other evidence surfaced, there would be no choice but to charge the young agent with attempted murder. Chief Resident Agent Paul Ewell concurred with the assessment.

Joe Earle Hope also remained in critical condition at Charity Hospital. He was found to have a broken leg, broken pelvis, several broken ribs, and a chipped vertebra. He was under sedation and unable to communicate very much. His brother, Johnny, was in Parish Prison on multiple charges of car theft and accessory to murder. His sister, Arthel Dandy, visited him every day, and sat with the unconscious Joe Earle part of each night. Her world had been shattered, and she didn't know how she would ever repair it.

Wesley Farrell spent much of the following week with Savanna, letting her sure touch and quiet strength help him get over all that he had been through. She had seen him like this before—outwardly calm and steady, but with a strange, indefinable look in his eye that reflected back the shock of a fight and the terror he had ignored to survive it.

They were lying on her bed with the window open one evening. The weather was perfect—a cool breeze swept down from the north and for once, the humidity was below fifty percent, making New Orleans a temporary paradise. Music that was like a sweet wine floated up to them from the open doors of clubs all along Rampart Street.

"Ever thought of going somewhere else?" Farrell asked as he lay tight to her side, her hand captured in his.

"Where would I go? I got everything I need here."

"Havana."

She raised up to look down into his face. "Havana? Cuba? What are you talkin' about?"

"It's where Dad and Mother went to get married. It's where they lived for the first couple of years."

She smiled. "How would we get there?"

"I know a man with an airplane who owes me some favors. He could fly us over there and we could take a vacation. Walk around the city, dance in a nightclub."

As he talked, she realized he wasn't joking. She sat up, turned, and stared out the window. To walk down a street with him, hand in hand, to dance in his arms to the music of a live orchestra, was like a dream to her. It didn't seem real.

He watched her, and imagined the things she might be thinking. "It's different there. People are a lot of different colors in Havana. We'd fit in."

As the image took hold, she looked down at him, her mouth open and her eyes wide. It still didn't seem real, but he was talking like it was fruit on a tree—hanging there waiting for your hand to pick it. She couldn't speak, couldn't do anything. She lay down against him again, wrapped her arms around him and held him as tightly as her strength would allow to still the trembling she felt inside.

The next day, Farrell drove across Canal Street to Charity Hospital on Tulane. He parked his car on a side street, then went inside and asked for James Schofield's room. He was directed to the fifth floor, and after an elevator ride and a short walk, he found himself at a door flanked by two uniformed police officers. Through the open door to the room, he saw a well-built blonde man in khakis on a chair watching the unconscious man. After he identified himself, the police officers let Farrell go inside.

The blonde man heard his footsteps and stood up. His insignia identified him as a Coast Guard lieutenant commander.

"I'm Wesley Farrell. How is he?"

"Commander Emmett Kelso." The blonde man offered his hand. "He's still in a coma. They can't tell me for sure if he'll make it or not. I can't believe how badly this all turned out. His brother was my best friend, and Jimmy is like a kid brother to me."

"I knew his brother slightly," Farrell said. "I'm sorry I wasn't more help to this man. Things didn't work out like I hoped. They tell me he's under suspicion for the shooting of a Commander Bracken. What was his connection?"

Kelso shrugged. "Jimmy was looking for somebody with a reason to kill his brother. Bracken had been an intelligence officer during Prohibition, and because Bracken's name figured in the notes George left behind, Jimmy was suspicious of him. I don't know—he must've found out something about Bracken that made him flip his wig." Kelso's face wore a mournful look. "If I'd just kept a closer eye on him, this would never have happened. I could've—" He broke off, took out a white handkerchief and blew his nose. He was wiping his eyes when he turned back to Farrell. "It was bad enough losing George. To lose Jimmy, too, is a hell of a blow."

Farrell nodded. He still felt his own sense of failure that the last piece of the puzzle had eluded him. "I'll be on my way. I hope he'll come out of this somehow."

Kelso nodded. "Thanks. Thanks a lot for everything. I heard about all you did. George would be grateful."

Farrell nodded, shook hands again, then left the room.

He was on his way out of the hospital when he saw Israel Daggett come into the lobby. Daggett spotted him at the same time, and came over to him.

"Didn't expect to see you here."

Farrell shrugged. "Well, I got restless. There're things that I don't know, and I guess I'm still hoping—" He made a face and shook his head.

Daggett gave him an understanding look. "We have to go through a lot of that. I must have a filing cabinet full of unanswered questions and cases that didn't quite come together. I was on my way up to see Joe Earle Hope."

"He's the kid who was so banged up—the brother of Johnny Hope, right?"

"Yeah. I think the kid got hurt trying to help his brother. Johnny says he had nothing to do with the gang, but he may be trying to protect him. They're both lookin' at a stretch at 'Gola." He paused to scratch his neck, then said, "If you're not doin' anything, why not come upstairs with me for a minute. Joe Earle's probably still out cold, and if he is, we can go somewhere and you can tell me the answers to some questions *I* didn't get answered."

"Sure. I've got nothing else to do."

The pair went to the elevator and took a car to the seventh floor, where the male negro ward was located. After Daggett showed the head nurse his badge, she conducted them to the end of a ward where a bed sat with privacy screens around it. The nurse moved a screen and gestured to them to go in.

The boy was flat on his back with a leg in traction. His eyes were closed, and his face wore the look of someone under considerable strain. Daggett frowned and shook his head. "He's awful young. I hate to see all this trouble piled on a kid." He pulled up a chair and indicated that Farrell should do the same.

"What do you know about this boy?" Farrell asked.

"Not much. He hasn't got a record. Been a mechanic and body-work man at a few garages—mainly pick-up work here and there. Nothing that would've kept him from acting as a full-time member of the gang, even though his brother claims he had no part of it. From what I can tell, they all lived double lives to keep people from asking too many questions."

The boy's breathing changed and he gave a sigh. His hands stirred beside him, and a groan came from his mouth. Daggett turned his attention to the young man and spoke to him. "Joe Earle. Joe Earle, can you hear me?"

The boy's eyes opened to a slit, and he seemed disoriented. He coughed and cleared his throat. Daggett poured some water into a glass, then held the glass so the young man could get the straw into his mouth. He drank steadily for almost a minute before he signaled that he'd had enough.

"Who're you?" Joe Earle's eyes opened a bit wider now.

"I'm Sergeant Daggett with the police. Mr. Farrell is the one who rescued you about a week ago. You've been in a pretty bad way."

"Johnny. Is he—?"

Daggett nodded. "Johnny's alive, but he's over in Parish Prison. He's been arraigned and charged with car theft and accessory to murder."

Joe Earle struggled to push himself up, but Daggett restrained him. With Farrell's help, he arranged the pillows so Joe Earle was propped up a bit more comfortably.

"Johnny ain't killed nobody," he said in a rasp. "It was Mercer and Hines went after that brutha and killed him. Johnny ain't never hurt nobody in his life."

"How do you know?"

"I was there. I seen Hines bring the brutha in. Boxcars Perry— he was in the gang with us—like to blew a gasket when he saw the man, 'cause he knew him for a cop. He told Mercer. The murderin' bastard took out after him with Hines and that shotgun, and when they come back, I was there. I seen the looks on their faces. Johnny wasn't nowhere near—" The effort of defending his brother was almost too much for him. His complexion grew waxy and he sank back against the pillows, exhausted.

"Okay, okay." Daggett put a restraining hand on his shoulder. "If you're willing to testify to that, you'll keep your brother out of the chair."

"What about Mercer and Hines?" The young man's voice was a harsh whisper.

"From what we can tell, Mercer killed Hines, and later Mr. Farrell killed Mercer in a fight. August Milton was killed by Luke Peters, and Peters is dead, too. Ring-around-the-rosy." Daggett sat back in his chair.

"Mercer dead." Joe Earle closed his eyes. "He's got to be in hell now, the filthy cruel bastard. I seen him—I seen him go after the cop and I seen him kill the other one, too."

Farrell's eyes widened, and he leaned forward. "What other one?"

Joe Earle laid a hand across his eyes. He was exhausted from the talking, and his words were coming out slurred. "The—the sailor. Coast Guard man. Was years ago. Made me go along, but— but I couldn't shoot nobody."

Farrell was standing over him now, his hand on the boy's wrist. "Listen to me. It's important. You and Mercer were in the car— was there anybody else? Was there anybody else?"

Daggett knew Farrell was on to something, but he kept silent, his eyes shifting quickly between the other two men.

"Yeah. Other man—the driver. He—he's the one set up the hit. Heard Mercer say so."

Farrell put a hand under the boy's neck and leaned down so his face was close to Joe Earle's. "What was his name? Tell me his name."

∞∞∞

Frank Casey and eight uniformed policemen were waiting outside when Lieutenant Commander Emmett Kelso walked out of the front door of Charity Hospital. Close behind him were Israel Daggett, Wesley Farrell, and Treasury Agent Paul Ewell. Kelso was adjusting his cap when he looked up and saw the police. He continued walking, not looking at any of them, his thoughts fixed on returning to the Coast Guard Station and on some monthly reports he had to file.

"Commander Kelso," Frank Casey called. "Stop where you are, please."

As Kelso slowed to a stop, he looked around with an unconcerned look. He stood straight and tall, like an officer on parade. His uniform was starched and pleated according to regulation. His physique was perfection itself from his regimen of the right foods, plenty of exercise, and no liquor or cigarettes. He could have been an image in a recruiting poster.

"Are you talking to me?"

"You're under arrest for the murder of Commander George Schofield," Casey said. "I have to warn you that anything you say can be used against you later."

"And you'll also be charged with multiple violations of the Volstead Act, divulging classified information to a criminal organization, accepting bribes, and Goddamn near anything else I can charge you with, you son of a bitch," Agent Ewell said through clenched teeth.

Kelso regarded the two men with a bland expression, as though they'd done no more than comment on the weather. "You shouldn't let yourself get so steamed up, Agent Ewell," Kelso said mildly. "A man's got to take care of himself if he expects to live to a ripe old age. Losing your temper like that—it could do bad things to you."

Casey looked at Ewell. "He's as loony as a bedbug. Put some cuffs on him, Sergeant, and take him to headquarters."

A uniformed sergeant stepped forward, pulled Kelso's wrists behind his back, and snapped the cuffs around them. Kelso stood there, looking at Casey and Ewell, saying nothing as he was taken away.

Casey looked at Farrell. "You satisfied now?"

Farrell nodded at his father. "Yeah. I'm satisfied.

Epilogue

Some days later, James Schofield came out of his coma, and found the world considerably changed. He'd lost consciousness thinking he was dying, awakened to find that he'd briefly been a murder suspect, and was told that a person he'd liked and trusted was in jail with numerous charges against him.

It took him a while to gain enough strength to talk, but when the police and Treasury men were through questioning him, he asked to speak to Farrell.

"I don't get it," Schofield said when Farrell explained his brief acquaintance with his brother. "You knew him for less than half an hour, but you went to all this trouble, risked your neck—and after I gave you the third degree." He shook his head. "I guess that makes me a prize chump."

"Let's say you were no dumber than any other young cop with a chip on his shoulder. But you came to town to find a killer and you had to suspect everybody. That's the way it works—at least, so the cops tell me."

Schofield was rueful. "I suspected everybody except the person I should have. I still can't believe it was Emmett. He was like a brother to us. He loved George."

"He might've loved George, but he fingered him and drove the car the night of the hit. Once Joe Earle Hope identified him as the driver of the Pontiac the night your brother was killed, the cops stopped taking some things for granted. For instance, when they realized that he'd quietly moved you into his house, it didn't take the cops long to figure out that he'd used the opportunity to take your service gun from your valise to use on Bracken. It's just dumb luck the bullet didn't penetrate Bracken's skull."

"So he's gonna make it. I'm glad, but it's one more person I've got to eat crow in front of."

"Kelso worked you and Bracken—he set things up, egged you on—and under interrogation, he admitted it. He hadn't liked Bracken very much—he envied him in some respects. He got a kick out of the idea that by murdering him, it might cast suspicion on Bracken's activities during Prohibition. And, he figured that by using your gun, he'd make you the patsy and put an end to your investigation."

Schofield groaned. "I'm the one who told him where the gun was. I remember telling him that Ewell had ordered me to leave my service revolver in my valise." He sank back on the bed and threw an arm over his eyes. He lay there like that for some time, Farrell watching him quietly.

"Sure, you didn't know him as well as you thought, but there was no way you could have. He was two people in the same body. The cops had a doctor who specializes in psychiatry talk to him for a long while after they arrested him. He says Kelso is a psychopathic personality. I don't know all the fancy terminology that goes with that—the simple explanation is that he doesn't know the difference between right and wrong."

"How could he fool George like that?"

"The way I understand it, people like him are smarter than average and have a natural charm—even a seductive quality. But they also lack a moral compass. They've been talking to people he served with and served over, and they started to uncover the ways he always got what he wanted—cheating when he had to, lying when that's what it took, even making other people look bad so he could shine by comparison. He sabotaged anybody who was in competition with him while he was passing every test and winning every commendation. He wanted it all, and he wanted it fast, which is how such people are, so the head-shrinker says."

"What good did it do for him to betray my brother and the service to people like Peters and Milton? Was the money that important to him?"

"It was another trophy to him, sure. He was able to buy himself a house, a fast car. He envied people like Bracken who had a lot of nice things, things that a guy from a poor family, like him, could never have on a military salary. He was probably looking for a guy like Luke Peters long before Peters found him."

"That still doesn't explain why he helped them murder my brother." Farrell noticed that the anger that had marked Schofield on their first meeting was gone now. He looked prematurely aged, his eyes filled with regret.

"The psychiatrist said people like him can even kill what they love if what they love gets in the way of what they want. Ultimately, Kelso wanted a real command—your brother's command. He figured it was owed to him.

"When he realized your brother was wise to the fact that somebody was tipping Milton and Morrison's gang as to where the patrols would be on given nights, it all came together for him. He knew he had to kill George to cover himself, and at the same time, he also knew he'd step into George's shoes. With his record and the consistent A-One fitness reports your brother had written, the odds were good that he'd be promoted and given command of the unit."

"And George must've shared his suspicions about the information leak," the young Treasury agent said bitterly.

"You said it yourself, kid. He and George loved each other like brothers. Sooner or later, George had to share his suspicions with Kelso—the man he trusted implicitly—his second in command. Then you came to town and shared what you knew. You were next on the list—one way or another."

Schofield shrugged. "I was no smarter than George. I believed everything Emmett said—I followed his lead when I went to interrogate some of the people on George's list. I figured if a natural leader like Emmett saw something wrong, there must be something wrong. Jesus, I'm a sap."

"But you were determined to find the killer," Farrell reminded him. "The very fact of your going around trying to force confessions out of people made Kelso consider the possibility that you might eventually figure out the truth—so he did the only thing he knew—after he helped engineer the blow-up at Commander Bracken's home, he lured him to the docks with a telephone call, waited for him there, and shot him with your gun. Afterward, he pitched the gun where he was pretty sure it would be found. Once it was, naturally you'd be blamed." Farrell got out his cigarette case, took one, and lit it. As he expelled the smoke from his lungs, he looked over at Schofield. "It's all over. You got what you came for. So what are you going to do now?"

Schofield's mouth had a brittle look. "Well, I haven't exactly covered myself in glory as a detective. I was so busy trying to get revenge that I let it override everything I'd ever learned about making a proper investigation." He paused for a moment, staring off into the room. "A few days ago, a man told me that he'd been a flop as a sailor, and that he'd been lucky enough to find something that he was a lot better at. It may be too late, but maybe I could get back into the Academy, and do what I wanted in the first place—follow my brother into the service. To paraphrase what that man said to me, 'as a detective, I stink.' If I go quietly, maybe it'll keep them from sacking me."

Farrell got up and held his hat down alongside his leg. "Don't be so tough on yourself, kid. Believe it or not, the cops are crediting your help in cracking the case."

Schofield's mouth fell open. "You're joking."

"Nope. True, you left foot tracks on people, and Commander Bracken's wife would still be happy to roast you over a slow fire, but according to Ewell, you're supposed to get a commendation for helping to crack a five-year old murder and expose corruption within the Treasury Department. He's recommended to Washington that you be transferred down here to his section." He put on his hat and grinned at the younger man. "If you decide to continue with Treasury, though, try not to lead with your chin anymore, okay? Your head's pretty hard, but sooner or later you'll put some permanent dents into it."

Schofield offered a wan smile. "Thanks, Farrell. For me, and for George."

Farrell nodded. "Call me when they let you out. I'll buy you a drink and you can tell me more about him."

"I'll do that."

Farrell paused at the door and looked back at Schofield. "They tell me Kelso said a funny thing as they were taking him to his cell."

"What?"

"He said George was a hero, that he died a hero's death, and that he—Kelso, that is—was proud of him. Maybe we all should be."

The young man watched as Farrell left the room, then he closed his eyes and drifted into a deep, dreamless sleep.

⋙

The Café Tristesse hummed with its normal Saturday night crowd. Frank Casey sat across from his son at Farrell's private table at the back of the club.

"So what's going to happen to the Hope brothers?"

"Well," Casey said, "Johnny's going to serve time for car theft, there's no getting around that. He's a two-time loser, so the best he can hope for is a five-spot at Angola. He wasn't much more than a flunky, and he's got no history of violent crime, so at least he'll avoid the chair."

"What about Joe Earle?"

Casey smiled. "Well, I called a friend at the Urban League to see if they'd be interested in helping Joe Earle out. I told him that he was a young man who'd gotten into trouble because of his brother's influence, and said that since he'd helped us crack the Schofield murder case, he deserved a chance to straighten himself out."

"So are they going to help him?"

"Matthew Meriweather said he'd take the case. He's one of the best attorneys in the city, and somebody they respect in the District Attorney's Office. He thinks he can get Joe Earle off with a probationary sentence."

Farrell nodded. "That's good. If he needs any money, let me know. I owe Joe Earle, too, for answering that five-year-old question for me."

"I'll tell Meriweather what you said." Casey paused to take a sip of the martini in front of him, then he sat back and regarded his son. "This has been some week. Thanks to you, five murders have been cleared up, and you kept Chauchaut out of the governor's mansion. Considering what his winning the election might have meant for the state, you deserve a medal, but I guess you'll have to settle for my thanks. And thanks, too, for trusting me, for confiding in me. That means more than I can say."

"Forget it, Dad. I'm glad that, for once, there's no kick-back, and no need for you take the heat for the laws I bent. I owed you that—for some time now."

"I never thought to hear anyone call me 'Dad'—it sounds fine. Thank you, son."

"It sounds fine to say it."

They were interrupted by the arrival of Brigid Longley, who favored each of them with a radiant smile as Casey stood to hold her chair. "Are the two of you finished telling your dirty jokes?"

"We're too old and dignified for that, Brigid. I was just tying up a few loose ends for my partner."

She smiled at him, then looked at Farrell. "You know, Wes, it's the strangest thing."

"What's that?"

"There are times when the two of you are together—you resemble each other in funny ways. You even have some mannerisms in common. A person might think you were related."

"Did you know that Wes is about to take a little trip to Havana?" Casey said quickly. "By the way, when are you leaving, Wes?"

Farrell smiled at his father and his new ladyfriend. My family is growing, he thought to himself. "I was thinking of leaving next week. A friend of mine with a twin-engine seaplane offered to fly me across the Gulf. I might be gone for a while."

"How lovely," Brigid exclaimed. "Are you going alone?"

Farrell grinned. "No, not this time."

To receive a free catalog of other Poisoned Pen Press titles, please contact us in one of the following ways:

Phone: 1-800-421-3976
Facsimile: 1-480-949-1707
Email: info@poisonedpenpress.com
Website: www.poisonedpenpress.com

Poisoned Pen Press
6962 E. First Ave. Ste 103
Scottsdale, AZ 85251